# CARAVAN TO ORENDIA

## SEQUEL TO THE RUNAWAYS OF PHAYENDAR

Carol Strote

authorHOUSE®

*AuthorHouse™*
*1663 Liberty Drive*
*Bloomington, IN 47403*
*www.authorhouse.com*
*Phone: 1 (800) 839-8640*

*Published by AuthorHouse 02/13/2017*

*ISBN: 978-1-5246-7088-7 (sc)*
*ISBN: 978-1-5246-7087-0 (e)*

*Print information available on the last page.*

# CONTENTS

# DEDICATION

To all of the oppressed, abused women on planet earth,
I wish you health, healing, forgiveness and love.
May your light grow and shine on all of the dark places.
May happiness be yours.

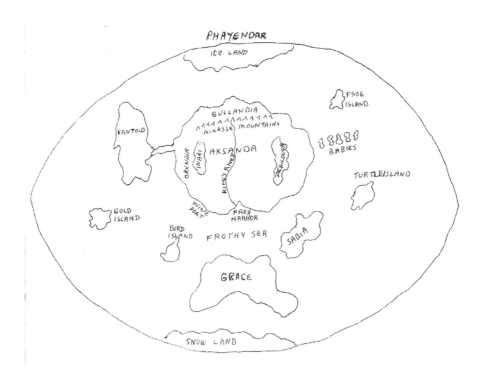

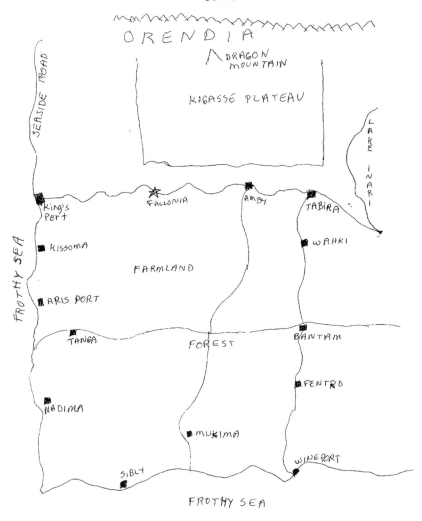

# CARAVAN TO ORENDIA

Tall Sky groomed the horses and Melody oiled the tack. The horses needed brushing and bathing and it was a perfect day for it. "We may have to replace some of this tack," said Melody. "Our wagon looks nice painted blue with pretty designs on it and I like the ruffled curtains at the windows. Are you sure that the roof won't leak?"

"It will keep us dry," said Tall Sky.

Tall Sky and Melody had enjoyed some time off from their adventures around their country of Aksanda. It had been a long winter, but a productive one. The slave trade had been laid waste largely due to their efforts last autumn when they and King Aryante's army had destroyed the slave markets around the country and freed many potential slaves who had been stolen from their families. Many of these girls had found husbands through the efforts of Beldock in Loadrel and Rando at Home Fire. This summer Rando's efforts to create a town out of the camp at Home Fire would continue along with his work with the runaways of Gullandia, north of the mountains.

Melody and Tall Sky were getting a little restless. They had managed to create a book about the world of Phayendar including maps, thanks to Malding, a mariner who had traveled the ocean and had mapped it. Now a more difficult task needed their attention. King Aryante wanted them to accompany a caravan to Orendia to recover girls who were sold into slavery and taken from Aksanda. The foreigners who bought the girls were an unscrupulous bunch of cutthroats who would do anything for their masters in Orendia. Many of these men were killed when King Aryante's soldiers raided the auctions throughout the country, but many had already left Aksanda carrying with them the precious children stolen from their homes. Tall Sky and a regiment of Bright Elves had been involved with this problem for some time. His wife Melody had counseled these girls. She knew the pain and humiliation they felt and the hopelessness that their parents experienced. Tall Sky and Melody would journey to Vivallen to speak with King Aryante about the caravan and their assignment.

"Tall Sky, should we take everything we will need for the caravan?" asked Melody.

"Yes, I think we will be leaving from Vivallen right away. We should pack our wagon," said Tall Sky. Ulrick, the town's carpenter, had helped Tall Sky create a wagon that was enclosed with wood to form a roof for protection and privacy. They did have some merchandise for sale, having made puzzles of the world all winter, but there would still be enough room for them to sleep inside. They had painted the wagon blue with some flower designs on it.

Tall Sky was a tall Bright Elf with long blonde hair and blue eyes. Melody had long, curly, red hair with big green eyes and long eyelashes. Her miniature dragon Daisy liked to sit on her shoulder partially under her hair where she could watch everything that was going on, make chirring sounds and rubbing faces with Melody. Daisy was a very loving little dragon, but she could be fierce. Just a few months ago at Home Fire, when the witch Avidora attacked Melody, Daisy had jumped on Avidora's face, clawing her eyes out, while Trag had stabbed her, preventing her from setting everyone on fire. Melody had found Daisy in a yet unhatched egg in Malwood Forest where she had met Tall Sky. It was love at first sight and they had been inseparable ever since.

The packing went smoothly and soon they were ready to bid goodbye to their friends. They walked to Trag's store to see Trag and Arinya. "Hi Trag, would you two like to come to breakfast with us? We are leaving for Vivallen today. Trag, did you decide to come with us?" asked Tall Sky.

"Sure," said Trag. Arinya and Trag walked with Tall Sky and Melody to the Laborer's Reward stopping next door to get Liadra, Elise and Laskron. They chose to sit at the long table in the back where they and their friends had visited so many times. Beldock, the owner of the inn and their close friend, came out of the kitchen to greet them. "Good morning, my friends. Are you ready for a great breakfast? We have scrambled eggs with cheese, sausage, fried potatoes, and some good pastries from Jelsareeb." Mina came out with the Daisy plate and a very hungry dragon hopped down to the table.

"That's my good little dragon. Are you leaving for Vivallen today?" asked Mina.

"Yes, we are," said Tall Sky. "Our wagon is packed and we will be leaving right after breakfast. I just have to hitch up the horses to the wagon. Trag and Laskron will accompany us. They have some shopping to do for their store. It's cool and sunny, a great day for travel."

Mina served plates of steaming hot food and everybody enjoyed a good breakfast. Daisy curled up on Melody's shoulder for a brief nap.

Arinya said, "While Trag and Laskron are away, Liadra and I are going to decorate my nursery. My baby will be born in a few months and I want to get the nursery ready before I get too big to move around much."

"That sounds like fun," said Melody. "I wish I could help you. Would you like me to bring you back flying kittens? I was thinking if we had a male from one litter and a female from another litter, we could breed them. You wanted a cat and this way I could see them and pet them. I can't have any of my own because of Daisy. Faerverin wants one too and King Aryante said that she could have one. It would be a long trip for them, but, if I'm really careful, I think it would be alright."

"How exciting!" said Arinya. "I've been wanting a cat." Trag rolled his eyes and thought about a cat in the air and a toddler on the floor. He did promise Arinya anything that she wanted and, more than anything, he wanted Arinya to be happy. He could still see her tears as she was being auctioned at Malwood Market, and he could still see the man who bought her as he killed him during the Purge

3

of Malwood. Yes, she could have a flying cat if she wanted one. He was her hero and he wasn't about to stop being that now.

Liadra said, "We should go shopping now and get some paint and order a crib and a rocking chair from Ulrick. You said that you want a porch and we can order one of those, too. It might even be built by the time Trag gets home. That would be nice, wouldn't it?"

"I want you to stay with Liadra and Elise while I'm gone," said Trag.

"Of course I will," said Arinya.

Liadra said, "Don't you worry, I will take good care of her." Liadra had been a good mother to Laskron's little girl and she was a gracious, loving hostess to her guests.

"Melody, Laskron, Trag, it is time to be leaving," said Tall Sky. They all hugged and kissed goodbye. Beldock and Mina came out with lunches wrapped for them.

Beldock said, "Keep vigilant and stay armed. You never know who you might meet on the road. The best to you. Say hello to Aleph for me. Goodbye my friend." He hugged Tall Sky.

Everyone left and walked home to get their horses and wagons. Each one of them had extra horses ready to ride in an emergency. Tall Sky and Melody had packed extra clothing including special clothing to wear when they met the King of Orendia. They were ready to leave within the hour. Tall Sky led the way with Trag and Laskron following. They traveled south along Lake Perilough and turned right onto King's Road. They stopped at the ruins for lunch.

"Laskron, how is business?" asked Tall Sky.

Laskron replied, "Business is good. We completed all of Home Fire's orders and are now taking care of the usual orders from neighboring towns and from Loadrel. This summer, when more houses are completed and the inn is built at Home Fire, we will again be very busy. I'm very grateful to my apprentice Twilric. He is a good man and a hard worker. Without him I would not have been able to keep up. He is planning on marrying one of the girls we rescued."

Trag said, "The same goes for me. People like my store and the Home Fire people have bought many things for their homes. I am also expecting more business when more building is completed there. I have even seen people from neighboring towns. Our supplies are diminished now, so this trip is timed just right for us. We have sold most of what we bought on our last trip to Vivallen for Aleph and Faerverin's wedding at the castle. That was a wonderful time, wasn't it?"

Tall Sky said, "Yes, and Aleph was blessed by God to have the vision of Faerverin lost and half dead at the big rock with other slave girls. Father God actually told him that she was to be his wife. Now, if that isn't the story of the century, nothing is and that wedding was gorgeous with the royals all dancing and Quickturn's officers dressed in white with gold brocade. Melody and I had a wonderful time. But finding Faerverin's four year old sister left by the slavers was a miracle. I never cease to be amazed at God's timing. Speaking of time, we should really get going."

Everyone packed up, watered the horses, and climbed aboard their wagons. It would be another four hours to reach Vivallen. The sounds of the wagons and the creaking of the leather straps made Melody sleepy, so she went into her wagon for a nap. It was nice to have a bed with them. There were a few travelers who passed them but nothing out of the ordinary. It was good to have a normal trip for a change.

Melody woke when the wagon stopped at the gate to Vivallen. The guard remembered Tall Sky and motioned him through. This time he rode his wagon right up to the castle stables where he gave instructions and a message to Aleph. Then the four friends walked to the Golden Chalice to register for the night. They ordered dinner, hot baths and rooms for the night. They bathed, changed clothes and went down for dinner. Aleph had received the message and was already there sipping some warm berry wine. He ordered some for his friends. "Tall Sky, it is good to see you. I have much to tell you, but let's have dinner first. King Aryante will want to tell you most of it anyway. Have you seen Faerverin yet?"

Tall Sky replied, "No, we just arrived and bathed. We are very tired and probably won't be visiting anyone tonight. How have you been? I haven't seen you all winter."

Aleph said, "I've been busy with my job of helping people to make peace with each other and, with this caravan project, King Aryante has given me duties. You know he wants me to go with the caravan to present the Orendian king with a gift and a treaty with a trade agreement. Remember the grazing rights treaty with Gullandia? It's working out well for both sides. He wants foremost an agreement with this king that would include no slave purchases. It should be interesting, and could be dangerous. Some of Quickturn's regiment and some of the king's soldiers have been training all winter in the art of trading."

Tall Sky said, "It sounds good. Is Quickturn going with us?"

"Yes. He will be invaluable, since people there will probably be resistant to this idea, and getting the slaves back could be difficult and dangerous, even if we pay for them," said Aleph.

The waiter brought dinner and the Daisy plate that Melody had ordered. The cook brought it out just so she could watch Daisy eat. "I love to watch this darling little dragon eat her dinner," she said. The food was excellent consisting of meat, vegetables, freshly baked rolls, and pie for dessert.

After dinner Aleph excused himself to go home to Faerverin. They lived in the castle with her little sister Aranel, which means princess in Elven. Aranel bore a striking resemblance to Faerverin with blonde hair, blue eyes, fine features, and porcelain skin. She was delighted to have the Queen's daughter as a playmate and to finally meet her sister. Faerverin had wandered off as a child to follow a fairy who taught her how to paint and how to talk to animals. When the fairies left her, she was taken in by a couple who raised her until her stepmother died and her stepfather became abusive. At that point, Faerverin ran away and was captured by slavers who left her and several other girls in the countryside with no food or water. That is when Aleph found her. Aleph introduced her to King Aryante who asked them to marry in the castle and live there while Aleph was his advisor.

Melody, Tall Sky, Trag and Laskron bid Aleph goodnight and retired for a much needed sleep. The next morning they walked to the castle to see King Aryante. They were escorted into the study to await Aleph and Quickturn. When they arrived, they were joined by King Aryante dressed in his riding clothes. He was a tall man with slightly graying, shoulder length hair, blue eyes and a short beard that came to a point. "Thank you for being here," he said. "I have long looked forward to this meeting. Melody, Tall Sky, you did a wonderful job during our last campaign and I am sure your services will be most welcome on our caravan. Should we be successful in retrieving our children, they will certainly need counseling. You must study the language on your way. We have an excellent teacher with us who knows the Orendian language and the customs. We have fifty soldiers and twenty-five Bright Elves trained in trading and in the Orendian language and thirty wagons of goods ready for sale. Each man will have his own horse and there are extra horses. There is a cook's wagon and a wheelwright's wagon with extra wheels and parts. Several wagons are loaded with food supplies. There are wagons filled with hay and grains for the horses and each wagon carries water and wine. The caravan will leave tomorrow morning. Do you have any questions?"

Melody asked, "Will there be any fighting?"

King Aryante replied, "There are many unknowns in this endeavor. We have tried to anticipate problems, but in a new area you just have to be prepared. It is possible that there could be fighting at some point, and that is why all of our men are soldiers with battle experience. As far as I know, the Orendians have not been at war, but they do have a small army. Aleph has a treaty and a trade agreement to present to the Orendian king along with a substantial gift. Hopefully the king will accept the gift and sign the agreements."

Tall Sky said, "It sounds like a well thought out plan. I think that the king will have some problems with the slave owners. It will depend on how strong of a leader he is and whether or not he is willing to give up the slaves. He might have some of our girls working in his castle for all we know."

"Yes, he might. Like I said, there are many unknowns in this. All we can do is to present the king with our offer and bring back as many children as we can. I hate to go to war with a neighboring country, but that option is open," said King Aryante. "One thing I am sure of, we can't allow another country to steal our children. That is just not acceptable."

Tall Sky asked, "What do we know about the royal family?"

King Aryante replied, "King Jahiz is married to Queen Dara and they have a son Castiphon and a daughter Sestia. They live in a castle in the city of Fallonia, several days journey from the Aksandan border. The Jahiz family has been in power for centuries, ruling with an iron hand and has been at peace during that time. They trade with Fantolo and Gullandia, but have not made overtures toward trading with Aksanda. Since they do enjoy trading with several other countries, it is probable that they would consider trading with us. They do have ships that sail the Frothy Sea and may even trade with Grace Island. I know that we turned away one of their ships at Free Harbor because of the slave trade they were conducting."

Melody said, "I bought some of their things at Free Harbor in the shops there. I bought a carving of a flying cat, some pretty scarves with golden thread running through them and Tall Sky bought an ornate dagger for Trag. They must be doing some trading with us."

King Aryante replied, "Yes, they have, but only on a very limited basis, and only as a cover for their real purpose of buying girls. Just the thought of that still makes me angry."

Melody said, "I know. You had the captain of that ship hanged."

King Aryante said, "Yes, and I will do worse than that if they will not return our children. You see how important this mission is. I want to avoid war if possible, but I will not tolerate our citizens to be violated in this way. I truly love Aksanda and we have exceptionally good people living here."

Tall Sky asked, "Do you know if there are any Bitter Elves operating in Orendia?"

King Aryante answered, "Not for sure on that one, but our interpreter Gantio says he heard rumors of the presence of Bitters there. The Orendians don't like them because of their rudeness. The Orendians do have a developed sense of propriety and manners in their own culture. That is why you and Melody must learn all that you can about their ways. Now let's go to the caravan. It is located just outside the city. Tall Sky, you should bring your wagon and horses out there now. Your wagon will be the first one in line, because Gantio will ride with you as your teacher and he is also our leader since he knows the way to the castle in Fallonia."

They walked down the long, arched hallway to the castle's large front door, walked outside, and turned left toward the stables where Tall Sky had left their wagon. They mounted horses and Tall Sky and Melody tied their horses to the wagon and climbed up to the driver's seat. They followed the king out of town to the caravan. It was an amazing sight to Melody. "There are so many of them," she said, "and we get to be in the front. That's good because there won't be much dust that way." The soldiers had already been camping out there to protect the caravan, so there were many tents set up beside the wagons. The wagons were full of merchandise and supplies so there would be no sleeping indoors until much of the merchandise had been sold. "I'm glad that we won't have to sleep outside in a tent. It could be messy in the rain and I really like my privacy with you," said Melody. "Are there any other women in this caravan?"

Tall Sky said, "I think the cooks are women. At least I hope so."

"They must be very brave women to do this," said Melody. They drove their wagon to the front of the caravan and parked it. "We should go back and talk to Faerverin. I wonder how she has been doing all winter." Aleph rode to their wagon and told them to leave it and ride with him to the castle, so they mounted their horses and followed Aleph. It was a beautiful day with a soft spring breeze and a sunny, blue sky. Melody felt happy and hopeful riding next to her handsome Elven husband. Her red curly hair bounced in the wind and her little dragon rode confidently on her shoulder watching everything and chirring happily. Melody wore brown pants that met

9

her boots at the knees and a brown, fringed, leather jacket. They rode through part of the town and left their horses at the stables.

Aleph said, "Faerverin will be so happy to see you. She misses her friends from Loadrel. She has made several new friends here, but it's not the same." They walked down the long hall and up the stairs to Faerverin's room. She was putting away her paints. Melody hugged her and said, "Faerverin, it's good to see you. You look well. Is your sister here?"

Faerverin said, "She is with Princess Anya in the garden. She walked to the window and called to Aranel to come in. "She and Princess Anya have a wonderful time together. How do you like the caravan? Isn't it adventurous looking?"

"Yes, it is," said Melody, "and it's a little scary to be traveling into a different country not knowing if the people there will be friendly or not."

Faeverin said, "I'm sure it is. I can't go because of Aranel, but we will be spending a few months back home in our house in Loadrel. That way I can visit with our friends and Aranel can play with Elise. They are close to the same age."

"Great," said Melody. "Elise has missed Emmy since Steben and Amidra moved to Yardrel. She will be very happy to play with Aranel."

"When Aleph returns, we are going to spend the rest of the summer together in Loadrel, and he can recuperate from his mission. Then, in the fall, we will return to Vivallen to the castle and he can resume his position as advisor," said Faerverin. "Aranel, do you remember Melody and Tall Sky?'

"Yes, can I see Daisy?" asked Aranel.

"Sure. Sit down and you can hold her if you like," said Melody. Aranel held Daisy and Daisy rubbed faces with her and chirred. "Faerveren, are you still happy here in the castle?"

"Yes, but Aleph has been so busy with his duties and with the caravan mission. I do get a little lonely," said Faerverin. "It is certainly a lot better than the life that the slavers had planned for me. I sure hope that this mission is successful. I want to talk to those girls and show them that there are good lives for them after slavery."

"I do too," said Melody. "We will be bringing some of them back to Loadrel, but most will probably want to go home. It would be nice if they would settle in Home Fire. Did you know that Flint and Cliff were killed by the witch Avidora at Home Fire? She was taking revenge for Rando killing her sister and was throwing fireballs at everybody. Arinya's skirt caught on fire, so Trag sneaked up behind her and knifed her. She grabbed hold of me and Daisy jumped on her face and clawed her eyes out. The place was a mess. The tents had caught on fire. Avidora's bears killed Flint and Cliff before the archers shot them. We have had some amazing times together."

"Yes, you have. How is the construction going at Home Fire?" asked Faerverin.

"They have ten houses built and part of the inn. This summer they will finish the inn and build more houses," said Melody. "Runaways from Gullandia are still arriving there, so they have their hands full, and the place is developing into a ranch. They keep acquiring horses and reindeer. They have chickens and several cows. This summer should be interesting. The women will be gardening and the men will be cutting down trees. They are even going to ask the dwarves to help them build a water system for themselves, for the animals, and for irrigating the gardens. It's a big undertaking, but Rando is doing a great job of it. Rando's wife Alqua is pregnant and so is Trag's wife Arinya. I hate to be away from all this during the summer. You will have to keep good track of it so that you can give me a report when I come back. Maybe you could keep a journal for me."

"I will be happy to," said Alqua. "It will give me something to do in the evenings after Aranel goes to bed. I will also be painting and setting up my paintings for sale in the front room that Aleph ordered to be built."

Aleph said, "Let's go out for lunch to the Golden Chalice and then walk around the shops to buy some things for our Loadrel house."

"Oh, that sounds like fun," said Faerverin. They left the castle and walked to the Golden Chalice leaving Aranel with Princess Anya.

The Golden Chalice was just a short walk from the castle. Daisy was already doing her hungry dance on Melody's shoulder. She was very dependent upon her three meals per day as was Melody. They sat at a table and the cook immediately brought out the Daisy plate. A very happy dragon hopped to the table and ate her little pieces of meat and vegetables and pastry. Then the people were served a sumptuous plate of fish, potatoes and fresh vegetables steamed to perfection. The pastries for dessert were delicious. "This is my favorite place to eat," said Melody. "Are you ready to shop?"

"Oh yes," said Faerverin. "I'm getting excited about making our new house a home." The rest of the afternoon was spent shopping. Faerverin bought some new painting supplies, some summer clothes, and some decorative pieces for the house. She also bought new bedding. Melody bought a few clothes and mosquito netting for the windows of the wagon. She also bought a dagger for protection.

That night Aleph and Faerverin would spend knowing that they would not see each other for an unknown length of time. "Aleph, I'm so scared of you getting hurt on this trip. You don't know these foreigners. The ones you fought at the Purge of Malwood were horrible people," said Faerverin.

"I don't think that those mercenaries were representative of the general population. At least I hope they were not," said Aleph. "And don't forget that Father God will be helping us. He wants those girls returned to their homes."

"You must promise me to be careful and not get separated from your guards," said Faerverin. "We are elves and could have many years together if we are careful." They made love and held each other all night. When morning came, they dressed and packed. Aleph put her bags into a carriage along with Aranel and bade goodbye to them. They would travel to Loadrel with four soldiers to keep them safe. Trag and Laskron had a wagon full of merchandise and traveled behind Aranel's carriage. They would have a safe passage home.

Tall Sky and Melody put their things on their horses and rode to the caravan. The wagons were lined up in a long line with armed men riding horses around them. Some of the men were still eating around a campfire and welcomed them to have some breakfast. Aleph said, "I would like you to meet our wagon master Halden. Halden, this is Tall Sky and Melody. They will be traveling with us. Their wagon is parked at the front of the line. They will be counseling when we get to Orendian towns. In the meantime, they will be learning the Orendian language and customs."

"Welcome," said Halden. "Have some breakfast and tea. We have a good day for travel and plenty of good food. If the weather holds, we should make good time, but a wagon caravan does not travel fast. The men are anxious to be on their way, having trained for this all winter. Everyone here clears away their own refuse and washes their own dishes. That way clean-up after a meal takes very little time. There is some water for this by the fire. All of the wagons are equipped with hooks to tie hammocks to under the wagons in case of bad weather at night. The men can choose to sleep there or pitch their tents. Here is Gantio. Tall Sky and Melody, this is Gantio, your teacher. He will be riding with you."

"I am pleased to meet you. I will try my best to be a good teacher for you," said Gantio. "As you can see, I am dressed like an Orendian. I am comfortable in these clothes, and I will blend in well with the Orendians and make them feel more at ease with me." Gantio wore a turban, a green shirt laced up the front with puffed sleeves, a leather vest, and bright green pants with high boots. He had dark eyes and hair and had a beard and a mustache. "I am an Orendian, but, as young men will do, I wanted to travel. I have been to several other countries, but I like Aksanda the best, especially Vivallen." He smiled showing a gap in his front teeth and crinkles at the corners of his eyes. Melody was well pleased with her new teacher. They washed their dishes and walked to their blue wagon.

Halden rode to the front of the caravan and yelled, "Forward!" Tall Sky drove forward and the caravan was underway.

"It's so beautiful. I love the new spring green of the trees," said Melody. The land was mostly flat with many trees. Some of the trees were already flowering in pinks and whites emitting a beautiful fragrance. It was altogether a pleasant day to be riding outside. They were traveling west toward Lake Inari, a very large lake used by the people of the area for fishing, boating, and picnics. There were no towns near the lake, so the area was mainly pristine with wild animals like rabbits, squirrels, bears and mountain lions. "Will be staying at Lake Inari tonight?"

"I wouldn't be surprised," replied Tall Sky. "I can see that this caravan doesn't move very fast. If we were just riding horses, we could be there in a few hours."

"Oh, well," said Melody. "We have the whole summer and part of the fall. Besides, we need to learn some things about Orendia. Gantio, what is the land like?"

"It varies," said Gantio. "Near the coast the land is flat and verdant. The northern part of Orendia is a plateau with forests. As the land goes north, it has rolling hills that get higher as it approaches the mountains. We will go the southern route around the edge of the plateau toward the coastal plains."

"Maybe you could help me make a map of Orendia and I could make puzzles from the map. I would also like to draw some people showing how they dress. These make good puzzles too," said Melody.

Gantio said, "That's good, but first let's discuss some of their ways that are different. For instance, the women of Orendia don't ever cross their legs as men do. It is considered rude. Women don't go into public without a scarf covering their faces. These scarves are usually a lightweight, see through material of a pastel color. Women wear dresses that go from their necks to the ground and they wear slippers. They never wear shoes or boots. They never speak to men unless they are spoken to by men first. Women may speak to each other away from the men. Women are not allowed to read and write. They are strictly for the pleasure of men and for bearing children. Upper class women do not raise their children. Other younger women are hired to do that and these women are also used by the master of the house for pleasure. I really do not like the way women are treated there, which is one reason I choose to live in Aksanda. I like the company of women and the freedom of Aksanda. In Orendia women are property of the men. They do not own property and do not inherit property. She is property and when a man dies, she is part of the estate and is passed to the man who inherits the property. When a woman can no longer bear children, she is hired out to work to earn money for her master, or is made to work in the fields or with the care of animals. Disobedience is dealt with severely. Sometimes a woman is sent to a brothel or is made to work in rock quarries until she dies."

Melody was appalled by this and became very angry. "'This is not right! How can people live like this? What can we do to stop it?"

Gantio said, "It has always been so. I know of no way to change it. A whole country of people live with these customs. I understand your anger. I wanted you to stay at home for this reason. You must not show your displeasure about these ways, or it could bring the displeasure of the king. You will not be allowed into the king's presence and you must not talk to the women about your feelings regarding these matters. It would bring harm to both of you and endanger our mission. You must act as they do and dress as they do."

Tall Sky laughed and said, "Good luck with that. Really, Melody, your part in all of this will be to talk with our girls. They will need you."

"I know. We have to get our girls out of this. Just staying alive like that would be hard for an Aksandan girl. If it weren't for them, I would get down and walk home," said Melody pouting. "What is wrong with these men?"

"They need to change their hearts, and they need to know Father God. The change has to come from within each man," said Gantio.

"Do you know Father God?" asked Melody.

"Yes, I do. Aleph introduced me to Father God and He lives in my heart now. It was the best experience that I ever had," said Gantio. "I want so much to introduce Him to the king, but it would be very dangerous. If the king knew God, he could make changes. The first step has to be to get the girls back."

"Do the Orendians have any kind of religion?" asked Melody.

"They revere their ancestors and honor them at ceremonies. They bring food and gifts to their graves on special days. When the boys reach the age of thirteen, they are circumcised at the gravesite of their grandfathers. When the men drink ale, they pour some on the ground for their ancestors. They remember them in this way. If there is a dead enemy, they piss on the grave of the enemy. They have idols that they worship. There is an idol for fertility, for rain, for the growth of crops, and for healing. Life just goes on. I can't say that these things actually have any effect. The king dictates what is right and wrong. For instance, it is wrong to steal and to murder. Other than that, men have much freedom to do as they please," replied Gantio.

"Do they practice any spells or magic of any kind?" asked Melody.

"There are some who do, but I don't know much about it," said Gantio. King Jahiz has an advisor who interprets dreams and watches the stars for signs. He may do some magic."

"So, I have to wear a veil and a long dress, and I can't talk to Tall Sky in public. Is there anything else?" asked Melody.

"Yes, when you are in public, you will not touch him and you will walk behind him," said Gantio.

"That's not much fun," said Melody.

"I know, little one, but we don't want to attract negative attention," said Gantio. "God will help you to develop patience in this way."

"Spirit flowers," said Melody.

"Spirit flowers?" asked Gantio.

"That's what my mother called patience, kindness, love, forgiveness and charity," said Melody. "Some of these you get the hard way like patience."

Gantio laughed and said, "Your mother was a wise woman."

Halden rode up to them and said, "Pull over in the grassy area up by that tree and we'll have lunch. Tall Sky drove over to the tree and stopped. Within minutes the cooks were setting up sandwich ingredients for everyone. "Have you and Melody been learning a lot?"

"Yes, I have," said Melody. "I've been learning that this culture is going to try my patience, and that if I don't try really, really hard, I could get killed." Halden laughed.

"I guess it would try the patience of newlyweds. No mooning and spooning in public," said Halden. "You just have to be very careful. Did you see the lake?"

"No, we were too busy talking," said Melody.

"Look over there through the trees and you will see a little of it. We will be passing closer to it in about half an hour. Then you will get a good look at it. It's really large and you won't see the other side of it. Now let's get some lunch," said Halden.

Daisy had been napping, but at the mention of lunch, she did her hungry dance. Melody fed her first and Tall Sky made some sandwiches. Neither of them realized how hungry they were. They walked around eating their sandwiches and looking at the other wagons. Most of the wagons were of unpainted wood. Some of the soldiers had never seen a miniature dragon before and asked if they could see her, but she was shy and tried to hide behind Melody's curls. "Daisy never quite got over her encounter with Avidora," said Melody.

"Avidora the witch?" asked the soldier.

"Yes. Avidora grabbed me and Daisy jumped on her face and clawed her eyes out," said Melody.

"Wow!" said the soldier. "I guess I'll leave her alone."

"I don't think you have to worry about it. Avidora was throwing fireballs at the time," said Melody. "It was enough to unnerve anyone."

Halden walked by and said, "It's time to roll again." Melody and Tall Sky walked back to the blue wagon and climbed aboard. He pulled his wagon out to the road and they were off again.

"This part of the journey is kind of fun," said Melody. "It will be nice to sleep in our wagon tonight."

Gantio said, "I will sleep in my tent tonight. I'm used to it. It's quite comfortable."

Melody said, "You told us about the upper class. What are the average people like? Do they farm and fish like in Aksanda?"

"Yes, they do," replied Gantio. "Both men and women work hard on the farms. It is necessary. The women and girls work in the garden, do the laundry and the cooking, make cheese and butter and take care of the chickens. The men grow crops of grain and cotton and take care of the larger animals. They also maintain the buildings. When the women are at home, they do not wear the veils. They still mainly talk among themselves. The boys help their father and gather wood for fires. Often the man will take in another woman to help his wife as she gets older and tired. This woman will help the wife with chores, giving her time to weave fabrics and make soap for the family and for the market. In this way she is adding to the income of the family and she has another adult woman to talk to. The husband uses this woman for pleasure. So he is happy and the wife is happy. The arrangement is good for the family." Melody shook her head.

As the caravan progressed, more of the lake became visible. The land was grassy with trees and there were tall grasses and stones at the water's edge. The sounds of a waterfall became louder as they traveled west around the lake. Soon the waterfall became visible. It was water coming off the rocks of the plateau and tumbling down in three tiers, landing in a pond that drained off forming a creek. Halden rode up to Tall Sky and said, "Pull up to the creek. We will camp here for the night. That way we can water the horses, bathe, and top off our water containers. Tall Sky pulled up to the creek and helped Melody out of the wagon. They unhitched the horses, groomed them and led them to the creek for a drink. The fire detail made two fires for cooking and the cooks started filling two large pots with meat and vegetables. Then they made a type of flatbread.

Melody and Tall Sky decided to explore the lakeside and found bear prints which they reported to Halden.

He said, "I wondered when we would see signs of bears. I knew that there were bears in this area. We will have to be vigilant, but they usually won't come near a large group of people, so we might not actually see any of them. Thanks for telling me. Let me know if you see anything else like this. Our guards will be watching for wild animals tonight. There are also cougars around here."

"Oh great!" said Melody. "Cougars and bears. Let's hope there aren't any bandits hanging around, too."

"You never know about that one, but I doubt it. This road isn't traveled enough for bandits to make a living here," said Tall Sky. "We should keep a watch for snakes, though." Water lilies had already started to bloom and the frogs were talking to each other. Birds were singing their evening songs, and the light had lessened as the sun crept .closer to the horizon. They walked back to the wagons and strolled along the caravan. Then Melody got some warm water from a cook and bathed Daisy who was delighted to splash in the water. Then she dried her and oiled her. Tall Sky stood guard as Melody bathed in the pool by the waterfall, and then he bathed. "Stopping here was a great idea."

"Yes," said Melody. "The water was cold, but it felt really refreshing. I'm getting hungry. Let's see how the cooks are doing." The stew smelled good and Daisy became agitated. "Could I get some meat and vegetables for my little dragon?" asked Melody. "She is really hungry and she doesn't eat much." The cook gave her a small plate of food and Melody cut it into small pieces and set it on the ground for Daisy who greedily ate her food. Melody took her behind the wagons to relieve herself. Then Daisy took a nap in her velvet pouch. Melody and Tall Sky went to the wagon for their bowls and spoons. It was time for dinner at last. The stew with bread and butter tasted good after a long day of travel. They found a rock to sit on and watched the sunset of reds and golds while sipping on some berry wine. "How beautiful!" said Melody. "If Faerverin were here, she would want to paint it."

Tall Sky put his arm around her and said, "Did I tell you today how much I love you?" He kissed her over and over and said, "We have to retire early, because this caravan moves out very early in the morning."

Melody laughed and said, "OK, let's go to bed." They climbed into their wagon and went to bed happily holding each other all night.

The morning began with a bird fight in the trees near their wagon. Tall Sky dressed quickly and went to investigate. The cooks were preparing breakfast and the men were watering and feeding their horses which is what Tall Sky proceeded to do. Then he and Melody took their bowls to the breakfast line. Some men had already eaten and were hitching up their horses. Melody fed Daisy and took her food over to the rock to eat with Tall Sky. "Everything tastes so good when you eat outside," said Tall Sky.

"It sure does," said Melody. "I wonder what Gantio will teach us today?" Gantio was putting his tent away. He brought his food over and said, "Good morning, are you ready for another interesting day? I thought we would learn a little of the language today and some more about the culture."

"There's more?" asked Melody.

"We need to talk about merchants and fishermen," said Gantio.

The trio climbed up to their wagon seat and, with Halden's direction, Tall Sky drove back onto the road.

Gantio said, "Hello is achta. Please repeat this. Goodbye is nechta." Melody and Tall Sky both repeated the new words. "Mother is bamba and father is bambo." They repeated the words. "Try to remember these. Now, the town people are different from the farmers. Men live in towns because they like to drink and use women. They trade for a living and they gamble. You may have met some of these men in your town when they went to the Malwood Market. It is in these towns that we will find some slave girls. They will be in taverns, brothels and homes of the rich like the town chiefs. You will have to try to buy back these girls with gems, with things, and if need be with threats. If you leave them there, they will not live long, and, if they get pregnant, they could be killed or thrown out with nothing. I will help with these negotiations and I am good at doing so. There must not be any fighting until we are on our way home. We don't want encounters with the Orendian army. If it comes to that, King Aryante will have to start it."

"Why don't they use their own girls in this way? Why do they have to use our girls?" asked Melody.

"The men want grandchildren from their daughters. The women want their daughters," said Gantio.

"Tall Sky, we have to get these girls and take them home," said Melody.

"That's what we're here for," said Tall Sky.

"Fishing villages are a mix of good and bad. The men depend on their wives to help clean fish, get them ready for market and take care of the children and the gardens. It is not a bad life for them, but the men drink, gamble, and use other women. It is something that their wives have to tolerate."

"I definitely do not like Orendia. I think the flying cats are the only good part of it. Where do you find them?" asked Melody.

"Flying cats can be found anywhere, but mostly on farms," said Gantio. "There is a breeder of them who I know of in Fallonia. We will visit her before we leave Orendia.

Halden rode up and said, "We will stop for lunch up ahead at the cliff." There were large boulders off to the right of the road leading to a cliff that rose vertically to the plateau. The lake was behind them now and they were in Orendia. Tall Sky drove for a while and stopped at the cliff. They climbed down from the wagon and walked behind a large boulder to relieve themselves. Daisy was glad to walk on solid ground for a change. She walked about chirring and then wanted back up on Melody's shoulder.

"I'm ready for this trip to be over already. I can hardly wait to deliver a flying kitten to Faerverin and Arinya," said Melody. Halden walked up to them to let them know that as soon as they were ready, they would leave for another two hour ride.

They climbed back onto their wagon seat and waited for Halden. In a few minutes he gave the order to proceed. Tall Sky drove back onto the road and drove west. Gantio said, "If you want a drink of water, you say, 'ya vema lado agia'. If you want wine, you say, 'ya vema lado vin'. Now you repeat these." Tall Sky and Melody repeated them. "Yes is ya and no is note. Now you repeat. They repeated the words. Say them in your mind and remember them."

"Will we see a farm first or a town?" asked Melody.

"We will see a few farms soon and then a town. We will stop a short time at each one to sell and to ask about slave girls," said Gantio. "Then we will spend more time in the town. You will stay in the wagon. We do not need people to know that we have a pretty girl like you with us. You never know what a drunk may think to do."

"That's not fair," said Melody, pouting.

"Maybe not, but it is safe for you and for the rest of us," said Gantio. "Remember you are in a new place that is not favorable toward women. Besides, you will soon be busy with the girls we rescue."

"I guess it will be alright," said Melody. "I want so much for everything to be good."

"I will let you go in to see the cats," said Gantio. Melody smiled.

"I am so proud of you, Melody. You have become a heroin in more ways than one," said Tall Sky. "You are my one and only most important person in the world." Melody hugged him. Daisy chirred.

"I'm tired. Would you mind if I took a nap?" asked Melody. She climbed into the back and got comfortable in the bed.

Gantio had wanted to talk to Tall Sky about court diplomacy, and this was a perfect chance to do so. "Court is very formal and is not unlike court in Aksanda," said Gantio. "When you are introduced to King Jahiz, you will bow and say nothing. You wait to be spoken to. The king will lead the conversation. I will be doing the talking, since I am Orendian and I know the language. I will tell him about our mission and will offer him a gift and the opportunity to see the caravan goods as proof of our intentions to trade with Orendian merchants. He will like this and feel honored. He likes beautiful things and will be intrigued by a caravan full of goods. It is probable that he will want to ride to the caravan to see them for himself. You do not turn your back on the king, so when you exit the throne room, you will walk backward looking at the floor."

Tall Sky said, "Is this king rational and friendly? I'm used to King Aryante sitting at a table in his study and talking like a regular person."

"King Jahiz probably does so, but a first meeting would be very formal," said Gantio. "If he likes his present and the caravan, he might invite us to a dinner with entertainment. You just never know. The cliffs on the right continue along the road for a long time as do the low rolling hills. The road will go over some of those hills, but they aren't too steep for the wagons. I am looking for the first farm to appear. It should be in just a few minutes. I will ask the farmer if he needs anything and ask him about the slave girls. There, up ahead, do you see it?"

"Yes, I do," said Tall Sky. "Should I pull over closer to the farm, or will you be riding a horse over there?"

"I think we should stay on the road and that Halden and I should ride over there. A caravan just dropping by the house would be too intimidating. It is possible that we could water our horses, but I will ask about it and see if their well could handle that," said Gantio. Halden rode up and told Tall Sky to stop the wagon. Gantio climbed down and asked Halden to accompany him to the farm. The morning chores had already been done and the farmer was outside staring at the caravan. It was probably the only caravan that he had ever seen. There was a long horse trough near the well, a medium sized house with a thatched roof and a barn with several outbuildings near it.

They rode up to the farmer and dismounted. Gantio immediately bowed and greeted the farmer, telling him of his mission to see the king and to sell goods to the Orendians. The farmer asked Gantio and Halden into the house and told his wife to bring tea. The farmer was very interested in this caravan and asked questions about the type of goods that they were carrying. Halden told him that there were household goods, and fabrics that he and his wife might be interested in seeing and inquired about water for the horses. He said that his well could accommodate the water for their horses and that it would be wise to water them now, because there wasn't any natural water like streams between here and the first town Tabira. Halden rode back to the wagons and told the men to bring eight horses at a time for water. In the meantime, the farmer and his wife rode to the wagons to see the merchandise. They bought a bathtub, a large cauldron for boiling water, some pans and some fabric.

The soldiers helped them back to the house with their purchases. Halden asked if there were any Aksandan slaves in the town or on the farms. The farmer said that there were a few slaves in the town, but none on the farms. He said that the town chief had one, the tavern had one and the brothel had one. Halden gave the farmer some silver for the use of his well water and rode back to the wagons. "Tall Sky, we have three girls in Tabira. Let's go." He called, "Forward!" and Tall Sky pulled out toward the town of Tabira.

Gantio instructed Melody, "Melody, when we get these girls, they will ride in the wagon behind you. There are mattresses and men's clothing in there. You will wash them if need be and you will instruct them to keep to themselves. Pin their hair up and give them caps to wear. It must not be known to others that we have women aboard the caravan. I want you to dress like a man and put your hair under a cap also. Little Daisy must not be seen, so if you are outside the wagon in the presence of Orendians, keep Daisy in her pouch. It is for her own protection."

Melody answered, "I will. I am so excited about this. I can hardly wait." The air was cool, the sun was warm, and there were wildflowers blooming in the foot tall grasses in the land to the left of them. Big boulders led up to the sheer rock face of the plateau on the right. Their first encounter with Orendians had been successful and they were very hopeful. Another farm loomed up on the left and Halden again rode with Gantio to speak with the farmer who said that he would like to see some of their goods. He bought some pans and some fabric. The caravan proceeded down the road. The next stop would be the town of Tabira, a town of several thousand people with shops, taverns and an inn. The caravan stopped for lunch just outside of town.

Melody donned her man's clothing and a cap. She and Tall Sky walked to the cook's wagon for a sandwich of cheese and bacon. Then they sat on a boulder to eat their lunch. Daisy happily ate her portion and munched on some apple pieces. "This is great," said

Melody. "This is our first day in Orendia and we have already found three girls."

"We have to negotiate with their owners first," said Tall Sky. "It is good to be hopeful, but there is no guarantee that the owners will sell them."

"Just hearing the words 'sell them' makes me so angry," said Melody.

"Me too," said Tall Sky. "We must keep level heads in this and not show our anger. We don't want them to start hiding the girls and we will be coming back this way, giving us a second chance to get them."

After lunch Halden and Gantio headed for town. On their way through town, they noticed an Aksandan woman rummaging through some garbage for food. She was obviously pregnant. They picked her up and rode back to the caravan to deliver her to Melody. Then they rode back to the town and went into a tavern to talk to the owner. The tavern owner served them ale and sat down with them. An Aksandan woman asked if they would order some food. She was scantily dressed with a short skirt and a low cut, ruffled blouse. She had blonde hair and blue eyes. "What is your business here?" asked the owner.

Gantio answered, "We have a caravan just outside of town loaded with goods, many of which could be used right here in your tavern. We would also like to buy your slave. We will give you a good price for her, or you may trade her for goods."

"I don't know, she is worth much to me, but I will come to see your caravan first. They rode out to the caravan where the owner chose some pans and some decorative pieces for his tavern. He said that he would be willing to trade these things and silver for the girl. Gantio paid the man who said that there was one next door at the brothel. They went next door and bought the girl. Then they rode back to the caravan to deliver the girls to Melody.

Their next step was to recover a girl owned by the town chief. He had a large house surrounded by gardens on a hill overlooking the town. A slave girl dressed in a beautiful long gown, wearing jewelry and a veil answered the door and went to get her owner. A short, fat man wearing a turban and colorful clothing bid them welcome. Gantio introduced himself and told him about the caravan and the many useful and beautiful things he should see. Gantio wanted him to have first choice of these things before the rest of the town's residents had an opportunity to see the items. Gantio said that they would trade these things and some silver or jewels for the slave girl. The chief said that he would come with them to the caravan. He chose some pans, fabric, and several tapestries for his home. They rode back to his house and gave him an emerald for the girl. Then they rode back to the caravan with the town's last slave girl.

Melody quickly had the girl change into men's clothing and put a cap on to hide her hair. She explained that the slave trade had been abolished in Aksanda and that the caravan was in Orendia to rescue slave girls who had been stolen from Aksanda. The girls were amazed by this and very grateful to have been rescued. Melody said, "There are more girls like you in Orendian towns. This will be a long trip. We have to visit King Jahiz and get a treaty signed. King Aryante will resist the abduction of our children with force if need be, so this is a very serious matter. You three are the first of many more. I have been involved with this throughout Aksanda, where we rescued hundreds of potential slaves. We returned many of them to their homes and quite a few married and now live in Loadrel and a new town called Home Fire. In fact, the chief of Home Fire married a slave girl named Alqua. You all have new lives to look forward to."

The girls smiled, but Indra said, "Who would want a pregnant girl?"

"You will be surprised. There are single men from Gullandia who will not mind that you are pregnant. They need more people out there and there are other pregnant women there. These people will not hold it against you for being abducted and sold into slavery. In fact the men of Home Fire helped the Loadrel militia to destroy the slave auction at Malwood," said Melody.

"That's where I was sold!" said Indra. The people of Tabira were busily shopping at the caravan, so the girls remained in their wagon.

After the customers went home, the caravan moved away from town to an uninhabited area to camp for the night.

The girls walked with Tall Sky and Melody to the boulders where they sat down and relaxed with a cup of wine while they waited for the cooks to make dinner. Melody said, "The men in the caravan are all soldiers in King Aryante's army and are here on a mission to retrieve the Aksandan children. You are safe with them. They trained all winter to speak Orendian and to know how to trade with these people. The king made very good preparations for this. We carry merchandise for sale, and under these things are beds for the girls we will rescue. The men sleep in tents or in hammocks under the wagons. We carry food, water and firewood. It is a well thought out plan. We even have a wagon full of wagon wheels in case we have a broken wheel."

"What about wild animals?" asked Indra. "Did you know that there are large dragons on the Kigasse Plateau and that there are people who ride the dragons and take directions from the king's sorcerer? He's called an advisor, but he dabbles in the black arts. He frequented the brothel that I was in. He would drink with us and talk too much, bragging about his influence on King Jahiz. He said that if he didn't like someone, he would send the person out of town and have a dragon rider attack the person."

"Oh, my God!" said Melody. She looked at Tall Sky and asked, "Did you know about this?"

"No, I don't think any of us knew about it. Let's talk to Gantio," said Tall Sky. They found Gantio at the cook's fire. "Gantio, did you know about dragons living on the Kigasse Plateau?"

"Yes, I knew about them, but they shouldn't hinder us. They have dragon riders and mainly keep to themselves," answered Gantio.

"Indra knows the king's advisor Ahriman. He visits the brothel often and drinks with the girls and brags about how he directs the dragon riders to ride against certain people he sends out of town. In this way he controls people in power. The king is unaware of this. We could get into a lot of trouble with this man. Gantio, this man is a sorcerer. We must be very careful in dealing with him. He will probably not like our mission, but he does like his position to the king," said Tall sky.

Halden walked up and said that it was time to leave. Tall Sky told him about the dragons and Ahriman. Halden said that tonight they would have a meeting with the soldiers, so that everyone would be aware of the possible danger. They went back to their wagons. Halden called "Forward!" and Tall Sky pulled back onto the road.

Melody said, "Tall Sky, what are we going to do if dragons come after us?"

Tall Sky answered, "Pray, shield, and shoot arrows. Dragons are notoriously hard to kill. They have thick, hard scales, but there is usually a thin spot on their underbellies. The problem is that by the time they are close enough to kill, they have already loosed their fire at you."

"That does it. We should turn around now and go home," said Melody. "I had enough of fire with Avidora, and my little Daisy doesn't deserve to face this kind of danger."

"None of us do, but we are so close to getting the slaves out of here. I think we should give it a try, even if it is illogical. Ahriman may not even get upset by this. There are plenty of other girls in the brothels," said Tall Sky.

"I am riding back to Vivallen and taking the slave girls that we already have. Indra is pregnant and should be in a safe place anyway. If you want to go with me, we could put the girls in our wagon and let the soldiers handle this. There are plenty of bright elves who can use shielding. They don't need us," said Melody. Tall Sky was crestfallen. He knew she was right, but he still felt the urgent pull toward his goal, and he knew that Melody's help would be invaluable to the handling of so many upset women.

Gantio had been listening to this and said, "Ahriman will not want to displease the king, and is mainly concerned with diplomatic relations and maintaining his power. I think that he will let the king decide this matter. After all, Ahriman will have more power if we do establish trade with Orendia. He likes pretty things and we have a good supply of those. He will want some and will undoubtedly make purchases and want more. I don't think that he would jeopardize his ability to get more interesting things and an opportunity to exercise more control. I will play up these ideas to him and ask for his ideas about trading to make him feel important. We should continue our mission."

Melody thought about it and realized the logic of what he said. "All right, I'll stay."

Tall Sky was relieved. They traveled for another hour without saying anything. Then Gantio said, "This is how you say that the food is good: Chakima kitoru. I need food: Nini chakima. Please repeat these and remember. Our next town is Kisoma and is close. We will stop there and then camp further on. In a while Halden rode up and told them to pull over next to the town of Kisoma.

Halden, Gantio and several soldiers with extra horses rode into the town and walked into the tavern for directions and information about the slaves. The tavern owner said that he had one, but that she was pregnant and about to be thrown out. Gantio offered him ten pieces of silver for her and the owner gladly accepted them. He told them that a brothel in town had one and so did the chief. Nobody else could afford them. Gantio sent the amazed girl back to the caravan with one of the soldiers. Then they visited the brothel and bought a girl who went back to the caravan with a soldier.

Lastly they stopped by the house of the chief, who was not in the mood to sell his slave. She was very pretty and was not pregnant. They said that this would be the last time he could get money for her, since the king was going to outlaw slavery soon. He agreed to sell her for a ruby. They took her back to the caravan and delivered her to Melody. They now had six girls in the caravan and needed to unload another wagon of items, so they passed word of a sale around the town. Soon they had a large group of customers purchasing their goods. They made sure to save the best items for the King and his advisor. After the sale, they consolidated goods to have another empty wagon for slave girls. So far the mission was a success. They had purchased six slave girls before seeing the king. The capitol city would have the most girls because of the wealth in that city.

Melody told the girls that they would talk more after dinner. Halden called "Forward," and the wagons moved again. Soon they arrived at an empty area next to the cliff wall and pulled off the road to set up camp. The men unhitched the horses and fed, watered and groomed them. The fire detail made two fires and the cooks began making a stew. They had purchased some meat and vegetables in the last town. Six girls, Melody and Tall Sky sat on some boulders apart from the others to talk.

One of the new girls named Fauna asked, "Why are you doing this? Are we going to be sold again?"

Tall Sky answered, "No, we are taking you home to Aksanda where you will choose to go home to your parents or move to a town to marry."

"Who would want to marry us now? We have been with other men and two of us are pregnant," said Fauna.

"The men I speak of went to war for you," said Tall Sky. "They realize that you were abducted from your homes and were forced into slavery. They do not hold this against you. A pregnant woman is particularly good for a new town called Home Fire. This town needs more people for it to grow. The men out there are looking forward to finding wives. They are working hard to build houses for them. Already some have married rescued slave girls. None of what happened to you is your fault. Most of the men who abducted you paid with their lives. King Aryante sent us to get you back. You belong in your home country. Let's walk over to the cooking fire and see if the food is ready yet."

The girls were given some bowls and spoons and a cook ladled some stew into them. They also picked up a cup and a piece of flatbread. Then they walked back to their boulders to eat. "This food tastes so good after a long day of travel and negotiations. The sale went well. The soldiers are going to arrange the wagons so that we have another wagon ready for more girls. Tomorrow is a very important day. We will try to see King Jahiz and present him with a gift and a treaty from King Aryante. If he signs it, getting the girls back will be much easier," said Tall Sky. "Getting his citizens back is very important to King Aryante."

"I see men setting up tents by the wagons. Will we be sleeping in tents?" asked Lyndi.

"No," said Melody. "You will be sleeping in a wagon on a mattress."

"What if we are attacked by dragons?" asked Indra.

Tall Sky replied, "There are twenty-six Bright Elves with us who will stand before the wagons and shield them so that the dragons will not see them. We are all excellent archers and can do damage to the wings of the dragons or shoot them in the eyes. We will protect you and the other soldiers. I can also send sand and dust storms to them. I will ask Father God to protect us and to guide us in our negotiations with the king."

"Why are you called Bright Elves?" asked Adalia.

"Bright Elves follow Father God and are connected to him by having His Spirit living in their hearts. He gives us gifts of healing and discernment of right from wrong. He guides us and gives us visions when necessary. We are called Bright Elves, because, when we are in danger, we can become very bright to confuse and frighten our enemy. Bitter Elves, on the other hand, are bitter against Father God for keeping magic from them and for not giving them all the wealth and power that they see some humans having. Elves are supposed to be helping humans, not trying to take wealth from them and killing them and abducting their children for profit," said Tall Sky.

"I wish we could have God's Spirit living in our hearts too," said Adalia.

"Father God is not just for elves. He has three parts, God the Creator, God the Redeemer and God the Restorer. He wants to love you and forgive you and give you good gifts like love, patience, kindness and forgiveness. All you have to do is to ask Him into your heart and ask Him to forgive you for wrong doing or wrong thinking. Then you forgive those who have wronged you. When you pray to Him, talk to Him as if he were your best friend or your loving father. Would you all like to pray this prayer together?" asked Tall Sky. They all said that they would, so Tall Sky led them in prayer.

"Father God, please forgive me and come to live in my heart. I forgive those who wronged me as You have forgiven me. Please help me to be a better person and to help others. Guide and protect me."

"Now any time you have concerns, just talk to Him about them and He will help you. He is and always will be your best friend," said Tall Sky. "Now let's go wash our dishes and get ready for bed. Tomorrow starts very early around here."

That night Tall Sky held Melody, caressing her hair and tried to reassure her that everything would be alright. They fell asleep and the night passed quietly. With the dawn came bird sounds and the smell of bacon, which got everybody's attention. There was bacon and hot cakes with jelly for breakfast. Daisy loved this breakfast and so did everybody else. They sipped hot tea and talked after breakfast. Halden stopped by and asked if Tall Sky was ready to meet the king. He said it would take him a few minutes to change his clothes. He brought with the clothes he had worn to meet King Aryante. "I'll be back here in a few minutes and you, Aleph, Gantio and I will visit the palace. Eight soldiers will accompany us. It is close by. We will drive the caravan to the edge of the city.

Tall Sky changed clothes and waited for Halden's direction. Halden rode up and called, "Forward!" Tall Sky pulled back onto the road and drove over a low hill. The city of Fallonia stretched out to his right. It was very large. There was another road leading to the city and Tall Sky turned onto that road. When he reached the edge of the city, he turned to his left and stopped. Tall Sky kissed Melody. "I love you my darling. You are the bravest, most beautiful woman in the world and I am blessed to have you for my wife."

"I love you my husband. Go with God. I will be praying for your success and safety."

# KING JAHIZ

Halden rode up with the others and Tall Sky joined them. They rode off toward the palace located on the outskirts of the city on a hill surrounded by a low rock wall. Beyond the wall was another higher wall with an arched opening. Beyond that were gardens of flowers surrounded by low, sculpted hedges and a large fountain. Ten long steps led up to a large, heavy, ornately carved door with a guard standing at each side of the door. Gantio spoke to the guards saying that they bore a gift to King Jahiz from King Aryante of Aksanda and that they had official business to discuss with King Jahiz. They were told to leave their weapons outside and were then asked to come into the foyer, a large room with some chairs along one wall. They were told to sit while they were announced to the king. On the walls were paintings of men riding horses in the hunt, a bear being killed, soldiers in a battle, and some scenes of ladies around a fountain in a garden. These were painted on the walls, not on canvass. In a few minutes the guard came back to them and said that King Jahiz awaited them, but that only three men could go in.

Gantio, Tall Sky and Aleph followed the guard through another heavy door into the throne room. The king was seated on an ornate throne, intricately carved and gilded on a platform with three carpeted steps leading up to it. They were led down a carpeted path toward the king where they stood and bowed. The king wore golden clothing including his turban and wore a girdle of gold encrusted with jewels. He had a slightly graying, short beard that came to a point and a long mustache. He said to them, "You have a gift for me. You may show it to me now." The advisor walked to them, accepted the gift and took the gift to the king. King Jahis lifted the lid on the box and was visibly pleased. It was a large necklace of gold with many large, well cut gems that sparkled. He said, "A gift fit for a king. You honor me. What are these?" He held up two scrolls.

"Aleph said, "I am Aleph, King Aryante's advisor. These are a treaty and a trade agreement. King Aryante desires peaceful relations with your country, so that trade between us may flourish. If it pleases your majesty, we would like to sit at table with you and your advisor to discuss these matters."

"We shall do so. Ahriman, take our guests to my council chamber," said King Jahiz. They walked down a long hallway to the council chamber and sat at a table. King Jahiz addressed Tall Sky and said, "You are an elf. We have been having problems with elves recently. Yesterday five of them broke into a home, killed the man and raped the woman. They took all the valuables and we caught them. They are now breaking rocks in the rock quarry."

Tall Sky said, "We have had trouble with them in Aksanda too. There are two types of elves, the Bitter Elves and the Bright Elves. There are many Bitter Elves who steal, kill, abduct children and sell them, burn homes, and rebel against the king. They are called Bitter Elves because they are bitter against Father God for not giving them riches and power that some people have. Father God sent Elves to Phayendar to help humans, and the Bright Elves do that, but the Bitters rejected Him and sought after wealth and power. They studied the black arts of magic to use against men. Last autumn in Aksanda they organized into an army and attacked the dwarves in the Aikasse Mountains. King Aryante's army and the Bright Elves joined the dwarves in battle against the Bitters. We killed about a thousand of them and put a hundred to work in the king's rock quarry, but many escaped, heading south and west. These Bitter Elves used spells against us causing an earthquake, attacking birds, and a thorny hedge. Aleph and I counteracted these using God's power. At one point I became bright to get their leader's attention so that Aleph could shoot an arrow into his eye. His name was Tupragult and he has caused trouble for many years. Tupragult was actually in your country a few hundred years ago."

King Jahiz said, "I have read about an elf named Tupragult, an advisor to King Shaduram who was poisoned by some Aksandan ambassadors."

Tall Sky replied, "Yes, I have heard this story, but truth is not in it. His son wanted the crown and killed his father with the help of Tupragult who gave him a vial of poison to use against his father. Then Tupragult planted the empty vial in the amabassador's bag and accused him of being a murderer. Tupragult bragged to me about this. Tupragult killed his own family, too. He was a wicked, evil, selfish traitor who lived until recently."

"King Shaduram was a good man who knew and followed Father God. You are wearing the proof of this on your medallion. The three gems on your medallion mean God the Creator, God the Redeemer, and God the Restorer," said Tall Sky.

"King Aryante organized a campaign against the Bitters throughout Aksanda to close down the auctions and rescue the children. We killed many more Bitters and returned children to their parents. Losing children in this way is very traumatic to the parents, so King Aryante sent us here to buy his people back. The Bitters are here now because of the slave trade. If we encounter any we will kill them or give them to you for use in your rock quarry. I am so sorry they came to your country."

"I am interested in this God of yours. Tell me about Him," said King Jahiz.

Tall Sky explained, "He created all of us and he loves us and wants us to have good lives, so He gives us gifts like forgiveness, joy, patience, kindness and healing. He also gives us discernment between good and evil to help us make the right decisions. He wants us to communicate with Him, so He gives us His Spirit to live in our hearts. All we have to do is to ask Him for it and to ask Him to forgive any wrong doing or wrong thinking. I found Aleph almost dead by the side of the road from an axe wound. He was with a group of Bitters who stole from a dwarf. He asked God to forgive him and asked God to live in his heart, so I laid my hands on him and Father God healed him. Since then he has participated in a war, saved King

Farin's life in battle, negotiated a treaty with Gullandia, and has been the king's advisor since then. That is why he is with us. God told me that he would become a great Bright Elf and he has."

King Jahiz said, "I want this God to live in my heart too. Father God, please forgive me and live in my heart. I want to get to know you and I want all of your gifts to help me be a good king."

"Father God is now living within you and you can expect a wonderful life," said Tall Sky.

"Now I will read this treaty," said King Jahiz. "After a few minutes, he said, "It looks like he wants peace with us and he wants us to not buy slaves and to let you buy back slaves. He wants me to issue a decree making it unlawful for slave ownership. I have no problem with that, but how will you transport them to Aksanda?"

"We have thirty wagons waiting on the edge of town. Right now they are loaded with merchandise for sale, but we won't open them without your consent. Also, we have placed the most beautiful things in the last wagon for you and your advisor to have first choice of these things. Would you and Ahriman like to see them?" said Gantio.

"I want to see them," said Ahriman.

"I will send one of my men back to tell the merchants to make ready the tables," said Gantio.

King Jahiz signed the Treaty and perused the Trade Agreement. "It says here that we will be welcome to trade in your ports and on land without being charged for doing so as long as we do not rape nor take women from Aksanda. The same applies to your countrymen in Orendia. Both countries must treat each other with respect." He signed this agreement also.

"King Jahiz, I was wondering if you would issue a proclamation making it illegal to own slaves and making it mandatory for people to sell their slaves to us and giving us permission to sell our wares in other towns before going back to Aksanda," said Aleph. "That would make it much easier for us and we would use the empty wagons to house the girls."

King Jahiz instructed Ahriman to have a scribe prepare it. Soon they were ready to visit the caravan. They mounted their horses and rode out of the castle grounds. King Jahiz and Ahriman rode in a carriage. They stopped at the last wagon where there were many beautiful things arranged on tables. King Jahiz immediately chose a tapestry and several rings. He continued shopping for a while and then walked down the caravan to see the rest of the wares. Advisor Ahriman also chose some interesting items of great beauty. When they had finished, they thanked Aleph and King Jahiz gave him the signed agreements. He gave Gantio the permission to sell and the order to Orendians to sell them any Aksandan slaves.

Tall Sky went to Melody and said, "He signed the agreements and he asked Father God into his heart."

Melody hugged him and kissed him. "I'm so proud of you," she said.

"You must hide your hair now. There are many people coming to buy these goods," said Tall Sky.

He went to the next wagon and told them to cover their hair and stay inside. Soon the caravan was flooded with customers. Most of them were men and most of them bought things. Halden would use the silver to buy slave girls.

The customers bought so many things that the soldiers were able to empty ten wagons. King Jahiz sent couriers all over the city to announce the new anti-slavery law and to tell people that slaves should be brought to the Justice Center to be sold to the Aksandans. The first one to bring slaves was King Jahiz, who would take no payment for them. Ahriman brought several slaves. They were busy all afternoon purchasing slaves and bringing them to the caravan. By the evening, there were sixty-five slaves including several young children. King Jahiz said that he would have his soldiers to search the city for any more and that they could pick them up on their return trip.

Ahriman was very unhappy with this, but said nothing to the king. He liked the company of Aksandan girls and could see no reason why this should not continue. He became angrier about it as time went on. He was used to getting his own way and was a very selfish and vindictive man, indulging himself with every form of pleasure like food, alcohol, gambling and women.

# SIXTY-EIGHT SLAVES

Melody and her core group, the first six girls rescued and converted, had their hands full getting the new slaves dressed, fed, and counseled. The new slaves had been conditioned to be docile and obedient, so they presented no behavioral problems and were cooperative. They were all delighted with the prospect of going home.

When Aleph, Tall Sky, Halden, and Gantio returned, the light was fading and it was time to move on. Halden gave the order to get into the wagons and called, "Forward!" Tall Sky drove his wagon back to the road and turned west toward the sea. When they were well past the town he pulled over to a clear spot where there was room to camp. The fire detail built two fires for cooking and the cooks brought out twice as many pots full of meat and vegetables to cook. It took longer than usual to make the flat bread. A few soldiers brought the slaves some bowls, spoons and cups.

Tall Sky assembled the girls in a rocky area and bade them to sit down. Then he spoke to them. "My name is Tall Sky and I am a Bright Elf, not like the Bitter Elves who abducted you. Most of them have already been killed by King Aryante's army. The men in this caravan are King Aryante's soldiers who trained for this mission all winter. They learned the Orendian language and how to be merchants. The purpose of this mission is to rescue Aksandan children and return them to their homes. There are more of you in smaller towns around the country, and we intend to get them also. It will be a long trip, but we are prepared for it. You have had some pretty rough experiences, but that will change. Most of our freed slaves are already married.

While you are with us, you will dress as men and hide your hair under a cap. This is for your protection from onlookers. You will sleep six girls to a wagon. You will keep your bowls, cups and spoons in your wagon and wash them after every meal. You must not be friendly with the soldiers. They are here only for your protection and must be alert to dangers at all times. They must not be distracted from their duties. This trip should be safe, but it is not without danger. There is always a possibility of attack from bandits who see a caravan as an easy target. That is why a soldier will accompany you to stand guard when you walk away to relieve yourselves. Do not go anywhere alone. Another possible danger is flying dragons. Should this occur, do not run. Get into the wagons and be absolutely silent. We have twenty-six Bright Elves with the ability to shield. They will stand before the wagons and use this power so that the dragons will not see the wagons. Shielding is a power that Father God gave us to protect ourselves and humans. We are all trained soldiers who fought in a war against Bitter Elves. We will do our best to take care of you and to protect you.

I want you to know that nobody will blame you for what has happened to you. It is not your fault. Your parents and your king want you back. In a new town called Home Fire, there are men who would be happy to marry you if you want to marry instead of returning home. My wife Melody and I will talk more with you in small groups as our journey progresses, but for now, let's have dinner. They all followed Tall Sky to the cook's fire to receive food.

Soldiers were setting up their tents, eating and washing their dishes. Activities of the night had begun. Guards had already been posted at each wagon. They would change guards in the middle of the night.

Melody said, "Tall Sky, I am totally exhausted from this day's activities. Let's go to bed soon."

"We will," said Tall Sky. They sat down on a rock to eat.

"The girls must have been pretty scared when they were told that they would be sold," said Melody.

"I imagine they were," replied Tall Sky. "They were very quiet, and they could tell we were Aksandans, but didn't know that we were taking them home."

"I feel sorry for them. They were marched to a slave market, beaten, raped, and taken to a foreign country to be sold to another man to be used and passed around. It's a horror story," said Melody.

They got up and walked back to the fire to wash their dishes. Then they walked back to their wagon for a good, long sleep with Daisy curled up on the pillow.

Morning came too soon with the smell of bacon cooking. The cooks had been up for an hour, cooking bacon and pancakes. The soldiers were folding their tents and their bedrolls and packing them in one of the wagons. Birds were singing, the sky was blue, and the sun felt warm. Melody took a deep breath and said, "What a beautiful day! I'm starving." Daisy was doing her hungry dance on Melody's shoulder, so Melody went to the cook's fire and fed Daisy. Then she and Tall Sky walked to their boulder and ate breakfast. "I'll bet the girls were happy to wake up free this morning."

The girls sounded happy. They were talking and laughing and eating breakfast. One of them said, "I forgot what it was like to be outside and to talk with other people." Another one said, "It's so good not to be slapped around and talked mean to." Conversations like this were happening throughout the group.

After the dishes were washed, Halden told the girls to get back into their wagons and called, "Forward!" The wagons headed west once again toward the sea. There would be no more towns until King's Harbor on Frothy Sea. The land stretched out flat on either side of the wagon. There were some trees, but not a forest. There were long grasses and colorful wildflowers everywhere with breezes carrying a beautiful fragrance. Daisy rode on Melody's shoulder stretching her neck this way and that so as not to miss anything. Gantio was quiet, reflecting on yesterday's activities. Then he said, "I don't trust Ahriman. He was strangely quiet throughout our negotiations and was not interested in Father God. I feel that we may have trouble from him yet. I think he is an evil man."

"I hope not," said Tall Sky. "I so want to see these kids safely home. I am a bit worried about the dragons, though. He wouldn't have contact with dragon riders would he?"

Gantio replied, "It's possible. I've heard of people he owes money to for gambling debts going missing after he sends them on a mission out of town."

"Great. That's all we need. He was none too happy to give up his slave girls," said Tall Sky.

"Didn't you say that he dabbled in magic?" asked Melody.

"It is rumored that he is a sorcerer," said Gantio.

"Maybe we should hire one of those big ships to sail to Aksanda with the girls we already have. Then we know that they at least will be safe and the soldiers can travel around the country and pick up the rest of the slaves," said Melody.

"That is actually a good plan," said Tall Sky. "They could save time by sleeping in the wagons and traveling lighter and faster. I will talk to Halden about it. You and I and Aleph could take the girls back to Aksanda. They would be safe and their ordeal would be over sooner. Besides, it would be less likely for them to cause noise during a dragon assault."

"I know, and besides that, we have some pregnant girls who shouldn't give birth on a caravan. They couldn't be moved for several days and we don't even have a midwife," said Melody.

"Now, I just hope that there will be a ship's captain willing to do it," said Tall Sky. They soon pulled up to the town of King's Harbor. Tall Sky, Gantio and Halden rode up to the inn to talk with the innkeeper. Tall Sky said, "Do you know if there is a large ship for hire, or do you expect a large ship soon?"

"Yes, the Abbey is in the harbor now. Her captain is seated over there in the corner. His name is Captain Artiz," said the innkeeper. Tall Sky introduced himself and asked if the Abby was for hire to Free Harbor.

"What is your cargo?" asked Captain Artiz.

"We have sixty-five girls to take home to Aksanda and we have written permission from King Jahiz to do so," said Tall Sky. "King Jahiz has banned slavery in Orendia and has given us permission to buy back all Aksandan slaves. We are on a mission for King Aryante to do so, and we will pay you well."

Captain Artiz and Tall Sky agreed on a price. "We will leave as soon as you are ready," said Captain Artiz. Tall Sky walked back to the caravan and told the girls to take their blanket rolls and follow him to the ship that would take them to Aksanda. They followed him to the ship and boarded. Meanwhile, Gantio and Aleph visited the chief of the town and showed him the decree of the king. He sold them a slave girl and told them where to find three others in a brothel. They visited the brothel and bought the girls. They took them to the caravan for men's clothing and bedrolls and walked them to the ship. Aleph said goodbye, wishing him well, and boarded the ship. The girls were not allowed on deck, so they went to a large room below and spread out their blanket rolls, happy to be off the caravan and out of danger from dragons and bandits. It was another amazing day. The ship left the harbor heading south toward Free Harbor.

The caravan opened their wagons and sold more goods. Some soldiers had been talking to the people of King's Harbor and they had a good turnout of customers. They left with two more empty wagons. They had now sold more than half of their merchandise and were headed south, traveling along the coast toward the fishing village of Kissoma. On the right, they could see the water and on the left was grassy land. They saw a large farm with a big barn, corrals and a large house. They needed some fresh produce, meat, eggs and flour, so they stopped. Halden, Gantio and several soldiers with extra horses rode up to the farm. There was a thin, dirty, Aksandan girl with long, blonde hair and blue eyes carrying water into the house. She said that her master was in the barn, so they went to the barn and made a deal to buy a large basket of eggs, some meat, flour, and fruit. The farmer bought a wagon with a team of horses to use in taking his produce to market. They then showed him the king's decree and order to sell slaves to them. He sold the girl to them and they departed with the girl and the food.

They took the girl to the cooks who washed her and dressed her in men's clothing. They told her about the sixty-eight other girls who are now sailing back to Aksanda. She was so grateful that she cried. "I haven't told anybody yet, but I'm pregnant," she said. The cook said, "There, there. We all go through that at one time or another. It will be alright. You must eat as much as you can and put some meat on your bones. There are men at Home Fire who won't mind at all if you're pregnant and they need wives. It's a new town and you will be welcome there." The cook fed her and took her to a wagon near the cook's wagon. Then they talked. She said, "My name is Talla and I have been a cook most of my life. I have two grown sons and my husband was a fisherman who was killed in a boating accident. I came with this caravan to have an adventure and to help the girls. What is your name?"

"My name is Celia. I am an orphan, and I was staying with a family and working in the field when I was taken by some slavers."

Talla said, "Celia, I have always wanted a daughter of my own. Would you be my daughter and come to live with me? I have a nice big house in Loadrel. It's a good town with caring people who will make you welcome. I will help you with the baby and take care of you as if you were my own daughter. Would you like that?"

"I would love that!" exclaimed Celia hugging her new mother.

"Now, we cooks take naps after breakfast, so let's lie down and sleep for a while. I don't want you to be alone in here. There's enough loneliness in the world," said Talla. The two fell off into a dreamless sleep.

# KISOMA

The caravan continued south along the coast toward the fishing village of Kisoma. Gantio rode with Quickturn in Tall Sky's wagon. Quickturn was the head of the Bright Elf battalion in the service of King Aryante. He had distinguished himself in many campaigns and battles, including the Battle of Othrund. Quickturn asked, "How long before we reach Kisoma?"

Gantio replied, "We will have lunch there. It's a nice enough fishing village with an inn, a tavern, some shops, and a brothel. The men work hard and play hard."

"What do you think our chances are of avoiding the dragons altogether?" asked Quickturn.

"I think that Ahriman is angry, but did not want to displease King Jahiz, so he kept silent and stewed about it. He is a dangerous and unscrupulous man, devious in all his ways. He can be trusted to do whatever pleases him, misusing his power to benefit himself. He has no pity and no mercy. I think it is likely that he will send the dragon riders to pursue us. It is good that we do not have the sixty-eight girls with us now. Besides, they would be too many for us to care for properly, and we need empty wagons for those we will rescue. Melody must be glad to be off the caravan. She tried to talk Tall Sky into leaving as soon as dragons were mentioned. Of course she was worried about Daisy and the pregnant girls, but she was also terrified of fire breathing dragons. I think I am too," said Gantio.

"What of the Bitter Elves? Are there enough of them to cause problems for us?" asked Quickturn.

"There are enough of them and Ahriman knows some of them from frequenting the brothels and the taverns," said Gantio. "He could have them attack us. They like to steal things and they don't know that we are really a convoy of soldiers."

Quickturn sighed. "Nothing worth doing is ever easy," he said. "It looks like a fishing village up ahead."

"It is Kisoma," said Gantio. Quickturn drove up to the edge of town and stopped his wagon. Gantio, Quickturn, Halden, and several soldiers with horses rode up to an inn and talked to the innkeeper who told them where the chief lived and served them some ale. "Are there any slave girls in this town?"

"Yes, the chief has one and the brothel has two. I even have one. Nobody else in town has enough wealth to own one." Gantio showed the man the King's decree and orders. The innkeeper quickly sold the girl and called for her to come out. She was slight of build with brown hair and hazel eyes and was dressed in a ruffled, low cut dress. Halden sent her back to the caravan with a soldier. "We are inviting everyone here to come to our caravan to buy goods. You are welcome." They left and went to the chief's house where they bought another girl and sent her back to the caravan. The last stop was a little rough. The brothel owner was willing to sell at a high price and one of the girls was with a customer who did not want to change partners. He had to be restrained and the owner had to be threatened with bodily harm. They finally agreed to a price and they left with two girls who were glad to be with their own countrymen again.

A few soldiers went door to door informing them of their sale at the caravan, and before long, they had customers who were very interested. They bought household goods, but were mainly concerned with bathtubs, so the sale lightened their load considerably. They even sold several wagons and their teams of horses. After the sale, the cooks brought out sandwiches and poured wine. The new girls sat with Halden who told them the rules of washing their own dishes, staying indoors unless accompanied by a soldier, and being silent when under attack. He told them of their mission and that it would take a few more weeks to complete. Each of the girls thanked him for rescuing them. "It's wonderful to be away from those awful men," said one of the girls.

"Well, we must be going soon. There are more of you to find out there. We mustn't leave anyone here. All of your parents deserve to have the children they raised," said Halden. He walked away and told everyone to pack up. The girls washed their dishes and climbed into their wagon. Halden rode up to the front and called, "Forward!" Quickturn drove back onto the road heading south toward Aris Port.

"What is the next town like?" asked Quickturn.

"It's a small port town like a smaller version of King's Port. It has shops, a small inn, and a brothel. Only the smaller boats can dock there. They carry on a brisk business, though. We may be able to sell some wagons there. It would be good to reimburse the king for some of the silver he spent on this caravan," said Gantio.

# ARIS PORT

The caravan had progressed along the coast and they decided to go swimming to bathe themselves before stopping at Aris Port. The girls remained in their wagons while the men bathed and changed clothes. The women gave themselves sponge baths behind their wagons. Aris Port was very close, so within a half hour they arrived and parked the caravan on the edge of town. A boat had already gone before them and the captain had told the people news of the caravan. They were very excited to see it and started to meet it as soon as it arrived. Halden, Gantio, Quickturn, and four soldiers rode into town to see the town chief. Gantio showed him the king's decree and orders. He immediately got his slave girl and sold her to them. One of the soldiers took her to the cook at the cook's wagon. The chief told them where the brothel was, so they walked to the brothel and bought two more girls. They took the girls back to the caravan and told them to go into a wagon and put on men's clothing and caps to hide their hair. The town's people bought many things and again wanted bathtubs. Several men bought wagons. The caravan left with twenty-five wagons. They drove past the town and kept going until the light started fading. Then they pulled over for dinner and camping. The fire detail made two cooking fires and the other men ministered to the horses. Then they pitched their tents. The new girls had no idea of what was going on, so Halden asked them to step outside where they sat on some logs while he talked to them.

"We are here to take you home. The men in the caravan are King Aryante's soldiers who trained to be merchants for this caravan. We think that our country's children deserve to live in Aksanda. While you are with us, you must dress as men for your own protection so as not to attract any unwanted attention from the Orendians. I think you all know what that's like. You will have your own bowl, spoon, and cup which you will wash after every meal and keep in your wagon. You will be accompanied by a soldier any time you leave your wagon. You will not be friendly with the soldiers. They are here solely for your protection. Do you have any questions?" asked Halden.

"How long before we get home?" asked one of the girls.

"Several weeks," said Halden. "You wouldn't want to leave the rest of the girls here would you?" They all said, "No," at once. There is always a possibility of bandits on the road, but we are well equipped to handle that. Now, if there are no more questions, let's go get some dinner." They walked to the cook's fire, got some stew and flatbread and went back to the logs to sit down and eat their meal.

Celia said, "The people here are very nice. I'm an orphan and I'm pregnant. One of the cooks named Talla said that she would adopt me and help me with the baby. She said that she always wanted a daughter and that her husband had died in a boating accident and her sons are grown. I'm so grateful for this. I was really scared about being all alone and pregnant."

"That would be scary. I'm Aisha and I don't know if I'm pregnant or not. I was in a brothel and would have no idea of who the father might be. I hated being there and having to be with those men. They were smelly and vulgar and sometimes drunk. Some of them would call me names and hit me. What is the matter with these men anyway?"

Halden said, "They don't know Father God. If they did, they would stay at home with their wives. Have any of you prayed to Father God for help?" They shook their heads no. "It's easy. You just talk to Him like He was your best friend. You ask him to forgive you and ask Him to live in your heart and He will. He will love you and help you and heal your minds and your spirits. You will be like a brand new person. Then you forgive everyone who hurt you so that the hate won't hurt you anymore. This really works. You try it now," said Halden. There was much murmuring as the girls prayed to God. "What a beautiful thing," thought Halden. When the murmuring stopped, Halden said, "It's time to wash dishes and go to bed. Goodnight." They went to bed and the new girls slept like babies.

The next morning the girls awoke with a new perspective. They were happy and hopeful. Aromas of ham and hotcakes wafted about and they grabbed their dishes and walked to the cook's fire. "This is so good," said Celia. "Thank you."

Talla said, "Remember to eat as much as you can for now. You can cut back later after you put on some weight."

Celia whispered, "The new girls asked Father God into their hearts last night. Isn't that great?"

"Yes, it is. They will be alright, just watch and see," said Talla.

Soon they were on their way again toward a new town.

# THE VOYAGE

Melody, Tall Sky and Aleph had their hands full keeping the girls calm and fed and toileted. Food on board was not hot. They ate sandwiches, cheese, fruit, and raw vegetables. It took a while for the girls to become accustomed to the rocking of the ship. They ate below deck, but they used an outhouse on deck. There was one crew member in charge of emptying the bucket after every use. Tall sky and Aleph took turns helping the girls across the deck to the outhouse. They were all afraid of falling overboard even though there was a railing. Tall Sky, Melody and Aleph divided the girls into three groups to talk with them. Each girl had a story to tell, and it was important that she had a chance to tell it with others who would understand.

Tall Sky asked his group, "Were all of you taken from your homes?" They all nodded yes. "Were any of your parents killed?" They all said, "No."

"Were all of you sold at auctions?" asked Tall Sky.

They all said, "Yes."

"Did your captors hit you and rape you?" asked Tall Sky.

They all said, "Yes."

"It is a terrible thing to do to a young, innocent person, and it is an evil man who does such a thing. None of this was your fault. You are not to be blamed for things that men did to you. They are the ones who are to be blamed. King Aryante's army has already killed many of them. The auctions were cleared out and many slaves have already been returned to their homes. Then the winter came, and this mission had to be planned and soldiers trained and wagons built. As soon as it was possible, King Aryante ordered the caravan to leave for Orendia. I am sorry that we could not get here sooner. You must understand that you are very precious to your parents and to the king. Would one of you tell me what happened to you?" asked Tall Sky.

"My name is Alia. I was gardening when a Bitter Elf grabbed me and rode away with me. When he got me out in the country, he tore my clothes and hit me and raped me. After that I was scared and hurt and did whatever he told me to do. We joined several others and rode to an outside market where he put me in a pen with other girls who had the same experience and that night we were auctioned off. My new owner also raped me and made me to ride to Orendia with five other girls. He sold us to other men. I was sold to an innkeeper who used me for himself and some customers who paid him well for my company. I am so glad to be away from all of that."

"My name is Treya and the same thing happened to me except that I was sold to a brothel where men paid to use me. If I complained to my owner, he would whip me with a whip that didn't leave marks, but it hurt really badly. Some men who came in were clean and perfumed, but some were dirty and smelly. I had to do whatever they told me to or face the whip. I was thinking of ways to kill myself."

"My name is Lakia and I was stolen on my way to visit my friend at the next farm. There were three of them and they took turns with me until we reached the auction where I was purchased by an Orendian who brought me here and sold me to a farmer. He used me for pleasure and to help with chores. He wanted me to get pregnant. Thank God I didn't."

"My name is Rendy and I was stolen while pulling weeds in a field. I was beaten and raped and sold to an Orendian at auction. He made me ride with two other girls to Orendia and I was sold to the town chief who used me for pleasure. He dressed me in beautiful gowns and jewelry, but it was degrading to be used without being married."

The stories were much the same throughout the groups. All of the girls were happy to have been rescued.

Each of the team leaders recorded the girls' names, parents' names and addresses to be presented to King Aryante. Captain Artiz came down the stairs and said, "We will be dropping anchor at Wine Port over night. It is important to sail during the daytime to avoid any problems. We will be there shortly.

# TREACHERY AND SORCERY

Ahriman met with the Bitter elves Lyra, and Erspar at the ancient ruins behind the palace. Ahriman said, "I want to tell you about a caravan of merchants that has been selling many goods in the cities. These goods include jewelry, household things, and fine leather apparel like clothing and boots. They also have a fine selection of fancy knives. Have you heard of this caravan? The merchants of this caravan have also been buying our slave girls. Does this interest you?"

Lyrah said, "The jewels interest me. If they're selling things, they have silver. If they're buying girls, they have silver and jewels. Have you seen these jewels?"

Ahriman said, "As a matter of fact, I bought these from them." He showed them a very ornate necklace and some rings.

"Do they have more of these?" asked Erspar.

"They have plenty more. They have enough to sell all over Orendia and still take home much of it," said Ahriman. "I wouldn't mind having some of it by helping you. I could put a sleep spell on the camp and you could do what you want with the girls and take what you want when you go."

"Why don't you do it by yourself?" asked Lyra suspiciously.

"I can't be involved in these things directly," said Ahriman. "I'm the king's advisor."

"How many do you think we should take with us?" asked Lyra.

"About a dozen should do," said Ahriman. "Keep in mind, the more you take with you, the less you will have for yourselves, and I need a share of it too."

"Where is this caravan?" asked Erspar.

"My spies tell me that the caravan is just south of Aris Port where they will camp tonight," said Ahriman.

"Our band is camped near there," said Lyra.

"I know," said Ahriman. "That is why I contacted you at this time. You can be there in two hours if you ride cross country."

"Sounds good. We will leave now. You will have your share tomorrow at noon," said Lyra.

The two Bitter Elves left the ruins and rode cross country toward Aris Port.

Ahriman went to a tavern gaming table very pleased with himself.

At the caravan the cooks were preparing dinner, everyone not on guard washed up and the girls combed out their hair. The new girls were beginning to relax, thinking about going home. The cooks gave the girls some wine before dinner and they sat on some rocks sipping their wine and watching the sea birds wading in the froth at the shore line. It had been a beautiful day. It was the first time in six months that they weren't being abused, and they could hardly believe their good fortune. One of the new girls named Haley walked over to the horses and was petting one, when the tack man walked over to check the leather on the horse's bridle. He said, "Hello young lady. Do you like this horse? Have you ever had one?"

Haley said, "Yes, I have. I had a beautiful horse named Rosie at home. I hope she's still there. You aren't a soldier, are you?"

Marsten said, "No, I'm not. They hired me because I'm a tack specialist, and they have a lot of tack on a caravan that has to be in tip-top shape at all times. They didn't want to put all these beautiful women in danger, did they?"

"No, definitely not," she said. "Do you drive one of these wagons?"

"Yes, I drive that one. It carries extra tack and wagon parts. Where do you come from in Aksanda?" asked Marsten.

"I come from a farm near Talath. Where do you come from?" asked Haley.

"Actually, I spent my life in Vivallen and I now work there at the king's stables. It's a great job and I can exercise the horses, which I love to do," said Marsten.

"I love to do that too, but I haven't been able to ride for a while now. I can hardly wait to get back home and ride my horse again," said Haley.

"You're a sweet girl, Haley. If you were mine, I would take good care of you and protect you and love you. Would you like to sit with me at dinner tonight?" asked Marsten.

"It's too soon, but maybe someday," said Haley. "I have to go back now." She walked back to the cook's fire and got some dinner.

After dinner, while she was washing her dishes, Marsten asked her if he could come to visit her at her farm near Talath. She said that it would be alright if her parents were there with them. He smiled and walked away.

The soldiers hooked up hammocks under the wagons and helped the cooks put away things. They fed and watered the horses and went to bed.

Quickturn told his Bright Elves to remain alert for any signs of magic or of movement around the camp. Before long the soldiers on guard duty were fast asleep. Quickturn sensed a sleep spell and he and his Bright Elves shielded against it. The soldiers woke up just in time to fight off some Bitter Elves who attacked the caravan's guards. It was dark, so the fighting was hand- to-hand. Bitter Elves screamed as they were stabbed with knives. One of the guards was too sleepy and was killed. Other guards managed to wake up enough to defend themselves. Quickturn used his sword, killing one after another. Bright Elves went bright to shed light on the area. They counted the corpses. They had killed an even dozen of Bitter Elves. Searching the bodies, they found a note from Ahriman asking them to meet him at the ruins behind the palace. Halden said, "So, the plot is revealed and what we suspected is true. We will show this note to King Jahiz. The soldiers dug a large hole and buried the bodies. The silver taken from their pockets and saddle bags was put aside for the purchase of more slaves. The rest of the night passed peacefully and most of them awoke rested and ready for a new day.

The cooks made a special breakfast of the eggs bought at the farm and sausages and hot cakes. It was welcome and heartening to eat well after the night's battle. Marsten sat beside Haley on a nearby rock and said, "Did the fight waken you last night?"

"Yes, it did. I heard that they were Bitter Elves. They must all be dead," said Haley.

"Yes, we buried them last night. One of the soldiers was sleepy from a spell that Ahriman used and he was killed. He was a friend of mine and I will miss him. He was a good man and did not deserve to die that way. I would like to kill Ahriman for this," said Marsten.

"The king will deal with Ahriman. Halden will show Ahriman's note to the king," said Haley.

Halden walked by and said that they should get ready to leave. "I'm already tired of being inside the wagon, but I know it's necessary in order to go home," said Haley.

The men fed and watered the horses and hitched them to the wagons. Halden rode up to Quickturn's wagon and called out, "Forward!" Gantio said, "Our next stop is just a fishing village named Nadima. It is small and quaint with a tavern and some stores. There is no brothel there, but the tavern has some rooms in the back. The owner usually has a few girls there. We should be in Nadima in time for lunch." The sun was sparkling on the sea and the air was cool. "There are more trees to the left," remarked Quickturn.

"Yes, there is a forest over there that stretches into the middle of Orendia. Creatures living there are better left alone. Some of them are large and very dangerous," said Gantio. "There are huge mantises that date back farther than anyone can remember. They spew acid that burns right through the skin and they can leap far into the air."

"I'll be happy to leave them alone," said Quickturn. "We don't need any more complications."

"Remember, we have a sorcerer mad at us, and he can reach us with his magic," said Gantio.

"And we have Father God on our side. He can warn us of impending danger, and can help us to repel evil spells," said Quickturn. "We will get these children home safely."

The girls looked out the windows and talked among themselves about their experiences in Orendia. Celia said, "My master's wife had a flying cat. She was multi-colored and so soft. I loved to pet her. Of course she spoke Orendian, so I couldn't understand her very well, but she liked me and would land on my shoulder and purr. I wish we could have brought her with us."

"My master's wife had one, too. I loved that cat. She was black with green eyes. I sure would like to get one and take it home to the farm," said Lelia. "Can you imagine my mother seeing a flying cat that talks?" They all laughed. "We have regular cats, a dog, horses, and a cow on our farm. It was a lot of hard work, but it sure beats having to let men hurt you and get all personal with you." They all agreed with that. "It's embarrassing. Are we going to tell people about it?"

There was a resounding, "No." "What will we tell them that we have been doing?" asked Lelia.

Celia answered, "We tell them that we were made to work hard in fields. It is something that they will understand, and it will stop their curiosity. Then they can't talk about it with neighbors who would look at us funny."

"I agree," said Lelia. "They would never understand this and it would only hurt them to know the truth."

"I love being able to go home. I had resigned myself to living this kind of life forever," said Celia.

"I was thinking about running away, but I didn't know which way to go and I had no food and no silver," said Lelia.

Soon the caravan pulled over on the edge of the fishing village Nadima and Halden, Quickturn, Gantio, and two soldiers rode to the tavern. There were only a couple of old men drinking ale at a table. The barkeeper served ale to the men and asked them if they wanted a woman. Halden replied, "Yes, but you had better first see this decree from the king regarding slaves. We are here to buy back our Aksandan citizens. The barkeeper went to the back rooms and brought out two slave girls and accepted the silver that was offered for them. He told them that the villagers were too poor to afford to buy slaves, but that the town chief had one. They sent the girls back to the caravan with the soldiers and bought a third girl from the chief. They told the chief that there was a sale of goods at the caravan and that his men would be telling the villagers about it. Halden rode to the docks and made a deal to buy all the fish they had for dinner that night. The fishermen were delighted and brought their fish in carts to the caravan where they purchased goods and bathtubs.

The new girls were put one in each wagon so that the other girls could explain the rules to them and let them know that they were going home. They were amazed by this and so grateful that they cried. After the sale, they drove away from the town and pulled over for lunch. Even at lunch the soldiers were vigilant and guards were posted.

After lunch they turned the caravan around, heading north toward a new road where they headed east toward the town of Tanga, a short distance down the road. It was a farming community with some industry like paper making, a lumber mill, and a grist mill. Gantio said that he was not familiar with this town, never having a reason to visit it. They didn't have to leave the rode to visit Tanga, as the edge of the town was right on the road. Halden, Gantio, Quickturn and two soldiers rode into town to visit the local tavern, ordered ale and asked the whereabouts of Aksandan slave girls. He brought out two girls and apologized for one being pregnant. Gantio showed him the decree of King Jahiz and offered to purchase the girls. The barkeeper told them that the town chief had one and so did the grist mill and the lumber mill owners have one. They purchased the girls with no problems and brought them back to the caravan where they put them in a wagon and had Celia to tell them the rules and get them changed into men's clothing. Soon the town's people came to the caravan and bought household goods and a couple of bathtubs.

"We have done very well," said Gantio. "Our sales have been great and we are purchasing slaves without many problems, thanks to that decree of King Jahiz. We have fewer wagons and have rescued eighty-eight girls. We regretably lost one man, but our losses could have been much worse. I am very encouraged."

"It is good. What is our next destination?" asked Quickturn.

"We will drive to Ari Road and turn right. Then we will travel the same distance to Mukimi. The problem with this is the amount of time spent in the forest. You have noticed that the amount of trees has been increasing since we left the Shore Road? There will be no more opportunities to purchase slave girls here because of the forest dangers. Nobody lives here. There are bears, and cougars, but there are also giant mantises and great wolves. We must not camp here, so I recommend that we have sandwiches on our persons to eat when necessary. I must talk to Halden."

Halden rode up and told them to move the wagons further down the road away from the village. Quickturn drove down the road for a while and stopped. He did not pull off the road close to trees. Gantio told Halden about the dangers and Halden called together the soldiers to discuss the defense of the caravan. Halden told them about the forest and said, "The only safer way to go would be to avoid the denser part of the forest by backtracking and taking the Shore Road south and then east to Sibly. Then we approach Mukima from the south. There is forest near Mukima, but not the worst part." The soldiers felt that it would be better to not endanger the caravan, so they decided to avoid the forest as much as they could. They turned the wagons around and headed for Shore Road. It was a wise decision. Ahriman was getting ready to use mantises against them.

That evening they camped on Shore Road near Nadima. Clouds gathered and the cooks fried fish for dinner. "We will sleep in and under the wagons tonight. We have six empty wagons for the soldiers to use. We will tie up the horses really well tonight. When dinner was ready, everyone got their food and ate seated on boulders watching the clouds rolling in over the sea. They drank berry wine for warmth and relaxed talking about their day and wondering about the forest. "I would rather face a storm any day than to be attacked by those forest animals and giant insects," said Gantio.

Halden said, "Yes, we're here to rescue girls not to get them killed." The storm began over the sea with lightning in the clouds and thunder. Some soldiers helped the cooks pack things back into the wagon and put out the fire with buckets of sea water. This kept the wind from blowing sparks into the caravan. Then they hooked up the hammocks and many soldiers entered the wagons for protection. They drove the wagons close to Nadima and some of the soldiers went to the inn to spend the night. The girls were excited and a little afraid to be spending a stormy night in the wagons. The wind buffeted the wagons making them rock and the rain battered the roofs and walls, but the wagons did not leak. The girls cuddled warmly into their covers and fell into a deep sleep.

The next morning everyone felt rested and hungry. The cooks fixed breakfast and the men used dry wood from their stored wood to build the fires. "That was quite a storm we had last night," said Halden. "Did everybody stay dry?"

"We were very snug and comfortable," said Lelia. They poured some hot tea and some hot porridge. It was a perfect breakfast after a stormy night. The sky was clear and blue and the sun was sparkling on the water. "It feels so good to be out and free."

"It sure does, and Halden said that we will meet King Aryante when we get back," said Haley. After breakfast the men bathed in the sea and the girls went in after the men were through. The men stood guard with their backs to the sea. Then they packed up, fed and watered the horses and hitched them to the wagons. They traveled south along the shore all day.

Meanwhile, Melody and Tall Sky had weathered the storm in the belly of a ship that rocked to and fro all night. They managed to get some sleep, but were awakened by the thunder quite often. Captain Artiz assured them that they were in a safe harbor and that there was no danger of sinking. Still, everyone was grateful for the morning to come and still waters. They could see Wine Port and wondered how many slave girls were there. Captain Artiz said, "We will be in Free Harbor by nightfall. I'll bet you are all looking forward to planting your feet on solid ground. You are welcome to spend one more night here. There may not be sixty-eight rooms available." There was a collective groan from the crowd.

"We will take you up on that," said Tall Sky. "Aleph and I will go into town and bring sandwiches back for everyone. It would be unsafe for all of you to be in this town without proper supervision. Tomorrow morning we will hire boats to take us up the river to Loss Port and hire some wagons to take us to Vivallen. There we will shop for new clothes and visit the castle. You must be patient for just a few more days." Captain Artiz told his crew to unfurl the sails and raise the anchor. They sailed out of port and followed the coast toward Free Harbor in Aksanda.

Traveling in wagons took more time. They wouldn't reach wine port for two days. The girls amused themselves by looking out the windows and talking about their plans for the future. Some of them wanted to go home and stay with their parents until they were married. Others wanted to live at Home Fire or another town and get jobs. They also shared some of their experiences with each other making fun of the Orendian men and calling them idiots.

At lunch time Halden found some of the puzzles and the toy house making kits and gave them to the girls. They would have hours of fun playing with these. Halden saved a world puzzle for King Jahiz. He also put aside a narrative about the islands and the people of the world that Melody had made for King Jahiz. Halden said, "We will be in Sibly for dinner, camp there and send some soldiers to Mukima to check for more slaves. I will not take the entire caravan up that road. It is too close to the forest and there are too many seriously dangerous beasts in that forest. Normally they would probably leave us alone, but with Ahriman's urging, they could come after us. Now we had better pack up and move out.

They watered the horses and headed down the road toward Sibly. The girls worked the puzzles and put together various types of toy houses. Hours later they arrived at Sibly, another fishing village. Halden, Quickturn and Gantio rode into the village and stopped by the tavern. The owner sold them one slave girl and sent them to the chief's home where they bought another slave. There was only one brothel and they bought two more girls there. They delivered four girls to the caravan, placing each one in a different wagon with other girls to get to know the rules and the routine of the caravan. The villagers came out to see the caravan out of curiosity and ended up making purchases. They spent enough to cover the purchases of the girls with silver left over. When the soldiers consolidated items, they had one more empty wagon. Everything was going as planned and

Halden was pleased. Halden asked the villagers about the forest and Mukima, their next stop. They confirmed what he had heard about the forest beasts, and told him that Mukima had some problems with them, but not many. Mukima was right on the edge of the forest.

Quickturn led the caravan past the village, close to the turn off to Mukima and pulled off the road in a clearing. The girls climbed out of the wagons and walked about stretching their legs. The fire detail made two fires and the cooks brought out the cooking pots filled with meat and vegetables. They made flatbread, placing it in a large basket. The girls walked over to the water's edge, waded in the foam, and picked up seashells. Being farm girls, this was a real treat for them. "I love the sea," said Haley. "When we get back, I want to live near the sea or a big lake like Lake Perilough. Halden says that Home Fire is on the lake and so is Loadrel. That's for me. I love the water."

Celia said, "I'm definitely going to live in Loadrel with Talla until I have my baby. After that I might get married to someone at Home Fire."

The soldiers fed and watered the horses and curried them. Then everybody ate dinner sitting on the long line of large rocks behind the wagons. Halden said, "Who are we going to send to Mukima tomorrow?"

Quickturn replied, "I thought that we should ask for volunteers, but we should have some Bright Elves and some soldiers. They would be risking their lives against unknown beasts. Hopefully none would attack until after they talk to the villagers about how to kill them. I'm thinking that carrying torches on the way back would be a good idea. Most animals are terrified of fire. They should also ride our swiftest horses and carry lances and swords. I am pretty sure that Ahriman has been monitoring our progress and will make an attack on us at this point."

"I'm thinking that fifteen men would be a good number," said Halden.

"That sounds good," said Quickturn.

The rest of the evening passed with the girls talking and enjoying themselves on the beach. They played like children making sand castles. Night came with a beautiful sunset that stretched across the sky and reflected in the sea. They all went to bed happy and hopeful, knowing that tomorrow morning they would not have to travel.

After a good night's sleep, there was breakfast and decisions to be made. Quickturn received his fifteen volunteers and armed them well. Then they rode down the road toward Mukima, watching the woods on both sides of the road. The woods would not be dense as they were on the northern side of Mukima. In about an hour of riding, they approached Mukima and rode up to the local tavern. Quickturn spoke to the owner who told him that he had a girl, the chief had one, and so did the owner of the lumber business.

"What problems have you had with forest creatures here?" asked Quickturn.

The tavern owner replied, "There are some terrible creatures, but they mainly stay away from people. We kill any of them that we find. There is an insect called the mantis that is very large. It leaps high and far, and it spews acid that burns the skin. It is hard to kill, but a well placed arrow can kill it. If it kills a person or an animal, it eats it with very strong mandibles. Carrying torches will help to scare it away. The wolves in the forest are three times the size of a normal dog and they hunt in packs. The best thing to do is to ride away as fast as you can. There are also large birds of prey. Again, moving quickly is one of the best things you can do. There are bears and lions, but you should be safe from them on the road. Why did you come to Mukima?"

Quickturn said, "We come on a mission for the King of Aksanda with the decree of King Jahiz. Here it is. It declares that slavery is illegal and that slaves should be sold to us so that we can return them to their parents. You see, Bitter Elves and slavers stole them from their homes in Aksanda and sold them to slavers from Orendia. We are here to offer you a fair price for your slave."

He paid the man and walked over to the chief's house to buy a second slave. Then they did the same with the owner of the lumber business. They told the girls that they were taking them home, but may have trouble on the road and to be ready to ride at a gallop. The girls were delighted with the prospect of going home and understood the dangers of being on the road.

They lighted their torches and left Mukima trotting their horses. About half way to the caravan, wolves started chasing them and they increased speed to a gallop. Then a high pitched buzzing sound added to the confusion and the wolves stopped chasing them, turning off the road to avoid the mantises. About five large insects pounced onto the road and ran after the horses. Quickturn called out, "Shield!" His Bright Elves shielded and rode to the sides of the road where they released a volley of arrows aimed at the mantises' foreheads. One by one the mantises shrieked and collapsed on the ground. The riders continued at a gallop until they reached the caravan. The soldiers were already on the road and pulled away as soon as the girls were safely aboard. They continued down the shoreline heading for Wine Port.

Before Wine Port they stopped for lunch and briefed the new girls about their mission and the required behavior aboard the caravan. They changed into men's clothing and hid their hair under caps. Lunch consisted of sandwiches of bread and cheese and dried fruit with wine. It felt good to be out of the wagons for a time, walk around and feel the breeze on their faces. The new girls were amazed to hear about the sixty-eight other slaves who were bought and sent on a ship to Aksanda. The new girls had traveled by ship to Orendia last fall. "We have a far way to travel still," said Halden. "We have to travel to other towns and buy back more slaves. Without King Jahiz' decree this would have been much more difficult. So far nobody has denied us the purchase of their slaves. King Jahiz has an evil advisor named Ahriman who has tried to kill us twice. We have to deal with him somehow, but that's for another day."

It was a great day to travel away from the woods and toward a large town. Wine Port was a good sized city for Orendia. Large ships could sail into port and a bustling trade took place there. Halden called the soldiers together and said, "There may be Bitters in this town, so be aware, but I would like you to go into the town, ten at a time, to have a mug of ale, listen to the talk in the taverns and report back to me. All of you deserve a break from your caravan duties. Quickturn, Gantio and I will visit the usual places and buy back slaves. We will do these things first and then let the villagers know that we have goods for sale. There should be a good turnout and more slaves here than usual. Let's move this caravan. We are very close to Wine Port." The girls climbed back into the wagons and Quickturn pulled back onto the road. They traveled for about a half hour and pulled over at the edge of town. It was a large town sprawling out along the coast.

The first thing that Quickturn, Gantio, and Halden did was to locate the chief of the town. Halden brought ten soldiers with him and five extra horses. Gantio told the chief about King Jahiz' decree and asked him the whereabouts of the slaves. The chief was very cooperative, listing all the places they should visit. The chief said, "I am tired of my slave anyway and I am tired of my wife. Would you buy her too? Shasta, come here and bring Lindel with you." Gantio was impressed with the beauty and demeanor of Shasta and said that he would buy her and marry her providing that she had a writ of divorce. The chief gladly wrote it and gave it to Gantio. The chief told her to go get her clothing and put it in a bag. They agreed on a price and Halden paid him for both women. When they were outside, Gantio put his arm around her and said, "Don't worry. I will be kind to you and protect you. We will go to Aksanda where you will live with me in King Aryante's castle." She smiled and thanked him. Halden sent the women back to the caravan with a soldier and told him to come back with the horses.

Their next stop was a brothel. There were men sitting in the waiting room drinking wine. Presently they were greeted by the owner. Gantio showed him King Jahiz' decree and he frowned. "These girls make me a lot of silver. I don't want to sell them, but if I have to, you must pay a fair price. Gantio told him what he was willing to pay and they haggled about the price until Quickturn told him that they could just take the girls and leave. The owner agreed on the price and brought out three girls dressed scantily. Quickturn gave them some men's clothing and told them to get dressed. Then two soldiers escorted them back to the caravan. "Gantio, you did very well. I probably would have paid more. Where do we go next?"

"We go to another brothel," said Gantio. He led them down the street to another brothel. The owner had five slaves. He said, "Two of them are pregnant anyway and I would have to throw them out next month. The other three are still good. Replacing these girls will cost me much silver. They don't come cheap, you know." Gantio and the owner agreed on a price, and the owner had the girls brought into the office. Quickturn gave them men's clothing to put on and they left on horses going to the caravan.

Gantio said, "The next place is a tavern with rooms. It serves mostly the sailors who need a place to stay overnight. We must talk only to the owner apart from the customers, because the sailors can get pretty rowdy. These men are not fond of elves, so Quickturn should wait outside. Halden and I will bring the girls to you." This arrangement worked out fine. The owner did not want any trouble from two kings and quickly closed a deal on two girls. Gantio had the girls change clothes and led them to their horses.

Halden said, "We're doing well today. We've bought fourteen slaves and a wife. That brings the total to thirty-nine." Gantio and Quickturn laughed. "I wonder how Tall Sky and Melody are doing. We should ask the harbor master if he knows anything about their ship, the Abby with Captain Artiz. We should visit the last two taverns and then visit the harbor master." The next two taverns yielded four more girls whom they sent back to the caravan. The harbor master said that the Abby anchored there and stayed the night during a bad storm. Then they bought about a hundred sandwiches and left for Aksanda. They rode back to the caravan with the good news.

Halden gathered the soldiers and asked what news there was of Bitters. They reported that there were Bitters around and that they had done some damage and had robbed a few places. Halden said, "On a brighter note, the ship carrying the sixty-eight girls safely weathered that storm right here in Wine Port. The next morning they bought a hundred sandwiches and sailed for Aksanda. Everyone applauded. We have now saved one hundred and seven slaves. Also, Gantio has bought a wife. They applauded again. We have thirty-nine slaves on our caravan. We had better stop selling wagons. Now let's get our merchandise out on tables. Customers will be arriving soon. Customers were only allowed near the wagons that held merchandise. They bought enough to unload another wagon. After the sale the soldiers packed up the wagons and drove further down the road to camp for the night.

The new girls were still confused and worried, thinking that they were going to another auction. Halden asked them to sit outside so he could talk to them. He said, "Welcome to our caravan. We have come to Orendia at the order of King Aryante to rescue you and bring you back home. It has been a mission long in the making, beginning last fall when the king's soldiers trained to be merchants and learned the Orendian language. These wagons were made especially for this journey. We have a decree signed by King Jahiz that makes slavery illegal in Orendia. This has enabled us to buy back the children that were stolen from their homes in Aksanda. You will travel with us in men's clothing to avoid any unwanted attention from Orendian men. We have already sent sixty-eight slaves home on a ship and have thirty-nine slaves with us now. We have other towns to visit where we will buy back more girls. The men in this caravan are soldiers here to protect you. You are not to talk to them, as they must remain vigilant at all times. There are Bitter Elves, bandits, and wild animals to watch out for. You will go nowhere alone. A soldier will accompany you. You will be issued a bowl, a spoon and a cup which you will wash after every meal and keep in your wagon. Are there any questions?"

One of the girls said, "Thank you. I am so glad to be going home. I thought I would never see my parents again." The girls applauded. The new girls were given their bowls, spoons and cups. Wine was poured and they relaxed, watching the sea and sipping wine. The fire detail made two fires and the cooks brought out pots filled with food to cook.

Two new girls, Brindie and Sal talked about this experience. Brindie said, "I never thought anything like this was possible. The Orendians are so evil that I can hardly believe they would let us go."

Sal said, "I know what you mean, but remember how they talked about King Jahiz? They just about worship the king and would do anything he says without question. This is a miracle. We don't have to wake up and have a man paw us and have his pleasure at our expense. I didn't think that I would ever be loved again. I thought that I would get pregnant and be thrown out to die of hunger."

Brindie said, "I might be pregnant. If I am, how do I explain it to my parents? What can we tell them that won't horrify them?"

"You could get married soon and tell them that you worked as a housekeeper for an old lady," said Sal.

"That would work if I can find someone to marry me," said Brindie.

"You know, we all have to do that and there are a lot of us. Let's talk to Halden about it," said Sal. They walked over to Halden and asked him how they could find husbands quickly so that they wouldn't have to tell their parents everything.

Halden said, "If you had boyfriends before you left, they might marry you. If not, you are welcome to start a new life in a town and get a job and meet someone like that. If you are pregnant, there is a new town of men who want wives and will not care if you are pregnant."

Brindie said, "I think that I am pregnant, so I want to go to the new town and get married. I lived on a farm, so I know how to do many things like gardening, making cheese and butter, and sewing."

"Brindie, it sounds like you would be a perfect wife for a man at Home Fire," said Halden.

"I thought I would tell people that I worked for old people keeping house and cooking," said Sal.

Halden said, "There is no reason to tell people all that happened to you. Just act the same way that you acted before you were stolen. You are that same person after all. Let's get some stew." They walked over to the cook's fire and got in line.

"This smells good. How do you get fresh meat?" asked Brindie.

"At every town and sometimes at a farm, a few soldiers buy from the local stores," said Halden. "Since we are on the shore, we can get as much fresh fish as we want." They took their food over to the rocks and sat down.

"It's fun to eat outside and watch the sea. This is the first time that I have seen the sea. It's beautiful," said Sal.

"You will have a chance to bathe in it. It's a little cold, but refreshing," said Halden. "When the girls bathe, the soldiers stand in a long line with their backs to the water."

"May we bathe after dinner?" asked Sal.

"Of course. I will announce it," said Halden. The girls quickly finished their dinner and grabbed some towels. Halden explained how the bathing was done and the rest of the girls got their towels and soap and headed for the water. The soldiers stood guard while the girls bathed, laughing and enjoying the frothy water.

After bathing, the girls sat outside behind the wagons combing their hair and letting it dry while the soldiers bathed. "It feels good to leave the caps off for a while," said Sal.

After a while, Halden said that it was time for bed and the soldiers hooked up the hammocks under the wagons. They still had to be watchful and ready to do battle should the Bitters strike. The Bitters were aware of the caravan's wealth and it was a big draw for them. When it was dark, the Bright Elves who were standing watch sensed a sleep spell and shielded it. The Bitter Elves attacked, thinking that their spell had worked, and were surprised by a full force of soldiers who fought with far more skill than the Bitters had. After killing the Bitters, the soldiers took their valuables, tied their horses, and put the bodies in a pile beside the road. There were twenty-five Bitters in all. Halden said, "We will leave the bodies for the villagers to bury. They will be happy to know that they don't have to deal with this band of Bitters again, and it may give them an idea of what to do with any more of them."

The rest of the night passed quietly and soon the smell of ham frying and hot cakes on a griddle woke the girls. Sea birds were calling and flying about and the sound of the surf made everything seem normal. The girls heard the battle last night, but stayed snugly in their wagons. This morning they noticed a large pile of bodies and realized what protection meant. Several of the soldiers wore bandages on their arms, but no soldiers had been killed in the battle. Today promised to be more peaceful as it was a day of travel.

After breakfast, Halden instructed the girls to relieve themselves as they didn't expect to stop until lunch. There were pots in the wagons if they needed them. The girls thought, "Well, this is a caravan not an inn." Back in the wagons, Quickturn drove the wagon back onto the road going northeast toward Fentro. The girls put together puzzles and told stories. They imagined what life would be like when they were married and some of them took naps. Soon the caravan stopped to pick up two pregnant girls walking beside the road. The girls did not know where they were going. Their owner let them go because they were pregnant and his customers didn't like that. Halden took them to Talla, who bathed them and gave them clean clothes. She fed them and took them to a wagon where there were several girls to talk to. Talla told Halden that she wanted to start a home for pregnant girls and take them into her home until they find husbands. Halden said that he would set aside the silver and gems they found on the Bitters who attacked them and she could use it for the girls. Then he told the caravan to move forward.

"This journey keeps surprising me," said Quickturn. "How can people be so cruel?"

# RIVER BOATS

Tall Sky, Melody and sixty-eight redeemed slaves stepped onto a pier in Free Harbor. They were tired and sore from sleeping on the floor and they needed baths, but they felt hopeful and glad to be free. Tall Sky reserved five passenger boats to go to Loss Port. They would have to wait for some of them to come in. He took them to a used clothing store where they chose clothing for the trip while Melody purchased cakes of soap and towels. Then they walked along the shore and found a sheltered area where they could bathe and change clothes. Feeling a whole lot better, they walked along store fronts looking for a place that could sell them enough food for their trip. They chose to order sandwiches from several places and skins of wine from a third place. They bought fruit and candy, and extra bread and cheese. Each of them carried their own bag of food for several days. When they finished shopping, they boarded the five passenger boats and headed up the river. It was a beautiful day for boating. The sky was clear and blue, the birds were singing, and the air was filled with the fragrance of wildflowers. The girls had never been on a boat, so they were really enjoying this.

Tall Sky and Melody were in the lead boat. Daisy was on her shoulder looking at the shore lines and chirring. She remembered her last trip on the boat, so she was perfectly happy with this. "I wonder how the caravan is doing," said Melody. "I hope they didn't have any bandit attacks or dragon attacks."

Tall Sky said, "I would have known if anything really bad had happened. If there were bandit attacks, they would be able to handle it. I think that having less people to deal with would make it easier for them."

"The shopping went well," said Melody. "I'm glad they could take baths, even if it was in the sea. The girls really enjoyed it. None of them had seen a large body of water before."

Tall Sky said, "I enjoyed getting clean again too." Tall Sky laughed.

"It feels good to be out of that ship," said Melody. "You know I didn't like the ship we saw the last time we were in Free Harbor. I said that I would not like to ride in a ship, and, of course, the next spring came and there I was in that very uncomfortable ship. It was worth it, though, to be out of the caravan and away from Orendia."

"You didn't get your flying cats," said Tall Sky.

"I didn't even see one," said Melody, "but rescuing these girls was worth it. What should they tell people about their experience in Orendia?"

"I've been thinking about that and I think that they should not tell them everything. I think that they should make up a story about being worked hard and skip all the sexual stuff. Parents would have a real hard time with the whole truth. Even the pregnant girls should downplay the sexual involvement. The girls need people to treat them normally, not having people thinking about them being raped all the time," said Tall Sky.

"Definitely," said Melody. "I'll bet these rowers will be tired. It's a long way to Brown Bear. I'll bet the tavern owners will be surprised to see so many of the slave girls being returned." Tall Sky laughed.

"They will be glad. Remember how they called slavers scum and slime?" asked Tall Sky.

"Yes, and they said that King Aryante should do something about it and that they would help if they could," said Melody.

"You said that we should buy them back and King Aryante had a plan to do just that. I am married to a very smart woman," said Tall Sky and he kissed her on the cheek.

"What's really amazing is King Jahiz believing in Father God and signing the treaty. That should please King Aryante. I can hardly wait to see his face when he sees all these girls. Don't forget, we have three little kids too. Their parents are going to be so happy to see them," said Melody.

"Yes, these people have some very interesting experiences coming their way," said Tall Sky. He looked behind him. The girls were peacefully enjoying their trip up the river.

# FENTRO

The caravan stopped before reaching Fentro and pulled over for lunch. Everyone was tired and hungry. The men watered the horses and the cooks brought out sandwiches. The girls walked behind some brush to relieve themselves and walked up and down the caravan for exercise. Then they sat down on some rocks and logs to eat. They were in a wooded area, so the soldiers were armed and kept watch for any dangers. They were about six hours away from that area, though, and should be safe from the mantises. Halden took a few minutes to reassure the new girls that they were safe and would be taken back to Aksanda to reunite with their parents or to go to a town to be introduced to prospective husbands. The soldiers were there for their protection at the order of King Aryante. The girls relaxed and thanked them. Soon the caravan continued down the road toward Fentro.

They were about a half hour away. "What is Fentro like?" asked Quickturn.

"It is a medium sized town supported mainly by a paper mill and some farming. There are two taverns and a brothel, so we will probably find some slaves there," replied Gantio.

When they arrived at the edge of town, they stopped and Gantio, Halden and several soldiers rode into town to the nearest tavern to find the whereabouts of the town chief. Gantio showed the decree from King Jahiz and asked about slaves. The tavern owner brought out one slave girl and told them that the chief had one, another tavern owner had one and the brothel had two. They sent the girl back to the caravan and proceeded to the next tavern where they purchased another girl and sent her to the caravan. Their next stop was the chief's house who warned them that they may have trouble from the brothel owner. They sent the chief's slave to the caravan and told the soldier to bring two more soldiers back with him. They spoke with the brothel owner and showed him the king's decree and order to sell. He said, "What do you want them for? They ain't nothing but whores and fit for nothing else. When they get pregnant, I'm going to kill them."

"No, you are going to sell them to us. They are going back to their parents. They were stolen from farms as they were doing chores. If you don't, I have soldiers with me who will give you the thrashing you deserve and then take them." He looked at the soldiers and agreed on a price for the girls. They took the girls back to the caravan. They were thin and had visible bruises on their legs and arms. Talla washed them and gave them clean men's clothing and told them that everything would be better now. Talla said, "You poor children have been through an awful time. Nobody should be able to hurt a girl like this. I want you to eat as much as you can until you have more meat on your bones. Your bruises will heal. I can tell that you are pretty girls. Did you come from farms?" They nodded yes. "That says a lot to me. You are good girls from good solid families and you will be alright again. Just give it some time and you will feel like yourselves again and you don't have to tell everyone about what happened to you. You just tell them that your master made you work very hard. You are going to put all this behind you and you will find husbands and live a normal life. Do you understand?" The girls nodded yes again. After lunch, Halden told them to return to their wagons for the sale. Customers bought a fair amount of goods and the caravan moved on to the north headed for Bantam.

Gantio said, "Bantam is an interesting town. The people there make their living by making material out of cotton and wool from the surrounding countryside. Melody would like to shop here. They make beautiful fabric. There are seamstresses who make clothing. There is a net making shop that trades with fishermen on the coast. They make rope and tapestries. The people there are very creative."

"It sounds like a place where we could do some real trading and bring back some things for Melody, Amidra, Arinya, Liadra, Faerverin and Queen Svetlana. Also, we could get enough fabric and thread for the girls to make clothing in the wagons on the way home. They get bored in there all day. This way they can start thinking about the future and they can tell their parents that they learned to sew in Orendia. Talla is interested in helping the girls. Maybe the cooks could let her teach the girls how to make dresses. Your new wife could teach them also," said Quickturn.

"This is a great idea," said Gantio. "When we stop again, I will talk to Halden about it. We will be there before dinner." The woods had diminished and there was rolling farmland on all sides. It was a beautiful clear day with a cool breeze. The road was smooth and traveling went quickly. It helped having so many empty wagons. The new girls talked with the others in their wagon and learned more about what was expected of them. They shared openly some of their stories of abuse and neglect and the other girls sympathized with them and told them that day by day they felt better.

"There is a large farm. We should send some soldiers over there to see if they have any slaves or if they know of any farmers who might have slaves," said Gantio. They stopped the wagon and told Halden, who said that they would check it out and just stop for a while. Halden, Gantio and two soldiers rode to the farm and spoke with the farmer about slaves in the area. He did own a slave and sold the girl to them. He said that he did not know of any others at farms nearby. They took her back to the caravan and Talla talked with her and gave her some men's clothing to wear. She was thin and tired. Talla wiped her face and arms and gave her some food. Talla said, "You make sure to eat all the food we give you so that your body can recover and ask the other girls what the rules are. You get in a wagon and relax. Everything will be all right and we will be in Aksanda before you know it."

Halden called out, "Forward!" Quickturn drove ahead and the caravan moved ahead toward Bantam. The new girl visited with the girls in her wagon and they told her about the mission and the rules of the caravan. When they reached the outskirts of Bantam, Quickturn told Halden about his plan to buy fabric for the girls to use to make clothes. Halden thought it was a good idea for them to have a productive skill to report that they had learned in Orendia. They decided to shop in Bantam before talking to them about slaves. They visited several shops and bought many bolts of fabric, scissors, needles and thread. After this, Halden and Gantio showed the chief the decree from King Jahiz and agreed on a price for his slave girl who gladly went to the caravan with a soldier. The chief said, "There are three girls across the street helping to make fabric. There are two girls making nets and there are two girls at the brothel. If you stop at the tavern, there is one there also." They had to pay a good price for these girls, because they were skilled workers. One of the girls at the brothel was pregnant and he was glad to give her away, but the other one they paid for.

After the nine girls were safely in the wagons, they pulled the caravan a safe distance from the town and set up camp. Soldiers pitched tents, made fires, fed and watered the horses and washed up for dinner. The cooks made a good stew and flat bread. The ten new girls sat on some logs outside while Halden spoke with them. "We will be taking you home, but first we have to visit several more towns and get whatever slaves they have. Then we will travel to Aksanda to visit King Aryante at his castle. This is his mission. He planned it and paid for it and wants to see each of you. He is a kind man and wants only the best for you. We have fabric and scissors, needles and thread for you to make clothing for yourselves. Talla and some of you will teach others to sew. When you get back home, you will be able to truthfully say that you learned to sew and made clothing in Orendia. You have all been through some very bad experiences, but Father God will help to restore you inside and out. He loves you even more than your parents do. He will send His Spirit to live inside of you and give you many good things like hope and love and healing. He will lead you and show you what decisions are good for you. To get this, all you have to do is to ask Father God to forgive you and to come into your heart. Will you do this?" The girls answered yes and proceeded to pray. Halden said, "I will be available to answer any questions you might have, but for now, let's have dinner."

The new girls received their bowls, cups, and spoons and went to the cook's fire for food. They sat down to eat and talk. "This sounds very interesting." said Thely "We can go back with some nice new clothes. That would really help. I want to make some pajamas and a wedding dress. My boyfriend was going to marry me this year. If he is still single, we could get married when we get back."

Nadene said, "I want to make some every day dresses and a dress for worship day, and I want to make a dress for my mother. She must be so sad with me disappearing like that." All the girls were having similar conversations and some of them already knew how to sew and said that they would help the other girls. They could hardly wait to choose fabrics. "Halden, when can we look at the fabrics?"

"Right after dinner we will look at the fabrics. Talla will decide what to make first. You may want to start with something easy like an apron or pajamas until you get accustomed to sewing. Then choose a fabric for a dress," said Halden. He went to get Talla to help with this and put a soldier in her place with the cooks.

It had been a long day, but the girls were definitely excited about making clothes. Talla first chose one bolt of fabric for practice and said that their first project was to make an apron. This would give them practice stitching, gathering and attaching ruffles, making straps to be tied, and attaching a top to a bottom. These were all important steps in dress making. They each cut three pieces of fabric for their aprons using Talla's apron for a guide. She handed out spools of thread and needles so they would be ready for tomorrow and told them they could get ready for bed. Talla asked the girls who knew how to sew to come to her and placed each one in a wagon so that there would be at least one person who knew sewing in each wagon. Then everyone went to bed.

The next morning began with a good hot breakfast of porridge and honey cakes with dried fruit and tea. The girls were really excited about learning to sew and talked about clothes and what they wanted to make. Many of them wanted to make a wedding dress, but realized that they needed to practice making a regular dress first. When breakfast and the morning chores were done, the soldiers hitched up the horses to the wagons and Halden called out, "Forward!" Quickturn led the wagons back onto the road heading north toward Wahki, the last town they would visit before heading back to Fallonia and King Jahiz.

Quickturn asked, "Does Wahki also make fabrics?"

Gantio said, "Yes, they do, but they make only silk fabric which they make from cocoons of the silkworm in mulberry trees. The process is very time consuming and is secret, but the fabric is very beautiful. If they will sell any to us, it will be at a high price. It would be a fitting gift for Queen Svetlana. We should try very hard to buy some of this."

"We should buy some of it for our girls back home, too. Liadra, Melody, Arinya, Faerverin and your wife would all like some," said Quickturn. "We must also make sure to get the thread that goes with it."

The girls were having fun learning to sew the important stitches like the straight stitch, the gathering stitch, and the slip stitch used in hemming. They learned quickly and by the time the wagons stopped for lunch, they had completed their aprons. Talla was very pleased with their progress and had them choose a fabric for nightgowns.

The caravan had pulled over close to the town and Halden and Gantio took two soldiers and extra horses into town to the nearest tavern to ask the whereabouts of the chief. They asked the tavern owner about slaves and he brought out his slave girl. He didn't want to sell her, but Gantio showed him the king's decree and he accepted payment for her. He said that the silk maker had two girls and that the brothel had two, but that the chief had none. They sent the girl back to the caravan and rode to the silk maker. His girls were busy on hand looms. He said that he would have to train more girls, and that he didn't want to be without his slaves, but agreed on a price and sold them. It was always sad to go to a brothel to retrieve Aksandan girls who should be at home with their mothers, but that was their last stop. The brothel owner showed them his two girls who were thin and scantily dressed. Gantio paid for them and escorted them back to the wagons.

Then they talked to the silk maker and arrived at a price for some bolts of silk. It was very expensive, but the silk maker accepted jewels in trade, making the purchase possible. They purchased enough for all the women they cared about in their personal lives. After taking the silk back to the wagons, they had lunch and waited for customers.

The customers were very impressed with the caravan and wanted to buy something for their homes. There were several wagons full of goods. The chief wanted to buy jewelry so they showed him some of the better pieces and he bought them. So far this had been a good and profitable day. The chief warned them of bandits on the road from Wahki to Fallonia. It was well known that people who traded with Wahki carried jewels and silver with them which made them prime targets for assault. Of course, most of these traders did not have so many men with them. He wished them well and said goodbye.

The caravan pulled back onto the road heading north toward Tibera. Quickturn said, "We already visited Tibera so we can travel past it and Kisoma. How long do you think it will take us to get to Fallonia? I am so ready to go home. Dealing with these Orendians has tried my patience and made me angry. If it wasn't for the women and children, I would like to fight these men in an all out war."

"I understand, but it would be better to introduce them to Father God and let the transformation take place. Then the women and children would have good men to help take care of them," said Gantio.

"I agree, but how do you do such a thing? There are so many of them and we would have to know their language," said Quickturn.

"Aren't the Bright Elves capable of moving into the cities and talking to the people about Father God?" asked Gantio. "You have many Bright Elves at your disposal. Ask King Aryante for permission to take them to Orendia on a teaching mission. I'm sure that King Jahiz would approve."

"I really don't want to come back here, but you are right. It is very much needed," said Quickturn.

The afternoon passed pleasantly for the girls as they practiced sewing and talked with each other about home and their families.

# DRAGON RIDERS

Meanwhile on the Kigasse Plateau, the dragon riders had received a message from Ahriman by carrier pigeon. The women had just come back from a good ride and had fed their dragons. Rana said, "We got a message from Ahriman. He must owe somebody else some money that he doesn't want to pay. He is revolting."

"What does it say?" asked Carwen.

"He says the king has outlawed slavery and there is a caravan of about a hundred slave girls he wants us to torch. He says the caravan is returning the girls to their parents. Two of those girls were his. He will deliver a wagon of food to us if we do." said Rana.

"This is pure evil. It's the worst thing he has ever asked us to do," said Chara. "He wants to kill all those girls because he lost a couple of his lays? Is he insane?"

"I think so," said Rana. "I hate him. It's time we gave him a piece of our minds."

"How can we get him up here?" asked Bander.

"We make him a very attractive offer. You know the basket of gems we have? We tell him that he has to come get them to trade them for silver in town and that he can have one fourth of them and that when we get the silver, we will torch the caravan," said Rana. "We'll tell him that we need to buy more grazing land for our goats and sheep. It's one thing killing a worthless man who wastes his money gambling and drinking, but torching a caravan full of girls is something I can't do."

"I can't either," said Chara. "Orendian men think that they can do anything to women. It's a good thing we have our dragons. It keeps men from carrying us off to some brothel."

"I know," said Bander. "I've been worried about him taking offense at us and hurting our dragons. He is just that petty and vengeful. Anyway, we are women. Why would we want to torch a bunch of women who never did harm to anyone?"

Carwen said, "I remember him threatening to hurt our dragons if we didn't do his bidding. We really need to end our relationship with him. I'll write the letter and send it to him. I'll tell him to maintain absolute secrecy or the deal is off. We don't need people to think we're sitting up here with a horde of treasure even if we are." Carwen wrote the letter and attached it to the carrier pigeon. The dragon riders went to the dining room for a sumptuous dinner.

# UP THE RIVER

The five boats carrying Tall Sky, Melody and their precious cargo of sixty-eight girls including three young children stopped at Brown Bear where they changed rowing teams. The tavern owner came out and said, "What do we have here? I have never seen so many people going up the river together."

"These are the slaves bought back from Orendians," said Tall Sky.

The tavern owner said, "I'm so glad. I don't know how you managed it, but I thank you for it. I have worried about these children ever since last autumn when the soldiers killed so many of the slavers at the market. I have fresh cookies baked and I want to give them to the girls. May I? It's not much, but I want to do something for them."

Tall Sky replied, "I'm sure that the girls will appreciate it. They've been worried about how people would receive them."

He passed out the cookies and told them, "Welcome home. We are glad that you are here."

Tall Sky bid him farewell and the boats headed up the river toward Windy Port. The girls were hungry, so they ate a sandwich from their food bags. They felt like they were on a wonderful adventure, never having ridden in a boat before. They enjoyed watching the little animals at the water's edge and seeing the pretty flowers. It was all deeply relaxing, and after eating and drinking some wine, some of them took naps.

Melody said, "I am so proud of you, Tall Sky. You have accomplished a lot in one year. It is like you did the impossible."

"All things are possible with Father God's strength and guidance. For one thing, He gave me the perfect help mate. Then He worked through two kings to accomplish this," said Tall Sky. "Our compassion is even something that he gave us, and knowing right from wrong."

"I know," said Melody, "but you were willing to do all of this and to put your life in danger to help all these people. I still say that I am proud of you."

"Well, thank you, my darling. I love you and I am proud of you, too." Tall Sky put his arm around her and kissed her. "You know, on this trip we won't have to go to any of the outlying towns, so it won't take so long. We should be in Loss Port tonight and we can rent some wagons."

When they reached Windy Port, they all left the boat to walk around for a while. Melody and Tall Sky told the barkeep that these were all slaves being returned to their homes and the barkeep insisted on serving them ale. He offered them his barn to sleep in, because it was a long trip to Loss Port and he didn't think they would make it by nightfall. Tall Sky thanked him and told the girls. He took them to the barn where they made themselves mats of hay to sleep on. With their pillows and blankets, they should be quite comfortable. They ate some of their food and went to bed.

At first light in the morning, the rowers had assembled and were ready for their passengers to board. The barkeep had steeped a large pan of tea and served it to them in their own cups. Everyone thanked him and they boarded the boats. Tall Sky called out, "We will be in Loss Port for lunch! Then we will ride in wagons to Vivallen!"

The air was cooler, so they wrapped up in their blankets, leaned back against their pillows, and ate some bread and cheese for breakfast, followed by some candy. After that, they took naps. Daisy was still enjoying the boat ride. She hadn't liked being confined in the belly of that ship, so she was really liking the freedom of being outside, feeling the breeze, and watching the shore line. As they traveled north, there were less flowers and cooler air. Daisy wore her sweater to feel comfortable and sat on Melody's shoulder. Melody was glad to have this much of the trip done. She was weary of the traveling and the worry and of the fear of being attacked. She longed to sleep in a real bed after a hot bath and cuddle up to Tall Sky in privacy.

# BANDITS

The caravan turned left at Tabira and traveled west toward Kisoma. The Kigasse Plateau cliff rose straight up to the Kigasse Plateau. To the left was hilly farmland rolling into the distance. The road was solid, but hilly. They had passed Tabira and were heading for Kisoma and the light was dimming as the sun descended toward the sea. Quickturn said, "We had better find a place to camp for the night. I see a good level place up ahead." Quickturn pulled off the road and talked to Halden. He said, "I thought this looked like a good place to spend the night. What do you think?"

"It looks good," said Halden. "I'm ready for a rest and some good food. I'll tell the girls to come out and enjoy a walk before dinner." The soldiers unhitched the horses, fed and watered them. The fire detail made two fires and the cook brought out pots of stew and baked flatbread. Some of the soldiers set up tents and others hooked up hammocks under the wagons. All of the soldiers remained armed throughout the night. The Bright Elves would stand guard. They had seen dragons circling overhead and wondered if they would be attacked, but the dragons flew beyond them and then back to the plateau as if they had satisfied their curiosity.

The Bright Elves sensed a sleep spell and shielded it. Then a large group of bandits assaulted the soldiers using swords and knives. When confronted with so many soldiers at once, who were unaffected by Ahriman's sleep spell, they ran. Dragons swooped down on them releasing fire. Quickturn and his soldiers stood there amazed, watching their enemies go up in flames. Then the dragons flew over the wagons and ascended to the plateau. Halden said, "I hardly believe my eyes. The dragon riders defended us! All this time I thought they would attack us and we would be fighting them."

Quickturn said, "Did you notice that the dragon riders are women? Could they somehow know of the girls we are carrying?"

Gantio said, "They could know about it. We have been all over Orendia, and they probably have contacts out there. You know how Ahriman sent the Bitters to attack us? It's just possible that he tried to send the dragon riders after us and they decided to watch us instead."

The girls had been peeking out the windows, and asked if they could come out. "Sure, come on out. We have good news. It seems that we have some friends for a change. The dragon riders incinerated the bandits! The dragon riders are women. It makes sense that they would want to save you," said Halden.

Quickturn said, "I am very happy about this, but I am still concerned about Ahriman's influence over the king. We shall see him tomorrow. That will be very interesting. We have had a very successful trip so far in spite of Ahriman's interference. I hope and pray that it continues."

The girls were very relieved about the dragon riders and thanked Father God for this in their bedtime prayers. Likewise did the soldiers. The rest of the night was spent peacefully sleeping.

Morning came with a renewed feeling of hope and well being. They ate a delicious breakfast of ham and hotcakes and tea. They were looking forward to beginning their first dresses. Talla helped them to choose fabrics for dresses and the girls returned to their wagons to begin. They would be sewing all the way to Fallonia.

# AHRIMAN

Ahriman woke in the morning exhilarated with the idea of becoming fabulously wealthy from the dragon riders' jewels. He would be unstoppable at the gaming tables for performing a simple task for the dragon riders. He skipped breakfast and slipped out of the castle and into his carriage without telling anyone and drove his carriage up the road to the plateau. In two hours he arrived at the meeting place. The dragons touched down a short distance from him and Rana climbed down and set before him a large basket and a small basket filled with jewels. He said, "You must really want that grazing land. Why don't you just take it?"

"They are our friends! We couldn't hurt them. It's a whole family and we love them," said Rana.

"Women," he said derogatorily. "I will get these traded for you and be back tomorrow morning, but you had better do a good job on that caravan. I've already sent mantises, wolves, Bitters, and bandits after them and none of them could get the job done. Torch the whole thing including the men."

"Of course," said Rana. She climbed back on her dragon and said, "Fire!" At that, all four dragons blew fire at Ahriman, who resisted the fire with a shield spell. They called out, "Fire!" again and incinerated him where he stood. As he died he screamed, "Melki-resha!"

"Problem solved!" said Rana. The girls picked up their jewels and put them in a sack. Then they rode back to their home to feed their dragons and bathe them in the lake. When the dragons were comfortable, they took naps in their dens in Dragon Mountain on the plateau. Rana, Bander, Chara, and Carwen met in the dining hall for lunch.

Bander said, "I am hungry and tired. We've done a lot today already, but I don't mind. Apep loves his bath so much."

Chara said, "I can't stop thinking about the caravan. I would really like to talk to those girls and find out what has happened to them. They're from Aksanda. I wonder what that country is like."

Bander said, "And those men! What kind of men travel to another country just to rescue girls they don't even know? I would like to talk with them."

Rana said, "They have to be brave and determined. They didn't stop no matter what Ahriman tried to do to them. In fact, they are headed back to the castle. Why are they doing that? It's a good thing we torched Ahriman."

"I'll tell you what," said Bander. "I want to meet those girls. Why don't we visit them on their way home? They will be traveling past the Plateau Cliff. We could bring them some meat as a parting gift. That many people must go through food quickly."

"Great idea," said Rana. "That way we can find out what kind of men they are."

Carwen said, "I feel really sorry for those girls. It would be terrible to be stolen from their homes and sold to men in a foreign country to be used by them. I hate it. I want to do something for them."

"Think of their parents. They are bonded to their children like we are to our dragons. If something happened to Kerberos, I would be in so much pain," said Rana. "It's a wonder those girls are still alive."

"Orendian men are horrible. They need to learn something from Aksandan men," said Carwen.

"Think about it," said Rana. "What kind of men could win battles against Bitter Elves and bandits and be so disciplined as to rescue beautiful women and not touch them?"

"Soldiers. They are soldiers!" said Carwen. "Their king must have gotten so angry with slavers that he sent his soldiers to bring the girls back home. I'll bet King Jahiz doesn't even know."

"Sure. They wouldn't want to cause a war, so they pretended to be merchants. It's a brilliant idea. I love this!" exclaimed Bander.

"We'll fly down and visit them tomorrow," said Rana. "They should be back by then."

# KING JAHIZ

King Jahiz sat in his library reading scrolls of ancient wisdom. He had never before been interested in studying these things, but now he had an insatiable desire to know what wise men knew about love and justice and God. He asked Father God to give him understanding of the deeper things in the writings. He was glad that Ahriman was not there to interrupt with his hateful ideas. King Jahiz had decided to dismiss Ahriman and find an advisor who was kind and insightful and not interested in drinking and gambling. King Jahiz was truly interested in something for the first time in his life. He wanted to find a way to improve his country by improving his countrymen. His tribune walked in and announced the arrival of visitors from the caravan. King Jahiz told him to bring them into the library. He wanted to speak with Halden, Quickturn and Gantio.

"Come in my friends. I want to show you something. I have been reading the wisdom of the old ones. These scrolls are filled with writings about love and justice and forgiveness. They are very old. Were you successful in your search for the slaves?" asked king Jahiz. "Sit at this table with me and we will talk."

"Your majesty, we were very successful thanks to your decree banning slavery. I can't thank you enough for that. We have rescued about sixty more girls. They are learning to make clothing. We stopped at Bantam and bought fabric for them. They are feeling better every day."

"I am glad to hear that," said King Jahiz. "I am grateful to you for introducing me to Father God. It is like I can see for the first time in my life and things are making sense to me. Now I grieve for my countrymen. They are living lives that are empty in comparison.

They need Father God. Is there some way that you could help me with this?"

"It is possible," said Quickturn, "but we would have to get the girls back home first," said Quickturn. "I have been thinking about this already and have been praying to Father God. I believe that a large group of Bright Elves could help to introduce your countrymen to Father God. Right now we work for King Aryante, but I think he would like this idea. Did your soldiers find any more slaves?"

"Yes, they located twenty more slaves. I have them here in the castle and you may take them with you when you go," said King Jahiz.

"I have something for you," said Quickturn. "It is a puzzle of the map of Phayendar." He handed the puzzle to King Jahiz. "And here are some navigational charts of the lands showing the depths of the water on the coasts for help in sailing near the lands. Here is also a scroll telling about the people who live there. They were made by a mariner who sailed the sea."

"This is wonderful," said King Jahiz. "Thank you. I will have my scribes copy them and give them to the captains of our ships."

"We have many old gowns in the castle. I will have them brought down to your caravan," said King Jahiz. "Would your girls like that?'

Gantio said, "You are most generous, your majesty. I'm sure that the girls will be delighted to have them."

"Make sure that you have King Aryante seriously consider having your people to help mine get to know Father God," said King Jahiz. "It has done me much good. I have an idea. I would like the girls and your men to come to the castle dining hall for a feast. They can bathe in our pool and the ladies here will help them get ready. It should be a great time for all of us. Would you be willing to do this?"

Quickturn said, "We accept your gracious offer. I will tell them now." Quickturn left and told the girls and the soldiers about the feast. The king called the tribune and told him what to do.

The women bathed first in an indoor pool made for bathing and some servants helped them with the gowns and their hair. Then the men bathed and put on clean clothes.

Food was brought in by cooks all over the city and, when all was ready, they were led into a large dining room filled with platters of food. King Jahiz sat at the front table with Gantio, Halden and Quickturn. The girls felt like princesses. They were in awe of the proceedings. King Jahiz stood and addressed the girls. "I want you to know that I am truly sorry for what happened to you. I have met Father God and I know now that slavery is wrong. My sincere wish is that you will have good lives when you return to your families. Now eat and enjoy yourselves."

Gantio spoke to the king about Melody and Tall Sky. He said, "Your majesty, I have friends who want flying cats. Is there a possibility that we could take some home with us? We have no flying cats in Aksanda. We would like a good breeding pair and some kittens if possible."

"This is not a problem," said King Jahiz. "I will send a man in my carriage to get them for you. He will also bring cages and other things you will need."

"Thank you," said Gantio. "I really appreciate it." King Jahiz sent a tribune to accomplish this task.

In the dining hall the soldiers sat with the girls and they felt safe and protected. After dinner they went to the ballroom for dancing. King Jahiz enjoyed watching everybody dancing. He even asked his wife to dance. They danced and talked and he began to know this woman he had been married to for years. That night he prayed with her and she asked Father God to live in her heart. It was a new beginning for them.

After the dance, they said their farewells and went back to the caravan. The next morning everyone had breakfast and Halden spoke to the new girls about the mission and the rules of conduct. Then the cats were delivered in cages and placed in an empty wagon with some food and water. They drove down the road heading east toward home. Halden said, "I didn't expect all that. It was a fine send off."

Gantio said, "You can tell that King Jahiz is already changing for the better. He was reading those scrolls and he danced with his wife. They were talking together. It may have been the first time he spoke with her and they were laughing."

"The girls and the soldiers were enjoying themselves too," said Halden.

The girls talked about last night's activities. "I had a wonderful time," said Haley. "I really liked the bathing pool and those gowns."

"I liked dancing with the soldiers. I wish that we could all just marry them," said Lelia. They both laughed.

"That would be fun," said Haley.

The caravan stopped for lunch at the scene of their encounter with the bandits. There was a long, flat area where they could pull off the road. The cooks set out sandwiches and wine so there was no need of fire. The soldiers watered the horses and the girls walked around for exercise.

Of a sudden, four dragons flew over dropping flowers. The flowers fell in a shower all over the caravan. The girls laughed in glee and picked up bouquets of flowers. Then the dragons sat down a safe distance from the caravan and the four dragon riders dismounted, took down some bags and walked toward the caravan. They told their dragons to stay. The dragons laid down on their bellies and curled their tails around themselves.

Halden, Gantio and Quickturn walked toward the dragon riders waving and called out, "Welcome," in Orendian. They set their gifts on the ground. Gantio translated.

Rana said, "We thought you could use some fresh meat. You have a long way to travel. We are happy to meet you and we would like to talk to your girls. You won't have to worry about Ahriman any more. He tried to get us to torch you, so we torched him instead."

Halden laughed and said, "Thank you. He tried to kill us a number of times. I wondered why he wasn't at the castle. You have done us all a great service. Come over to the caravan. You are welcome to take lunch with us.

"Thank you," said Dana. Halden told the girls to remove their caps and there was an audible sigh of relief as they removed their caps and fluffed out their hair. "Why do the girls wear caps?"

"They wear caps and men's clothing for protection from curious men," said Halden.

"I can understand that," said Carwen. "We know that you are soldiers from your success in fighting, but it is better to not start fights in a foreign country."

Halden said to the girls, "I would like to introduce the dragon riders of Orendia. We will be staying here for a while so that you can get to know each other. Gantio will be translating for those of you who do not speak Orendian well."

"I am Rana and I ride Kerberos," said Rana.

"I am Bander and I ride Apep," said Bander.

"I am Chara and I ride Alvoh," said Chara.

"I am Carwen and I ride Cheesah," said Carwen.

"How did you choose their names?" asked Celia.

Rana answered, "When a dragon is hatched, it bonds with a human and tells the human its name by thinking it. That bond is something like a mother and a child, only stronger."

"What is it like to be a dragon rider?" asked Celia.

"It is a lot of work. A dragon needs care like bathing it in the lake and feeding it regularly and spending time with it talking to it and loving it. A dragon needs to fly, so we fly our dragons once a day. It feels great and exhilarating to fly through the sky with wind blowing through your hair. I really love to fly," said Rana.

Quickturn said, "I have a friend who has a miniature dragon. It is with her always and in the winter, the dragon wears a sweater, a fur cloak and fur booties. The dragon loves this. Do you dress your dragons in the winter?"

Rana said, "We do put a fur cloak on them in the winter, and we give them fleece hides to sleep on."

Celia asked, "How does a person become a dragon rider?"

"A person would first ask us and then that person would be put through a rigorous training for strength and endurance. The person would have to learn to fly on another dragon and would learn by doing all the care that a dragon needs. It is not easy to become a dragon rider," said Rana.

"We have questions for you, too. How did you become a slave?" asked Bander.

Telia answered, "I was captured by slavers as I worked out in the garden. They made me walk a long way without food or water. They hit me and raped me and sold me at an auction. Then I was taken to Orendia and sold to a tavern owner who also raped me and made me give pleasure to other men. It was about the same with all of us, but since then we have all asked Father God into our hearts and He has taken away the pain and has given us hope. He sent you to help protect us and we love you for it."

Haley said, "We had a wonderful time at a feast and a dance last night in the castle. King Jahiz gave us all gowns to wear and I saw him dance with his wife and he talked to her like people in Aksanda do. He asked Father God to live in his heart too and he wants all of the Orendians to do the same. You see, when you do, Father God gives you gifts like love, compassion, patience, healing and inner strength. He forgives you and you forgive others letting go of hate that can hurt you. It really works. I feel like a new person since I've known Father God. It's easy to do. All you do is talk to Him and ask Him to live in your heart. Would you like to do this?"

"Yes, I would," said Rana.

"Alright, let's pray. Father God, please forgive me for anything I have done wrong and please come into my heart to live. Please teach me and guide me and love me," said Haley. The dragon riders all prayed this and said, "Thank you." Haley said, "When you die, you will go to Heaven where you can live in a beautiful place, and you can have your dragons with you." The girls hugged the dragon riders.

"Oh, I almost forgot. We have a gift for each of you." The dragon riders gave each of the girls a gem to help them get started in their new lives.

Halden was speechless. He thought, "Father God does move in mysterious ways. He amazes me with His kindness." He felt as proud of these girls as if they were his own daughters.

The dragon riders bid the girls farewell, thanked Halden, Gantio and Quickturn and departed on their dragons waving goodbye. Halden said, "Everyone back into the wagons. It's time to go home." They climbed back into the wagons and he called, "Forward!" The wagons were now moving toward Lake Inari. As they traveled, the land became greener and the trees were more numerous. It was a beautiful day with a clear blue sky, warm sun and cool breezes.

# FROM BEYOND THE GRAVE

Quickturn closed his eyes and appeared to be dozing for a while. When he opened his eyes, he said, "Father God has given me a vision. I saw Ahriman on fire and screaming the name Melki-resha. Then I saw a dark cloud and out of it came a demon, great and terrible. It blew smoke from its nostrils onto the forest near Lake Inari and the beasts of the forest became enraged. They attacked a small village west of Lake Inari. The demon growled out the name of Ahriman. Its purpose is to draw us into the wild land to be destroyed. Father God wants us to help the villagers by fighting Melki-resha. It is an ancient demon from another world far away from Phayendar. It is a mighty demon of vengeance. Ahriman is reaching out from beyond the grave to complete his vengeance upon us. Gantio, I will need you and Halden to take the caravan to Vivallen. I will send enough men with you to guard the caravan and keep it safe. The rest of the men will come with me to defend the villagers. The Bright Elves I leave with you should be able to fight the demon if it attacks. Stop the wagons. I will tell the men. Quickturn gathered the soldiers and told them of his vision. He said that in his vision he saw them killing beasts and fighting the demon. He chose half of the soldiers and Bright Elves to ride with him. He said, "We will prevail, but it will take some time and I don't want the caravan put in danger, so the rest of you will take the caravan as quickly as possible to Vivallen. You must not take extra time for walks and bathing. Eat as you travel. You must reach Vivallen soon."

"Now, quickly, men! To the village!" Half of the soldiers and the Bright Elves followed Quickturn northwest toward the village. The caravan kept on the road passing Lake Inari and on to Vivallen.

When they arrived at the village, they saw beasts clawing at the houses. Bears were growling and cougars were snarling. Remains of people lay scattered about the ground. Anyone still alive was barricaded in their homes. A woman and a child did not get into their home in time. They were burning refuse outside when the beasts came and were keeping the fire burning for protection. Bright Elves loosed their arrows killing wolves that were circling the woman and her son. Soldiers threw spears at the larger animals killing bears and cougars. All of this infuriated Melki-resha who sent a swarm of bees at the soldiers. The Bright Elves countered the attack speaking to the bees, "Father God commands you to return to your hives. The bees turned around and flew back to their hives. Melki-resha sent hail to pelt the soldiers. Quickturn spoke to the hail clouds commanding them to leave.

Finally, Melki-resha appeared as a large, bulbous being with fiery eyes and a mouth filled with pointed teeth. He roared and snarled. The Bright Elves stood in a line, went bright, and held their hands out toward the demon, sending one beam of light that wound round and round the demon like a rope. Quickturn said, "I bind you in the name of Father God. Father God commands you to leave this world and never return." The demon shrieked and flew up into the sky until it disappeared from sight. The animals went back into the forest and all was calm. The villagers came outside to meet the soldiers and thank them. Quickturn and his Bright Elves ministered to the wounded. They stayed and helped the villagers with the clean up, burying the dead, dressing out the dead animals and skinning them for fur pelts. They had bear meat for dinner and stayed the night in the barn. The next morning they headed for Vivallen.

The caravan had traveled as fast as they could and still be safe. They reached Vivallen by nightfall and pulled into the king's stable area to let the girls out. Halden reported to the king who told him to bring the girls into the dining area and told the cooks to bring food and wine out to the girls. He told a servant to take the girls into the baths when they had finished eating. Talla gathered the girls' dresses and had some soldiers help to carry them in to the girls. When they had bathed and dressed, they sat in the dining area to rest and await the king. Tall Sky and Melody had arrived a few days ago and went to the dining area to see the girls and to write down their names and home towns. In total, the caravan mission had saved one hundred and forty-three girls and three small children. Melody was very pleased. "Tall Sky, we did it. It seemed impossible to do such a complicated thing, but it worked. I hope we got them all."

Tall Sky said, "If we didn't, it's not for lack of trying."

"Where are all these girls going to sleep?" asked Melody.

"They can sleep in the wagons," said Tall Sky. "We can empty out the rest of the merchandise and other things and they can sleep on the mattresses that were stored under it. Also, many of the girls will be going home soon."

"When can we go home?" asked Melody.

"After the ball and the conference," said Tall Sky. "We can help take some pregnant girls to Loadrel with Talla. There may also be some girls who want to go directly to Home Fire. Rando probably has his inn built by now. Then there is Yardrel and Talami. Some soldiers will come with us to escort the girls to the northeast sector. We could have a large amount of people going with us."

Gantio found Melody and said, "I've got a present for you. Remember what you wanted to take with you from Orendia?"

"Flying cats," said Melody. "You brought flying cats?!"

"King Jahiz sent some and they are in the last wagon on the caravan. With all this activity I almost forgot them," said Gantio.

Melody ran out of the castle and over to the stables where the wagons were parked. Gantio followed to translate for her. "You know, these cats speak Orendian," said Gantio. "They want to know your name. They are concerned about your dragon. They want food. They want to know why you're crying."

"Tell them I love them. Daisy is their friend," said Melody. She pointed to herself and said "Melody."

The cats said her name in kitty voices that sounded like meows. Daisy was curious, looked the female cat in the eyes and chirred. The cat said, "Daisy."

Gantio said, "It appears that Daisy can communicate with them mentally. This is very interesting. They eat meat and fish. I will get them some. Don't open the cages."

Melody sat in the wagon watching the cats. There were four kittens of varied colors. The mother was calico and the father was black. There were two orange kittens, one black kitten, and one calico kitten. Melody reached her hand into the cage and petted the mother cat. There was another cage with a male and a female cat. The male was black and the female cat was calico. She said, "Achta, bamba," which means hello, Mama in Orendian. The cat responded, "Achta, Melody." Gantio brought the cats some food and fresh water. Then he cleaned out the sand box. "They're beautiful," said Melody. "Thank you for bringing them to me. We have to show them to Faerverin. I haven't even talked to her yet. Would you go get her?"

"Sure I will," said Gantio. He brought Faerverin to see the cats. Gantio said, "We must set up a breeder in this area who will monitor the breeding of these cats. We have two pairs of cats and their kittens must be bred carefully so as not to get inbreeding. This needs to be done right away. I will talk to King Ayrante about this."

Faerverin said, "We will bring these cats up to my room for now. It will be getting too warm to keep them in here. They asked some soldiers to bring them in.

King Aryante talked to Tall Sky and said that he wanted a meeting right away to discuss the mission. "I want representation from the girls. Would you please choose several girls to attend the meeting? Bring them to my study in a few minutes." Tall Sky brought Aisha, Haley, and Lelia. He also brought Halden, Gantio and Melody. King Aryante asked Quickturn's second in command Pentigard to attend. They met in his study and sat around a long table.

King Aryante said, "Welcome. I have asked you here to tell me about your experiences. It has been a very successful mission and I thank you for all of your hard work. Quickturn, I understand that you took about half of the slaves on a ship from King's Port in Orendia to Free Harbor and then took boats up the river to Loss Port. Why did you do that?"

Tall Sky said, "We were worried about dragons attacking and we had sixty-eight girls by then, so it just made sense to get them out of there. We still had most of the country to travel and more girls to acquire. This way we kept them safe and freed up the space for more girls."

"Good thinking," said King Aryante. "Halden, did you have trouble getting the slave owners to sell them to you?"

"For the most part, the owners sold them because of the decree from King Jahiz, which outlawed slavery and instructed them to sell the slaves to us. The main trouble came from the king's advisor Ahriman, a sorcerer who was angry with us for buying two of his girls. He sent Bitters, bandits, and wild beasts to attack us throughout our journey. His last ploy backfired on him. He asked the dragon riders to torch our caravan, and they torched him instead. As he died, he called on a demon Melki-resha and it attacked a village near Lake Inari to get us to come to their rescue. Quickturn and half of our soldiers went with him. He has not yet returned."

"Kineol, what was your master like?" asked King Aryante.

"I belonged to King Jahiz. He was kind to me and I lived in the castle. I am pregnant with his child, but I didn't tell him, because I wanted to come home," said Kineol.

"We will talk more of this later," said King Aryante. "Haley, what was your experience like?"

"I belonged to a tavern owner who raped me and was paid by other men to use me. He hit me if I objected to anything. It was horrible," said Haley. "I have to say this. I wanted to kill myself until I met Father God and asked Him to live in my heart. Now I feel better – happier and stronger. I believe that Father God is the key to this whole thing. If people in Orendia would come to know Father God like I do, the whole country would change for the better."

King Aryante said, "I believe you are right. Lelia, what kind of experience did you have?"

"I lived in the house of the chief of Aris Port. He had a wife and a flying cat. I was used by him and I helped his wife with the chores. My experience wasn't as bad as the other girls had, but I was lonely for home and felt bad that I wasn't married. If I would have gotten pregnant, I would have been let go and probably would have died of hunger. The men do that with pregnant girls, or they kill them," said Lelia. I wanted to bring that flying cat home with me."

Gantio said, "We will be breeding flying cats and I will make sure that you get one. We have kittens right here in the castle and I will show them to you after this meeting."

"Oh, thank you," said Lelia smiling.

"Of course, the next step is to return these girls to their homes," said King Aryante. "I want to talk to them and throw a party for them with a dinner and a dance like the one that King Jahiz gave them. Do all of them have gowns for that?"

"Half of them do, but the ones who came by ship do not," said Halden.

"We will round up as many as we can here in the castle, and buy what we don't have," said King Aryante. Each woman in the castle has a wardrobe of gowns."

"King Aryante, we have all been wondering if there could be something done to help the men of Orendia to know Father God. When I talked to the dragon riders, they asked Father God into their hearts right away," said Lelia.

Halden said, "King Jahiz was open to it, too, and he wants our help with this."

King Aryante asked, "Do you have any ideas about how to do this?"

Lelia answered, "I do. If the Bright Elves could go into the country and take jobs in the towns, they would have opportunities to talk to the regular people about Father God. Those men are bad because they don't know any better. They aren't stupid, but they don't have the knowledge of anything better. They need to be taught and they need their hearts to change."

Kineol said, "There are seventeen main towns in Orendia. If you placed ten Bright Elves in each town it would take one hundred and fifty Bright Elves. I've noticed that when someone asks God into their hearts, they right away want to share it. If that happened there, before long the whole country would know Father God and a lot less bad things would be happening."

"They would stop hurting girls and value human life," said Haley. "It would be fun to see Orendian men actually talking to women."

"It sounds like a great plan. I will talk with Quickturn about it when he returns," said King Aryante. "I want to thank you for your ideas. You are a credit to your country. Now let's adjourn this meeting. Kineol, I would like a word with you and Tall Sky and Melody. Kineol, you said that you are carrying King Jahiz' child. This could be important in the future. This child, being Orendian royalty, could have a future in relations between Orendia and Aksanda. If you are willing, I would like you to live here at the castle where the child could have the advantages of education and royal conduct. Of course, you may still marry and both of you live here. It's not a command, but it surely is a strong recommendation. Tall Sky, what do you think of this?"

"I think that you are a wise man to think ahead like this. What do you think of this, Kineol?" asked Tall Sky. "I can introduce you to Aleph's wife Faerverin and you can talk to her about life at this castle."

"I would like that," said Kineol. "Thank you for your kind offer, King Aryante."

"Think about it and let me know tomorrow," said King Aryante.

Melody, Tall Sky and Kineol walked upstairs to Faerverin's room.

Princess Anya was already drawing the cats, and Faerverin was holding a kitten. Has Aleph seen the cats yet?" asked Tall Sky.

"Not yet," said Faerverin.

"Gantio says that he is going to set up a breeder to keep track of the kittens to prevent inbreeding," said Melody. "This is Kineol. King Aryante has asked her to live here because she is carrying King Jahiz' child. He says it could be important to the future relations between Orendia and Aksanda. She hasn't decided yet, but would like to talk to you about life in the castle."

Faerverin said, "It's nice here. It's calm and quiet. There are beautiful gardens, and you have time to paint or read or embroider.

Aleph and I are very happy here. He is an advisor to the king. If I were you, I would accept his offer. You may even find a handsome young man to marry."

"It sounds good. I will accept his offer. Will he let my parents come to visit?" asked Kineol.

"Of course he will. You may also visit them if you like. You are living here, not a prisoner," said Faerverin.

Gantio said, "Faerverin, we bought some silk in Bantam, Orendia for you and Queen Svetlana. It is still on a wagon. I'll have it brought in later. It's for really fine gowns and pajamas. It is beautiful and the most expensive cloth. I had better get back to the girls in the dining hall. Someday all of this will be over and there will be a new problem to solve."

Gantio went back downstairs where girls were choosing dresses to wear to the party. They were all excited talking about dresses and hair. He found Aleph and Tall Sky sitting by the wall trying to look inconspicuous. "Want to go out for a mug of ale? I don't know about you, but I need to get away from all this fluff," said Gantio.

"Let's go," said Tall Sky. They walked out of the castle and down the road to the Golden Chalice where they ordered mugs of ale. I wonder how Quickturn and his soldiers are."

"They should be on their way back by now," said Aleph. "I haven't gotten a message about them or from Quickturn, have you?"

"No," said Tall Sky. "That usually means that everything is all right. I can hardly wait to find out what it was like fighting that demon. It's a particularly strong and nasty one. Those poor villagers. There had to be casualties from all those beasts. I'll bet they stayed to help with burial and clean up."

Gantio said, "Melody is crazy about those cats and one of them was communicating with Daisy. She looked the cat in the eyes up close and chirred. The cat said, 'Daisy'. You might end up with a flying cat. It can sit on Melody's other shoulder or on one of yours." They laughed.

"If I'm not careful, I could end up with a house full of animals," said Tall Sky. "We don't stay home that long, though. I would have to hire a person to take care of them while we're gone."

"That's what people do," said Gantio. "Faerverin's got two pairs of cats and a litter of kittens in her room right now. The cats talk to each other in Orendian. The girls are up there petting them as we speak. I promised Lelia one of the kittens. I think lots of people are going to want them. King Aryante said that Faerverin could have one."

"Gantio, when are you going to marry Shasta? You should do it at the party. She must feel abandoned right now," said Aleph.

"Yes, Gantio. Marry the woman at the party. Make her happy," said Tall Sky.

"Alright, I'll do it," said Gantio. "I did promise her that I would marry her. When is the party?"

"Probably tomorrow. King Aryante is waiting for Quickturn to return with his men. It's only fair," said Aleph.

Tall Sky said, "We have to give some silk to Queen Svetlana and to Faerverin before we forget. When should we do that? We could do it now or at the party."

Gantio said, "We should do it at the party before my wedding."

"Sounds good. Are you ready to go back yet?" asked Gantio.

"Yes, I have to find a place for those cats. I can't have them talking in my room all night," said Aleph. Everyone laughed and walked back to the castle. When they arrived, the girls were in their regular clothes and they were taking their party dresses out to the caravan. The cooks had already prepared dinner. Later on Quickturn and his men showed up. They went to the cooks' fire and had some food. They were tired and hungry. They had bathed in Lake Inari so they were ready for bed. Tall Sky and Melody slept in their own wagon and the soldiers slept in their tents.

The next morning was full of promise and excitement about going to a ball at the castle. After breakfast, the girls wanted to go shopping. They had some silver and gems given to them by Halden and the dragon riders and they needed clothing like undergarments, shoes and dresses. They divided up into groups of five and a soldier accompanied each group to go shopping. None of the girls had been to Vivallen before, so they were amazed by all the shops and the abundance of pretty things for sale. The pregnant girls went to a special shop where they bought maternity clothing. When they finished shopping, they ate lunch at the Golden Chalice. Feeling tired and happy and full, they returned to the caravan with their purchases.

Later that afternoon they returned to the bathing pool where they bathed and dressed for dinner. The dining hall was decorated with flowers and table cloths and beautiful dishes. The girls wore gowns and the soldiers wore their dress uniforms. The Bright Elves wore white with gold brocade. King Aryante and Queen Svetlana walked in with Prince Rauthomir Prince Haldovar and Princess Anya and sat at the first table in the front facing the guests. King Aryante wore burgundy velvet with a heavy gold necklace and his crown. Queen Svetlana wore a light blue gown with a tiara. Princess Anya wore a pink gown with a tiara, her brown hair falling freely down to her waist. Prince Rauthomir wore a bergundy shirt with puffed sleeves and a gold necklace. King Aryante stood and addressed the guests.

"My honored guests, I welcome you to our celebration of a successful mission, 'The Caravan to Orendia'. Soldiers, I congratulate you on your bravery and your hard work. You performed well, doing your best to rescue our girls from the clutches of evil men in a foreign country. It was a valiant effort worthy of our country's best men. I thank you for this. Girls, I understand the horrible things you had to endure and I am truly sorry for this. I have thought of nothing else for a long time. I hope that you will lead good and happy lives from this point forward. Now let's have dinner. He clapped his hands and from the front on both sides walked in waiters carrying platters of food. They walked down the sides to the back and placed platters on each table. When they had done this, they returned for more until everyone had been served. Quickturn and Dawn Lace, Tall Sky and Melody, Aleph and Faerverin, Gantio and Shasta, and Halden and his wifeTilly sat at a table to the right of the royal family. To the left of the Royal family sat Grendamore, the royal family's spiritual advisor, and officials.

Quickturn said, "Dawn Lace, you look like your name. How do you come to be here tonight?"

Dawn Lace said, "I was in Vivallen shopping and heard about the caravan parked behind the castle. I just had to see it and I wanted to meet the girls, so I talked to Queen Svetlana about it. She said that you were involved in the mission and that I could come to the ball and sit with you at dinner. It pays to know people in high places." She laughed, her blue eyes sparkling. Dawn Lace and Quickturn were friends from long ago. She had long, blonde hair, long eyelashes, fine features and was tall and slender. "I understand that you've been fighting bandits and Bitters and even a demon. You are really a hero. It's a story I would like to hear."

"Yes we have. They were all orchestrated by a sorcerer named Ahriman who was King Jahiz' advisor. Four dragon riders finally torched him when he asked them to torch our caravan," answered Quickturn.

Tall Sky said, "Dawn Lace, I remembered you when a counsel was held involving several of these girls yesterday. Remember the Elf council that you were a part of when you were only ninety years old? I recommended you for that and you proved to be worthy of it. These girls did a fine job of crafting a mission to Orendia of Bright Elves introducing the Orendians to Father God."

Dawn Lace said, "Yes, I do remember that. It was very exciting to me. I see you have been married since I saw you last."

Tall Sky said, "Yes. This is Melody, my wife and her little dragon Daisy." Daisy chirred.

Dawn Lace said, "I knew her name. She told it to me. She is lovely. It's rare to see a pet miniature dragon these days. Where did you find her?"

Melody said, "I found her egg in Malwood and her egg hatched in my pocket. We have been partners ever since. She actually saved my life once. Avidora was getting ready to incinerate me and Daisy jumped onto her face and clawed her eyes out. Then Trag knifed her from behind."

"Avidora the witch? Daisy is a handy little friend to have," said Dawn Lace.

"How long have you known Quickturn?" asked Melody.

"We have known each other for about a hundred years. We met through your husband who is my uncle," said Dawn Lace. Tall Sky smiled.

"What have you been doing all this time?" asked Tall Sky.

"I stay home and garden and paint," said Dawn Lace.

"You'll have to see Faerverin's paintings. She has been teaching Princess Anya to paint," said Tall Sky. "Faerverin and Aleph married a while ago. He is an advisor to King Aryante."

"Dawn Lace, I would like you to meet Gantio who was with us as a guide and interpreter on the caravan. He rescued Shasta and they will be married here after dinner," said Tall Sky.

A trumpet sounded and King Aryante stood up and said, "Tonight we will witness the marriage of Gantio and Shasta. Grendamore, Gantio and Shasta, would you please come up here?"

Grendamore said, "Gantio, you rescued this woman and told her that you would marry her. I am pleased to officiate at your wedding today. Shasta, are you entering into marriage with Gantio of your own free will?"

Shasta replied, "Yes."

"Gantio, will you love and protect Shasta from this day forward leading her into a deeper walk with Father God?" asked Grendamore.

"Yes I will," answered Gantio.

"Then I pronounce that you are married. Please sign the wedding book in the chapel," said Grendamore. The guests applauded.

King Aryante said, "We will all go to the ballroom for dancing and wine."

The royal family, the newlyweds, and the people at the two front tables walked down the aisle toward the ballroom. Down a long hallway, there was a very large room with columns and a platform in the far right corner with musicians playing. The walls were lined with tables and there was an open space in the middle for dancing. The newlyweds danced first and were joined by King Aryante and Queen Svetlana. Then the soldiers asked the girls to dance and soon the floor was filled with swirling skirts of different colors. Melody and Tall Sky were dancing close and she said, "I'll bet these girls are totally amazed by this. It will be something they will never forget."

"I know," said Tall Sky. "I love you Culina. I hope that these girls will have wonderful marriages like ours." He kissed her and she blushed.

Quickturn danced with Dawn Lace who was wearing a light blue flowing gown with a low cut neckline. "Did you wear this gown just for me?" he asked.

"Yes, I did. Do you like it?" she asked.

"I like it very much," he said, thinking about slipping her straps over her shoulders. "You have matured nicely since I last saw you. I should have made time to visit you. How long will you be in town? Perhaps we could have dinner tomorrow at the Golden Chalice."

"I would love to have dinner with you," said Dawn Lace. "My schedule is open. I am on a long deserved vacation. Where do you live?"

"I stay right here at the castle," said Quickturn.

"I am a guest at the castle," said Dawn Lace. "Queen Svetlana asked me to stay for a while. We haven't visited for a few years, so she wanted me to stay to catch up."

"She is a wise woman," said Quickturn. "I can't believe you are still single. I would think you would have suitors camping on your doorstep."

"Well, I've been interested in flowers, reading, writing poetry, painting and playing the harp. I keep busy at home and I am very happy with all of that," said Dawn Lace.

"Beautiful and cultured, too," said Quickturn. "A nice combination. Do you have any pets?"

"Not yet, but I haven't seen the flying cats yet. Cats that talk are intriguing. I want to see Faerverin's paintings, too," said Dawn Lace.

"There is one over there on the wall. King Aryante wanted one of her and Aleph dancing," said Quickturn.

"How did she learn to paint like that?" asked Dawn Lace.

"She learned how to paint from a fairy child who asked her to stay with her when she was a child. Her story is interesting. Ask her about it sometime," said Quickturn. "Let's sit down and have some wine."

Faerverin and Aleph were dancing. Aleph said, "I missed you when I was on the caravan. It was really a busy time trying to take care of the girls and I grew tired of being on constant alert. The men of Orendia are not to my liking. They have a different value system than we do. I never want to return. I hope the king doesn't ask me to."

"I would go with you if you have to go," said Faerverin. "Being without you was very difficult and sad."

"The country is not yet safe for women. I wouldn't expect you to go with me," said Aleph.

"I would like to meet the dragon riders," said Faerverin. "I could make a painting of them and their dragons. Don't worry. I wouldn't want to ride one."

"There's Gantio and Shasta. I'm glad that Gantio has a wife. He is a really good man and Shasta is quite a lady. He promised to marry her right after he bought her. She will fit in very well here at the castle," said Aleph. "The girls and the soldiers seem to be enjoying themselves. Tomorrow we start the relocation process. If a number of girls are from a certain town, the soldiers will probably use a wagon or two to take them home."

Marsten asked Haley to dance. "You look beautiful tonight, Haley. I'm glad to have the opportunity to dance with you. I enjoyed our conversations on the caravan and I am sincerely interested in coming to see you at your farm if you would like me to."

Haley said, "I think it would be nice to see you again, so you are welcome to visit me at my parent's farm. I didn't know if you were serious about that."

"I am. I really like you, Haley," said Marsten.

"I like you, too," said Haley. "Let's go outside and walk in the gardens. They are so beautiful with new flowers this time of year."

They walked around the gardens breathing in the fragrant air. Then they sat down on a bench watching the butterflies and the birds.

"I'm going to miss you when you go home tomorrow. I wish you could stay a little longer. Maybe I could volunteer to help escort your group home. Would you like that? I could meet your parents and get their permission to see you again," said Marsten.

"I would like that," said Haley. "I think my parents would like it, especially if you brought them some new tack."

"I would be happy to," said Marsten. "Let's go ask Quickturn for permission."

Quickturn was seated at a table with Dawn Lace, Aleph, and Faerverin. "Quickturn, could I have your permission to help escort Haley and others from her area tomorrow? I would like to meet her parents and ask them for their permission to see Haley on a regular basis," said Marsten.

Quickturn said, "And it begins. That's a great idea, Marsten. Haley is a very good choice for you. She helped to create the plan for evangelism of Orendia. King Aryante is very impressed with her. You have my permission." Marsten virtually glowed and said, "Thank you." They resumed dancing on the dance floor. The soldiers were enjoying themselves dancing with the girls they had protected for weeks. The girls were having fun finding out that there was a whole new world for them to explore.

Tall Sky and Melody were dancing. Melody said, "This is one of those times that I wish would never end."

Tall Sky said, "It's a very special time, but tomorrow we head back to Loadrel with two new cats, one for Arinya and one for us."

"Oh, Tall Sky, we can really have one?" asked Melody.

"Yes, I think it will be alright since Daisy communicates with them," said Tall Sky. "Do you know which one you want?"

"No. I think I will see if there is one that Daisy likes. Let's go see them now," said Melody.

Tall Sky and Melody went upstairs to see the flying cats. Aleph had located them in a room near his own room where Faerverin could keep an eye on them. Oh, I love them! They are so beautiful.

She took Daisy out of her pouch and set her down near the cage of kittens. The mother cat said, "Achta Daisy." A calico kitten walked over to Daisy and said, "Daisy." Melody said that the calico kitten was the one she wanted, so Tall Sky took the kitten out of the cage and let Melody hold her. The kitten purred and enjoyed Melody petting her. Daisy walked up to the kitten and rubbed faces with her and chirred. The kitten fluttered her wings and Daisy fluttered her wings. Then they cuddled up together on Melody's lap. Melody felt full of joy and awe.

Quickturn and Dawn Lace walked in to see the cats. Dawn Lace sat down by the cages and just watched in amazement. "I want to hold the orange one," she said. Tall Sky gave her an orange kitten to hold. "She is so soft," said Dawn Lace.

Melody said, "Teach her your name."

Dawn Lace said her name while holding the kitten up to her face and the kitten said her name. "I want this kitten," said Dawn Lace.

"You will have to get a cage and a sand box and two bowls for food and water," said Melody. "They are old enough to be away from their mother."

Quickturn said, "I will have a tribune get some cages and sand boxes. Celia and Lelia want a cat, too."

The tribune had already determined the need for these things and brought them in. "Thank you," said Dawn Lace.

Faerverin walked in and said that she wanted one of the adult pairs so that she could have the fun of having a litter of kittens. She thought that Haley should take the other pair since she would probably end up living close by with Marsten. If they don't get married, she lives in Talath, the closest town to Vivallen.

Being pregnant and about to deliver, Arinya could wait to choose from the next litter. "Tall Sky, let's get packed and be ready to leave tomorrow morning. Do you have the list of people who ride with us to Loadrel and Home Fire?" asked Melody. "We should probably check the wagons and clean them. They got some pretty hard use on the caravan."

# GOING HOME

Quickturn, Halden and Tall Sky assigned girls from certain areas to certain wagons and they all slept in their designated wagons. When morning came, they left for their various home towns. Melody's company included Talla and her pregnant girls, and about one third of the others who came from the northeast sector of Aksanda. Some of the girls went directly north to Talath and farms in the northwest sector. A major part of the girls went south into the Angvar Province.

Melody had her new kitten with her in the wagon. It couldn't fly yet, so she could safely hold it in her lap. Daisy sat on her shoulder enjoying the breeze and the scenery as they traveled the familiar road back to Loadrel. She felt happy and contented to be next to Tall Sky on their way back to their very own house. "I'm so happy I can hardly stand it," said Melody. "Our mission was successful, I now know two kings, and I have a flying cat and a dragon, and I'm married to the most wonderful elf in the world. God has been so good to me. Now we get to see our friends in Loadrel and give them some silk. Mina should have some to make pajamas or a nightgown. Arinya, Liadra and I will make gowns and night gowns. Alqua should have some for a gown, too. It will be fun to go to Home Fire and see what new buildings they have. I wonder if they have more Gullandians there yet."

Tall Sky said, "I'm sure they do. Remember how often people told us about seeing Gullandians heading south? I'm really looking forward to talking to Rando. The dwarves should be helping with projects there. Some of these girls want to go to Home Fire. I hope everyone is ready for a big surprise when we get to Loadrel. There are quite a few people with us. If there aren't enough rooms for them, we still have wagons with us for them to sleep in. The soldiers will take some of them to the Yardrel and Talami areas, so we won't have to go that far, but I want to go with them to Home Fire if for no other reason than to see the look on Rando's face." They both laughed.

"I want to help Talla get her place ready for the pregnant girls. She has ten girls to settle in. Each one is going to need baby beds and baby clothes. She has to get beds for all of them," said Melody.

"They could use the mattresses from the wagons until we could get Ulrich to make beds for them," said Tall Sky. "I wonder how he's doing with the Home Fire furniture. He had a big order to fill for the inn out there."

Tall Sky pulled over next to the ruins for a rest and some lunch. They had with them ten soldiers, seven wagons, six extra horses, and thirty girls. Each one of them carried their own bag of food and a skin of wine. They spread out blankets on the ground and sat there having lunch. It was a beautiful spring day with a blue sky and warm sun. The girls talked about last night's festivities and going home. They decided to tell stories about being made to work hard as servants and skip the sexual abuses. They would get busy on their families' farms and fit in again to that routine. Some of them wanted to get married right away to feel safe. Others didn't want anything to do with men for a while.

Talla spent some time talking with Tall Sky and Melody about getting beds for her home. She needed ten baby beds and eight more regular beds. "Don't worry about that. I will have Beldock put out the word to the villagers and people will loan or sell you the beds you need. If not, Ulrich will make you some. The soldiers will bring in the girls' mattresses tonight. I will get a work crew to your house tomorrow to build another room onto your house. It can be done in a week. We had better get the girls back into the wagons. There are four more hours to reach Loadrel. We might want to spend one more night in the wagons."

Tall Sky pulled back onto the road and headed east again. The girls spent their time sewing and napping. "I wonder how Halden is doing," said Melody. "He has a long journey ahead of him with over eighty girls to return. There will be celebrations throughout the whole province."

"I'm sure there will be," said Tall Sky. "Halden handles a caravan very well. He talks well with the girls and they like him. He has plenty of help with him including cooks and soldiers just like we did. I'll bet he will be good and tired when he's done with this journey. I'm already looking forward to a rest."

"Me too," said Melody. "I want to see what my kitten does in the house."

"Have you named her yet?" asked Tall Sky.

"I'm going to call her Shelly. I have always liked that name," said Melody. "I'm going into the wagon and take a nap. Wake me if anything happens."

The light was waning as they pulled into Loadrel. It had been an uneventful trip, but the sight of a small caravan accompanied by soldiers brought out the onlookers. Beldock came out of the Laborer's Reward along with his dinner customers. "Tall Sky! Good to see you my friend." He hugged Tall Sky and Melody. I'll bet you need a mug of ale. Come in. How many people do you have with you?"

"We have forty-three People. Don't worry, we can cook outside like we did on the caravan," said Tall Sky. "The girls have been sleeping in the wagons and the soldiers have tents or they can sleep in hammocks under the wagons. Talla has decided to have the pregnant girls stay with her. She doesn't have beds yet, but they could put their mattresses on the floor until we can round up some beds from people who have extras or have Ulrich make some. We need eight beds and ten baby beds. She has silver to spend on the girls."

Beldock said, "For now you can have them stay here. I have enough rooms for them."

"That sounds good. I'm sure they will appreciate it," said Tall Sky. "Talla will make dinner for the girls and the soldiers. Melody and I will eat here and tell you about our journey. After dinner I will bring the pregnant girls into the inn." Tall Sky moved the wagons to an empty area south of the inn and told Talla to begin making dinner. Then he and Melody returned to the inn and gave Mina her silk. "It's beautiful and so soft. I was so worried. I prayed for you every day. I'll get a plate for Daisy." Mina brought Daisy her food and said, "I have missed this little dragon. She is the highlight of my day."

"Mina, I have a kitten too and when she is older, she will fly. She's outside in my wagon," said Melody. "She is in a small cage. Should I bring her in?"

"You bring her in. I will get your food and a plate for your flying kitten," said Mina. Tall Sky went to the wagon and brought in the kitten and her cage. Beldock walked next door and brought Laskron, Liadra and Elise. Everyone wanted to touch the kitten, so Melody took her out and said, "One at a time you can pet the kitten while I hold her. This worked out well, but she let Mina hold her. Then Mina set her down in front of a saucer of milk and a few little pieces of meat. Shelly was hungry and she ate it all. Then she walked over to Daisy and said, "Daisy," and rubbed against her.

"I'm glad to see them getting along so well," said Mina.

"Daisy and Shelly communicate mentally. Daisy told Shelly her name," said Melody. She put Shelly back into her cage and sat down for dinner and conversation.

Laskron ordered dinner and ale for his family and said, "We will eat first and then you can tell us about your journey. I'm really glad you're home. I have missed you." Elise finished eating and sat down by the kitty cage with Daisy. When they finished eating, they listened to Tall Sky tell of their adventure through Orendia. "We found some girls right away at the first town, but when we reached Fallonia and King Jahiz signed the treaty and the trade agreement, things really picked up. He asked Father God into his heart. King Jahiz ordered all slaves to be sold to us and that day we ended up with sixty-five girls. Fallonia is a large city like Vivallen. King Jahiz was the first to turn in his two girls. One of them is pregnant, but he didn't know that. King Aryante asked her to stay at the castle so that the child will be afforded a good education and learn proper court conduct. King Jahiz had an advisor named Ahriman who was also a sorcerer. He tried to kill us by sending bandits, Bitters, wild animals, fire breathing dragons with dragon riders, and a demon."

"Melody and I thought it best to bring home the first bunch of girls by ship to Free Harbor, and then by river boats to Loss Port. While we did that, Halden and Quickturn took the caravan around Orendia selling goods and buying slaves. It was very successful. Gantio, our guide, even bought a wife and married her in Vivallen. We had the girls to wear men's clothing and hide their hair under caps to avoid attention. They had to fight off two sets of Bitters and lost one of our soldiers in the first battle. Ahriman sent sleep spells to disable the troups, but Quickturn sensed them and repelled them. Next, Ahriman sent beasts after them in the forest. One of those beasts was a giant mantis that could leap through the air and spew acid at its victims. The Bright Elves shielded themselves and sent arrows into the mantises' heads. The soldiers and several girls galloped away back to the caravan."

"One of the most interesting things to happen was an encounter with the dragon riders," said Tall Sky. "Ahriman had hired the dragon riders to torch the caravan, but they torched him instead. Then they attacked the bandits. On their way out of Orendia, the dragon riders swooped down on the caravan dropping lots of flowers, set their dragons down and walked over with gifts of meat. They wanted to meet the girls. The dragon riders are women. At that, everyone laughed. In talking to the girls, they all asked Father God to live in their hearts."

"The last problem encountered was a demon sent by Ahriman. The Bright Elves went to the rescue of some villagers near Lake Inari. They killed the beasts and bound the demon with bands of light and commanded it to leave Phayendar in the name of Father God. I'm glad that Melody, Aleph and I came home with the first group of girls. King Jahiz has asked King Aryante for help in introducing Father God to his countrymen, so there may be another campaign in Orendia. Then there are foreigners who took girls from Aksanda to Fantolo. King Aryante is already talking about getting them back. It's not over yet. We rescued one hundred and forty three slaves on this mission," said Tall Sky.

Melody said, "Liadra, would you like to go out to the wagons and meet some girls? I have to bring the pregnant girls into the inn. Beldock is putting them up for tonight and tomorrow Talla is taking them home with her."

"I would love to meet them," said Liadra. They walked out to the wagons where the girls and some soldiers were eating dinner. Melody introduced Liadra and they sat down on some logs. "The pregnant girls will be staying at the inn tonight. Wash your dishes and bring them and any of your belongings with you. Let me know when you are ready."

Liadra said, "I was with Melody, Amidra and Trag when we entered Malwood Forest. Trag was enslaved by Avidora, and Rando let us stay at Home Fire which was just a camp at that time. Tall Sky liberated Trag and brought him to us. I think that without Tall Sky's help, we would all be in your situation now. As it is, we are all married and living in homes. Trag liberated Arinya at the Malwood Auction and she will be having a baby this summer. Will any of you be staying here?" Four girls raised their hands. "Who will be staying at Home Fire?" Four girls raised their hands. "So, the rest of you will be going home to your families." They nodded yes. "The four of you who are staying here may move into my house for the night, so if you would, please get your things and come with me. The rest of you will stay in the wagons tonight and leave tomorrow morning." The four girls brought their things over to Liadra's house where they washed up, changed clothes, and went to bed.

Tall Sky and Melody drove their wagon home, bathed and went to bed. "It feels so good to be home again. Liadra really surprised me by taking in four of the girls. I'm really proud of her," said Melody.

"She is a nice lady," said Tall Sky. "We are all grateful to have found each other and we know that these girls can find mates, too." Melody put Daisy and her kitten on her pillow and both of them purred her to sleep.

Not having food in the house, the next morning, Tall Sky and Melody headed over to the Laborer's Reward for breakfast. Mina saw them and quickly brought out the Daisy plate and the Shelly plate.

She put her kitten into the cage for a while. They had a big breakfast of scrambled eggs, hot cakes and sausage. Melody felt like she hadn't eaten for days. She ate it and went to the bakery for some pastries. "I have missed Jelsareeb's pastries. Want some?" asked Melody.

"Yes, I would," said Tall Sky.

As Melody lifted the pastry to her mouth, Daisy bit it, so she broke some little pieces for her dragon with a sweet tooth. Trag and Arinya walked in and sat at the table. "Arinya, I've got a kitten and when we go somewhere you can watch it for me if you would," said Melody. "King Jahiz gave her to me. There are others. If you like mine, Faerverin has a pair of adult cats who will mate and have kittens and you can have one."

Arinya said, "She's darling. May I hold her?"

"Sure," said Melody. "How have you been feeling? Can you feel the baby kick yet?"

"Yes," said Arinya. "I've been feeling fine, but Trag has been very protective. He doesn't want me to do any work. How was your trip?"

"It was dangerous and I rode in a big ship with sixty-five girls to Free Harbor. We thought it would be safer than traveling all over the country with them. We were right. The caravan was attacked by Bitters, bandits, and giant animals. The king's advisor was an evil sorcerer, and when he tried to pay the dragon riders to torch us, they torched him instead. They are women and they ride these huge dragons who love them. I didn't get to meet them, but I want to," said Melody.

Trag said, "How many Bitters did the soldiers kill?"

"About forty," said Tall Sky. "I'm going for a walk by the Lake. Melody, would you walk with me?"

"Always," she answered.

"You can leave the kitten with me," said Arinya.

"Alright, but she needs a sandbox in the room with her," said Melody.

"I'll get one for her," said Trag.

"Trag, we're going to Home Fire today. Would you keep her until tomorrow?" asked Tall Sky.

"No problem. Have fun," said Trag.

Tall Sky and Melody first stopped by the caravan and asked when they would be ready to go. The girls wanted to bathe and wash their hair before arriving at Home Fire, so he said they would stop on the way for them to bathe in the Lake. Melody and Tall Sky walked back to their wagon and stopped at a few stores for food and supplies. They bought a few kegs of ale and some wine and the soldiers filled the water containers and hitched up the horses. Tall Sky called, "Forward!" and pulled onto the road heading north toward Home Fire. They stopped by Ulrik's and picked up a baby bed for Alqua.

"I'm so excited," said Melody. "It's been a long time since we were at Home Fire. I wonder how Alqua is. She and Arinya got pregnant about the same time. Does she know about the bed?"

"No, Rando ordered it as a surprise. He sure does love that woman," said Tall Sky.

"We have some silk for her, too," said Melody.

It was another good day for travel. Spring breezes, fragrant flowers, new green leaves and warm sun made everyone feel happy and hopeful. Children were returning home and some were starting new futures in a brand new town. Daisy sat on Melody's shoulder watching everything and chirring at the birds and the squirrels. They would be at Home Fire in time for lunch. Now and then there was a friendly passerby, but they were few. Tall Sky said, "Remind me of what you know of Fantolo."

"It is a land mass connected to Orendia by a land bridge. It is very cold in the northern part where they herd reindeer. The main part of the land has marshes, lakes and rivers. They grow lilies that are edible and rice. Of course they fish. The people are dark skinned and gentle and are hospitable. They worship idols and believe that you can come back as another person after you die. I'll bet that Gantio knows more about the Fantolese people. Malding didn't spend much time there," said Melody.

"I want to know as much as possible before we go to that place. What about the animals?" asked Tall Sky.

"There are different animals there. There are lizards and snakes of various sizes and there are different dragons. There are animals that we have never heard of. Are you sure that we will be going there?" asked Melody.

"I'm not sure, but King Aryante said that he wants our girls back from there. He must have information about it from the ships' crews who sailed that way. I want to be prepared with as much knowledge as possible. The Gullandians at Home Fire may know something. There are reindeer herders in Fantolo in the northern region."

Lelia and Cassia rode in the second wagon. "You know what's strange?" asked Lelia. "Talking to boys normally like we used to do before we were stolen. It's like pretending to be innocent and shy. It's hilarious if you think about it. Do you feel it too?"

"Yes, I do," said Cassia. "I think being slaves made us grow up. You can only be a child so long. I'm not afraid anymore. I feel like nobody can fool me and they had better not try. The worst has been done to us and I'm not putting up with anything anymore!"

"Good," said Lelia. "We're going to be alright. I think we made the right choice to start in this new town. The people there are strong, too. They have to be."

"I'm almost done making these pants. I think it's important to have protective clothing in the country, especially for riding horses and working outside and walking through woods," said Cassia.

"I agree." said Lelia. "We're turning! We must be there." The wagons pulled up beside Home Fire and stopped. The girls were so excited that they climbed down right away and waited for Tall Sky.

Rando came out to greet them. "Tall Sky! Good to see you. What's all this?"

"This is part of the caravan that we took to Orendia. Most of these girls are going north to their families, but I have some who want to settle here. They are farm girls with some good skills. Do you have the inn finished yet?"

"We do," said Rando. "We finished it last week and have some Gullandian men who would like to meet your girls."

"Lenma, Kayla, Lelia and Cassia, I would like you to meet Rando, the chief of your new town. He and his men helped in the destruction of the auction at Malwood. They also killed many Bitters who were on their way to destroy Loadrel," said Tall Sky. "Have a seat around the fire and we will bring out the food."

"Come with me and I'll show you around. Have you had lunch yet?" asked Rando.

"No, but we have food with us. We'll bring it over to the fire and a keg of beer, too. Rando, your baby bed is in our wagon. Let's take it to Alqua," said Tall Sky.

"Great!" said Rando. Tall Sky and Rando carried the bed to his house and knocked on the door. Alqua opened the door very surprised. "What's this?" she asked.

"Our first present for the baby," said Rando.

"It's beautiful," said Alqua. They brought it in and placed it in the nursery. Alqua hugged Rando and said, "Thank you my darling."

Melody thought, "Now Rando is a darling."

Rando said, "Tall Sky brought us four girls who want to settle here. Come meet them. They're at the fire having lunch. Do we have rooms ready at the inn?"

Alqua said, "Yes we do. I'll meet the girls and have lunch, and then I'll get them settled in their rooms." They walked over to the fire. "Where are the rest of the girls going?"

Tall Sky said, "They are going north of here to their homes. They want to see their parents before deciding what to do. Some of them may decide that Home Fire is for them. They aren't little girls any more. They have been through a lot and they have seen a lot since they were stolen."

"I can imagine," said Rando.

"These girls met the dragon riders of Orendia and attended balls at King Jahiz'castle in Fallonia and at the castle in Vivallen. They were in a meeting with King Aryante to create a way to evangelize Orendia. They're smart and they have very good skills that they learned on their parents' farms," said Melody.

The soldiers brought over the keg of ale and poured ale for everyone. After lunch Rando led his guests around the town. Fifteen houses and the inn were finished and there were three more houses under construction. There were corrals filled with horses, reindeer and several cows and a chicken coup. Alqua showed her new girls to their rooms.

Melody said, "Rando, this inn looks really great. Do you have other guests staying here now?"

"Yes, we have two couples and five Gullandian men. I will introduce them at dinner. They are working with the construction crews right now," said Rando.

"Will you be staying here tonight?" asked Alqua.

Tall Sky answered, "Yes, we will. I thought we would try out your inn."

Rando laughed. "I kind of hoped you would. Let's sit here in the dining room and sip some ale and talk. I want to know more about Orendia."

Tall Sky said, "Orendia has a variety of land. There is farmland, a forest and a plateau in the northern part. The western side of it is the sea. We visited fifteen cities. They plaster their buildings and cover them in paintings of scenery, battles, people and hunting scenes. The fishing villages and farms are much like ours. The Orendian men are dominant over the women. They use them for pleasure and for having children. The women are their slaves. When they tire of their women, they put them in a brothel, hire them out for working in the fields, or kill them. Women are not allowed to talk to men and they walk behind the men. They do not know Father God. There is nothing good in this culture."

"Did you have any problems with Bitters or bandits?" asked Rando.

"Yes, but Melody, Aleph, and I took the first sixty-five girls on a ship to Free Harbor. After meeting with King Jahiz and getting the treaty and trade agreement signed, we heard about the king's advisor Ahriman who was also a sorcerer. He would send dragon riders to torch men he owed gambling debts to. Ahriman was angry with us for taking away his slave girls. As it turned out, Ahriman sent bandits, Bitters, wild animals, giant mantises, and dragons after the caravan. Halden and Quickturn traveled the country buying back slaves. Most of the men in Orendia are devoted to their King, so they sold the slaves without too much trouble."

"What about the dragons? Melody said that our new girls met the dragon riders," said Rando.

"Ahriman wanted them to torch the caravan and those women didn't want to, so they torched Ahriman instead. Then they swooped down on the caravan and dropped flowers all over it. They set their dragons down and walked over to the caravan with baskets of meat. They wanted to talk to the girls about their experiences. The girls told them about Father God and prayed with them. Then the dragon riders gave each of them a gem to help them get started when they got home," said Tall Sky.

"So you didn't have to worry about dragons after all," said Rando.

"No, we didn't, but there were too many girls to carry all around the country, so it worked out alright," said Tall Sky.

"I have to meet those dragon riders!" said Melody. "I wonder how Daisy would react to seeing a full sized dragon."

Tall Sky said, "You might get a chance to find out. We could get assigned to the mission to Fantalo."

"When does this one start?" asked Rando.

"As soon as these girls are returned to their homes, the next caravan could commence to Fantolo. Also, King Jahiz has requested that King Aryante send about a hundred Bright Elves to introduce his countrymen to Father God. The Orendian men are extremely cruel to women. That's why the dragon riders don't marry. Quickturn's soldiers killed about forty Bitters and they were fighting a large group of bandits when the dragon riders chased the bandits away torching many of them," said Tall Sky.

Rando laughed. "We could have used them during the Battle of Othrund."

"We sure could have," said Tall Sky.

"Are there any more girls staying in Loadrel? We need a few more," said Rando.

"There are ten pregnant girls staying with Talla, the caravan cook, and there are four staying with Laskron and Liadra," replied Tall Sky.

"Good. I will talk to our single men about it," said Rando. "I don't think it will matter to them if the girls are pregnant. Did you know that Vanya and Almarie have remarried since Flint and Cliff were killed by Avidora's bears? They married two of the Gullandians."

Melody said, "Oh, I'm so glad. I've been worried about them. I think I'll go talk to them."

Rando said, "They're probably helping with the laundry. Today is laundry day."

"Alright, I will see you later," said Melody.

Melody walked past the cook's building to the laundry area where there were clothes lines strung up between trees and several bathtubs of water. Almarie and Vanya were hanging up wet clothing. "Hello, you two, got a minute to talk?"

"Melody!" they said and hugged her. "We were wondering how you were and how the caravan trip was."

Melody said, "It was successful. We brought back over a hundred slaves. I was wondering how you were and if you got over the deaths of your husbands."

Almarie said, "We were really sad for a while, but time passed and we met some Gullandian men who came to us last winter. They are very nice men and they spent time with us and we fell in love with them. We are very happy now."

"I'm glad to hear that. Whatever happened to Shandra and Callie? Did they ever marry Salek and Parin?" asked Melody.

Vanya said, "Yes, they did. They married last month. They are very happy and living in the houses they built."

"How is Brilley doing?" asked Melody. "Has she been doing any doctoring?"

"She delivered a baby last month," said Shandra.

"Great," said Melody. "What about Indra? She liked working with children."

"Indra holds classes to teach the children how to read and about many interesting things," said Callie. "She teaches them how to sew and how to draw and make things."

Daisy started doing her hungry dance on Melody's shoulder. "I've got to feed Daisy. See you later at dinner." Melody stopped at the cook's kitchen and made a Daisy plate for her miniature dragon. Tall Sky walked up to her and said, "Culina, I was missing you. Would you like to go down by the lake and put your feet in the water?"

"Sure," said Melody. "As long as we keep a look out for grustabists." They both laughed and walked toward the shore of Lake Perilough. "Liadra, Amidra and I once bathed here. Vela loaned us some of her soap that smelled like flowers."

"Let's take a bath now. It will feel good. Daisy might enjoy it too," said Tall Sky.

They took off their clothes and walked into the water. Melody held Daisy while she flapped her wings and splashed in the water. It felt cool and refreshing. Melody put Daisy in her pouch for a nap while she and Tall Sky swam in the cool, clear water. "This is wonderful," said Melody.

"Let's go back to our wagon and take a nap," said Tall Sky. They put on their clothes and walked back to the wagon. Melody oiled Daisy and they all took a nap. They woke to the sound of the dinner bell. "I feel so relaxed," said Melody.

"That swim really helped. Let's see what they have for dinner," said Tall Sky. They put on some clean clothes and walked over to the cook's area to receive their food. They sat on the logs around the fire and ate their dinner. "It has been fun catching up on all that has happened this summer. Everyone is doing well. Brilley delivered her first baby, Almarie and Vanya are remarried, and Indra is teaching reading to the children and they are all married and in homes," said Melody.

"Any messages sent to us will be sent through Beldock, so we should probably be going back home tomorrow," said Tall Sky.

"Yes," said Melody. "I want to check on Talla's project and see how she and her pregnant girls are getting along."

Rando sat down next to them and said, "I'm planning on building a Vision Hall as soon as we can. With this many people here and more coming, we need a spiritual center to this town. We also need a spiritual leader like Laskron, so keep a lookout for one."

"I will," said Tall Sky. "Have you prayed for one yet?"

"I have and will continue to do so," said Rando.

"Father God will send you the right person for Home Fire. You will be pleasantly surprised," said Tall Sky. "Have you spoken with King Farin about getting help with your water system yet?"

"I plan to do so next. I wanted the inn finished first so that any water system would include the inn," said Rando.

"When you build Vision Hall, build a house next to it or as an addition to it for your spiritual leader," said Tall Sky. "Rando, there is a girl staying with Laskron who is very small. Her name is Jalia and she belonged to King Jahiz. She wants to come out here. She is pretty and very sweet and helped to take care of a princess in Orendia. I wonder if you could look out for her and have her to help with the care of the baby and of Alqua while she recovers from childbirth. She could do the same for other new mothers. She would also be a big help to Indra with the teaching of the children. Since she is so short, she might become friends with the dwarf who comes out here to design your water system. She will be arriving here with the next work crew. Have Indra to meet with her."

"Sure, I'll keep track of her for you and I will tell Indra to work with her when she arrives," said Rando. "I haven't been away from here since Aleph's wedding at the castle in Vivallen and I would like to meet King Farin at Othrund and see his water system. Would you consider taking me there? It would only take a few days and it might be the only way for me to meet him."

"I hadn't thought of that, but it's a good idea. We could stop off at Yardrel and visit Steben and Amidra. You haven't seen Steben for a while either. What do you think, Melody? Would you like to visit

Steben and Amidra and little Emmy?" asked Tall Sky. "It would probably be the last time we could see them this year."

"That sounds like fun," said Melody. "I would like to see them again."

"Shall we leave in the morning, then?" asked Rando. "I think Alqua would like to go with us."

"She could ride in our wagon with us," said Melody. "That way, if she gets tired, she can lie down on a mattress inside the wagon and take a nap. That's what I do."

"That sounds good. I'll go tell her to pack some things," said Rando. "She'll be happy to go on a short vacation. I'll see you in the morning."

# A PROVIDENTIAL MEETING

Tall Sky and Melody went back to the wagon and got ready for bed. "I can hardly wait to see the dwarves and their tunnels. I want to thank King Farin for my ring. We should give some silk to his wife and some to Alqua and Amidra. We have a whole bolt of silk still in the wagon."

"Yes, and it is a gift fit for a Queen," said Tall Sky. "I would also like to buy a few other things to trade with them like I used to do. I think I will have Rando drive the extra wagon and I will fill it with vegetables, fruits and other things for the dwarves. It will be a good trade and will please King Farin. His wife Heiki will love the silk. They have given us so much. It will be good to do this for them."

Melody fell asleep thinking of gems and silk and tunnels. Tall Sky was very happy at the prospect of seeing his friend King Farin again and spending more time with Rando.

Morning began with the rooster crowing. "Oooh. I forgot about that. I'm glad we don't own one," said Melody. Tall Sky laughed.

"Are you hungry? They make great breakfasts out here. Let's see what they have this morning," said Tall Sky. Rando and Alqua were already at the circle of logs around the fire eating ham and blueberry pancakes. Melody brought their plates over and sat next to them. Tall Sky brought the tea. "Rando, would you drive the extra wagon? I want to fill it with things to trade with the dwarves. I usually fill a wagon with vegetables and other things for them. They really appreciate it and I get some gems for it."

"Maybe I could ride with you for a while and let one of my men drive the wagon. I would like to talk with you some more," said Rando.

"That sounds better," said Tall Sky. "Are you packed and ready to go?"

"Yes, and I have three of my men ready to go with us for protection," said Rando.

"Great. It's a good idea to be safe with our wives along," said Tall Sky. "The other wagons will be with us for a while, but they will turn off one at a time to take the girls home. Let's put your stuff in the wagon."

"I want to give King Farin a gift from Home Fire. One of my men carved this figure of a dwarf with a crossbowon a pony. I also thought to give him two ponies. Would he like that?" asked Rando.

"He will love it," said Tall Sky. "He doesn't get many gifts and he has been curious about you and Home Fire." Tall Sky helped Rando with his bags and spoke with Halden about the caravan. "Halden, I am bringing Rando and Alqua with us to Othrund and I need the use of the wagon that our four girls rode in. Would you mind if we led the caravan? When we get to Yardrel, we will be staying the night at Steben's farm."

"It sounds like a good plan. We are ready to go when you are," said Halden. Everyone boarded their wagons and Halden called, "Forward!" Tall Sky drove onto the road heading north toward Yardrel.

Melody and Alqua rode inside the wagon. Alqua said, "This is fun. I haven't been anywhere since Rando and I were married, and after the baby is born, we will be staying home for a year or so. That baby bed makes it seem more real. I wish we knew if it would be a boy or a girl, so I could make baby clothes for it."

Melody said, "When a baby is little, it really doesn't matter. The baby will wear loose clothing and you will have time to make special outfits for the baby as it grows."

Alqua said, "I'm glad it isn't here now. I want to plant a garden, swim and explore the area on foot with Rando. I love the land, the woods and the water out here. Do you mind all the traveling you do with Tall Sky?"

"No. I enjoy seeing new places. I could have done without the voyage on that ship, though. Ships are not that comfortable and you get the feeling that you're in danger all the time. I have met two kings and have helped to rescue many slaves. It has all been worth it. I am happy as long as I'm with Tall Sky," said Melody.

Alqua said, "I really want to meet King Farin and Queen Heiki. The Gullandians who were married at Othrund said that the King and Queen were very gracious and generous. They gave the couples wedding rings and a big party with dancing afterwards. How long does it take to get there?"

Melody replied, "It will take about four hours to get to Yardrel and we will stay overnight there to visit with Steben and Amidra. It sometimes takes more than a day to get to Othrund. It takes four more hours to get to Talami, and after that about six more to Othrund. We will stop at stores in Yardrel and Talami to buy things for the dwarves. I am excited to meet them too. King Farin gave Tall Sky this ring for me for our wedding."

"It's very beautiful," said Alqua. "I love emeralds. Could I hold Daisy for a while?"

"Sure," said Melody and handed her to Alqua. Daisy crawled up Alqua's arm and rubbed faces with her and chirred."

Tall Sky and Rando rode up front enjoying the morning air and the woods on either side of the road. Rando said, "Tall Sky, I have some questions. As Home Fire gets bigger, there could be problems among people that I will be expected to solve. So far I have simply used the force of my will and position as chief to say what should be done. This is why I want a spiritual leader out here."

"There is a lot of pressure in leadership. You have some experience and a sense of fair play that will come to your aid, but we have time to talk about these things," said Tall Sky. "Your most immediate problem will be to talk to your men about how to relate to the girls. They must never lay blame on them. If they tell the men they feel guilty, the men are to say that what happened to them is not their fault and it doesn't make them less desirable or lovable. Some of these girls have been mistreated very badly and the pain of that goes deeper than the physical pain. They will need reassurance and tenderness. These men must be compassionate and thoughtful. You planted flowers for Alqua and she appreciated it. That made her feel loved. It is this type of thing that these girls need. A pregnant woman would appreciate a man making her a special spot for the baby, getting her a rocking chair and a small bathtub for the baby. Things like that will make her feel wanted and accepted by her man. Pregnant women sometimes get cravings for a particular food and it helps to cater to those needs. They must make her feel that they want this baby and that they look forward to being the baby's father. The baby is part of her and that's what is important. After a baby is born, the woman must not have sex for several weeks. She must have time to heal. After the baby is born, it would be good for the husband to buy his wife something pretty and some good smelling soap and candy. It would also be good for him to buy the baby some special clothes and a baby toy."

"I'm going to be doing these things for Alqua. I want her to feel loved and happy," said Rando. "Do you think that the pregnant women should be out there before the babies are born?"

"That depends on the men," said Tall Sky. "It may be helpful to have them there when Alqua is pregnant. It might make them feel more comfortable. Alqua would have more women to talk to about it and be able to lend emotional support to them. The men would have time to get used to the idea of being a father. It definitely has some advantages. Talla is willing to have them stay there until after the babies are born, so it will really be up to the individual couples."

"How does work get done if all the women are watching babies?" asked Rando.

"That is an important question. You could make a building for training of the children and have the older children watch them and teach them for a morning or an afternoon each day. That way the mothers would have some time to churn butter and do laundry and make soap when they need to," said Tall Sky.

"Having water running close to the town will be a big help. It will make everything easier from cooking to bathing," said Tall Sky.

"I know. I can hardly wait," said Rando. "While we are building this town, we don't have the firewood ready for next winter."

"You may want to buy the firewood you need for next winter. That way you can continue to create the town," said Tall Sky. "There is only so much time in a summer and you really do need to create right now."

"I agree," said Rando. "I'm really looking forward to this winter. I will have more time to spend with Alqua and the baby."

"What are you girls doing back there?" asked Tall Sky.

"We're making a baby dress," said Melody. "Are we close to Yardrel yet?"

"We will be there soon. Are you hungry yet?" asked Tall sky.

"Not yet," said Melody. "I'm ready for a nap, though."

Melody and Alqua decided to rest for a while.

"Rando, there are ways of handling certain situations that can be very helpful to know. For instance, if someone is making you feel very angry so that you are tempted to yell or strike the person, it is best to step back and imagine a wall between you and the other person. Then think about what the person said to make you feel angry. Was he attacking your pride? Was he so amazingly wrong? You must see that person as separate from you and answer him with a calm voice. Ask him questions that will make him think about his situation. Then offer him possible solutions. Anger is something that is usually not productive," said Tall Sky.

"I've noticed that," said Rando. "Anger seems to get more and more until whatever caused it is lost. It makes me feel like I am not in control of myself. I really don't like that feeling. I will try this method of yours. It has to be better than being angry."

"It is. Someone told me about it long ago and it has been very helpful to me," said Tall Sky. "When you counsel two angry people, you have to get them to practice this and to say how they feel without yelling at each other or accusing each other and calling each other names. It does help to have a spiritual advisor at this point to keep everything calm."

"How am I going to get a spiritual advisor?" asked Rando.

"I actually had a vision about this. I'm glad that you have a mind that is not judgmental about others. We are going to Othrund to find a good engineer for your water system, but this person is also a wise and devout man who has counseled many people at Othrund. I saw him, in my vision, speaking at your Vision Hall. Remember the small girl I told you about named Jalia? She will marry this man," said Tall Sky.

Rando laughed. "I am delighted…. and relieved. My life just gets more and more interesting. I liked having the dwarves at Home Fire."

"It is possible that a few others may join you. Some of them do like the outside. Hundreds of years ago during the age of the giants, the dwarves retreated to the tunnels in Othrund to avoid being killed. Before that they lived as we do," said Tall Sky. "We had better wake the girls. Yardrel is just up ahead. We will be turning off to the east at the next road."

Melody and Alqua combed their hair. In about fifteen minutes they pulled up to Steben's farm. There were horses and a cow in the corral and a wagon parked near the barn. There were chickens wandering about and a cat on the porch. Emmy called in, "Mama, there are two wagons out front!" Steben and Amidra came out to meet them.

"Tall Sky and Rando, I am happy to see you," said Steben. They all hugged and Amidra invited them into the house for lunch. Rando's three men brought in some blankets to sit on and some food. "How is everything at Home Fire?" asked Steben.

"It's pretty much the same except for all the building going on. We finished the inn and have two couples, five Gullandians and four girls staying there. More houses are being built. We will build Vision Hall next and a place for our spiritual advisor to live. We are on our way to get a dwarf to help us set up a water system. We will soon be in need of more furniture. Do you think that your father would want to make some furniture?" asked Rando.

"I'll have to ask him," said Steben.

"We need enough for seven houses and the Vision Hall," said Rando. "It's a big order, but we won't need all of it at once. Only three houses are partially built."

Steben asked, "Where did you get the four girls?"

Tall Sky said, "We found them in Orendia. We brought back one hundred and forty-two slave girls with us. Half of them Melody and I brought back on a ship to Free Harbor and then up the river to Lossport. The caravan bought the rest of them in towns throughout the country. Halden and Quickturn had bandits and Bitters, wild animals and giant mantises and even a demon to battle. There was an evil sorcerer who kept sending enemies after them. The last one he sent was flying, fire breathing dragons, but the dragon riders were women and didn't want to torch a caravan full of girls, so they torched him instead. As he died he called on a demon and it attacked the Bright Elves near Lake Inari. The Bright Elves bound the demon in bands of light and commanded it to leave Phayendar in the name of Father God. The dragon riders swooped down dropping flowers on the caravan and set their dragons down. They wanted to meet the girls and give them gifts. The girls introduced them to Father God. Melody likes this story so much that she is ready to go back to meet them."

Amidra said, "Melody, you would. I can still see you chasing a cat toward a razor tree in Malwood and picking up a miniature dragon egg and running toward a Grustabist to save a little boy in Loadrel. You have no fear, do you?"

Melody said, "I have fear of big ships, but I rode in one just the same. I guess I should be more careful, but I don't think I can."

Amidra said, "I didn't see this one, but you tried to stop Avidora from throwing fireballs. Thank God that Daisy jumped on her face and that Trag knifed her. Your mother would have fainted."

Melody said, "Well, it all turned out alright, didn't it?"

"Yes, Culina, it turned out fine, and I am very proud of you," said Tall Sky. "Don't worry. I will keep her safe."

"Could I have a little plate for Daisy?" asked Melody.

Everyone ate lunch and drank some wine. Daisy ate her lunch with some fresh milk.

"Does Emmy have any friends here?" asked Alqua.

"I have two friends who come over and stay with me overnight sometimes," said Emmy. "We have a lot of fun. I have a pony that

I brush and bathe and lead around. She is my friend too and I call her flower."

Steben said, "Come outside and I will show you around the farm. We have a garden that is doing well and we planted some fruit trees. We also planted some nut bearing trees. There is a good well on the farm. The barn is in good repair. I didn't have to do much to the farm except for planting."

Rando said, "That's good. I'm glad you're doing well here, but I must confess to missing you. Alqua and I will be parents this fall. You should bring Emmy out to visit us and try out our new inn. We have lots of animals for Emmy to see. Have you ever seen a reindeer, Emmy?"

"No, but I would like to see one. Can you pet them?" asked Emmy.

"Yes, you can and you can also ride them," said Rando.

"Oh, Papa, when can we go?" asked Emmy.

Steben said, "We can go after a while. You know that Rando and Alqua won't be there for a while because they are on a trip to Othrund to visit the dwarves. We could go to Home Fire next week."

"We could stop and get you on our way back home. That way you wouldn't have to travel alone," said Rando.

"Could I ride in the wagon?" asked Emmy.

"Yes, and we will bring your horses with us for the return trip," said Rando.

"Rando could keep the wagon. It is a handy thing to have and Grandpapa can use it for transport of furniture to Home Fire," said Tall Sky.

"Othrund is a long way from here to travel all in one day. Talami is the half way point. I think that it would be wise for us to travel to Talami and spend the night there. We will be back here in a few days anyway," said Tall Sky.

"It makes sense," said Rando. "Let's do this. Steben, make whatever preparations you need to make and we will be back to get you in a few days."

"Sounds good," said Steben.

Rando and Tall Sky rode in the driver's seat of the first wagon with two of Rando's men in the second wagon and the third man riding about. The extra horses were tied behind. It was a nice afternoon with mild weather, sunny and not too hot. Tall Sky said, "As Home Fire grows, you will see some change from communal to more individual ownership happening. Right now everyone is still working together to build the town, but in the future, there will be less of that. It would be good to keep that communal feeling going as long as possible so that when new people come, there would be plenty of help to get them settled. There is plenty of wealth right now and this is very helpful. I would suggest creating a building fund from which newcomers can draw to buy necessary items to create homes. They also need a way to create income for themselves. Necessarily, the community will feed off of itself with people trading with each other and with other communities. The creation of food supplies for the winter must be done as it has been done so far only in a larger way. Division of duties in this is important and you should put someone in charge of this.

You also need to put someone in charge of town maintenance including the new water system, the road, and the waste dump site. If you try to be in charge of all these things, you will find yourself overworked and less effective. I know that right now you can handle it, but as the town and your family grow, you will be much happier with a division of responsibilities. You will have regular meetings with your managers to make plans and keep track of things. If you start this right away, your managers will get used to it before any new problems arise. Rando, I know that this sounds like a lot, but you are very capable of doing this, and there is no one more capable than you are."

Rando said, "This sounds much better. I had given some thought to this, but hadn't made any solid plans. Should I hold a meeting and ask for volunteers for these positions?"

Tall Sky replied, "That's a good idea, and if there are more than one wanting a position, call for a vote. To make everyone feel a part of the town and take ownership of that, you might consider asking everyone to sign up under one of the departments. That way if something needs doing, the department head has a group of people to ask for help."

"How did you learn all this stuff?" asked Rando.

"I've been around for several hundred years," said Tall Sky. "You just naturally pick up on things."

"What about the defense of the town?" asked Rando.

"I think that at this point every able-bodied man should be a part of the militia," said Tall Sky.

"I agree," said Rando.

"When we get to Talami, I would like to see Vela and Rusken. Vela was an important part of Home Fire for ten years and I miss her. She will be surprised that I am married and that Alqua is expecting a baby. She will be happy to hear the news about Home Fire," said Rando. "She was like a mother to all of us sewing and cooking and bandaging our wounds. I am really grateful to her. I would like to bring her a gift. Maybe we could stop at a place in Talami and buy something for her."

"Showing appreciation is always a good thing," said Tall Sky. "I know just the place to shop for something special."

The wagons pulled into Talami and Tall Sky stopped on the main street to do some shopping. Alqua and Melody helped by looking through a few shops. Alqua asked Rando, "Do you want something personal or something for the house?"

Rando answered, "Yes," and Alqua laughed.

"I think that both would be good. After all she did take care of you for ten years," said Alqua. "How about a new bathtub, some towels, and some good smelling soap? Also, there is a necklace with a heart shaped pendant that would be a good remembrance."

"That's fine," said Rando. He asked the shopkeeper, "Can you inscribe something on the front and on the back? I would like a campfire on the front with the words Home Fire under it."

"Let's also eat dinner at the café. They have good food there," said Tall Sky. "He can inscribe the heart while we have dinner."

They paid for their purchases and walked into the café to order dinner. The waitress brought out stew, fresh bread, and pie for dessert. She also brought Daisy a plate of stew cut up into tiny pieces. Daisy hopped onto the table and gulped down her food. Then she climbed into her pouch for a nap. "Now that's what I feel like doing," said Melody. "Let's turn in early tonight." After dinner they loaded their purchases into the wagon and climbed in. They drove to Vela's house and brought their gifts to the door and knocked. Rusken answered the door and both he and Vela were pleasantly surprised by the gifts and the company.

"Rando, it's so good to see you," said Vela. She hugged one after another. Rando put the necklace around her neck and said, "Thank you for all your hard work and the care you gave to all of us."

Vela said, "I love it. Thank you."

"Alqua and I are having a baby this fall," said Rando. "You and Rusken should come to Home Fire and see us then. You could bring Steben and Amidra, Emmy, and your children and stay at our new inn. The place has really changed. We have houses and more people and more animals. We are on our way to Othrund to ask help from the dwarves to create a water system. We are building a Vision Hall as our next project."

Rusken said, "We would be happy to visit Home Fire this fall. So, do you still use the fire for cooking and sitting around the campfire in the evening?"

"Yes, we do," said Rando. "We function the same way that we always have. It's convenient and efficient and gives us enough time to create the town. How have you been doing? Have you rested from the war enough to begin some type of work here?"

"Yes, I have been working in the field like I used to do. It feels really good to be out of the army," said Rusken. "It's great to be home with my family again."

"How did your caravan go? Did you get any of the slaves back?" asked Vela.

"We brought over a hundred girls back from Orendia," said Tall Sky. "It was a very successful mission. Melody and I brought half of them back on a ship and the rest came by caravan with Quickturn. King Jahiz signed a treaty and a trade agreement outlawing slavery in his country. He gave us written permission to buy back the slaves and accepted Father God into his heart. There is another mission planned for a caravan to Fantolo and King Jahiz wants about a hundred Bright Elves to help evangelize his country."

Rusken asked, "Did you encounter any Bitters or bandits?"

"Quickturn battled both Bitters and bandits. He only lost one soldier and he killed many of the enemy," said Tall Sky.

Melody said, "The girls are being returned to their homes now. Four of them are staying at Home Fire, and some are staying in Loadrel at Laskron's and with Talla. Talla was our caravan cook and she is housing ten pregnant girls until they can be married. Vela, you would like Talla. She is very much like you."

Tall Sky said, "We need to get to bed soon because we will be leaving early in the morning. We have beds in the wagons."

Everyone went to bed for a good night's sleep.

A rooster's call heralded the morning. Vela had already made a big breakfast of eggs and hotcakes with sausage. Her guests sat around on blankets eating breakfast and visiting. Melody was still feeling tired and went back to bed for a nap in the wagon. After breakfast they said their farewells and climbed aboard their wagons driving through Talami to buy supplies for the dwarves. They stopped at the grocer's and purchased fresh fruits and vegetables and then at a store to purchase fabrics, thread, needles, and towels and washrags. They also bought some tools and nails. Melody wanted to buy Queen Heiki a special gift, so she found a beautiful painting of flowers for her. After shopping, they continued northwest toward Othrund.

Rando said, "That was a good visit. They liked their gifts."

"Yes, they did. That necklace was a perfect gift for her," said Tall Sky. "Rusken looks better than when I last saw him. Married life agrees with him."

"We all seem to be much happier married," said Tall Sky.

The land became hilly as they journeyed north and the trees became more numerous. The road was good and the air was cooler.

Rando was still thinking about the water and sewage systems. He said, "I would like to have water available inside the houses. Do you know of any way to do that?"

Tall Sky said, "Well, obviously the first step is to bring water from a stream into the town or just behind the houses. If the stream is sufficient, there could be smaller outlets to the corrals and to the garden areas to irrigate them. This is a large project and will take some time, but it is well worth it. Bringing the water from a stream flowing over the cliff above Lake Perilough will provide enough force to drive the water through the trough and enter houses. It would also be good to make a water storage unit. Of course, in a time of drought, you always have the lake."

"I hope the dwarves have some ideas about how to handle waste products. So far we have used out houses, but it is something that needs to be changed. I really don't like them and they have to be filled in and redug. It's just a mess," said Rando.

Melody said, "We want to ride up front for a while. Could Rando and Alqua drive the second wagon for a while? We're feeling lonesome."

Tall Sky stopped the wagon and Rando and Alqua took control of the second wagon. "Did you miss me?" asked Tall Sky.

"Yes, I did," said Melody as she cuddled close to her husband. "It's really a nice day, and Daisy is so happy to be out here looking at everything."

"I see that. Rando and I had some very good talks about Home Fire, town government and water systems. It was well worth you being back there for a while. You didn't mind, did you?" asked Tall Sky.

"No, I didn't mind. It was good getting to know Alqua better," said Melody. "It's been fun visiting our friends again. I wish we could all live close together like we did in Loadrel."

"That was a good time, but these are good times too and we have each other," said Tall Sky. "Home Fire is not so far away from Loadrel, and Rando has an inn now." He kissed Melody and said, "I love you, sweet one."

"I love you, too," said Melody. "We will be back with Liadra and Trag pretty soon, won't we?"

"Yes, we will be back home in about four days," said Tall Sky. "Is my Culina home sick?" He put his arm around her and hugged her close. "Are you excited to be visiting the dwarves and their tunnels in Othrund?"

"Yes, I am. I would like very much to see how people live inside of a mountain. Is it dirty and smelly?" asked Melody.

"Actually, it's quite clean and has fresh air," said Tall Sky. "You'll like it and you will like the dwarves. They are good hearted people, kind and charitable."

Time passed pleasantly as they traveled through the countryside of beautiful rolling hills and trees. They stopped for lunch in a clearing under some shade trees. "It feels good to walk around for a bit," said Melody. She put down Daisy so she could walk around for a while and relieve herself. They brought out bread and cheese and some dried fruit and wine and had a satisfying lunch sitting on some blankets under the tree. After lunch Rando laid back and watched the sky for a few minutes. "It looks like we could get some rain by this evening. Those fluffy white clouds are starting to accumulate."

"That could be," said Tall Sky. "We will be safe and cozy in the Othrund tunnels by then."

Melody looked at him dubiously and said, "Tunnels and cozy just don't sound like they go together."

"But they do. You'll see. The place is very homey and comfortable," said Tall Sky. "They even have indoor toilets and a large, warm pool to soak in. You will really like that."

"This has certainly been an enjoyable trip so far," said Melody. "Rando, I love what you've done with Home Fire, and I am happy that you kept the name of Home Fire for your town. It's a great name and no other place is called that. It's wonderful how you have helped so many people."

"Thank you, Melody. I'm glad you like it. Home Fire has been a passion of mine for a long time. It is a real pleasure for me to see it develop into a permanent town. I hope everyone there will not forget the difficulties they came out of and continue to help others get established," said Rando.

"From what I know of those people, they will continue to help others," said Tall Sky.

"We should probably move on," said Rando. "We don't want to get caught out in the rain." They all climbed back into the wagons and drove on toward Othrund.

With the appearance of clouds came colder air. Melody brought out their cloaks and put on Daisy's cloak, too. Daisy loves clothes, so she rubbed her cheek against Melody's and chirred. Daisy was happy looking at the foliage by the road for any little animals she could see. When she did see one, she would call out to it and chirr at Melody, who would then make a comment about it. Melody and Tall Sky felt happy and hopeful this morning anticipating their visit with the dwarves. The cool wind buffeted the wagons as they moved across the land that became increasingly bumpy as they neared the mountains. Melody and Daisy retreated into the wagon to avoid the wind. Alqua did the same. Rando and Tall Sky rode together on Tall Sky's driver's seat and two of Rando's men sat on the driver's seat of Rando's wagon with one man riding alongside of the wagons.

"I can hardly wait to see Heiki's face when she sees the bolt of silk. She has never had silk and it is so beautiful. I don't think the dwarves have any paintings either, so she will be delighted with Melody's gift. You know, after the Battle of Othrund, King Farin gave Melody her wedding ring, so she feels grateful to him," said Tall Sky. "I think she will be favorably impressed with the place and the people."

The wind became stronger as they approached the mountains. When they reached Othrund, they pulled Rando's wagon into the cave next to the tunnel entrance. Above the entrance were the words, "THESE ARE MY PEOPLE. AWAKENING NOW," inscribed by God during the Battle of Othrund. Tall Sky remembered it well, since he was standing in front of the tunnel when it occurred. Rando was duly impressed. He said, "Those words were inscribed by lightning?"

"That's what it looked like," said Tall Sky. "The battle stopped for a few minutes when it happened."

"I wish I could have seen that, but I had people to protect at Home Fire and Loadrel," said Rando.

"You did what Father God wanted you to do and we will always be grateful to you for that," said Tall Sky.

Tall Sky and Rando, Melody and Alqua walked into the tunnel entrance where they were greeted by two guards who escorted them into a waiting room with a table and chairs. Tall Sky told them that they were there to conduct trading and would need to see King Farin and Queen Heiki to present gifts and to propose a business arrangement. One of the guards went to get the King and Queen and the dwarf in charge of trading. The other guard had a woman bring wine and goblets. In about fifteen minutes, King Farin and Queen Heiki walked in and greeted them. King Farin was wearing his crown and a large gold necklace with the pendant of a battle axe crossed by a pick axe. He wore bloused sleeves with a leather vest and pantaloons tucked into his boots. His beard was clean and fanned out at about ten inches. His blue eyes sparkled. His hair was shoulder length. Queen Heiki had brown hair down to her waist and a pleasant face with brown eyes and a ready smile. She wore a blouse with puffed sleeves, belted at the waist and an ankle length skirt.

"Tall Sky, my friend. It has been too long since I saw you last. This red haired beauty must be Melody. Welcome to you Melody. I trust that you had a comfortable trip?" asked King Farin. Melody curtsied and said, "Thank you, I did. This must be your wife Heiki who I have heard is gracious and kind. I brought you a gift."

She handed the painting to Heiki, who smiled and took Melody's hand. She said, "How beautiful and thoughtful. I will hang this in our bedroom."

Tall Sky gave her the bolt of silk, a beautiful shimmering blue color. She said, "I have never seen this kind of fabric. Wherever did you get it?"

Tall Sky said that the caravan master found it in Orendia and that the fabric is made by a secret process from the silken webs of silk worms. It is highly prized and mostly the royal families have it, so he thought that Queen Heiki should have some. She laughed and said that she was delighted with it.

Melody thanked King Farin for her ring. Tall Sky said that there were some new tools for him and asked if he would send some men out to the cave to unload fruits and vegetables for trade. King Farin did so, and then sat down to talk to Tall Sky and Rando. King Farin, I would like you to meet the chief of Home Fire, Rando. He is the one who has been getting the Gullandian runaways settled down."

"Nice to meet you, Rando. I really appreciate you helping those kids," said King Farin.

Rando said, "I enjoyed meeting your pony riders and I want to give you this carving of one. I also brought you two ponies as a gift," said Rando. King Farin smiled and thanked Rando.

"Was your mission a success?" asked King Farin.

"Yes, it was. We brought back over one hundred slave girls and the king of Orendia asked Father God to live in his heart. We encountered and killed many Bitters who attacked us. We also battled bandits and were helped by four women riding fire breathing dragons. Melody and I didn't get to see them because we had already sailed on a ship with sixty-five girls. Quickturn and Halden, our caravan master, the soldiers, and a caravan full of girls met these dragon riders when they flew over the caravan releasing flowers and set down their dragons. The dragon riders wanted to meet the girls and they gave them each a gem to help them get started when they reached Aksanda. They also gave the caravan cook bags of fresh meat. The girls talked to them about Father God and the dragon riders asked Father God to live in their hearts. Melody and I will have a chance to meet them, because we will be taking a caravan through Orendia to Fantalo to search for more slaves."

"Where do these dragon riders live?" asked King Farin.

"They live on a plateau on the northern part of Orendia in caves in a mountain," said Tall Sky. "There is a lake nearby where they bathe their dragons."

"I would like to see this," said King Farin.

"It would take you three or four days to reach it if you traveled at the foot of the mountains. I don't know if there is a way to travel the top of the mountains, but if you could, you would be at the plateau. Another way would be to have some Gullandians take you through the southern part of their country. Of course you are welcome to travel with us, but it will take weeks for us to search Fantolo," said Tall Sky.

"I will consider these ideas," said King Farin. "I would like to know about this business proposition of yours."

Rando said, "Tall Sky has told me about your water system. It intrigued me so that I just had to come and see it and I would like to talk to your engineer about my new town of Home Fire. We need a water system including irrigation and a waste system. I would like to hire him to help us with it. Would that be possible? We have an inn that he could live in and plenty of food. I thank you for sending Gullandians to us. Two of the newcomers married two of our widows and they each have a house of their own. Home Fire used to be a camp with tents, but we have an inn and fifteen houses now and three more being built. People settle with us for a variety of reasons. It is well situated just above the lake with plenty of room for gardens and corrals. Our next project is the building of a Vision Hall for worship."

"Rando, I can see that you are a good man and that you have the best in mind for your community. I'm glad that our Gullandians are doing well at Home Fire. I became rather fond of them when three Gullandian couples married here. The decision as to whether or not our engineer will go with you is entirely up to him. I personally think that it is a good idea to strengthen our bond with you. Heiki, let's show our guests our home," said King Farin.

Heiki said, "Melody, I have wanted to ask you about your little dragon. Does she always sit on your shoulder?"

"Yes, she does for the most part. At home she has her own nesting box that she is fond of for naps, but when we are out and about, she likes to be where she can watch everything. I found an egg in Malwood and put it in my pocket where she hatched and we've been fast friends ever since," said Melody. "Her name is Daisy."

143

"She is very well behaved," said Heiki.

"Yes, she is unless someone attacks me. Once a witch attacked me and she clawed her eyes out. The witch had been throwing fireballs at everybody and she grabbed my arm. That was enough for Daisy. I'm really proud of her for that," said Melody. "It gave a friend of mine just enough time to knife the witch. Usually Daisy is a happy, loving dragon who likes everybody."

"I think she takes after her mommy," said Queen Heiki.

As they walked down the first tunnel, King Farin showed them an apartment that had several rooms with beds, table and chairs, and shelves to put things on. It seemed comfortable. Then he said that for every ten rooms there was a bathroom with running water to carry away waste. He then escorted them down another tunnel to the kitchen where there was a long oven with spaces for a number of pans. There was a boy minding the fires and four cooks preparing dinner. There were baskets full of freshly baked buns. King Farin took them to the large dining hall that was filled with tables already set with metal plates, cups, and silverware. He then walked them down a hall and down some steps that led to a pool of warm water. "This is where we soak our sore muscles and bathe. It has water that is constantly replenishing itself. There is another smaller one where we wash our clothes. Now, let's sit in the dining hall and wait. It is time for dinner and our engineer will be here."

Thogul Okri walked into the dining hall and King Farin called him over to the table. "Thogul, I would like you to meet some new friends. I believe you know Tall Sky. This is his wife Melody. This is Rando and Alqua from Home Fire come to see your handiwork and ask for your help in creating a water and waste system at Home Fire."

Thogul shook hands with Rando and said, "I would be happy to help you any way that I can. I have heard much about Home Fire and I admit that the place intrigues me."

Rando said, "I remember Greta telling me about you helping her when a snake wrapped around her in a swamp outside of Othrund."

"Yes, I did," said Thogul. "She had just arrived and was scared of us at first so she ran into the swamp."

"Thogul, would you consider staying at our inn at Home Fire while helping us make a water and waste system? You already know the six people who were married here. We really need your help. We have good cooks and the inn has a woman who keeps it clean and would do your laundry. All you would have to do is to help us design and implement a system," said Rando.

Thogul said, "I would be happy to do whatever I can do to help you with these projects if King Farin can spare me for a length of time."

King Farin said, "I would very much like you to help Rando create a good town at Home Fire."

Rando smiled and said, "I'm so glad! I have been worried about this ever since we started building. We have a wagon and a driver at your disposal whenever you need them, and you are welcome to bring a friend with you if you like."

"I would like to bring Hafka. He can translate for me and teach me the language. While we are there, we can learn more words, and when we come back, we can conduct classes in the language here," said Thogul.

"I would like more of our people to know the common language. We should communicate more with the outside world," said King Farin.

While they were talking, a crowd of dwarves entered the dining hall and took their seats. King Farin stood and prayed for blessings on their food and gave thanks for their friends. Bowls of food were set on the tables and wine was poured. The men all wore beards and the women had hair down to their waists. They were dressed in colorful clothing and wore jewelry in honor of their guests. Word had circulated that Tall Sky had brought his wife and his friends to dinner. To them this was a special occasion and after dinner there was music and dancing. The dwarves formed a circle including their guests and everyone danced in a circle and then broke off into couples whirling 'round and 'round the dance floor. Several dwarven women asked the single men to dance and they did, holding hands and moving 'round and "round. Rando and Alqua sat back down and

Rando said, "King Farin, your people are wonderful. They are warm and happy and welcoming. Thank you for this party. I loved it."

"You are welcome," said King Farin. "I have something special for the wives of my friends. Alqua, this is for you." He gave her a necklace with a pendant shaped like a shield which held a sparkling blue gemstone. He gave Melody a necklace with a pendant shaped like a dragon set with green gemstones for eyes. They were both delighted and thanked King Farin for his beautiful gifts. He next called over Gromdar Durak to complete a trade with Tall Sky. Gromdar and Tall Sky went back to the tunnel entrance where they completed the trade of goods for gems. Tall Sky was well pleased with the trade.

Having completed the business and festivities, Heiki showed them to their rooms for the night. They would spend the night comfortably sleeping in beds with furs for covers. Alqua said to Rando, "This was a wonderful night. I love this necklace; it looks regal. These people are so generous. Hieki said that we could use the bathing pool when we get up in the morning. That sounds really good to me."

Melody and Tall Sky cuddled under the covers and slept like babies all night. In the morning, everyone headed down to the bathing pool. Nobody was there, so Melody and Alqua went in first. The water was almost hot. They washed their hair and Alqua swam around the pool. Afterwards the men went in and bathed. The water soothed away all the soreness in their muscles and they felt envigorated and ready to meet the day's challenges. They met King Farin and Queen Heiki in the dining hall for breakfast of pastries covered in jam, scrambled eggs with sausages, and tea. Daisy really enjoyed this combination, and wanted to be in her pouch afterwards for a nap. Heiki said, "I love that little dragon. Please bring her back when you visit us again."

"I loved visiting with you and I will come back at the earliest opportunity," said Melody. "We have to go on another mission soon where I will see large dragons and women who ride them. I'm looking forward to that. They are fire breathing dragons, but their riders are friendly toward Aksandans. Then we will travel in a caravan to

Fantolo and we really don't know what kind of reception we will get there, but we will have soldiers disguised as merchants with us, so it should be safe."

Thogul and Hafka approached and asked how soon they should be ready to leave. Tall Sky said that they should leave after breakfast. Hafka asked, "Would it be all right if I brought my wife? She really wants to go with."

Rando said, "That would be just fine. Bring her. What is your wife's name?"

"Her name is Kiley. We have no children yet. I will tell her to pack our clothes. Thank you," said Hafka.

Soon all was ready and the travelers boarded the wagons. Tall Sky said farewell to King Farin and promised to return as soon as possible. The dwarves rode in the second wagon and Alqua and Melody rode in the first wagon with Rando and Tall Sky driving. Heiki had made sure to send with them provisions of food and wine for their journey. They were all happy, well fed, and excited to be on their way home.

Rando said, "That went better than I had imagined, and we have three dwarves with us. Our people at Home Fire will be delighted, especially the Gullandians, who were helped by the dwarves. My Alqua is an amazing woman. She likes the dwarves and speaks ill of no one. She accepts them just as they are. She has been a perfect wife for me."

"You are truly blessed," said Tall Sky. "My trading went very well, and since I have no need for the profit, I will donate it to the building of your Vision Hall."

"Thank you, Tall Sky. That will really help. I am much encouraged by all of this. I think that by this time next year, Home Fire will be a very pleasant place to live," said Rando.

"I'm sure it will be," said Tall Sky.

The dwarves sat on the chairs they brought with them and talked of what it would be like at Home Fire. Hafka told them of the big fire in the center of the camp and how everyone sat on the logs around the fire to eat and fellowship with each other. He told them of how everyone shared in the daily chores and helped each other. He said that there was a young woman named Brilley who did all the doctoring and that another young woman taught the children every morning. He told them about the reindeer, horses, milk cows, and chickens and about the houses that were recently built. Thogul and Kiley were favorably impressed and looked forward to seeing the inn.

"What is it like being with people who are so tall?" asked Kiley.

"It makes you feel like a dwarf." said Hafka and they all laughed. You will feel much better about it when you learn the language. We will ask Indra, the teacher, to help us learn the language. I know her. She is kind and thoughtful. You will like her. You might enjoy helping her with the children."

"I think I would like that," said Kiley.

Thogul said, "I can't stop thinking about ways to bring water into the houses. I know what we can do to bring water close to the town and how to make irrigation ditches, but I want to bring water into the houses. There has to be a way." He decided on making a water pump to pull water through a pipe into the house. The pipe would go down to the water level, into the water that would be flowing past the house. He would have men dig a channel from the waterfall pond to the houses. They would put wood into the channel and set it on fire to bake the clay hard and the water would flow through the channel which would have to be covered to keep it clean. They could also make smaller channels for irrigation purposes and for the watering of livestock. The pond at the base of the waterfall has a stream flowing from it into Lake Perilough. That stream would be dammed up causing more water to flow down to Home Fire. The sanitation could be done in much the same way with a channel carrying waste to a pit downstream from the water channels. It might take a whole year to do it, but Thogul thought it well worth doing. The left over clean water would flow to Lake Perilough.

They stopped for lunch just short of Talami. They climbed out of the wagons using a step ladder. Hafka told Rando that Thogul had decided on ways to make the water and sewage system work. Rando was delighted and poured the wine for everybody. They brought out some delicious pastries, meat and cheese sandwiches, and fruit. "We are just a short way from Talami now. We will stay overnight there and head for Home Fire in the morning," said Rando. "How are you faring in your wagon?"

Hafka said, "Pretty well. When we get tired we will take a nap."

"If you feel like being out for a while, you can take turns sitting up front with the driver," said Rando.

"I would like to do that," said Hafka. "Thank you."

Melody said, "Kiley could sit in our wagon with us for a while. We're going to make some baby clothes. Ask her if she would like to sew with us or just be with us and we can teach her some words."

Hafka asked Kiley and she said that she would like that. They sat on the rocks by the side of the road eating their sandwiches and enjoying the warm sun and the cool breeze. They had seen no other travelers on this stretch of the road. Daisy was happy eating her pieces of food and drinking water. After lunch the three women climbed into the first wagon. Tall Sky and Rando sat in the driver's seat.

Melody showed Kiley the baby gowns that they were working on and Kiley smiled and examined them. Then she took some fabric and began cutting out some pieces for a baby gown. She gathered the sleeves to make puffy sleeves and stitched the pieces together. It was obvious that she knew how to sew. She made tiny gathers across the front of the gown and, with her own colored thread, made a flower design. By the time they reached Talami, her baby gown was looking very nice. In the meantime, she learned words like stitches, needle, thread and fabric. She also learned hug, kiss, hi, and bye. They were making great progress when the wagons stopped in front of Vela and Rusken's house. Tall Sky wanted Vela and Rusken to meet their new friends. They stayed overnight there, sleeping in the wagons and got an early start in the morning with a breakfast made by Vela.

"Vela, this breakfast should last us well into the day. Thank you," said Tall Sky.

"You are very welcome, and thank you for bringing your new friends to meet us," said Vela. "I hope that everything goes well with your water system at Home Fire." She hugged Rando and said goodbye to everyone.

The travelers boarded the wagons and they were back on the road again headed for Yardrel. The girls sat in the back of the first wagon so they could make more baby clothes. Kiley made a baby bonnet and some booties. Melody made a baby cloak like the one she made for Daisy. Then they all decided to make some summer clothing for Daisy, and the little dragon was in her glory with all this attention.

Rando and Tall Sky talked about God and the need for fairness and justice in the world. Rando was determined that his little corner of the world would be fair and just. He had great respect for Beldock and the way that Beldock handled Loadrel.

In Yardrel they stopped at the café for dinner and spent the night parked in front of Steben's home. They all had a good breakfast together. Steben said, "We are packed and ready to go. I can hardly wait to see Home Fire again." Steben and Amidra drove their own wagon and Emmy rode with Melody, Kiley and Alqua. Emmy was entranced with this small adult woman. She wanted to ask her questions, but Kiley couldn't understand her, so she just sat next to her and watched her sew and embroider. Kiley decided to make a rag doll just small enough for a baby to play with. She used the scraps of material and when she was done, she showed Emmy how to make one. Their little caravan stopped for a break after a few hours and everyone walked about for a while. Then the girls decided to take a nap and before long, they were turning left into Home Fire.

This time the guards were welcoming their town chief. They were relieved to be home after such a long journey. Rando and Tall Sky helped the girls down from the wagon and invited them to sit around their fire for some wine. Alqua went into her house with her things and came back to sit by the fire. After getting centered, Rando asked his guests into the inn to see their accommodations. He gave the first two rooms to the dwarves and the third room to Steben and Amidra. Emmy would sleep in their guest room. Melody and Tall Sky would stay in their wagon, which was truly their home away from home.

Axel and Aela had married and were managing the inn at Home Fire. They brought ale for their guests and for Rando and Alqua. They sat at a long table in the dining area and relaxed. Rando brought out a drawing of Home Fire and the surrounding area including buildings that were still in the planning stages. Tall Sky explained the drawing to Hafka who in turn explained it to Thogul. Thogul nodded and smiled. Thogul wanted to walk around the area, so Rando, Steben and Tall Sky took him and Hafka for a walk up to the waterfall and the pond. Thogul explained his ideas and Hafka translated. Thogul said, "There is clay between here and Home Fire. We should dig a channel for water, fill it with wood, and set it on fire. This will bake the channel hard. Then we dig channels to the garden area and do the same. We also do that for watering the animals. We control the water flow with doors that we raise and lower. Before we fire it, we lay pipes from the houses into the channel. You can plan ahead with this too by laying pipes to where houses will be. This whole system has to be in place before letting water in."

Steben asked, "How do we keep the water clean from debris like leaves in the fall and from animals getting into it?"

Thogul answered, "That could be a problem. We will need to cover the channels, maybe with wood covers or with some other material. The last two steps will be to dam up the stream that leads from the pond to the lake and open the door to the channel. At the sink in the house will be a hand operated pump that will bring the water from the pipe into the sink. I have a design in mind that should work well. Do you have a smithie here?"

"Yes, we do," said Rando. "He makes horseshoes, tools, and swords."

"I will talk to him about making the pumps," said Thogul. "Do you have enough men to do this work? If not, we may have to hire labor from another town."

"We can do that if need be. What if there is too much water?" asked Rando.

"That is a good question. We will have a trough ready for runoff that would be a stream to Lake Perilough. Also, a second trough could be used for waste which would end in a pit downhill from town. If the flow of water is managed correctly, there shouldn't be any problems," said Thogul.

Rando laughed and shook Thogul's hand saying, "Thank you, Thogul. I am so happy. Let's walk back and get some dinner. Is anybody else hungry?"

"I am," said Thogul. The men all walked back to Home Fire to get ready for dinner.

While the men were busy with their discussions and plans, Alqua, Melody, Kiley, Amidra and Emmy visited the various animals. Emmy wanted to ride on a reindeer, so one of the Gullandians put her on a reindeer and led her around the corral. Then she milked the cow and gathered eggs. Kiley was impressed with the way things were done at Home Fire. Some women were washing clothes in tubs bought in Loadrel and others were cooking and baking bread in and near the cookhouse. One woman was churning butter in front of her home. The men were busy building the houses and chopping down trees. Several men were making shakes for roofing. When Steben arrived, he looked for Amidra and found her at the inn.

Alqua introduced Emmy and Kiley to Indra in the children's classroom at the inn. Kiley felt quite comfortable sitting at the children's table on a low chair. Class was over for the day, but Indra showed Emmy what they had been working on. They were making a model of Home Fire using the building kits that they had bought in Loadrel. After they finished the houses, they were going to make an inn and a Vision Hall. For these they were going to find their own sticks and materials. Indra showed Emmy the words they were learning to print. She showed Emmy how to print her name and Emmy said that she would practice it and the alphabet. Indra asked, "How did you get Emmy?"

Amidra said, "We were on a trip with Tall Sky and Melody when we noticed a small group of slavers just a short way off the road. Several of our soldiers went to investigate and killed the slavers, rescuing Emmy. Steben and I decided to adopt Emmy as soon as we were married. She has been a blessing to us ever since."

"What of her parents?" asked Indra.

"Emmy had been an orphan living in a barn and performing chores for the farmer's wife to pay for her food when the slavers caught her," said Amidra.

"I'm glad that you found her. She is very smart. I wish that she could be a part of my class. If you could leave her with me for a few months, I could teach her to read and write and how to doctor people and animals. I think she could learn here and then continue learning at home," said Indra.

"We will have to talk about it," said Amidra.

Steben said, "Emmy, what do you think about vacationing here for a few months and being in Indra's class? You would come back home after that and we could find books and paper and doctor's things for you to use so that you could have them when you come home. I will have Grandpapa make a desk and chair for you and put up a shelf in your room where you could keep your supplies. Would you like that?"

"I will miss you," said Emmy.

"We will come to visit you. Keep in mind, this is where I grew up," said Steben.

Indra said, "You could stay with me right here in the inn. I know the other children would love to have you here. Everyone knows your daddy and they all like him."

"Alright. I will stay here, but just for a few months," said Emmy.

"When we come to visit you, we will bring things for your classroom. Melody and Tall Sky made maps and a book of people around the world. We could also bring more paper and some paints for painting," said Steben.

The dinner bell rang and everyone gathered around the fire to get their food. Daisy was doing her hungry dance on Melody's shoulder, so she fed Daisy first. Melody told Tall Sky about the classroom and he said that he had some maps and a copy of her book in the back of the wagon. He went to get them and brought them to Indra, who immediately placed them in her classroom. Dinner was good, consisting of stew, bread and ale. After eating, Rando stood up and explained Thogul's plan for the water system and the waste system. He said that he didn't want the construction projects to be halted, so he would hire workers from other towns to work on this project. He told them that Vision Hall would be built with silver that was donated by Tall Sky. Everyone applauded. Tall Sky stood up and introduced Thogul, Hafka and Kiley. They applauded again. Then musicians played some dancing music and people danced including Hafka and Kiley.

A very small young lady named Jalia asked Thogul to dance. He was amazed by her beauty. She had long, silken blonde hair and big blue eyes and she was only about a head taller than he was. Thogul stood up, bowed, and kissed her hand. Then they danced, smiling and laughing. After the dance, he led her over to Hafka for some translation. She told them that she had been at Home Fire for one week and was helping Indra with the children in the classroom. She said that she had been a slave in the royal household in Orendia and had been assigned to be a helper to the king's daughter. She said that, since her parents were no longer alive, she would come to Home Fire to begin a new life. She had asked Father God to live in her heart and wanted to learn more about Him. This pleased Thogul very much since he was devoted to Father God. She said that she would help him to learn her language and asked him to visit her classroom right after breakfast to devise ways for him to learn and to set a regular time for him to work with her. Since she had to get up early and get the classroom ready, she would go to bed now. They said goodnight to Rando and walked to the inn.

The next morning at breakfast, Indra taught Thogul the names of his food. Rando had scheduled a meeting with some volunteers for the water system and wanted Thogul and Hafka to explain it to them, so Indra said that they could meet in the classroom in the afternoon. She went back to the classroom and had her students to make small cards with words and little pictures on them for the dwarves. That way they could learn to read at the same time as they learned the names of things. Indra was a naturally gifted teacher.

Thogul and Hafka met with Rando and his men and explained the water and waste systems that they would create. Rando told them that they would have to hire workers to help with the digging of the canals and they were very relieved by this. He said that Tall Sky would be going to Loadrel and that he would hire some men for this task.

Tall Sky and Melody said goodbye to their friends and left for Loadrel after breakfast. They wanted to help Rando with hiring men, but they also wanted to see if King Aryante had sent a message to them through Beldock. Melody said, "I can hardly wait to get back to see my new kitten Shelly. I didn't get much time with her before we left on this trip and we hadn't planned on being gone this long. I hope Arinya isn't worried about us. She is probably having fun holding the kitten."

Tall Sky said, "I'm sure everything is fine. Are you ready for our next adventure?"

"I think we should rest for a while in Loadrel, don't you?" asked Melody.

"Yes, but when King Aryante says so, we have to be ready to go, so when we get back, we should pack and get things ready," said Tall Sky.

"I want to buy some paper and other supplies for the Home Fire School," said Melody.

"We should do that and we could send the supplies back to Home Fire with the work crew that we will hire for Rando," said Tall Sky.

"It was nice of King Farin to be so cooperative with Rando," said Melody. "Our necklaces were very thoughtful, too."

"It has been a very productive trip. Emmy will be learning to read and write, Rando will get his water system, and Thogul and Jalia have started their relationship. I couldn't be more pleased," said Tall Sky. "When we get home, I am going to ravish you. Then we will pick up your new kitten." Melody laughed. For now she had to be contented with petting her dragon. Daisy was happily watching the scenery pass by. Soon both of them would take a nap.

# HOME TO LOADREL

Tall Sky drove for about three more hours and pulled up in front of the Laborer's Reward for dinner. Melody had slept most of that time and was hungry. Beldock saw the blue wagon and brought out two mugs of ale for them and told Mina to bring food. Melody and Tall Sky sat down and drank some ale. They asked Beldock to get Laskron and Liadra and send someone to get Trag and Arinya. Mina brought the Daisy plate right away and Daisy ate her food like she had been starving. Mina and Beldock joined them for dinner. They ate dinner first and then told their friends about their trip. Tall Sky said, "First, our friends are all doing well. Amidra, Steben and Emmy are at Home Fire right now for a visit and Emmy will stay there for two months to learn reading and writing with Indra and Jalia in a classroom at the inn. Vela and Rusken are happy living in their home in Yardrel. Rando bought Vela a necklace with a heart pendant and had the shopkeeper etch a campfire on one side with the name of Home Fire under it. He also bought her a new bathtub and towels. He said that he was grateful to her for taking care of all of them at Home Fire."

"It took us extra time because Rando wanted to be introduced to the dwarves to ask for help with his water and waste systems. We drove to Othrund and took them a wagonload of food and goods for trade. We met Thogul who is an engineer in charge of the water system at Othrund and is a kind of spiritual advisor there. He agreed to come to Home Fire to devise water and waste systems there. He and his interpreter Hafka came back with us to Home Fire. Jalia likes Thogul and agreed to teach him our language. I think the two of them will get along quite well," said Tall Sky.

Melody asked, "How is my kitten doing?"

Arinya said, "Shelly is an adorable kitten and she is doing just fine. I hold her and pet her and she has learned to say some words."

Liadra said, "I am interested in this classroom at Home Fire. Is there anything we can do to help?"

"Yes, there is," said Melody. "They are really short on supplies like paper and anything written like scrolls. Indra is doing a great job with what she has, but she could use some paints and canvass and pens and ink."

"Beldock, Rando needs to hire some strong young men to dig a long canal. Would you put the word out? When they go to Home Fire I want them to take school supplies with them. Home Fire is planning on buying firewood for the winter, so you could put out the word about that, too," said Tall Sky. "I left a wagon out there, so they can use it to help haul wood, furniture and people. They are going to spend the summer building houses and a Vision Hall. I believe that Thogul and Jalia will marry and that Thogul will be the spiritual advisor that they need."

"Rando never ceases to amaze me," said Liadra. He has developed into a caring person. Is Alqua still happy out there?"

Tall Sky said, "She is well and very happy with Rando. I never saw such a loving couple. Arinya, is it alright if we pick up the kitten tomorrow? We are both really tired from the trip."

Arinya answered, "That would be fine. I like taking care of her."

"Then I think we will be going home now. It was good seeing you again. We will be staying in town until we get word from King Aryante. He has to get the girls delivered safely to their homes before he can launch another caravan. We will see you tomorrow," said Tall Sky.

The friends all got up and walked home. Tall Sky and Melody drove their wagon home and went to bed.

Melody said, "I want to thank you for my life. It has been exciting and worthwhile since I met you. The first day I met you I was looking for fun. I had no idea how much fun it is to help others. You introduced me to God that day and He has shown me how to experience the gifts of the Spirit. I am so happy. You are my hero."

Tall Sky hugged her and said, "I couldn't love you any more than I do. We will have a child someday. I have seen it. He will look like me, but will have your red, curly hair and green eyes."

"Oh, Tall Sky, how exciting! When will we have him?" asked Melody.

"We must finish the work we started. There are still slave girls out there and their lives are terrible. We will bring them home to their parents and then God will give us our child," said Tall Sky. "After the campaigns, we will spend more time helping out at Home Fire. Is that alright with you?"

"Of course," said Melody. "I always like helping Rando and his people at Home Fire. The place is like a miracle in itself."

"It is definitely God's work. Now I need some sleep," said Tall Sky.

Morning began with a knock on the door. Trag and Arinya wanted Tall Sky and Melody to go to breakfast with them. Arinya was craving pastries and Trag was craving a man sized breakfast. Melody and Tall Sky dressed quickly and they walked to Jelsareeb's bakery. Jelsareeb said, "Good morning. I heard that you made it safely back. Did you enjoy your trip to Othrund?"

Tall Sky answered, "Yes, we did. Rando got himself an engineer and a spiritual advisor to help out at Home Fire."

Melody said, "King Farin gave me this dragon necklace with green eyes like Daisy's."

"That's really pretty. What are you hungry for today? I have some fresh pastries with berry jelly," said Jelsareeb.

"We'll take ten of those," said Tall Sky. "We're headed over to the inn for a big breakfast with Beldock and we'll stop and get Laskron, Liadra and Elise."

"How is Ulrick doing? I have to talk to him about making more furniture for Home Fire," said Rando.

"He's doing just fine. Did you know that Ulrick and I will be married?" asked Jelsareeb.

Tall Sky laughed and said, "No, I didn't. He's a good man. I'm glad you're getting married to him."

The friends walked to Laskron's and invited them to breakfast. They all walked to the inn and sat at the long table in the back. Mina brought the Daisy plate and Melody gave Mina one of the pastries. "Thank you," said Mina. "These are so good and I haven't eaten yet. I'll bring your food out right away." Beldock brought out cups and a pot of tea.

"Did you sleep well last night?" asked Beldock.

"Yes, we did," said Tall Sky. "We're glad to be home. Please tell me that you haven't heard from King Aryante yet."

"I have not, but I think it is too soon for that, don't you?" asked Beldock.

"Yes, it is too soon," said Tall Sky. "Have you heard from any young men who want to work this summer at Home Fire?"

"I have started a list. How many will Rando need?" asked Beldock.

"He will need as many as you can get. There is one long canal to be dug and several other short ones. He will also need lumber enough to cover the canals to keep the water clean," said Tall Sky, "and don't forget to let everyone know about Home Fire buying firewood for the winter."

"I've already passed around the word on that," said Beldock. Mina and Beldock brought out plates of eggs, bacon, fried potatoes and hot cakes and everybody enjoyed a good breakfast.

"Melody has been homesick and has missed our friends. Do you feel better now, Melody?" asked Tall Sky.

"I feel much better now," said Melody. "You all mean a lot to me. We started out together, we got married together, and we will have babies. Tall Sky said that I will have a baby after we finish getting the slave girls home. Liadra will have a baby at close to the same time."

Liadra was delighted. She said, "Do you know what I will have?"

Tall Sky answered, "You will have a baby girl." Liadra laughed and said, "Laskron, we will have a baby girl! I can hardly wait. First I had to help raise my five brothers, and now I get to have two little girls. I am so happy. Elise, did you hear that? Next year you will have a baby sister. Isn't that great?"

Elise said, "What are we going to name her, Mommy?"

"Joy," said Liadra. "She will bring joy to all of us."

Laskron said, "I think that Joy is a perfect name for her. She can use the baby bed we used for Elise. I have kept all of Elise's clothes just in case she would have a sister some day. We can repaint one of the rooms and make a baby room. Elise, you can help to make it nice and use the room for your baby doll until Joy arrives."

"It would be a good idea to make the room now, because Home Fire will double in size this year and they will have lots of orders for you to fill," said Tall Sky. "We will need to do that too."

"Ours is ready," said Trag. "You can see it when you pick up your kitten."

"For now we will have to do some shopping for the Home Fire classroom so that the work crew can take the supplies with them. I think the town of Loadrel could use a school house. What do you think, Laskron?" asked Tall sky.

"Absolutely," said Laskron. "It would be a big help to the parents. All the children could learn to read and write and to do other things like sewing and net mending and cooking. Children need to know all these things and it would give the parents a break, too."

"Let's go shopping. Who wants to come with us?" asked Melody. Laskron and Trag had to go back to work, but Liadra and Arinya said that they would go with. Liadra looked for paper and charcoal spears, pens and ink. Arinya gathered things to make the classroom look interesting. She found a painting of Lake Perilough, a carving of a lion, and a tapestry depicting scenery with animals. Melody found sewing supplies like thread for embroidery, knitting, and tatting. She also found some carving knives for the boys to use. Tall Sky found paints, canvasses and brushes. Emmy found several scrolls of children's stories. Altogether it was a successful trip.

They took the supplies back to the inn and placed them in the storage room. Beldock said, "Don't worry. I won't forget to send them with the work crew. I think that I have enough men to send tomorrow, but he may want to hire some from Yardrel, too. He may want to lay in more food supplies. This is going to just about double their food needs. They will probably have to use tents for these men.

During storms they could always sleep on the inn floor. I will send him a message about these things."

"Beldock," said Tall Sky. "I think this town needs a school. We could start out in the Vision Hall and build a schoolhouse after that. I would like to see Elise and other children learn to read and write and learn useful skills. It will help them to develop their talents. Do you know someone who could be a teacher for half a day?"

"The widow Marion might do it. She can read and write and when Faerverin returns for the summer, she can teach painting. I will talk to her about it tomorrow," said Beldock.

"We should get it set up and running before Faerverin returns. I will contribute by writing some scrolls about Father God and about the history of Aksanda. There is much to be told. I'll get started on it tomorrow morning," said Tall Sky.

"I want to see my kitten now," said Melody. "Let's get her and go home. I have to help her and Daisy become friends."

Melody and Tall Sky walked with Arinya to Trag's Store. "Your store looks good, Trag," said Rando. "We're here to pick up the kitten," said Tall Sky. Trag handed the kitten to Melody who cuddled her and kissed her. Tall Sky picked up the cage and they left for home.

At home, Melody held her flying kitten and talked to her while Daisy sat on her shoulder watching. The kitten crawled up to Daisy and spoke her name. Daisy rubbed cheeks with her and both of them purred. While she enjoyed this, Tall Sky gathered writing materials on the table and began writing a scroll about the history of Aksanda.

He wrote about the giants and the dwarves and about how the dwarves had retreated to the mountains to avoid the onslaught of the giants. He wrote about the foolish way that the giants used up the resources of the land and moved on to do the same until they ended up on a volcanic island that erupted and sank into the sea. He wrote about the humans who were created to inhabit the world starting on Grace Island and how they had migrated to Aksanda, Gullandia, Orendia, and Fantolo. The inhabitants of the world were fewer then and were living in small groups. As the population increased, there was need for small governments called chiefdoms. Then disputes arose over land ownership. At that time they did not trade with each other.

When trade developed, greed became the driving force of men. God sent elves to help mankind to remember Him and to worship Him. He wanted men to realize the purpose and meaning of life and not to be preoccupied with the gathering of wealth. The trouble came when some elves decided that wealth was what they desired and that they could take this wealth from the humans. These Bitter Elves grew in numbers and power until the Bright Elves confronted them during the War of the Elves. It was a terrible battle causing many deaths of men and elves. As a result of this battle, men banded together forming a larger government with a king at the head.

At that time, there were two kings, one in the Northern Province and one in the south called the Angvar Province. These two provinces functioned well until the king of the Angvar Province became greedy for power. He had an advisor who was a Bitter Elf feeding him with desire for more wealth and power. His queen was beautiful and full of pride. She also wanted to be queen of all of Aksanda, so she talked her husband into attacking the Northern Province with the intention of killing their king.

King Lantomere was the king of the Northern Province. He was a tall man with impressive fighting abilities and led his own men into battle. He had already trained a good army of his own and they were fiercely loyal to him. King Lynton of the Angvar Province had Bitter Elves in his army and attacked King Lantomere at night using sleep spells, but King Lantomere's Bright Elves shielded the spell and turned it back onto the Bitter Elves causing them to sleep. Without this advantage, King Lynton's army retreated and King Lynton was killed by his own advisor. King Lantomere placed one of his own trusted men in charge of the Angvar Province and put many of the captured Bitters into service breaking rock for use on the roads.

Tall Sky and Melody worked on the history of Aksanda for three days, writing and producing copies of it. They wanted copies to give to the schools of Home Fire and Loadrel. They knew that their friends and their own children would need this knowledge.

They also made copies of their previous work on foreign lands and peoples. They would encourage Brilley to make copies of the medical information that they had given her last year. They would ask Indra to have the children make a project of making a scroll about the animals with pictures and information about them. Tall Sky wanted to take copies of these to the kings of Aksanda, Orendia, and Fantolo. He also wanted to take puzzles with them to Fantolo. They now have puzzle maps of Aksanda, Orendia, and Phayendar. The schools would have scrolls from which to teach children about their world. In a town meeting Beldock introduced the plan for a school and the people voted for building a separate facility for it. They would all donate labor and silver to this project. Tall Sky and Melody shopped for supplies for the school and put them in Laskron's storage room. They wanted everything in place before leaving for Vivallen.

When all of the slave girls were safely delivered to their parents, King Aryante sent a message to Tall Sky in care of Beldock. The message was an invitation to join the caravan in five days. This would give Tall Sky and Melody just enough time to finish their school preparations. They wrote a letter to Indra about the children helping to create scrolls for the school and about having Brilley teach a class in animal care and the care of wounds. He also wanted Hilda to teach a class in the making of creative things and sewing. He would ask Hilda to learn painting from Faerverin so that she could teach that at the school. He found people in Loadrel who could also teach these things in the Loadrel School. Tall Sky wanted the Loadrel School to be fully developed by the time he and Melody had a child.

Melody continued bonding with her kitten and teaching her to say words. She also exercised Daisy so that Daisy would be able to fly. Daisy and the kitten were friends spending much time together running around the floor, hopping up on things, and taking naps together. Melody taught Daisy to throw a little ball of yarn for the kitten to chase. Daisy also learned to use the litter box. Melody decided to take the kitten with them in their wagon. She would take the kitten's cage with her and she made a harness and a leash for Shelly.

# TO VIVALLEN

Soon preparations were done for their trip and they boarded their wagon and drove out of town, not knowing when they would return, but confident that they would have an interesting journey. It was hard to say goodbye to their friends. They promised to bring gifts back for them from Fantolo.

Melody said, "You know, I started out running away from home and it seems like I have been running away ever since."

Tall Sky put his arm around her and said, "Culina, I know that we have been traveling a lot, but after this trip we will stay in Loadrel for a long time. We will make our house a warm and happy place with our flying cat, our little dragon, and our child. You will like that, won't you?"

"Yes, I will, but I have liked being with you on our journeys, too. I'm not really complaining. I know how important it is to get the slaves back so that they can lead normal lives," said Melody. "I would like to amaze King Aryante again by bringing back many slave girls."

"Yes, and don't forget the dragon riders. I am hopeful that we will get a chance to meet them," said Tall Sky. "It's starting to cloud up. I hope it doesn't rain before we get there."

"I like Vivallen. I like shopping there and the food at the Golden Chalice is so good. We should get Faerverin and Aleph to come to dinner with us," said Melody.

"We will, and if we have time, we will go shopping for some new clothes and new bedding for our wagon. I think Aleph and Quickturn will come with us to Fantolo. They have the experience with meeting all those strangers in Orendia and, since Fantolo is so close to Orendia, there should be some Fantolese who know Orendian. I hope Gantio will go with us. He was really good at negotiations in Orendia," said Tall Sky.

"Maybe they will bring their wives with them this time," said Melody hopefully.

"They could. I know that Faerverin wanted to meet the dragon riders," said Tall Sky

"She would like to make a painting of them," said Melody.

They pulled over to the ruins for lunch. She fed Daisy and the kitten Shelly first. Then she let them be down on the ground for a while, keeping Shelly on her leash. They had sandwiches that Mina had packed for them and a pastry from Jelsareeb. Then it was back onto the wagon for the rest of their trip. Melody climbed into the back to take a nap with her pets.

Four hours later they stopped at the Vivallen gate where a guard passed them through. Melody climbed back onto the seat with Tall Sky to see the shops as they drove through the city to the castle, where they parked their wagon near the stables and walked to the Golden Chalice. They paid for a room with a bath and dinner and proceeded to sit down at a table. Aleph heard about their arrival and walked in with Faerverin. "We were just hoping that you would walk in. It's good to see you Aleph and Faerverin. Have a seat. Will, you have dinner with us?" asked Tall Sky.

"Yes, we will," said Aleph. "How have you been?"

"Very busy," said Tall Sky. "We introduced Rando to King Farin and he talked them out of their engineer Thogul. He is going to help Rando to create a water system at Home Fire. Rando has completed the inn and already has boarders there, so Thogul will stay there with his interpreter Hafka and his wife. Thogul will be the first spiritual advisor there and Rando is building a Vision Hall. Melody and I are helping to put together schools at Home Fire and Loadrel. We wrote a history of Aksanda to be used in the schools. We lined up some teachers who can read, write, and teach painting and other crafts like the making of lace and embroidery. We thought that Faerverin could be involved in this. What do you think, Faerverin?"

"It sounds like a great idea, but I would have to train an adult to work with the children. I would like to paint at home if I don't go on this caravan," said Faerverin.

"How are your cats doing?" asked Melody.

"They're fine. They talk a lot and Gantio has been teaching me their language. The female cat is pregnant, so I have been thinking about staying home with her at Loadrel," said Faerverin. "Also, I don't want to leave my sister, so I think that I won't go on the caravan."

"I totally understand," said Melody. "I'm going to be missing all our friends, but it is important to get these slaves back home."

Aleph said, "We will be leaving the day after tomorrow. King Aryante wants to meet with us tomorrow to go over the plans." The waitress brought mugs of ale and a Daisy plate followed by plates of steak, potatoes and stewed vegetables.

"This food looks so good after traveling all day," said Melody. Daisy ate her food and climbed into her pouch for a nap. Melody gave some of her meat to the kitten and she ate it and went to sleep on Melody's lap.

"I think you should leave the kitten with me. I can take her to Arinya to keep for you until you get back. It would be safer for her. You don't know what complications you will have out there," said Faerverin.

"She's right, you know," said Tall Sky. "You should leave her with Faerverin for a few weeks."

"I'll miss her, but I know you're right. I'll leave her with you," said Melody. She felt relieved.

After dinner, Tall Sky and Melody went upstairs to their room, bathed and went to bed for a well deserved rest. "It's like we're on vacation," said Melody. "We have no work to do and we can cuddle up in our bed and..." Tall Sky interrupted her with a kiss.

In the morning after breakfast, they walked to the castle to deliver Shelly to Faerverin and to meet with King Aryante. They were met by Quickturn and Aleph who led them into the study. Gantio and Halden were there seated at the table. "The wagons are clean and in good repair," said Halden. He looked at Tall Sky and Melody and laughed. "Are you two ready for another adventure? I understand that you have been busy since Orendia. You've been helping Rando and talking with King Farin and organizing schools and writing history. I thought you two would be resting up for our next caravan."

"All of that was fun. There was no danger, and there's nothing like creativity and friendly company to rejuvenate the mind and body. What do you think, Melody? Are you ready?" asked Tall Sky.

Melody answered, "I feel great and I am very excited to meet the dragon riders and to see the country that Malding told us about. I have a copy of his descriptions of the lands of Phayendar so that I can add to them as we travel. The King of Fantolo may like to have a copy of that and of Malding's navigational maps. He made a copy for this new king. I just hope that there aren't too many scary creatures living there like those mantises that chased Quickturn."

King Aryante walked in and greeted them, "Hello my friends. I've just returned from my morning ride. The caravan looks good and the soldiers are ready. Melody and Tall Sky, it's good to see you again. When you get back from this journey, I would like to talk to you about starting a school in Vivallen. I think that it is important for all children to learn to read and write so that they can contribute to the good of all. The soldiers are well equipped with as much knowledge about Fantolo as Gantio could provide. Of course they have the experience gained in Orendia. Gantio knows some of their language and customs. Again, he will inform you of these on the way. This time I have commissioned an artist to accompany you. She will record as much as she can of the sights including the dragon riders of Orendia, the people and the animals of Fantolo. I dare say she will be very busy. There is a wagon full of nothing but art supplies. We have a new cook. Her name is Jalia. She is strong and has much experience cooking for large groups of people. You will be traveling straight through Orendia, stopping only to see King Jahiz. I would like a drawing of him and I would like to give him a gift. King Aryante gave Tall Sky a jeweled brooch for his turban. He was very cooperative during the last trip. You will then travel up the coast to the Isthmus of Fantolo and on into the country. From there you will inquire about the whereabouts of slaves and trade with the villagers. You will make contact with the king of Fantolo and deliver him gifts including a treaty, a trade agreement, and a copy of the navigational maps. That country has been peaceful for many years, so I do not expect any military problems. You will leave at dawn tomorrow. Are there any questions?"

"If for some reason we need to hire a ship to take some of the girls to Free Harbor, would that be alright?" asked Tall Sky.

"Of course," answered King Aryante. "You must do what you see fit to do. I have complete confidence in you. Make sure that you have clothing for all weather. It is still cold in the north near the mountains. Now, I have promised Svetlana to spend time with her and the children today, so I bid you farewell. When you return, we will have a celebration as we did last time."

Tall Sky said to Quickturn, "I trust that the caravan is equipped as it was last time?"

Quickturn answered, "Yes, we have a wheelright, a blacksmith, medical supplies, food, goods to trade and a tack man. We are truly ready for this one especially since we already did this once."

"May we go shopping now?" asked Melody. "I told Faerverin that we could go shopping today for our trip."

"It needs to be done," said Tall Sky, "so let's go get Faerverin." Aleph walked them upstairs to see his wife and she promptly showed them her two flying cats. "Are you ready to go shopping with us?" asked Melody.

"Yes, let's go," said Faerverin. They walked down stairs, through the long hallway, and out of the castle into a sunny day full of promise. Melody and Tall Sky bought new clothes and bedding for their wagon. Faerverin bought a few new decorations, some clothes and many painting supplies for herself and for the new schools. By lunch time they headed for the Golden Chalice and ordered lunch. Daisy was doing her hungry dance on Melody's shoulder, so the waitress brought her a plate of meat, vegetables, and cheese with a small bit of pie. After enjoying her meal, Daisy took a nap in her pouch. She brought plates of food and mugs of ale for everyone. "Melody, did you get everything you wanted?" asked Tall Sky.

"Yes, and I particularly like the gown I will wear to meet King Jahiz," said Melody.

"You will look like a person of royalty," said Tall Sky. "It is perfect."

"Is there anyone in Loadrel who can make paper?" asked Faerverin

"Ulrick made our puzzle boards. I think that he could make paper. You should talk to him," said Melody.

"I will. The school will need a lot of paper," said Faerverin. "Students need to practice drawing before they learn to paint. That's how Azurie taught me."

"I will find out how they make paper in Fantolo and bring back any information I can," said Melody. She now had another purpose for going on the caravan. She was going to document everything she could, just like Malding did on his voyages. "I think we should get started now and spend our first night at Lake Inari," said Melody.

"I understand your impatience, but we will wait until the appointed time tomorrow morning. After all, there are many soldiers involved and they are already following this plan," said Aleph.

After lunch, they walked to the castle so that Melody could pet her kitten for a while. Then they put their new clothes and bedding in the wagon. They decided to spend the night in the wagon so that they would be ready to leave in the morning.

The next day they awoke to the sounds of men talking and hitching horses to wagons and the smell of ham, eggs, and hot cakes being cooked. Tall Sky and Melody fed and watered their horses and hitched them to their wagon. Then they walked to the cook's fire and filled their bowls with food and their cups with tea. "It looks like a good day for travel. The air is cool and there are a few clouds in the sky to keep the sun from getting too hot," said Tall Sky.

After eating, they washed their dishes and climbed back onto the wagon. Halden rode up and called out, "Forward!" Tall Sky drove forward and a long line of wagons followed him. The road was dry and solid and there were trees on either side of the road with grasses and wildflowers. Daisy sat on Melody's shoulder happily chirring and watching everything. Halden and Quickturn scouted the road ahead looking for any signs of danger. The road was clear and there were no travelers for at least a mile ahead. The morning passed quickly and they stopped in a clearing for a rest. They could just see part of the lake through some trees. After walking about and having a sandwich, they resumed their journey around the southern edge of Lake Inari. The air was cooler near the lake and the foliage was denser. They pulled up to park for the evening near the pool in front of a waterfall where they could water the horses and bathe.

They filled up all the water containers first and watered the horses. Then the women bathed in the pool while the men bathed in the lake. Shanteel, the artist, said that she was excited to have the opportunity to draw everything on the trip. She had already sketched the caravan and Halden riding on his horse. "I will sketch you and Tall Sky sitting on your wagon. I will also sketch Jindra cooking at the fire. I want to put all of the sketches into a book to give to King Aryante," said Shanteel.

"That's nice, but I will need copies of those for a book I'm writing to be used in the schools," said Melody.

"What a great idea!" exclaimed Shanteel. "I am very willing to do that, and especially the new animals and Fantolese people we meet and the dragon riders should be documented."

"There is so much in the world to know about and I think that children should learn as much as they can," said Melody. Shanteel and Melody would work closely together to create a narrative to go with each sketch as she did with Malding. When Jindra and the other three cooks finished bathing, the cooks checked on the pots that were simmering on the fire. Dinner was ready and they rang the dinner bell.

Shanteel and Melody walked to the cook's fire to get their dinner. Melody took a Daisy plate back to the wagon where the little dragon waited impatiently. Shanteel, Melody and Tall Sky sat on logs to eat and were joined by Halden. "Did you see any bear tracks this time?" Halden asked smiling.

"No, we didn't. Maybe they were killed by the Bright Elves when Quickturn saved those villagers."

"That is possible," said Halden. "This stew is good."

After dinner they washed their plates and watched the sunset which was always beautiful at the lake. Then they cuddled up under their new quilt and made love listening to the night sounds. They slept well, but were awakened by thunder and lightning. The wind rocked the wagon, but they were warm and dry. Daisy cuddled close to Melody and they went back to sleep. The next morning there was hot porridge and tea for breakfast. It was comforting after a night of storms. Melody said, "I am so ready to travel again." She washed her dishes, and fed the horses while Tall Sky watered them. Then they hitched them to the wagon and waited for Halden who rode up presently and called, "Forward!"

"We will reach the Kigasse Plateau by lunch. It is there that we might see the dragons flying. They take them for flights every day," said Tall Sky. "We shouldn't have trouble with bandits this time, but with them you never know."

"At least it doesn't look line rain today," said Melody. "I wonder if the dragons can fly during the rain."

"I'm sure they can if they want to. It would probably feel good to them," said Tall Sky. "We will stop to see King Jahiz before going to Fantolo. We can tell him about King Aryante's plan to send Bright Elves to Orendia to teach the Orendians about Father God. That will make him happy."

"When will we be there?" asked Melody.

"We should be at Fallonia by tomorrow evening," said Tall Sky. "Gantio, do you know much of the Fantolese language?" asked Tall Sky.

"I know some, but not much. I will ask King Jahiz if he knows of someone who can be an interpreter for us. We will see some farms on the left soon and then the town of Tabira. You probably remember Tabira from the last time we came to Orendia," said Gantio.

"Yes, I do," said Melody. "It was there that we bought back our first slaves. As I recall, the land gets more hilly until we reach the plateau."

Melody decided to join Shanteel, who was sketching in the back. "Hi, Shanteel, I thought that I would write some narrative about the sketches you already made."

"Good idea," said Shanteel. "I don't want to get too far ahead of you. Here are the sketches. I think you should start with the one of the caravan with Halden riding horseback in front."

Melody described the caravan, its contents, and its purpose. By the time they stopped for lunch, she had three pages of writing completed. Tall Sky pulled off the road and stopped. The cooks brought out sandwiches and fruit for lunch and everyone sat on the boulders next to the road and ate lunch. They watered the horses, but left them hitched to the wagons. "How's the writing coming along?" asked Tall Sky.

"This is going to be a good story for the kids to read in school," said Melody. "I've written three pages describing the caravan and its purpose. Most people in Aksanda have never been this far away and I think that they will be very interested in this story."

"I think that each school should make a copy of the maps and stories and pictures and be responsible for starting a school in another town," said Tall Sky. "Home Fire could help start a school in Yardrel. Yardrel could help start a school in Talami. Loadrel could help start a school in Vivallen. Talami could help the dwarves start one in Othrund."

"What a great idea!" said Melody. "Children from one town could get to know children of another town. When they create something new like the record of the local animals, they can share it with their sister school. When knowledge is shared, there is more to learn. They can get together for a picnic once a year. That would help promote good relations between the towns. If someone discovers a new way to make something, he shares it with the sister school. Pretty soon everyone knows how to make it."

"How many subjects do you have so far?" asked Shanteel.

"We have reading, writing, art, sewing, history, cooking, doctoring, soap making, cheese making, the care of horses, tack making, and whatever else they think of. Recipes need to be written down and shared with other schools," said Melody.

Halden rode up to them and said, "It's been a nice break, but it is time to move on." Everyone climbed back into their wagons and Tall Sky pulled out onto the road.

They could see the sheer rock face of the plateau reaching about two hundred feet into the sky. Along the road next to the rock face was a long line of boulders and to the south stretched rolling hills. The road was rough with many rocks. Ganto said, "We should stop at the first farm to water the horses and fill up our water containers." Shanteel and Melody resumed their drawing and writing. Melody was almost caught up to Shanteel. Within the next hour Tall Sky stopped near the first farm and Gantio talked to the farmer who gladly gave him permission to water the horses if he could see some of their merchandise. They watered their horses eight at a time and made their first sale of the trip. The farmer wanted another bathtub. He also bought his wife some material for a new dress. Soon it was time to head west again toward Tabira.

# THE DRAGON RIDERS OF ORENDIA

Tabira was a small town only an hour away. This time they wouldn't stop at Tabira. They had already bought the slaves from there, so they drove right past Tabira heading toward Amby where they stopped for dinner and camping. Halden rode up to Tall Sky's wagon and told him to pull over on a level spot to camp. The fires were made, the horses were unhitched and fed, and the cooks filled the pots with meat and vegetables. Some of the men pitched their tents beside the wagons as did Gantio. Shanteel and Melody took a leisurely stroll down the wagons. They needed to exercise their muscles after sitting for hours in the wagon. Shanteel said, "Melody, look!" She was pointing at the sky where four dragons were circling high overhead. Gantio, Halden and Tall Sky joined them to watch as the dragons flew lower and lower, finally landing a safe distance away. Gantio, Halden, Tall Sky, Melody and Shanteel walked out to meet the dragon riders.

Gantio said, "Welcome to our camp. Would you like to stay for dinner?"

Halden said, "Ask them if they would like some wine." Gantio asked them and they said yes. Gantio said that he would translate for everyone.

Melody said, "I am Melody and this is Daisy." Daisy chirred.

Rana said, "She is beautiful. Where did you find her?"

Melody said, "I found her in Malwood forest while riding away from the slave auction. She was in an egg and she hatched in my pocket. I would love to pet your dragon. Would he let me?"

Rana said, "My dragon's name is Karberos and if I bring you to him, he will let you pet him, but first tell me why you have returned to Orendia."

Melody said, "We are traveling through Orendia to get to Fantolo where we hope to recover more slave girls. We are also going to talk to King Jahiz about helping him to introduce his countrymen to Father God."

Rana smiled and said, "That's the best news I've ever heard. Orendian men need to change. They're pigs!" and she spat.

"I have heard enough from our girls to understand that," said Melody.

Rana took Melody by the hand and led her to Kerberos who stretched his neck out to sniff Melody. He seemed to like her long red curls. Melody reached out to gently touch his nose. She couldn't help herself. She put her arms around Kerberos' neck and hugged him. Kerberos emitted a low hum something like a purr. "Kerberos wants to meet Daisy. She smelled Daisy in your hair. She won't hurt Daisy if you bring her over here." Melody kissed Kerberos on the nose and walked back to Tall Sky to get Daisy. Daisy was very curious about this large version of herself. Kerberos stared at Daisy and said her name.

"Your dragon can talk?" asked Melody.

"Yes, but he doesn't talk a lot. He is very impressed with your Daisy. He likes her," said Rana. Gantio was translating, but would not get really close to Kerberos. On the other hand, Daisy wanted very much to get close to Kerberos and stretched her neck out to rub cheeks with him.

Melody asked, "Do you know anything about Fantolo?"

"Let's go over to the boulders and sit down and then we will talk," said Rana. The dragon riders walked with Gantio and Melody over to the long line of boulders where they sat down with Halden, Quickturn, and Alelph. One of the cooks poured wine for them and they talked about Fantolo.

"Do you ever fly over Fantolo?" asked Halden.

Rana said, "We don't fly over Fantolo often, but we have done so. It's a long way for us, and we have to stop to rest our dragons. Fantolo is a wild place full of some very dangerous animals. We have seen dragons flying, but no dragon riders. We have seen large cats, bulls, and hogs. There are many people who grow crops and some who live in towns, but we didn't get a chance to talk to any of them. There are reindeer herders in the northern part of Fantolo much like in Gullandia. You will have to watch Daisy closely. There are small dragons there also and she is old enough to mate. If she does so, you will have to stop until she returns to you."

Bander asked, "How are the girls who you returned to Aksanda?"

Tall Sky answered, "They are healthy, happy, and back home with their parents. Some have married, and some of the pregnant girls are staying with Talla until they have their babies and get married. When we arrived in Vivallen with them, King Aryante threw them a dance like King Jahiz did, and before they left for home, they went shopping and bought new clothes with the gems you gave them. They are very grateful to you and send you their thanks."

Bander said, "I'm glad. I really liked those girls. I don't know if there are any in Fantolo, because we don't keep a very good watch on that area. If there are, I hope that you find them. We will watch you as much as we can, but we can't get close to other dragons and risk the safety of ours."

"I understand," said Tall Sky. "Do you ever take people for rides with you?"

Bander said that they have taken their neighbors up with them. "Would you like to ride with us?"

Melody said, "Please, please, please."

Tall Sky said, "Do you have extra harnesses?"

Rana said, "As a matter of fact we do. What about Daisy? Do you have a harness for her?"

"Yes, I do," said Melody. "I'll get it." She put Daisy in her harness and walked to the dragons. She rode with Rana and Tall Sky rode with Carwen. Daisy's harness was affixed securely to Melody's harness. Kerberos took a running start, flapped his wings, and took to the air. Melody could feel the strength of the dragon's muscles and she heard the dragon's wings pushing against the air making a whooshing sound. As they climbed higher and higher, the caravan looked smaller until it looked like a toy caravan. The air felt cool against her skin. She loved the freedom of flying through the sky and she loved this dragon. She thought, "There has to be a way to be Tall Sky's wife and a dragon rider, but what about the schools? Aksanda needs schools and I am writing information to be used in the history classes. I will talk to Tall Sky about this." Daisy was enjoying this ride, stretching her neck to see in all directions. The descent was smooth and effortless as they glided in circles until touching down on the ground.

Tall Sky dismounted and, facing the dragon, said, "Thank you, Cheesah, most beautiful and gracious of dragons." She blinked her big eyes at him and said, "Tall Sky."

"What do you think? Did you like flying?" asked Rana.

"I loved it so much that I want to be a dragon rider," said Melody.

Tall Sky said, "I loved it too, but we have duties to perform before we could ever consider this type of lifestyle. We are also going to have a child someday."

Rana said, "Being a dragon rider is a full time commitment. Once you bond with a dragon, you belong to it and you have to care for it always."

Halden said, "Would you stay for dinner with us?"

Rana said, "Thank you, but we have to get our dragons back to the mountain and feed them."

They said goodbye and mounted their dragons. Melody and Daisy watched them fly high into the sky and disappear over the Kigasse Plateau.

"I'm happy," said Melody. She and Tall Sky walked to the cook's fire for some food. There was stew and flatbread. They sat on some boulders to eat and drink some wine. Daisy happily ate her food and crawled into her pouch for a nap. "This stew is great and I'm hungry enough to eat a grustabist."

"You are an amazing girl, said Tall Sky. "You not only pet a full sized dragon, but you kissed it and rode it."

"And it was the most fun I ever had," she said smiling. "Did you like it?"

"I agree with you. It was the most fun I ever had, but don't pester me about becoming full time dragon riders," said Tall Sky. "We have a long way to go and a lot to do."

After dinner they washed their dishes and sipped on the wine watching the sunset and thinking about their flying experience. "Maybe we can do it again on our way back," said Melody.

"I hope so," said Tall Sky. The soldiers were pitching their tents and the cooks were putting away their pots and pans. Tall Sky and Melody fed and watered their horses, unhitched them, and retired for the night. Melody fell asleep dreaming of flying on a dragon.

The next morning after breakfast, the caravan drove past Amby. Shanteel drew pictures of the dragons and the dragon riders while Melody wrote a narrative about their encounter with the dragon riders. She included in their story what she was told about the experience of the last caravan and the way that the dragon riders had defended and treated the girls of that caravan. Shortly past Amby, they stopped for lunch. Several Orendian men rode up to the caravan wanting to sell a slave girl they had found. Halden paid for her and Melody cleaned her up a bit and gave her the men's clothing and a cap. The girl had long brown hair and brown eyes. She was thin and tired. Melody gave her some wine to drink and a sandwich.

"My name is Andra. I was a slave in a brothel and I tried to run away. I suspected that I might be pregnant and thought they would kill me."

"You are safe now. We are here to bring slaves back home to Aksanda. You must eat well and rest to regain your strength. If you are pregnant, there is a woman in Loadrel who will take care of you and help you to find a husband," said Melody. "We have already helped several hundred girls in this way."

Andra smiled and thanked Melody. "Why do you travel through Orendia again?"

Melody said, "We have traveled all around Orendia before and are now headed to Fantolo to buy back their slaves."

"I am so happy to be with Aksandans again. You wouldn't believe how awful the Orendian men are," said Andra. "They enjoy hurting women and using them for anything."

"I have heard many stories from the other girls we rescued," said Melody. "King Jahiz has outlawed slavery in Orendia and has asked for help in introducing his countrymen to Father God. Have you ever prayed to Father God?"

"I have prayed, but I don't know if He heard me. Maybe that's how you found me," said Andra.

"I'm sure it is," said Melody. "Have you ever asked Him into your heart?"

"No, does that help?" asked Andra.

"If you ask Him into your heart, He will be with you always helping you in many ways. He will give you the gifts of love, forgiveness, health, compassion, and so much more. All you have to do is to ask him to forgive you and to live in your heart."

Andra prayed. Melody said, "Now, why don't we eat our lunch? The caravan will move again soon. You may ride with Shanteel and me until we get more girls. Melody fed Daisy and ate her sandwich. Then they all climbed into the wagon. Daisy was very curious about Andra and curled up beside her while they both took a nap. Shanteel and Melody continued working on their project.

Gantio rode with Tall Sky on the wagon seat. Gantio said, "Fallonia is our next stop. I wonder if they found any more slave girls. It's possible since Fallonia is such a large city."

"I know," said Tall Sky. "I wonder what changes there are in the castle and in King Jahiz. I was thinking of asking him for a treaty to present to the king of Fantolo just like the treaty and trade agreement we presented to him from King Aryante. It worked with King Jahiz and certainly made it easier to trade with the locals for slaves."

"True enough, and I would like to explain this to King Jahiz. It should be to his advantage to have formal relations with the Fantolese. I know he trades with them. I hope he has a good interpreter for us."

Tall Sky said, "I have to decide if I should tell him about his slave girl being pregnant. She will have a son and King Aryante wants to raise him in the castle and groom him to become a liaison between Aksanda and Orendia. King Jahiz could become angry with this and want the child raised in his castle, but the mother does not want to live in Orendia. She plans to marry an Aksandan man and rightly so. King Jahiz has been so gracious and cooperative; I just don't want to impede our progress at this point. I also don't want to be deceptive in any way. What do you think, Gantio?"

"After we get the interpreter and give King Jahiz the good news about the campaign planned for Bright Elves to come to Orendia, we should tell him about his son. It is the right thing to do. He will appreciate your honesty and I think that he will like the idea. After all, he does already have an heir to the throne," said Gantio.

"We will do it this way. You are a wise man, Gantio," said Tall Sky.

"I miss my wife. She is beautiful and gracious. She fits in well at the castle. Everyone likes her. I am truly fortunate to have her," said Gantio.

"You made a wise decision to buy her. Her husband was an idiot. He didn't even realize what he had. She is truly a great treasure," said Tall Sky.

"Yes, and I want to bring her back something special," said Gantio.

"We may find something in Fantolo. Every country has its artisans," said Tall Sky.

"I already know what Melody wants. She wants her very own dragon. If she finds an egg, I'm in trouble," Tall Sky said laughing. "If she had a dragon, we would have to move to the mountains."

"The dwarves would probably like to have that kind of protection," said Gantio.

"If Melody adopted a dragon, I wouldn't want to live in the Aikasse Mountains. It's too far north. It might be possible to live at Home Fire and keep the dragon in a cave in the cliff above Home Fire," said Tall Sky.

Gantio said, "King Aryante could build a shelter on top of the castle and you could live in the castle."

"Actually, either place would work, but I prefer Home Fire. We could keep sheep to feed the dragon and we could bathe it in Lake Perilough," said Tall Sky.

"It sounds to me like you wouldn't mind having a dragon," said Gantio.

"I loved riding the dragon, but caring for one is a big tie down. It's time consuming and you can't leave it alone for long before it goes hunting on its own. You know, I have a hard time saying no to Melody. We will have a child and he will probably be like Melody and want to be a dragon rider. If I ever have to make the decision, it won't be an easy one," said Tall Sky.

"The houses are becoming more frequent. Fallonia is up ahead," said Gantio. "Let's pull over and have lunch before going to the castle." Tall Sky stopped the wagon in a flat area just off the road and told Halden that they needed to eat and clean up before going on to the castle. The soldiers fed and watered the horses and the cooks set out sandwiches.

Melody, Shanteel, Tall Sky and Gantio walked around the caravan to stretch their legs, got a sandwich and some wine and sat down on some boulders to eat. "I thought I heard something about dragons at Home Fire," said Melody.

"We were discussing where dragons could live in Aksanda. It's probably not a good idea. Dragons can be dangerous if they grow up wild, and, as you found out, they can lay their eggs anywhere. Of course, if the mother dragon is tamed and has her own home, she will lay her egg there," said Tall Sky.

After lunch, Gantio, Tall Sky and Aleph washed up and changed clothes. They rode to the castle and announced themselves to the castle guards who announced their presence to King Jahiz. The king told the guards to show them into his study where they sat at a long table. King Jahiz walked in smiling and said "Welcome my friends. Did you get your girls safely back to Aksanda to their parents?"

"Yes, we did with a little help from the dragon riders who chased away a large contingent of bandits," said Tall Sky. "Aleph and I took the girls from this city by ship to Free Harbor. That went very well."

"What did King Aryante say about sending Bright Elves to help introduce my countrymen to Father God?" asked King Jahiz.

Aleph answered, "He is very interested in this and is preparing a plan to do so. You may expect help from him soon."

"Ah, he is a wise king. I would like to meet him someday. Perhaps we could arrange a meeting near Lake Inari. I have been there before. It is a pleasant place to visit," said King Jahiz.

"I will mention it to him. I think that he would very much like to meet you," said Aleph. "King Jahiz, we are traveling by caravan to buy back slaves from Fantolo much as we did here in Orendia. We would like the king of Fantolo to sign a trade agreement and a peace treaty with you and with Aksanda. Would you like to do this? I think that formal relations between countries is always a good thing."

"Yes, I will have the papers drawn up immediately. I have never met the king of Fantolo, but the nation has been at peace for many years. You will need an interpreter, and I know just the man. He is Fantolese, and knows the country and the language. He will be a great help to you. I will be back in a minute." King Jahiz left for a while and returned with a man named Trinian, who was dressed in silken clothing and a turban. He had olive complexion, a short beard and mustache, and brown eyes. "This is Trinian. He will represent me in these negotiations. He knows both Orendian and Fantolese languages, and with Gantio, you should be able to accomplish your purposes. Trinian will write the treaty and trade agreement in Fantolese and will be ready to go with you shortly." Gantio presented the king with the thank you gift from King Aryante.

Aleph said, "King Jahiz, I have more news for you. Kineol is pregnant and King Aryante wants her to stay in his castle and raise the child to be part of his royal household to receive the education and training that his own son has received. That way he can become a laiason between our two countries. The child will be a boy. Would you be agreeable to that?"

"It sounds like a good plan. Will I be able to see the boy? I would like to visit with him sometimes," said King Jahiz.

"Of course you will. He is your son and Gantio will teach him your language and customs," replied Tall Sky.

"I am very pleased with this. Now I will take my leave of you. I wish you success in your mission," said King Jahiz as he left the room and they waited for Trinian to finish the papers.

"That went smoothly enough," said Aleph. Soon they were ready to leave with their new interpreter. Trinian brought his bags and gave the papers to Aleph. They walked out to the horses and rode to the caravan. Trinian and Gantio rode with Tall Sky so they could discuss Fantolo as they drove west toward the Frothy Sea.

"We have a good day for travel," said Tall Sky. "This breeze feels good and I can already smell the sea."

"We will be camping by the sea tonight," said Gantio. "I'm going to explain more about our caravan to Trinian now, and then you can ask him questions about Fantolo."

# FANTOLO

**M**elody, Shanteel and Andra rode in the back of the wagon quietly drawing and writing. Andra read the history that Melody had written and said that it was good. Andra asked, "So does anyone know about Fantolo?"

Melody said, "Fantolo has a variety of creatures and plant life, and some of them are very different from the ones in Aksanda and even in Orendia. Some of the creatures are very large and dangerous. For instance, they have a variety of lizards and dragons. The country has been at peace for many years. It has climates ranging from hot in the south to very cold in the north. We don't really know much about the people yet, but Trinian will be telling Tall Sky about them, and he will tell us when we camp tonight. Have you ever seen the sea?"

"No," answered Andra. "What is it like?"

"It's big and beautiful," said Melody. "The waves crash into the shoreline bringing shells and seaweed. The water is salty and cold, but it feels really good to bathe in. Everyone who sees it is amazed by the sea. Tall Sky, Aleph and I sailed on a ship to Free Harbor with sixty-eight slave girls. Ships aren't all that comfortable, but it was pretty exciting during a storm. We anchored at a harbor during a storm."

"Is there anything that I can do to help you with your project?" asked Andra.

"If you can write, you could copy the history for King Aryante. I would like to present him with a copy when we return," said Melody.

"Really? I would love to do that," said Andra.

Trinian spoke with Gantio using the Orendian language, describing the Fantolese people and their customs. After each description, Gantio translated to Tall Sky and Aleph who would later explain it to the soldiers. Gantio asked Trinian, "What are the Fantolese people like?"

Trinian answered, "The Fantolese are quiet and gentle for the most part. Along the coast, they fish for a living. In the southern areas they raise rice and water loving vegetables. They live in homes that sit on sticks above the ground to avoid the water. At times the land floods and it is necessary to use boats to get around. There are predators living in the waters, but they stay mainly in the major streams. There are trees there with moss hanging down to the ground. The men are allowed to have as many wives as they can support. Most men have several wives so that they can help with the work and with watching the children."

"What about the middle part of Fantolo?" asked Gantio.

"The land in the middle part of Fantolo has forests and farms where they raise crops and animals. The forests are filled with very dangerous large beasts that are best to avoid whenever possible. Farmers in Fantolo use slaves for work in the fields and for pleasure. In towns there are craftsmen who make many beautiful and delicate things. Townspeople make their livings by making and trading these things. They work with metals and fabrics. Some create beautiful paintings and tapestries. The most successful of these artisans train slaves to do most of their work. They aren't cruel to the slaves, but they are very demanding," said Trinian.

"Does the northern part of Fantolo have mountains like Orendia does?" asked Gantio.

"Yes, there are rolling hills that get higher as they reach the mountains. Of course it gets colder the farther north you go. The people who live there raise sheep and reindeer. In the towns of the north are taverns and brothels and stores," said Trinian.

"Do any of the Fantolese know Father God?" asked Gantio.

"Not that I know of," said Trinian. "They use idols to put in their fields to help with the crops. They worship a god to help with the weather. There is a goddess to help women in childbirth and for fertility. I have met Father God and now feel that all these other Gods are silly."

"I understand completely," said Gantio. "Having a real relationship with the true God makes everything else pale to insignificance. I wouldn't give Him up for anything."

"Nor would I," said Trinian. "Father God causes everything to make sense."

"What do you know of the royal family?" asked Gantio.

"I will give you their names. King Narendra, Queen Darshana, Princess Nalini, Princess Vala, and Prince Ravi are their names. Prince Ravi was born first and is the heir to the throne. They live in a castle in Kunola named for the lotus that blooms there. It is the largest city in Fantolo and is located in the center of the country. It is my opinion that we should stop there as soon as possible to pay our respects to King Narendra and to get the treaty and trade agreement signed. He would consider it bad manners if we did otherwise. King Jahiz gave me a gift to present to King Narendra. It is a gemstone necklace and matching ring. The king is sure to like it and it will pave our way to negotiations. Family ties are strong in Fantolo, so he should understand your country's need for its children," said Trinian.

"Are the relations between men and women similar to those of Orendia?" asked Gantio.

"Yes, they are similar, but not quite as strict. Men can talk to women, but they prefer the company of men. Some men love their wives and some just use them for making babies and for the work that they want done. Women do not make decisions. That is the responsibility of the men. Women do not have freedom to come and go as they please. They do not attend school, so they don't read or write. However, the princesses are required to learn as much as possible in case one of them is called upon to rule," said Trinian.

Halden rode up and said, "We are close to King's Port. We will stop close to the city and camp. We don't want to be swarmed by a lot of people wanting to buy goods at this point, so choose a flat spot and pull over."

Tall Sky drove to a flat area and stopped. He then climbed down and helped Gantio and Trinian to feed and water the horses and unhitch them. The soldiers did the same and made fire for the cooks.

Everybody relieved themselves behind some boulders in the woods and walked around the wagons for exercise. "I think that Aksanda's soldiers are the best men in all of Phayendar to do this," said Andra.

"I agree with you," said Melody. "I was hoping that we could camp at the shore tonight, but we will see the ocean tomorrow and I will ask Halden if we can stop on the shore and bathe before we reach Fantolo. You just have to experience that. It feels so good."

They got some wine and sat down for a few minutes. Halden called the soldiers together and Gantio briefed them on the country of Fantolo and its customs. Trinian answered their questions. They were concerned about the military of Fantolo. Trinian said that there was a small army, but they would not engage in a fight without the consent of the king. The dinner bell rang and everybody got their bowls and cups and headed for the cooks' fires. There was a meat and vegetable stew and flatbread with honey cakes for dessert. Daisy ate her food and curled up on Melody's shoulder for a nap. It was altogether a good meal and afterwards they relaxed with some wine and watched a beautiful sunset of reds and golds. "It feels so good to be outside like this. I'm going to spend some time throughout the day on the wagon seat with you. It gets kind of warm in the wagon. We have made good progress with our writing and drawing, though."

"Gantio can spend some time with Aleph on the second wagon seat and Andra can ride with us for a while. Shanteel can ride on the third wagon seat. I didn't realize that you needed to be outside," said Tall Sky.

"It's alright. I was very busy writing for a while, but I've caught up now," said Melody. "Besides, I want to watch the sea and I want to bathe in the sea, so would you arrange it with Halden?"

"Sure," said Tall Sky. "I think we would all like a bath. We should wait until we pass King's Port, though."

Halden walked over and said, "We will be stopping at King's Port for groceries and ale, but we will not be selling goods there. Then we will travel north on Seaside Road toward the land bridge. When we stop for lunch, we will also bathe in the sea. Not many people travel to Fantolo, so we should have privacy and safety."

"It sounds like an enjoyable day," said Tall Sky.

"According to Trinian, it only takes about four hours to cross the land bridge, so we should be in Fantolo to camp tomorrow night." said Halden. "The next morning we will travel directly to the castle in Kunola where we will meet with King Narendra. We should be there by lunch of that day."

"It sounds like a good plan," said Tall Sky. "Did Trinian say anything about army patrols stopping us?"

"We could see army patrols, but Trinian is confident that he can explain the nature of our visit as one of trade and diplomacy," said Halden.

"Good," said Tall Sky. "What of bandits?"

"There are bandits, but they mainly leave King's Road alone because of the army patrols," said Halden. "We should be safe until we reach Kunola."

Melody exercised Daisy by raising her up and down so that she would flap her wings. Daisy was getting stronger and could actually fly for a short time. She would need to have her flying skills soon, because she was close to her mating time.

"Let's go to bed," said Tall Sky. "We have a big day of travel tomorrow and I want to be well rested for it."

"Yes, I am getting tired," Melody said, smiling. "Don't forget that baby you promised me."

"I won't forget," said tall Sky.

Everyone slept peacefully through the night and awoke with renewed optimism knowing that this day would be spent traveling the Seaside Road toward the land bridge. They had breakfast, fed and watered the horses and hitched them to the wagons. Tall Sky, Melody and Andra climbed onto the wagon seat and Tall Sky drove back onto the road. They drove past King's Port and turned right onto Seaside Road. Everything was going as planned. Daisy sat on Melody's shoulder enjoying the cool sea breeze and watching the waves of the Frothy Sea. It was a beautiful day with blue skies and wildflowers.

Melody said, "Well, Andra, you and I have a day off from writing. I think I'll ask Shanteel to draw a map of Fantolo with the help of Trinian and Gantio. It really helps to have a map to look at while you're traveling. Then you can copy it into the book you are writing for King Aryante."

Andra said, "I'll do my best. I love the sound of the waves crashing into the shore."

"I do too," said Melody, "but sometimes they can keep you awake or wake you up too early. The sea birds can also wake you up. What is really fun is to watch a storm come in. Because you can see far, you can watch the curtain of rain falling as it comes toward you and you can see the lines of lightning flashing across the sky and hear thunder cracking and rolling. It's thrilling! It's like you are a part of something much bigger than yourself and it makes you feel so alive."

When Halden told them to pull over for lunch, he said that they would be bathing. The women bathed first and then the men bathed. Then everybody made their own sandwiches and ate sitting down on the sand. The men fed and watered the horses and Daisy enjoyed stomping around in the sea foam at the edge of the water. Melody kept her harness and leash on for safety. Andra and Shanteel found some pretty seashells, marveling at their design and colors. When the men had finished attending to the horses, they climbed back onto the wagons and Halden called out, "Forward!"

They traveled north for another hour and turned west on the Isthmus road leading across the land bridge to Fantolo. Melody said, "I'm really excited. We will be in a new country soon."

"This is where are I start getting worried," said Tall Sky. "You are not to touch any animals without Trinian's consent. This is his country and he knows what is safe and what is dangerous or poisonous. They have very pretty, but very poisonous frogs. I'm serious, Melody. Trinian said that just touching one of them can kill you."

Melody said, "How about if I just touch animals that are furry?"

"Not without Trinian's permission," said Tall Sky. "This is a very different place with very old swamps and some animals that you have never seen before. We must exercise great caution the whole time that we are here. Do you understand?"

"Yes," said Melody pouting. "What if we find a dragon egg?"

"We ask Trinian first before touching it," said Tall Sky. "We don't want to offend a wild dragon."

"I don't want to offend one, but I sure would like to talk to one," said Melody.

"Melody, you know that I love you, but you must obey me on this one. Keep your mind focused on our mission. If we are harmed, we will not be able to help those girls. Remember the horrible situations they are in. Remember how hurt they are. Remember that they belong to us and that we are responsible for rescuing them," said Tall Sky.

"I'm sorry, Tall Sky. I will try harder to be more disciplined for their sakes and for your sake," she said smiling and gave him a hug.

Andra said, "I will help to remind you when I see you getting interested in something."

"Good idea," said Melody. "It's like when I see an animal, I lose all self control. I want to hold it and love it and pet it and I don't think about any dangers involved. All there is in the world at that time is this amazing, cute little creature who is looking at me. It would be very helpful for you to remind me."

"Andra, I would like to give you an assignment on this mission to watch over Melody when I am not with her. She is kind and compassionate, but, like a kite, the wind can take her in an unexpected direction when you least expect it. She is my beautiful wild child, but in this country, she cannot be that way. She must be disciplined and you can help with that. When we get more girls, you will see the importance of your assignment," said Tall Sky.

Andra replied, "I will do as you ask."

"It looks like I have a new best friend," said Melody.

"Yes, you do," said Tall Sky. The rest of the afternoon was pleasant with the breeze and the sound of the waves on either side of the land. The sea could just barely be seen, but there were curious sea birds flying above them. There were long grasses and wild flowers growing on the isthmus, but no trees. They reached the other side of the isthmus in time for dinner and looked for a good place to camp. There were trees on both sides of the road, so Tall Sky drove for a while until he saw a level piece of grassland big enough for thirty wagons. He pulled over and stopped. "We camp here," said Tall Sky, and they climbed down to take their walk around the caravan.

Gantio joined them and said, "Trinian says that we have to start being vigilant now. There are dangerous animals in these woods, so we must not go into the woods for any reason. Once we start a fire, we will be safer. This part of the woods goes on for several hours and then the farmlands begin. Shanteel has drawn a map for us. There are twenty-three towns on the map including some ports. There is a plateau near the mountains, some streams and a river. There are a number of lakes and a large swampy area and forest, as you can see. We are at the northern edge of the forest. Shanteel will make a copy of the map for you."

A gold and red butterly with a ten inch wing span wafted by and Melody held her hand out for it to sit on. Andra pushed her arm down and told her to ask Trinian about the insects first. Melody said, "Surely a butterfly isn't harmful, but I will ask him." Gantio asked Trinian who said that most insects are venomous, but that the butterflies are harmless. Melody spoke the elven words given to her by Faerverin, "Wilwarren, haara en lepta." The butterfly landed on her hand and watched her for a while. Then she said, "Amin mela il." and moved her hand up to let it go.

Tall Sky looked at Andra and said, "Good job, Andra. Now you see what I mean."

"Yes, I do. What did you say to it?" asked Andra.

"I told it to sit on my finger and told it 'I love you,'" said Melody. They are elven words. My friend Faerverin learned from the fairies how to talk to butterflies and she taught me," said Melody.

"You sure do have interesting friends," said Andra.

"When we get back to Aksanda, I will introduce you to Faerverin. She was caught by the slavers, but never made it to market. Aleph found her and married her. They are both elves and live in King Aryante's castle where she teaches Princess Anya how to paint," said Melody. "Aleph is with us and is representing King Aryante on this mission."

"Let's take care of the horses. Dinner will be ready soon," said Tall Sky. The soldiers were already setting up their tents and taking care of their horses. "This sure beats sitting around the house being bored."

"Maybe we should move out to Home Fire," said Melody.

"I've been thinking about it," said Tall Sky. "I wonder how Rando's water system is coming along."

"I'll bet it's done by the time we get back. He's got the best help there is," said Melody.

They fed and watered the horses and went to the cook's fire for some stew and bread. Melody fed Daisy first and then she ate sitting on a log with Andra and Tall Sky. Shanteel sat with Trinian and Gantio. She was trying to learn the Fantolese language. The air was humid and warmer in the woods. Melody felt tired and didn't need any coaxing to go to bed early. The wind picked up and there was thunder and lightning before the rain. Many of the soldiers climbed into the wagons finding places to sleep amid the merchandise. Others slept in hammocks under the wagons, and some stood guard around the wagons wearing rain gear. The forest creatures were pretty quiet during the rain. In the morning, however, there were lots of animal sounds and bird calls. The cooks made porridge for breakfast while the soldiers took care of the horses.

Shanteel gave Tall Sky a copy of the Fantolo map that Trinian had helped her to make. There was a straight road from their location to the castle. All the main roads in Fantolo led to the castle with some connecting roads. They had been well thought out and deliberately planned, which was necessary to avoid the most dangerous areas. The king was very proud of his road system and he made sure that road crews kept them maintained.

Halden rode up to Tall Sky and said, "It's time to move on. Pull out as soon as you're ready." They washed their dishes and climbed aboard the wagons. Halden called out, "Forward!" and the caravan moved down the road traveling west toward Kunola.

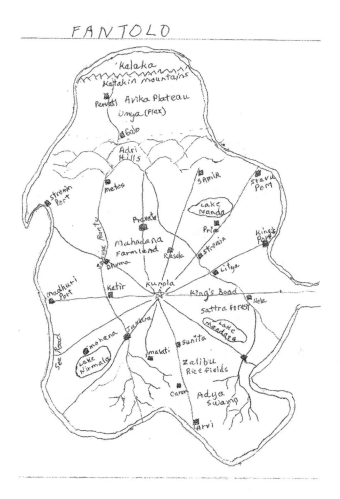

"This map is going to be very helpful," said Tall Sky. "Thank you, and thank Trinian for me, too."

"The Sattra Forest is mainly on our left and, from the looks of it, is getting denser every minute," said Melody. Daisy looked into the forest and chirred. Then she snuggled under Melody's hair for protection. "It seems that Daisy senses danger here and so do I."

"I think we will be alright as long as we keep on moving. I will not stop this wagon until we are clear of this forest," said Tall Sky. There were no houses on the road and no paths going into the forest. There were bird calls and animal sounds. At one point there was a crashing sound through the undergrowth and bushes, but the animal did not show itself. A brightly colored turquoise and red parrot landed on the wagon seat next to Melody's feet and squawked at her. The parrot turned its head this way and that and peered at Daisy who stretched out her neck and chirred at the parrot. "Has Daisy made a new friend?"

"It seems so," said Melody. She gave the parrot a piece of bread and the parrot ate it. "This parrot is so pretty. "May I touch it?"

"See that beak? It could really hurt you. You two are not good enough friends for touching yet," said Tall Sky.

"This place is going to try my patience," said Melody.

"How did you ever make it through childhood in one piece?" asked Tall Sky laughing.

In the second wagon, Gantio, Trinian and Aleph rode on the wagon seat. Trinian noticed the parrot flying to Melody and said, "I see we are going to have some interesting times in Fantolo with Melody along. She attracts animals to her without even trying. We must all keep a watch on her. She is likely to attract danger to us."

Gantio said, "She loves them and they know it."

"There are lizards and snakes that she must not touch. I will have Andra to write about them and Shanteel to draw them. That should help Melody to be able to identify the worst of them," said Trinian. "We should also do this for other people who wish to visit Fantolo and give copies to the schools that Tall Sky and Melody are starting."

"Yes, and you should teach our soldiers about them soon," said Gantio. "Let's go into the wagon and have Andra start the descriptions now, and, when we stop, we will have Shanteel draw them." Gantio and Trinian went into the wagon and asked Andra to begin writing. By the time they stopped for lunch, they had many descriptions with spaces left for Shanteel's pictures. Halden rode up to them and asked if it would be alright to stop for lunch. Trinian said that they were getting close to Kunola and that it should be alright.

The worst of the forest was behind them now and the trees were thinning out. Halden told Tall Sky to pull over at the next grassy area that he saw. The parrot was still riding on Melody's foot rest and Daisy was keeping a wary eye on him. When Melody started to climb down, the parrot flew to the roof of the wagon where he sat like a lonely sentinel watching the proceedings of lunch. While the soldiers took care of the horses, the cooks brought out sandwiches. Melody, Andra and Shanteel walked around the caravan. By the time they got back to the cook, sandwiches were out on a table. They ate standing up, not knowing what insects might be about. "I would really like to see some houses," said Shanteel. "These woods scare me."

"Trinian has been describing some of the forest creatures for me to write about and he will help you to draw them. You have a right to be scared of Sattra Forest, but we will be totally clear of it soon," said Andra. Halden said that it was time to go, so everyone got back onto their wagons and horses and Halden called out "Forward!" Tall Sky pulled back onto the road and drove west. The parrot stayed on the wagon enjoying the ride.

"What are we going to do with the parrot?" asked Melody.

Tall Sky answered, "Nothing. The parrot will fly away when he wants to."

"Do you think he belongs to anyone?" asked Melody.

"No, I think he is wild and we are not going to adopt him," said Tall Sky. "We will soon have more important things to worry about. We have to negotiate a treaty with King Narendra and rescue slave girls, and we will be there soon. You will have to keep the girls company in a wagon while we conduct business with the king. You can help with the book writing for the school we will start at Home Fire."

"Look, there are some houses," said Melody. "There are some kids playing outside. There are some goats and chickens and a cow."

"We are close to the castle. Keep looking for that," said Tall Sky.

# KING NARENDRA

The castle, which was situated on the far side of the city on a hill, was readily seen as it was constructed of white marble that reflected the sun. Around the castle was a mote of water with a drawbridge. To either side of the main castle were attached buildings to house the soldiers. Melody said, "It is breathtaking!"

Halden rode up and told Tall Sky that there would be an arched gateway through which they would enter the city. Trinian and Gantio traded places with Melody. Trinian would lead and Gantio would translate to Tall Sky. At the gateway they were met by two guards who questioned them. Trinian told them that he had gifts for King Narendra from King Jahiz and King Aryante and asked where he should park the caravan while he and several representatives visit King Narendra. The guards motioned to an open area across the street and Trinian related that to Gantio who told Tall Sky. Tall Sky drove the wagon into the open area and stopped. Tall Sky, Aleph, Gantio and Trinian assembled the documents and the gifts and rode through the gate accompanied by six soldiers.

The streets were narrow and lined with many houses. At the center of the city was an open air market with vendors set up in open, colorful tents with tables of merchandise. It was crowded with shoppers dressed in brightly colored clothing. The men wore beards and turbans and the women wore long, flowing dresses with pastel colored veils over their faces. The market was noisy with so many people talking at once. There was a minstrel playing a stringed instrument and singing. Five women dressed in veils were dancing to the music, entertaining the crowds. The people were only mildly interested in the strangers as they rode by. They rode by many stores as they approached the castle. The mote turned out to be a naturally flowing stream with a bridge to cross and beautiful gardens before the castle. The walls of the castle were ornately carved with figures of animals and people. There was a fountain with the statue of a woman holding a large shell with a single lily growing in it. Guards talked to Trinian and invited them into the castle where they were led into a waiting room. A guard then left to announce their presense and purpose to the king. When he came back, he told Trinian to bring Aleph and Tall Sky to the throne room.

The throne room was large with more carvings on the walls, statues of men and women, tapestries, and a burgundy carpet leading to a raised platform with two large chairs seated by King Narendra and Queen Darshana. The guard introduced Trinian as the advisor to King Jahiz, Aleph as the advisor to King Aryante and Tall Sky as the leader of the mission. Gantio translated. All three of them bowed to the king. "You may present your gifts," said King Narendra. Trinian gave him a gemstone necklace and a matching ring. The king said, "It is beautiful," and put on the ring. Then Aleph presented him with a copy of the navigational maps and the treaty and trade agreement. King Narendra read the documents and said that he saw nothing disagreeable in them. He signed them. Then Aleph had Trinian explain the purpose of their mission and showed him King Jahiz' decree outlawing slavery in Orendia and his order to sell the Aksandan slaves back to the Aksandans. He explained that the Bitter Elves had stolen these children from their parents and had taken them by force to foreign countries. He said that this was totally unacceptable to King Aryante, who wanted them back.

King Narendra looked frustrated by this and said, "Why would he want a bunch of slave girls back?"

"King Aryante doesn't see them as slave girls, but as the future mothers of Aksanda. He wants them to raise children to populate his land," said Trinian. "Also, he sees them as the children of Father God. Through the ages, the kings of Orendia and Aksanda have worshipped Father God, the trinity of God the Creator, God the redeemer, and God the Restorer. Your ancestors probably did, too.

King Narendra looked at his wife and asked her if she knew of this. Queen Darshana said that when she was a child she became sick and that her mother had prayed to Father God and He had healed her. King Narendra said, "What of the other Gods we worship? We bury fertility figures in with our plantings to help bring forth crops and there is the God of rain and fire and other gods."

Trinian said that Father God blesses the land He created and also gives the believers gifts like peace, love, forgiveness, discernment of right from wrong, and joy. Father God will send His Spirit to live inside you and will guide you in your decision making. He will lead you into all truth and will make you a great king.

King Narendra considered this for a while and said, "How do I get this? I want this Father God to live in me." Trinian led him in prayer and King Narendra smiled and thanked him. King Narendra immediately told his wife to ask Father God into her heart, too and she did. He said, "I feel better already!" He had his tribune to write up the documents which he signed and wished his new friends a good journey.

He also gave them permission to sell their merchandise and sent his messengers to post the new decree forbidding slave ownership and ordering them to sell their slaves to the men of the caravan.

Tall Sky, Trinian, and Aleph left the castle feeling happy and hopeful. It had been a successful meeting and the mission was off to a great start. He told the soldiers to spread the word about a sale at the caravan and rode back to get things ready. Then he sent some soldiers out to buy back slaves. This was the largest city in Fantolo and they expected lots of business. They would need to stay an extra day and consider sending the girls back by ship as they did before.

The king decided to get behind this and sent his soldiers into the city to bring girls to the caravan. Townspeople flooded to the caravan and bought merchandise. Before long, they had emptied ten wagons of merchandise and had filled those wagons with some very astonished slave girls. King Narendra arrived in the royal carriage to speak with Tall Sky. He had with him an interpreter who knew the Aksandan language. "Tall Sky, I have never been outside of my country and I would like to visit Aksanda and meet with your king. I would like to offer my ship to carry these girls back to Aksanda and personally present them to King Aryante. I have much to discuss with him."

Tall Sky was amazed at this suggestion and said that it would be an honor to introduce him to King Aryante. He said that it would entail taking river boats upstream and taking wagons to Vivallen, but it was a pleasant trip. "We will purchase blankets, mattresses, and pillows and the girls can sleep on the floor of the ship."

"That is a fine idea and we will stock the ship with water and wine and food supplies," said King Narendra. "I will get all of this ready and we can leave in the morning."

"It is a good plan," said Tall Sky. The king left and returned to the castle.

The soldiers packed up everything and the fire detail made two cooking fires. Halden asked the girls to get out of the wagons and sit down on some boulders beside the road. He said, "I am sure that you are wondering what all of this is about. We have purchased you to bring you back to Aksanda where you will be free." The girls laughed and applauded. "King Narendra has made it illegal to own slaves in Fantolo and has graciously offered the use of his own ship to return you. He will accompany us and will personally present you to King Aryante. We will be purchasing mattresses, pillows and blankets for your comfort on the voyage. King Narendra will stock the ship with provisions and we will leave in the morning. When we arrive at Free Port, we will take river boats upstream to Loss Port where we will rent wagons to Vivallen. This journey will take at least three days. When we arrive in Vivallen, you will shop for clothing. After meeting King Aryante, our soldiers will return you to your families or take you to a new town where you can work at a job or find a husband. We have people at Loadrel and Home Fire ready to help you."

A girl named Nanda asked, "What made King Narendra change his mind about slavery?"

Halden said, "He met Father God and asked Him to live in his heart. This changes people for the better. You see, when you ask Father God into your heart, He gives you spiritual gifts like love, compassion, patience, discernment of right from wrong, forgiveness, and healing. You can pray to Him for help whenever you want. Would you like to do this?" They all said yes at once. "Pray after me, 'Father God, please forgive me for all of my wrong doing and wrong thinking and come to live in my heart.'" The girls all prayed this prayer.

Halden said, "King Narendra signed a treaty and a trade agreement with Orendia and with Aksanda. We have already returned the slave girls from Orendia. While you are in the caravan, we ask you to refrain from speaking with the soldiers. They are here for your protection and must be constantly alert to dangers. You will be accompanied by a soldier whenever you leave your wagon. You will use a bowl, a spoon, and a cup and will wash them after each meal and return them to your wagon. Do you have any questions?"

"What about girls that were sold to people in other places in Fantolo? I have a friend who was taken out of the city," said Nanda.

"We will take the caravan to every town and village in Fantolo and we will buy them back. Then we will travel to Aksanda through Orendia, stopping to see King Jahiz. He has expressed interest in meeting King Aryante and may want to travel with us," said Halden.

"Please look for my friend and tell her that I am alright. Her name is Faervel and she is a Bright Elf. Her name means strong spirit," said Nanda.

"I will tell Quickturn and the soldiers to bring her to me as soon as we find her. There are many Bright Elves with us. We will keep her safe," said Halden. "I will place her in the second wagon with two girls who are writing an account of our journey. She may be able to help with that. Now, I want all of you to change into the men's clothing that you will find in your wagons. This will help to keep you safe until you reach Vivallen. Then report to the cook's fire to receive your food."

That night the girls slept safely with soldiers on guard. The girls awoke happy and hopeful. Some of them had been brought to Fantolo on ships and wondered what the king's ship would be like. After breakfast a king's messenger arrived to lead them to the King's ship. Ten wagons and six soldiers including three Bright Elves and Halden's second in command Adon followed him to Madhuri Port where the king's ship was anchored. It was a full day's journey to Madhuri Port, and King Narendra insisted on stopping for lunch just outside of the town of Katir. He took Tall Sky, Halden, Aleph and Gantio into town for lunch at a restaurant where they were served a sumptuous meal of lamb, potatoes and apple pie.

Then they left for Madhuri Port with the king riding in a carriage in the lead. They would reach Madhuri port in time to set up camp for the night. The king slept aboard his ship in his cabin, and his men slept in their bunks. The next morning there was much to be done. They loaded bedding and girls onto the ship. King Narendra greeted them and showed them the provisions and the sleeping area downstairs. The King had a cabin downstairs and a shelter on the deck. The ship was large with ornately carved wood on the sides and a dragon's head on the bow. The king ordered tha captain to get underway and the captain ordered his crew to unfurl the sails and raise the anchor. The sea voyage had begun.

Halden and some of his men bought mattresses, blankets, and pillows to replace the ones that were taken to the ship. Trinian, Gantio, Halden and several soldiers with extra horses rode into Madhuri to look for slave girls. Trinian took the lead in the conversations and Gantio translated. A tavern owner said that he had one slave, two brothels had some and the town chief had one. Trinian explained that it was now illegal to have slaves and showed him the king's edict. He brought out a pretty young girl and accepted payment for her. They sent her back to the caravan with a soldier. They did the same thing with the brothels and the chief and brought eight girls back to the caravan where Halden talked with them and told them to change clothes. Then they traveled east on King's Road to Katir where they purchased five more slave girls and on to Kunola to meet up with the main caravan. They pulled up to the main caravan. "Halden, what's this? Were there too many girls for the ship?" asked Tall Sky.

"No, these are new girls from Madhuri Port and Katir. I thought, since we were there, we should make a start," said Halden.

"Do you have a girl named Faervel?" asked Halden. "She is a Bright Elf and I promised her friend Nanda that we would look out for her. She should be in a wagon close to yours. I will introduce you to her." Halden brought Faervel to Tall Sky and introduced them.

"Faervel, welcome to our caravan. We will treat you well and keep you safe until we reach Aksanda. We will take you home. You can ride in the wagon behind ours. I'm sure my wife Melody will like to meet you. She has a friend at the castle in Vivallen who is a Bright Elf named Faerverin," said Tall Sky.

We have to decide on which area we should travel first," said Halden.

"I think we should tackle the most dangerous area first so that we will have fewer girls with us to protect from those dangers. Also, it is likely to be uncomfortably warm in the south. That is where we may encounter large animals and insects. We should do that area before we get tired out," replied Tall Sky.

"You are right. We will go south toward Lake Nirmala. There are several towns there. Let's start now and head for Jumara. We should be able to camp there after the sale." Tall Sky drove his wagon to Jumara Road and turned right. The wagons followed him and the caravan was once again on the mission. The air was warm and humid and the foliage was getting dense and had large leaves. There were groves of fruit trees and some small farms growing vegetables. They reached Jumara near dinner time and stopped the caravan. Trinian, Gantio, and Halden rode into Jumara and stopped at the local tavern. The tavern owner told them that there were several slaves at the brothel, but none at other places in town, so they rode to the brothel and informed the owner of the illegality of slavery, and he brought out two Aksandan girls and sold them to Trinian. They returned to the caravan and presented the girls to Melody, who helped them to change clothes and explained to them the purpose and rules of the caravan. The girls were delighted to be out of the brothel and on their way home.

At the sale, some things were purchased, but this was a small town and the sale didn't last long. By the time it ended, the cooks had dinner ready and the tired soldiers gratefully ate their food and relaxed for a while drinking ale. Halden said, "It's been a good day. We bought fourteen girls today and visited three towns. Tomorrow morning a group of soldiers will cross the Sakina Rantu River and visit the town of Mohana. It doesn't make sense to take all these wagons across the river. Then we will travel east from Jumara to Malati. The evening passed with fourteen girls visiting and laughing and sharing stories of their experiences. Melody shared her story of how she met Tall Sky and how he had shared Father God with her. She told them of how other girls had found Father God and had met men who married them after that. She told them of girls who had been badly mistreated, but after meeting Father God and asking Him to send His Spirit to live in their hearts, their pain went away and they became truly ready for love. Every one of them asked God for forgiveness and asked His Spirit to live in their hearts.

Everyone had a good night's sleep and woke rested in the morning. Six soldiers left for Mohana to buy back more slaves. It took them until early afternoon to return with two slave girls. They had been used to weave tapestries for a weaver whose hands had become arthritic. Melody told them the purpose and the rules of the caravan and gave them men's clothing to wear. After lunch the caravan resumed its journey southwest toward the town of Malati. The road was more a path with trodden down grass and the foliage became denser and larger with beautiful flowers. There were many birds and animals scurrying through the undergrowth. Daisy enjoyed looking out the window and watching all of this. Shanteel was busy drawing pictures of the plant and animal life. Melody wrote a narrative about it. Andra made a copy of Melody's writing and Faervel made a copy of Shanteel's pictures. Their project was progressing well. Melody also wrote a secret narrative on the evils of slavery including the stories that the girls told about their abuse. It was for the king's eyes only and did not include the girls' names to protect their privacy. She felt that the king should know the importance of his mission.

The girls practiced sewing by making nightgowns for themselves. They were beginning to feel calmer and more like themselves. They talked of what life was like on their farms with their families and wondered what their homecoming would be like. They all decided not to tell their families about the abuse that they had suffered. It would only cause them pain and worry. It would be much better to tell them that they worked hard for their owners.

Trinian said that Malati was located on a tributary of the Sakina Rantu. The land was flat and moist and the foliage was full of dangerous snakes and lizards. "Everyone must stay on the path and not leave it for any reason," said Halden. He rode down the line of wagons warning each driver. They traveled safely until reaching Malati. As they approached Malati, they noticed that the land had been tllled and planted with crops. The town was medium in size and had some stores, two taverns and a brothel. Trinian, Gantio and Halden with several soldiers and extra horses rode into town and stopped at a tavern. They ordered ale and talked with the owner showing him the king's edict about slavery. The owner said that he had one slave and that the town chief had one. There were two more at the brothel and one at the the other tavern. There was a maker of fish netting who had two slaves making nets and weaving rugs. Buying the slaves was almost effortless until the weaver, who did not want to sell his slaves. He depended on them for his business and had trained them well. Trinian explained to him that he faced time in the rock quarry if he refused to sell the girls. They reached an agreement, but Trinian had to pay the man well for the slaves.

Seven slaves were brought to the caravan where Halden told them the rules of the caravan. He told them about King Aryante's mission to return slaves to Aksanda. The girls were amazed by this. Some laughed and some cried. Halden introduced Melody and she explained that they would find men's clothing in a wagon and that they were to wear the clothes for their protection and that they were not to talk to the soldiers. Because of the area they were in, they could not leave the path to relieve themselves. There were buckets to use and then they would empty the buckets without stepping off the path. They washed clothing every three days and there were extra clothes for them to wear on that day. They would sleep six girls to a wagon. There was fabric to use to make nightgowns from and there should be one girl per wagon to help the others with this.

Trinian visited the town with several soldiers for protection. He told key persons about the sale at the caravan, and before long there were many people buying goods at the wagons. They sold enough merchandise to empty one wagon. They rented a cart, filled it with water kegs, and drove the cart to the town's well where they filled the kegs with water. Then they took the kegs back to the caravan and affixed them to the wagons. The fire detail made two cooking fires and the cooks made dinner using meat purchased from the town's grocer. By now they had twenty-one girls to feed and they had only visited five towns. Halden and Tall Sky were both feeling the weight of responsibility.

Halden said, "We have twelve more towns to visit and some of them are in areas with swamps and forests. I really didn't think that this many slaves would be in Fantolo."

Tall Sky said, "I know, but most of these slaves came by ships, so they didn't have that far to travel cross country. That made it much easier for the slavers. I am so disgusted with slave owners that it is hard to keep my peace. It is also hard for me to stay back at the caravan while you and Trinian do the buying."

"Trinian is the only one who knows the language, and we don't know how they would react to an elf. We also need you to stay and keep the girls calm. You also have to keep a special watch on Melody so that she doesn't interact with any more animals. Your little dragon might try a mating flight, and Melody might chase her into the undergrowth which could mean her death," said Halden.

"I will talk to her about that," said Tall Sky.

The dinner bell rang and everyone converged on the cook's fires to receive their food. Everyone ate standing up to avoid any insects on the ground. Tall Sky and Melody sat on the wagon seat and Tall Sky warned her again of the dangers in the area and told her that she was not to chase Daisy into the undergrowth. "I can keep her on the leash until we are in a better area," said Melody.

"You can do that," said Tall Sky. "When we are farther north near the forest, we might encounter wild miniature dragons. If one shows interest in Daisy, we could let her fly, but under no circumstances are you to chase her. Until then I will put up fish netting at your window. We should do that for each of the wagons tro keep out snakes and anything else while we travel through the south. I will get some soldiers to help me with it."

"What a great idea!" said Melody. She fed Daisy, put on her harness and leash and walked her up and down the caravan for exercise. Meanwhile, Tall Sky and some soldiers nailed fish netting to the wagon windows. After that they retired to their wagons for sleep. The soldiers took turns sleeping in the extra wagons and guarding.

The next morning after breakfast they headed east to Sunita traveling a dirt road. They arrived in Sunita before lunch and set up for a sale while Trinian, Halden and Gantio with several soldiers and extra horses rode to the town's only tavern. The tavern's specialty was rice wine which the tavern owner served them. The wine was good and very potent. Trinian and the owner conversed for a while and the owner went to the back and brought out a pretty Aksandan girl with long brown hair and blue eyes. She was surprised to see an Aksandan man standing before her. The owner said that she was the only slave girl in the town. He accepted payment for her and said that he would be happy to come to the caravan for the sale. Trinian visited other places in town letting them know of the sale.

Halden took the girl back to the caravan and delivered her to Melody who explained to her that she and other slaves were being returned to Aksanda by the order of King Aryante. She told her the rules of the caravan, led her to Father God and introduced her to the girls in her wagon. The cooks put out sandwich materials for lunch and everybody made their own.

"I sure am glad to have a good road to travel going south," said Tall Sky. "I'm always worried about rains making the ground muddy down here. It will be great to get to a more civilized area. I definitely do not like swamps and wetlands. They are too unpredictable. The weather is usually bad, and you can't live outside without being prey to everything that crawls, walks and flies. I really miss Aksanda."

After lunch the caravan traveled south on a main road that made traveling faster and safer. They were traveling past rice fields toward Curon. They could see people working in the fields harvesting rice. At one point Trinian rode over to a worker and asked him if they used slaves for this type of work. He said that only Fantolese worked in the fields and that he did not know of any slaves in the area.

They arrived in Curon in the late afternoon. Curon was a small town that catered to the rural community. There was one tavern and Trinian, Halden and Gantio with several soldiers and extra horses rode into town and talked with the tavern owner. He told Trinian that he had one slave and that the brothel had two slaves. There was a man who made rice paper who had one slave to help with the paper making. Trinian explained that having slaves was illegal now and that he was here to buy back the slaves for Aksandans who were returning them to their parents. He wasn't aware that they were children who were stolen from their parents. He gladly sold his slave girl Lindi to Trinian. He said that she was a good girl and a hard worker who helped his wife with the cooking and clean up at the tavern. Next they went to the rice paper maker and told him and he said that he didn't want any trouble with the king and sold them his slave girl. The last stop was the brothel and the owner did not want to sell his slave girls, but changed his mind when Halden asked the soldiers to come in. He arrived at a fair price with Trinian and they all rode back to the caravan. Halden then sent Trinian accompanied by several soldiers into town to let the people know about a sale at the caravan. Many of the townspeople came to the sale and purchased goods.

Because of the sale, dinner was later than usual but tasted better than usual. They had purchased meat and vegetables from the local grocer and had simmered them during the sale. They also made flatbread during that time. The new girls ate with Melody and Tall Sky. They still didn't know why they were there.

"It looks like a good part of Aksanda moved to Fantolo to live in wagons," said Lindi, the girl from the tavern.

"I'm sure it does," said Melody laughing. "We aren't moving here to stay. We are on the move through Fantolo to buy back our citizens and we intend to deliver them to their homes in Aksanda."

"That is a big job," said Lindi. "Why are you doing it?"

"King Aryante ordered it, trained the soldiers to be merchants, and bought all these wagons. He filled them with everything needed and signed a treaty with the Orendian king and King Narendra of Fantolo. We have already returned the slaves from Orendia and King Narendra has about sixty slaves on his ship taking them to King's Port. He plans to travel with them to Vivallen and present them personally to King Aryante," said Tall Sky.

"Why did two kings all of a sudden agree to sell back the slaves? Won't their people be angry with them?" asked Lindi.

Both kings asked Father God to live in their hearts and after that they saw you as children of your parents and children of God."

"How do you get God to live in your heart?" asked Lindi.

Tall Sky said, "Ask god for forgiveness and ask him to live in your heart. He loves you and wants you to know him and to live good lives. He will give you gifts of love, health, wisdom, patience, protection, guidance and will lead you into all truth. Would you please pray and ask Him for these?"

Melody led them in prayer and they all asked God to send His Sprit to live in their hearts.

Halden walked up and told them that it was time to go to bed. He briefly told them the caravan rules and escorted them to a wagon after showing them to the dish water.

"I am so happy," said Lindi. "I want to help. I've been helping to cook at the tavern all this time. Could I help with the cooking here?"

Halden said, "Change your clothes and we will talk with the cooks." Halden introduced her to the cooks who said that they would be happy to have her help them. She stayed in the cooks' wagon from then on.

Melody said, "Home Fire would love to have her." It was Melody's favorite time. At night she could cuddle with Tall Sky and have him all to herself. She thought that sleeping in the wagon was fun. It was like camping except that it was much safer and when it rained, it was cozy and dry. They slept well through the night and awoke to the sound of a rooster crowing.

The cooks had already been up preparing breakfast. There was ham and eggs and honey cakes. The new girls were surprised at how well all of this worked. It was fun to live outside. Breakfast was good and satisfying and after washing their dishes, everyone climbed back into their wagons and Halden called out, "Forward!" Tall Sky drove back onto the road and the caravan moved south toward Arvi and the Frothy Sea. Traveling toward the sea always gave Tall Sky a sense of freedom and expectation. The breeze coming from the sea was cooler than over the wetlands. Melody decided to sit up front and Daisy stretched her neck out sniffing the air and enjoyed watching the landscape. She saw a deer walking gracefully through a field and chirred.

The girls occupied themselves with sewing and teaching each other various kinds of stitches. They shared stories of their capitivity and marveled at their good fortune at being rescued. "Trinian said that Arvi is a seaport," said Hanna. "This time we will see a port without being a slave."

"I know. I remember being shoved and hit like I was a criminal being walked off the ship," said Shirl. "This time we have lots of soldiers to protect us. It feels good."

Within a few hours of traveling, the port town of Arvi came into view. Tall Sky pulled over across the street from the town. Halden said, "We will have lunch here and then take care of our business." The cooks brought out sandwiches and cold tea and everyone sat on the ground having a leisurely lunch. Then Trinian, Halden and Gantio took four soldiers and extra horses into town. They stopped at a tavern to get information. There was a healthy lunch crowd there. Trinian asked the owner to speak privately for a minute and they walked into the kitchen where he explained the mission and showed the owner the decree from King Narendra. The owner brought his slave girl to Trinian and accepted silver for her. He said that they should check with the chief of the town, the brothel, and the other tavern. Halden sent the frightened girl back to the caravan assuring her that they would take her home. Then they visited the chief and bought his slave. The other tavern was next and the owner was not happy to lose his girls, but he finally took silver for them. As usual, the brothel owner needed persuasion from the soldiers to sell his girls. In all, there were five girls rescued from this small port town. Trinian spread the word about the sale, and within the hour there were many customers buying goods from the soldiers. Trinian was busy the whole time answering questions and helping to make deals. He was a good trader.

After the sale, they packed up and drove east on the Sea Road until they were away from town and could have total privacy. Then the girls bathed first, the soldiers standing with their backs to the sea in front of them. When they finished, the men bathed while the girls waited behind the wagons. When bathing was completed, the caravan again traveled the Sea Road. The sea breeze was cool and the sea birds like gulls were flying about wanting handouts. There were fluffy clouds shading them from direct sunlight and the water was a turquoise blue. The land to the left was flat with long grasses and wildflowers. Melody said, "This is so beautiful that I would like to stay here and forget the inland part of the journey."

"That would be nice," said Tall Sky. "I'm not looking forward to being near the swamp and the forest, but I will do it for the girls. None of them deserved the treatment that they have endured."

"I know. It's amazing that they have survived it. I wonder how many of them died," said Melody.

"Culina, we cannot think about that. It is too sad, and we have rescued hundreds of slaves," said Tall Sky. "Now, just relax and enjoy the rest of the afternoon." The caravan traveled for several hours and stopped earlier than usual to wash clothing. The fire detail made two fires and heated up some water filling four bathtubs and everyone took turns washing their clothes. They hung them to dry on their wagons, or on lines strung between their wagons. While that was going on, the cooks made dinner. "We now have thirty-one slave girls and we have visited nine towns. I think we are doing very well," said Halden.

"Yes, I am very pleased with the outcome so far. With the girls from Kunola, we are close to a hundred girls," said Tall Sky. The laundry was done and the food was ready, so they brought their bowls to receive the stew and flatbread. It had been a good, productive day. After dinner the girls waded at the water's edge looking for seashells and letting the wind blow their hair dry. They were laughing and splashing in the water. It was as if nothing bad had ever happened to them. They could hear thunder in the distance so Halden ordered everyone into the wagons. The wind picked up and it started to rain. They would sleep well tonight.

The rain stopped before morning, so when they woke up, the sun was glittering on the waves of the Frothy Sea. The cooks had porridge with fruit and tea ready for breakfast. The girls ate their food and walked through the froth at the edge of the sea while the men fed and watered the horses. Melody put the harness and leash on Daisy and let her hop about in the water. The tide had brought in new seashells so she gathered some to take home.

It had been an exhilarating morning, but it was time to leave again, so everyone got back into the wagons and onto their horses, and they drove off, following the sea shore. They traveled on the Sea Road until they reached a road that turned to the left toward a town called Adya. They turned onto this road which passed by the Adya swamp. The air became moist and dense and they had to fend off mosquitoes. There was much standing water to the left with water lilies and algae and long reeds at the edge. They saw alligators swimming through the water lilies and watching them. One walked out of the water onto the road to get a closer view of the caravan. Large snakes swam through the water. There were trees growing out of the water with moss hanging from them and brightly colored birds perched there. Soon they reached Adya, a small town located near Lake Mandara.

Tall Sky drove up next to the outskirts of Adya and stopped. Trinian, Halden, Gantio and four soldiers with extra horses rode into town to the nearest tavern and talked with the tavern owner. He told them that there were two girls at the brothel and one at the chief's house. The net maker also had one to help make the nets. He had one, but he was going to keep her to help with the kitchen work. His was the only tavern in town, so he kept very busy. Trinian showed him the king's decree and order to sell slaves to the Aksandans, so he brought out his girl and sold her to them. The chief sold his girl to them without any trouble. The net maker was an old man who really needed the girl to help with knotting the nets, but he realized that he had to obey the king's order, so he sold his girl. The last stop was the brothel where they encountered the usual resistance. It took two soldiers to threaten him, but he finally relented and sold his girls. They left with five slave girls and took them to Melody.

The girls were scared and said nothing. Melody told them about their rescue and return to Aksanda. Their eyes opened wide and one girl said, "You mean that we won't be sold again?"

Melody answered, "That's right. You are free and we are here to protect you and to return you to your parents. These men are soldiers under orders from King Aryante. He believes that no one should have the right to kidnap children and to sell them into slavery. You are precious to him and that is why he created this caravan and trained his soldiers to be merchants. You will wear men's clothing for your protection and you will sleep in one of these wagons on mattresses. We have a long way to travel to buy slaves north of here. Do you have any questions? Some people from Adya will be coming to the caravan to buy things soon. After that we will have lunch. Until then, stay in your wagon."

Trinian had walked through Adya telling people about the sale, and soon people were making purchases. It had been a good day so far, especially since they would be leaving the swamp area that they had dreaded. After the sale, the cooks passed out sandwiches and fruit to be eaten on the way. The caravan drove north toward Nola, located on King's Road. They stopped near Lake Mandara to camp, not wanting to spend the night in Sattra Forest. They would rather do that part of the trip in the morning. Still, they were close enough to Sattra to stay vigilant and extra guards were posted. Not wanting to attract wild animals with the aromas of cooking, everyone ate sandwiches and fruit for the evening meal. They had some extra time now, so the soldiers groomed the horses and checked their hooves. The tack man checked all of the reins and straps and oiled them, replacing any of them that showed significant wear. The wheelright did the same to the wheels. They had traveled a long way and things needed maintenance for the second half of their journey through Fantolo.

The girls took off their caps and wandered around watching all of this. Being from farms, they were familiar with the grooming of horses and the maintenance of wagon wheels. They were beginning to relax and feel more normal. There were trees here, but they were sparse and they could see through them. There were armed soldiers on guard all around the caravan. They remembered the forest in Orendia and the giant mantises. At least this time they didn't have a sorcerer sending wild animals and insects after them. That night there were loud animal sounds like large cats shrieking, but the animals did not approach the caravan.

The next morning the cooks served porridge with fruit and tea, keeping cooking aromas to a minimum. The caravan traveled north toward Nola and the number of trees increased until the forest was dense on both sides of the road. About halfway to Nola, a pack of large wolves appeared on the road behind them wanting to kill one of the extra horses. The Bright Elves shot them with arrows killing them one by one until the wolves stopped chasing them and ate the fallen wolves. A cougar jumped from a branch onto one of the wagons, but jumped off after finding no food there. They increased speed until they reached Nola where they unhitched the horses, gave them a rubdown, and let them cool down. Then they watered the horses while Gantio, Trinian and Halden rode to the nearest tavern for information. They ordered ale and asked the owner about slaves in the town. The owner said that he had one, the brothel had three, and the chief had one. Trinian bought the slave and sent her to the caravan with a soldier. He bought the slave from the chief and talked to the owner of the brothel who was ready to toss one out for being pregnant, but he needed a good amount for the other two. Trinian paid the man and they all rode back to the caravan.

Melody had five new girls to counsel. Trinian rode back to town spreading the word of a sale at the caravan. He also purchased fresh meat and vegetables from the grocer. While he was gone, Melody told the girls about the purpose and the rules of the caravan. The girls from the brothel were so relieved that they cried and hugged Melody. The pregnant one named Chilia said, "I was supposed to be thrown out today. He said that a wild beast would probably kill me. Thank you for rescuing me."

Melody said, "We have other pregnant girls. Don't worry. There is a lady in Loadrel who has a big house with room for pregnant girls and there are men at Home Fire who want wives. You will be fine. We will be home before your baby is born. Two of my friends were slaves and they are pregnant and married. Now you girls should change clothes and stay in your wagon until the sale is over. It doesn't last long, but it does free up more wagons for people to sleep in. I see people coming now, so we have to get into our wagons. This one is yours. You will find the clothes in there." They got into their wagon and people showed up for the sale. The customers were very excited about the merchandise and purchased many things. Trinian helped with the bargaining and at the end of the sale, they had sold so much that they could rearrange things and free up several wagons.

After the sale, the soldiers were tired and hungry, so they drove the caravan across King's Road and traveled north for a short time where they pulled over to rest and have lunch. The girls were hot and tired and in need of water and food. They took off their caps to let their hair dry, drank some water and ate a sandwich sitting outside in some shade.

A red miniature dragon flew into camp circling around and around shrieking. Daisy became agitated and flew off Melody's shoulder to join him. Daisy landed on the ground and the male dragon mated with her. Then he flew away. Melody ran to her and picked her up and put her in the velvet bag so that she would calm down. She walked back to Tall Sky who said, "I knew this would happen and I am glad it happened here instead of in the Sattra Forest." Melody was shaking. She had felt the fear, anxiety amd excitement that Daisy had felt and she needed some wine. Tall Sky brought her some wine and told her to sit down on the wagon seat for a while. He brought a plate of food for Daisy and a sandwich for Melody. She put Daisy on her leash and gave her some food. Both of them became calmer. "What you were feeling is what Daisy was feeling because of the bond between you. If Daisy had been a full sized dragon, you would have felt that a hundred times more and you would have had to mate at the same time."

"I'm glad that she isn't a full sized dragon. She has never flown away from me before. Do you know how long it takes for her to lay an egg?" asked Melody.

"No, I don't," said Tall Sky. "We should make a nesting box for her. After she lays eggs, it will take two months for them to hatch, and we will want to give them to people who want them and will bond with them."

Halden walked over to Tall Sky and said, "You two had a bit of a scare. Is Daisy alright?"

"She's alright. She will be kept on a leash for a while, though. I would feel better if we were farther away from the forest. Some animals can range far looking for prey," said Tall Sky.

"I agree with you. There are about two hours of sunlight yet. I'll pass the word," said Halden.

Melody decided to get the new girls started on sewing projects. She gave each of them fabric suitable for a nightgown with needle and thread. She made sure that at least one girl in the wagon could teach the others how to sew. Some of the girls in the other wagons were finished with their nightgowns and they showed them to the new girls. The girls who were finished were given fabric for a dress. They had just finished when Halden said that they would be leaving soon. Everyone boarded the wagons and mounted the horses and Halden called out, "Forward!"

Shanteel, Andra, Faervel and Melody took advantage of the remaining light by documenting what had happened in the Sattra Forest. The girls worked on their sewing projects. Tall Sky drove until the light started to dim and there were fewer trees. He found a level grassy area and pulled over to camp. The soldiers unhitched the horses and fed and watered them, while the cooks fixed dinner. Halden said, "Tall Sky, we have made great progress. We have finished the south and are north of King's Road. We shouldn't find too many dangers from wild animals in the farm land."

Tall Sky replied, "I didn't like the south lands. At least we didn't see any mantises in the forest."

"Are the new girls settling in?" asked Halden.

"Melody has them making nightgowns. They are very happy to be away from their owners," said Tall Sky.

"We will be in Litya before lunch tomorrow and then it's King's Port for dinner," said Halden.

"Good. Our equipment is holding up well. The new tackman is doing a good job," said Tall Sky.

"He is. I can hardly wait to be on the Sea Road again. It's beautiful and refreshing to be by the Frothy Sea, and the girls love playing in the water. It's good for them." said Halden.

"The sea is healing for the mind and spirit. I love it," said Tall Sky.

"Why is it that you never settled in a port town?" asked Halden.

"I have been following the leading of God's Spirit," said Tall Sky. "He wanted me to travel and get to know the people of Aksanda and do what I could to help them."

"The people of Aksanda are lucky to have you," said Halden. The dinner bell rang and the campers lined up to receive their food. They had stew and flatbread for dinner with fruit for dessert. The girls spread blankets on the ground and sat on them while eating their dinner. Then they washed their dishes and got ready for bed. Everyone else did the same. It had been a tiring day.

# DEMONIC ACTIVITY

Tall Sky and Melody cuddled together with Daisy sleeping curled up on Melody's pillow. She dreamed of flying with her red dragon friend. Melody dreamed of the red dragon, too. The new girls found that sleeping on mattresses in a wagon was comforting. They felt hopeful for the first time since they had been stolen from their homes.

They woke to the smell of ham, eggs and hotcakes. The girls rushed to the cook's fire to receive their breakfast and tea. "What a great way to start the day!" exclaimed Chilia. They walked over to their wagons to eat. After breakfast, they washed their dishes and climbed into their wagons.

The men had taken care of the horses and hitched them up before breakfast, so Halden called out, "Forward!" Tall Sky drove back onto the road heading north toward Litya, a small town in the farming area. The road was good and there were wildflowers growing in the fields. In the distance they could see farm buildings. The sky was blue with a few clouds and the wind was cool. It was altogether a pleasant day for travel.

Tall Sky said, "How is Daisy today?"

Melody replied, "She is fine. She ate a good breakfast, and she seems to be happy." Daisy chirred and rubbed her face against Melody's cheek. Melody snuggled up to Tall Sky and said, "I love you."

Tall Sky replied, "I love you too, Culina," and he kissed her on the cheek. "We are blessed to have each other." They enjoyed the ride to Litya, which didn't take very long because of the drive the afternoon before. "See the homes up ahead? We are close to Litya." Soon they were on the edge of town and Tall Sky drove off the road to an empty area. Trinian, Gantio, and Halden took four soldiers with extra horses into town and stopped at the tavern.

Trinian told the owner of their mission and of the caravan of goods for sale. "Are there any slave girls in town?" asked Trinian. He showed the king's edict regarding the illegality of slavery and the order to sell slaves to the Aksandans.

The owner said, "I have one, the brothel has two and the bakery has one. I will get her." He brought out his slave who was dressed in work clothes and had been cooking in the kitchen. He sold her to Trinian and they left with her. Then they stopped at the bakery and bought the baker's slave and all the sweet rolls he had. They rode to the brothel and talked to the owner who said that one of his girls was pregnant, but two of them were still good. He wanted too much for them, but Trinian bargained with him and they agreed on a price. They rode back to the caravan with the girls and delivered them to Melody. Then Trinian and a soldier went into the town and spread news of the sale.

Melody told the new girls, "We are on a mission from King Aryante to rescue slave girls and return them to Aksanda. The men on this caravan are Aksandan soldiers and are with us to keep you safe. You will wear men's clothing so as not to attract any unwanted attention. From this point on you are free. When we return to Aksanda, you will have the choice to return to your families or to live in a town and work at a job. Our journey is long. We have bought back many other girls. There are about sixty girls on a ship to King's Port and we have about forty girls with us. You will each be given a bowl, a spoon, and a cup which you will wash after every meal and keep with you in your wagon. For now you must stay in your wagon during the sale." She took them to an empty wagon and told them to change clothes.

People arrived for the sale and bought the heavier items. They wanted the bathtubs, cauldrons for soap making, butter churns and cooking utensils. By the end of the sale they had emptied a wagon and lightened the wagons which would alleviate the strain on the horses. Melody gave fabric to each of the new girls so they would have something to do on the way. Halden told Tall Sky to drive down the road toward King's Port. They would have lunch close to there.

They were off again traveling happily toward the sea with some girls who had never seen it.

By lunchtime they were close to King's Port and they stopped for lunch. They could smell the sea on the breeze. The cooks passed out sandwiches and fruit and everyone walked about eating lunch and stretching their legs. When they had finished, they climbed back into the wagons and left. They soon arrived at the outskirts of King's Port. It was larger than other towns and stretched out along the seashore. There were several ships and smaller fishing boats in the harbor. People were out and about shopping in the town. The girls all wanted to go into town and walk around, but Halden said that this kind of action would draw the attention of unsavory people and he forbade it. They must stay in their wagons until after the sale. Then they would travel down the shore where they could bathe in the sea. The girls didn't like this, but they understood the logic of it.

Trinian, Halden, Gantio and four soldiers with extra horses rode into King's Port and spoke with a tavern owner who told them where the slave girls were. He had one working in the kitchen, the town chief had one, the brothel had three, and the net maker had two. Trinian explained the purpose of their mission and showed him the decree of the king and he immediately sold his slave girl who was busy making dinner. She was terrified until she saw Halden and the soldiers and heard them speak Aksandan. They next visited the town chief, who sold them his girl dressed in a beautiful gown. Next they visited the netmaker who just about cried when he read the decree because he was old and needed the girls for his business. Trinian offered him a generous price for the girls to make up for his loss. They sent the girls back to the caravan and brought back more horses. Then they visited the brothel and confronted the owner who was in no mood to sell his girls, so the soldiers came in and stood there looking threatening. He finally agreed to sell the girls for a high price and they took the girls back to the caravan. Trinian took several soldiers with him when he spread the word of the sale, and almost immediately customers came to shop. Melody took the new girls into a wagon and explained the purpose and the rules of the caravan.

The sale went very well and they were able to empty out two more wagons. Halden said, "We had a good sale and it's time to move on toward Stavu Port. We'll stop for bathing on the way. There's plenty of time to get near to Stavu Port to set up camp." He called out, "Forward!" and Tall Sky drove onto Sea Road heading north. Halden said, "I think we should stop about half way to Stavu Port for bathing. It will be a good refreshing time for everybody."

"I agree," said Tall Sky. "That way it won't seem like such a long trip to Stavu. Let me know when you're ready."

Melody was still in the wagon with the new girls. They were still getting used to the idea that they wouldn't be abused any more. Tiala said, "I didn't know how long I could survive living in the brothel. I thought that one day a drunk, angry fisherman might just kill me. I forgot what fun was and had lost belief in love or goodness. If it wasn't for memories of my family, I might have killed myself. I prayed sometimes and asked God to take me to heaven. I asked Him to not let me get pregnant and used lard and bathed a lot."

Melody said, "I think God must have heard you and sent us to help you. Tall Sky and I have had little else on our minds for about a year now. I think that Father God had King Aryante to create this mission. It took a whole winter just to get the caravan ready and to train the soldiers. He also gave us the money to buy back the slave girls and to buy all the merchandise and provisions. He said that if the kings would not sign the treaties, he was willing to go to war for you. Father God will guide and direct a king if the king knows Him."

"I was in the original group of runaways in Malwood Forest when I met Tall Sky. He helped one of our friends named Trag. Father God directed him to help us out of Malwood Forest where there was a witch named Avidora after us. When Trag was in the forest, he saw a girl being auctioned off and he and the Loadrel Militia and Home Fire men rode to Malwood Forest, killed all the slavers, and rescued the girls. Then there was a battle between the Bitter Elves and the king's soldiers, the dwarves, and the Bright Elves. Tall Sky had a leading role in that and God led him and directly helped in the battle. In fact, a bright light like lighting wrote above the Othrund tunnel entrance, 'These Are My People. Awakening Now.'" You see, Father God can be a great help to people."

Tiala said, "I must thank Father God for helping us. Also, I would like Him to help me to find a husband when we get home."

"Thanking Him is always a good idea. But to really honor Him, you could ask Him to send His Spirit to live in your heart. Then He will give you gifts of forgiveness, love, patience, charity and others. He will guide you into truth and give you discernment so that you can tell right from wrong and help you to make the right decisions. To have all of this, you just need to ask Him to forgive you and ask Him to live in your heart." Melody led them in prayer and all of the girls asked for God's Spirit to live inside of them.

Tall Sky stopped the wagon and everybody climbed out of their wagons. The cooks passed out sandwiches and everyone sat on the warm sand to eat. After lunch, the girls grabbed towels and soap and headed to the beach while the soldiers stood in a line facing the wagons. This was the first time of feeling the cold sea water for Tiala's group. They splashed each other and squeeled and then washed their hair immersing in the water to rinse. Afterwards they dressed in clean clothes and went back to the wagons. The soldiers bathed next. Halden noticed a ship on the horizon sailing towards them and ordered the girls back into the wagons and the men to don their weapons. The ship dropped anchor and lowered smaller boats to row into shore. They looked like a rough bunch of pirates. Halden, Quickturn and Trinian stepped forward to meet them with about forty soldiers standing at attention in front of the wagons. Trinian addressed the pirates asking them why they came to shore.

The pirates said that they wanted gold, silver and gems. They had seen the girls bathing and they wanted time with the girls. Trinian said no and that they were ready to defend themselves. The soldiers unsheathed their swords and the Bright Elves notched their arrows. Trinian said, "If you leave now, no one will be killed. We fight to the death!" The pirates were determined, thinking that a bunch of merchants would be no match for their fighting prowess. Also they had in mind taking girls to their ship, raping them and then throwing

221

them overboard. They drew their weapons and attacked. Ten of them caught arrows. The rest of them matched sword to sword in mortal combat. Only five of them survived the attack by rowing out to their ship.

"Well, that was a new one," said Halden. After checking the bodies for gems and silver and confiscating their weapons, they threw the bodies into the sea for the fish to enjoy. Then it was back to business. Halden called, "Forward!" Tall Sky drove back onto the Sea Road and they drove the last of the afternoon reaching Stavu Port before nightfall. They decided to camp just before reaching Stavu Port so that they could have dinner and recuperate from the day's activities. While the cooks prepared dinner, the men groomed and fed the horses and the tackman examined the leather straps and oiled them.

"This stew is really good," said Melody. Daisy had finished hers and was taking a nap in her pouch. "Were the pirates very good fighters?"

"They were fair fighters, but they lacked the skill and the strength of our battle hardened soldiers," said Tall Sky.

"Are you going to sell the weapons you took from them?" asked Melody.

"I'll have to talk to Halden about that," replied Tall Sky. "Why? Do you want one?"

"I might want to use them for a display to go with the pictures and narrative," said Melody.

"That's a good idea. I'll talk to him about it," said Tall Sky. "I think we should wash clothes now so we'll be ready to travel." Tall Sky mentioned it to Halden who gave the order to heat water in the tubs. The new girls learned what it was like to wash clothes outdoors and hang them up to dry on lines strung out on the wagons. While they were doing this, several travelers rode by coming from Stavu Port. Trinian spoke with them about the caravan and about the pirates. They said that the pirates had been troubling smaller ships that sailed out of Stavu Port and King's Port, but this is the first they heard of them attacking on land.

After doing laundry, everyone sat around sipping a cup of wine and enjoying the sunset colors reflecting off the sea. "This is so beautiful and I am so happy. The journey has been good and successful. We have a really nice bunch of girls with us." said Melody. "Halden, how long will it take to finish the northern area?"

Halden replied, "I've been studying the map and I think we should go directly to Samir next, then go south around Lake Nanda to Pria, and then continue south to Stromin and cross the river to Rasala. That will take care of the northeast area. You really don't know how long it will take until you do it. The northwest part of the country only has six towns, but two of them are north of the Adri Hills. I don't recommend taking the wagons through the hills, so we will have to send a detachment of soldiers to that part. There are Galo and Pervati north of the Adri Hills.

"It's getting pretty late. I think Melody and I will turn in," said Tall Sky.

"I'll tell the rest to retire, I'm tired too," said Halden.

The night passed peacefully with the sound of the surf lulling everyone into a deep sleep. The next morning came with the sound of sea birds and the aroma of hot cakes and ham. The girls were hungry and rushed to the cooks' fires for food. It was thoroughly enjoyable to eat outside and watch the waves. Tiala said, "This is like being on a vacation! I love this." After breakfast they straightened up their wagons and the men fed and hitched up the horses. Halden called out, "Forward!" and Tall Sky pulled onto Sea Road going north to Stavu Port.

Stavu was little more than a fishing village spread out on either side of a very small town and a dock for small boats. However, when Trinian inquired about slave girls, the tavern owner said that there were four slave girls in town, so Trinian, Halden and a few soldiers bought them and brought them back to Melody. The girls were scantily clad, so Melody immediately had them change clothes. She then explained about the mission and the rules of the caravan. The sale went well, but didn't last long, so they were able to leave for Samir hoping to be there by mid afternoon. While the wagons were moving, the cooks made sandwiches and passed them out when they stopped for a break. Halden told them to eat and relieve themselves now, because they would not stop until they reached Samir.

Halden said, "Tall Sky, we bought enough fish to have it for dinner tonight. There's nothing like freshly caught fish."

"I know, and it may be a week or more before we reach the western shore. I've been studying the map. I do wish there was a way to speed up this journey," said Tall Sky.

"There isn't. Most of us will have a few days of rest, though, while some soldiers go north of the hills to clear out two towns," said Halden. "I'm going to tell everybody to get back into the wagons. We need to keep on moving." Soon they were on their way again.

The caravan pulled up to the outskirts of Samir in late afternoon and Trinian, Gantio, Halden and four soldiers rode into town to visit the tavern. The owner said that most of the people who use the town are farmers and mainly bought things that they needed to run their farms. Most of them didn't use the brothel, but there was a small one. It had one slave girl, he had one, and the mill had one. Trinian showed him the decree of the king and he sold his slave to Trinian. Then they visited the mill where the owner had a girl working on filling bags. He didn't want to sell her, but he did. The brothel owner needed some physical persuasion, but he finally relented and sold his girl. Trinian and two soldiers visited the town letting everyone know of the sale, and soon the caravan was crowded with interested customers. It was a good sale, so the soldiers could rearrange things producing one empty wagon. They pulled on down the road looking for a good place to camp. The land was farmland, so it was easy to find a flat area for the camp.

The girls climbed out of the wagons, happy to be able to walk about. The fire detail made two cooking fires and the soldiers unhitched the horses, fed, watered, and groomed them. Then they pitched their tents and put their bedding into them. By the time chores were done, dinner was ready. They sat on blankets on the ground to eat. "This fish is delicious," said Melody. "Daisy likes it too."

"That's the benefit of being near the sea. I always enjoy it," said Tall Sky. "Do you know that we have fifty-eight girls now?"

"Yes," repied Melody. "What if we run out of room in the wagons?"

Tall Sky laughed. "Don't worry. We have enough wagons to house at least one hundred and twenty girls, and we also have tents."

"I forgot about the tents. It's a good thing the other girls went by ship," said Melody.

"That is a clear example of how God leads kings," said Tall Sky.

"I'm so glad," said Melody. "God has been very kind to us."

"I love you, my darling," said Tall Sky and he kissed her.

"I love you, too," she said. "Let's clean our dishes and go to bed."

The night passed quietly and peacefully. The new girls were happy to be starting new lives and slept well until the morning when they were awakened by the smell of sweet rolls and eggs. The world was looking better all the time. They were looking forward to seeing Lake Nanda. They had heard that it was a pretty lake and Halden said that they would camp there tonight. Tall Sky and Melody sat on the wagon seat to eat breakfast and drink tea. Melody said, "Daisy has her appetite back. She's eating more than usual and wants more of my sweet roll."

Tall Sky said, "She has eggs in her tummy now and she will slow down when the eggs develop."

"That makes sense," said Melody. They finished eating and washed their dishes. Halden ordered people back into the wagons and, in a few minutes, he called, "Forward!" Tall Sky drove back onto the road heading south toward Lake Nanda. The new girls busied themselves making nightgowns and the other girls made dresses. Shanteel, Faervel and Andra worked on the book. Shortly, Melody joined them to document yesterday's activities. Trinian and Gantio were sitting up front with Tall Sky. Gantio translated.

"Trinian, you handled yourself very well with those pirates," said Tall Sky.

Trinian laughed and said, "I'm not a soldier, but I managed to kill one of them. I have practiced with the sword and knife."

"I was surprised and I salute you," said Tall Sky.

Gantio said, "I waited it out in the wagon. The girls needed protecting." They laughed. "I just kept on telling them that everything would be alright."

"Trinian, tell us about Lake Nanda," said Tall Sky.

"Lake Nanda is very large and blue. From one side, you can't see the other. It has big fish that are good to eat. There is wildlife around it like bears, cougars, deer, and other animals," said Trinian.

"It sounds like a nice place to camp, but I think we should camp a bit away from it. I don't feel like fending off wild animals at this point," said Tall Sky. "We should camp near Pria after the sale. We can water the horses and renew our own water supply there and get back on the main road headed south to Stromin."

Trinian said, "This is farmland, but Prians make other things than farm products. They buy flax from merchants north of here and make paper, fabric, rope, and other things from it. There is a store full of scrolls that one can buy. The people who live there are very creative. They make beautiful things that can be purchased." This peaked Tall Sky's interest.

"I am definitely going shopping there," said Tall Sky. "Trinian, would you be willing to translate some of the scrolls for me? There might be some that we could use in our schools."

Trinian said, "I would be happy to. It will give me something to do on our journey. Gantio would have to help with it, since I don't know your language."

"I thank you," said Tall Sky.

When they reached the west side of Lake Nanda, they stopped for lunch. There were some trees here, but not thick forest. The cooks set out sandwiches and wine, and they walked along the shore eating and enjoying the view of blue water, reeds, long grasses and wildflowers. There were several fishing boats far out on the water. Halden told everyone to bathe here, because they wouldn't be able to bathe near Pria. The girls really enjoyed this. The water was clear and fresh and warmer than the sea water. When they had finished, Halden told everyone to get back into the wagons and called out,

"Forward!" They drove along the south shore of Lake Nanda until reaching Pria, where they pulled up close to the town and stopped.

Halden, Trinian, Gantio and several soldiers rode into town and stopped at a tavern. There were several customers having ale and talking. Trinian asked the owner if there were any slave girls there. The owner said that there were a few slaves working in small businesses and one in the brothel. One old man had a slave girl to help him make tents, ropes and nets. One slave girl worked at the grist mill and there was one at the brothel. Trinian told him about the sale at the caravan and about the king's decree regarding slavery. After Trinian helped with the purchase of the girls, he walked about the town telling people of the sale. Then he helped Tall Sky to shop for special items for his home and for the schools at Loadrel and Home Fire. He bought paper, pigments to make paints for the schools and for Faerverin, a painting of dragons for Melody, and some scrolls for the schools. By the time they took their purchases back to the caravan, the sale was in full swing.

Customers here were mainly interested in decorative items and bathtubs. Some jewelry was sold to a jeweler who wanted to reproduce the designs. After the sale, Tall Sky showed Melody what he had purchased, and she was delighted. She loved the painting of dragons flying and was keenly interested in the scrolls. Trinian said that he and Gantio would begin translating them for her. There were scrolls on history, animals, philosophy, and medicine.

While Trinian and Gantio were busy with translating, Melody talked with the new girls in their wagon. The girl named Ashya had worked at tent making. She said, "My master was kind to me and gave me fabrics to make clothing for myself. I was able to bring those clothes with me, so I can just help Nina and Larissa to make their clothes."

Nina said, "That's good, because I don't know much about sewing. I worked at the mill filling flour sacks and cleaning. It was hard work, but my master was not mean to me."

Larissa said, "I was in a brothel, and I didn't get beaten, but I had to put up with men using me. I would think about my home in Aksanda until they were done. Thank God I am not there any more."

Melody said, "I believe that Father God sent us here to rescue you. He loves you and wants you to be free to marry and live good lives. If you asked Him to forgive you and live in your heart, He would give you gifts of love, patience, joy, peace, and healing. All you have to do is talk to him like you would talk to a friend. Would you like that?" All three of them prayed with Melody and felt more happy and hopeful. "I am going back to my wagon now. It's time to leave."

Halden called, "Forward!" and Tall Sky pulled onto the main road heading south toward Stromin. They would be near Stromin for dinner. Passing near to a large farm, they stopped to buy eggs, milk, butter, meat, fruit and vegetables. The farmer was happy to sell to to them and he bought a tub from them. He said that none of the farmers in the area had slave girls. After loading their food, the caravan proceeded to travel toward Stromin assured of a good dinner and breakfast tomorrow. It had been a good day and everyone wanted to be done with Stromin and have a good dinner.

Stromin, being close to Kunola, was a fair sized town with lots of activity. People were bustling about conducting business, shopping and greeting each other. Tall Sky stopped very close to the town and Trinian, Gantio and Halden with three soldiers and extra horses rode into town to the nearest tavern where they inquired about slaves in the town. Trinian showed him the decree and he immediately brought out a slave girl and sold her to them. Then they visited the brothel where they purchased two more slave girls. Another tavern sold them one slave girl and the town chief sold them one. They returned the girls to the caravan and delivered them to Melody, who counseled them and told them about the rules of the caravan. She gave them each their dishes and some fabric and introduced them to the other girls. Melody said, "With you five, we now have sixty-one girls on the caravan and we have nine more cities to visit. We will stop at Kunola one more time to see if any more girls were turned in to the queen. King Narendra is escorting sixty of our girls on his ship to visit King

Aryante. The girls were totally amazed by this. When we get to the Aikasse Plateau in Orendia, we will probably visit with dragon riders. They are our friends. Let's all get into our wagons and wait for the sale to be over. Then we will travel a short way to our evening campground."

The sale was very busy with many customers wanting to buy. They bought a variety of things including jewelry, decorations, fabric, cooking utensils and bathtubs. Then the soldiers put things away and they had freed up another wagon. Halden called "Forward!" and the wagons turned south for a short distance where they set up camp next to a river.

The fire detail made two cooking fires and the cooks brought out big pots full of meat and vegetables. Meanwhile, Trinian, Gantio and several soldiers with extra horses rode into town to the bakery and bought all the baked goods that the baker had. Then they asked if she could bake thirty-five pies to be picked up in the morning. She said that she could, but she would have to hire some girls to help prepare the fruit. Trinian said that he would pick them up in the morning and he paid her half of the price so that she could buy ingredients. They didn't tell everyone because it was to be a surprise.

By the time they arrived at the caravan, dinner was ready and the horses were taken care of. They were very pleased with themselves when they handed the cooks bags of bakery. The sweet pastries and dinner rolls were a welcome addition to the meal. Tall Sky and Melody sat on a log and ate their food. Daisy particularly enjoyed the sweet pastry. After the meal, Melody put Daisy's harness on her and walked her about for exercise. It was a pleasant evening with cool air and a beautiful sunset. Then they sat up on the wagon seat sipping wine and watching the stars. There were myriads of stars twinkling in a clear sky. Tall Sky put his arm around Melody and they relaxed enjoying the sky. It was getting chilly, so everyone retired for the night.

Early in the morning, Trinian and some soldiers with extra horses returned to the bakery to get the pies. Trinian gave her some extra silver for the pie tins and took the pies back to the camp. The cooks were preparing scrambled eggs and ham and just about fainted when the soldiers opened bags containing apple pies. They served a piece of pie with every breakfast and everyone enjoyed the delicious food. Afterward the girls drank tea while the soldiers took care of the horses.

The caravan crossed the river over a bridge on the main road and then turned right on the road to Rasala. By the afternoon they reached the town, which was much like Stromin. Rasala was the closest town to Kunola. Like Stromin, it was a busy town with much actvity. Halden told Tall Sky to stop for lunch, and everybody took a walk around the wagons while eating their sandwiches. Setting up and conducting two sales a day was tiring for the soldiers, so they welcomed every break. They were thankful that the people of this country were more gentle than the Orendians, but they were in the heartland where most people were farmers.

After lunch, Trinian, Halden, Gantio and three soldiers with extra horses rode into town to the nearest tavern where they ordered ale and talked with the owner. Trinian told him of their mission and showed him the king's decree. He had a slave girl named Lidra helping his wife in the kitchen and he thanked her for her service and sold her to Trinian. He said that she should take her clothes and gave her some silver. She cried and hugged his wife goodbye. His wife had been like a mother to her.

Next they rode to two businesses and bought girls who were working there. The last place was a brothel. As usual, the brothel owner argued and complained, but he finally sold his two slaves. They were dressed in rather exotic costumes and were happy to meet Aksandans. The soldiers brought the girls to Melody, who talked with them, gave them men's clothing, and told them that they should stay in the wagon during the sale. She gave them fabric to use for the making of clothes.

Trinian, Gantio, Tall Sky and some soldiers with extra horses rode into town to buy some groceries and to spread word about the sale. They bought all of the bakery that the baker had and bought all the candy that the grocer had. Trinian was determined to show the girls that he liked them and sympathized with them. Tall Sky bought Melody a new nightgown. By the time they returned with the groceries, the sale was underway and the customers were buying things. Trinian spent the next hour helping with the bargaining. After the sale, the soldiers repacked the merchandise so that one more wagon was empty. Halden told Tall Sky to drive due east toward the road leading to Pravata. Halden called, "Forward!"

Trinian and Gantio spent the afternoon translating a scroll into the Aksandan language and Tall Sky really enjoyed listening to the history of Fantolo. It described kings and fights with the highlanders who lived in the northern Adri Hills and the Katakin Mountains. The highlanders were described as unruly roughians with no manners, who dressed in wool and animal skins. They fought with clubs, spears, and knives. They didn't bathe often, so they were smelly. They all wore unkempt beards and long hair. Their armor consisted of a breastplate made of thick layers of hide. They lived communally in buildings housing five families with no marital restrictions. Most Fantolese people considered them to be barbarians and would have nothing to do with them.

"Well, that was more than I wanted to know about the northerners," said Tall Sky. "I hope that we don't have to deal with them. I've got to tell Halden and Quickturn about this."

Gantio said, "There is more. They fought dragons on the Avika Plateau near the mountains. They lost many soldiers to these dragons, but they did manage to kill some dragons."

"Melody won't like this and neither do I," said Tall Sky. "I won't take her there."

"I see the beginnings of a town up ahead. It should be Pravata." Tall Sky pulled over on the outskirts of town and stopped. The soldiers began arranging the merchandise on tables while Trinian, Gantio, Halden and four soldiers with extra horses rode into town and stopped at the nearest tavern where they ordered ale and talked with the owner. Trinian informed him of the mission and showed him the decree of the king. The owner informed Trinian that there were two girls at the brothel and one at the bakery. He did not have one, but he could use the extra help. They bought the three girls and all of the goods at the bakery and returned to the caravan except for Trinian and two soldiers, who spread word of the sale.

The new girls were dumbfounded. "Why do these men want us?" asked one girl. "Where are we going?" asked another. "I'll bet I know why they want us," said a girl from the brothel.

"And you would be wrong," said Melody. "These are soldiers sent by King Aryante to bring his citizens back home to their families. King Narendra has decreed that slavery is illegal in Fantolo and he wants the slaves sold to us. Aksanda and Orendia are already slave free countries. We only have five more towns to visit and then we are going home. We sent about sixty girls home by ship from Fantolo and we have about seventy girls with us now. Your families will be so happy to have you back and we will talk about your experiences later, but right now I need you to go into this wagon and change into the clothes you find in there and put your hair under a cap. You must stay in your wagon until after the sale. Then we will drive a short way from town to camp and have dinner. When you are dressed, I will join you in your wagon for the duration of the sale."

People started coming to the sale, and Melody climbed into the wagon to talk with the new girls. "My name is Melody and this is my friend Daisy." Daisy chirred and rubbed cheeks with Melody. "I have not been a slave, but I have known and helped many slaves. My husband and I met in Malwood Forest when I was a runaway with my friends. He is a Bright Elf who Father God directed to help my friend Trag to escape from Avidora at the slave auction. I found Daisy's egg in Malwood. Since then, Tall Sky and I have been together helping slaves all through Aksanda, Orendia, and Fantolo," said Melody.

"Why is King Narendra freeing the slaves?" asked Lidra.

"We told him about Father God and he asked Father God to send His Spirit to live in his heart. That changes a person for the better and he realized that all of you are God's own children," said Melody.

"Would it help me? I have been miserable ever since I was kidnapped," said Lidra. "I don't know how to live after all this. I don't even know how to feel."

"You take one day at a time and live it. You will feel more like yourselves every day. It would make you feel better to talk to God. You ask Him to forgive you and to send His Spirit to live in your hearts. He will do this and give you gifts of love, guidance, knowing right from wrong, healing and patience. Your lives will change for the better. Just say the words after me." The girls prayed with Melody and then lay down to rest.

Soon the sale was over and the soldiers packed up. Halden called out, "Forward!" and the wagons moved back onto the road heading east toward the Sakina Rantu River. When they were clear of the town, they set up camp and the cooks made dinner while the soldiers took care of the horses and the girls took off their caps and walked around the wagons for exercise. "Halden!" called Tall Sky. "I need to talk with you and Quickturn together." They found Quickturn grooming his horse. Tall Sky said, "Trinian and Gantio were translating one of the scrolls we bought that spoke of past kings and wars. The scroll described the northern people who live in the hills and the mountains as being barbarians who were fighters with no manners. They lived communally in a building with five families, didn't bathe often and wore unkempt beards and long hair. They wore animal skins for clothing. They fought with knives and spears and wore breastplates made of several thicknesses of leather. Also, there were dragons that killed many of the soldiers. I have decided to not take my wagon and the wagon behind mine into the hills."

"Metos is our next town and is located near the Adri Hills. We have too many girls to take them into those hills. We can pay a farmer to let us camp on his land while we send in soldiers through the hills. Galo is located on the northern side of the hills, and near the mountains is Pervati. We may need to hire locals who really know the area to be our guides and scouts. Some people must travel that direction, or there wouldn't be towns there," said Halden.

"I agree," said Quickturn. "I really don't want to fight dragons, but I think we could if we had to. Guides would know the best way to avoid them and to hide if need be."

"We don't even know if slavers came this far north, and there is another possibility. It is possible to reach Pervati by sea," said Tall Sky.

"We will decide after talking with the locals in Metos," said Halden. The dinner bell rang and everyone converged on the cooks' fires.

There was stew, rolls, and apple pie for dessert. Apple pie was Daisy's favorite dessert, so she was a happy camper. They spread out blankets on the ground and ate dinner. The new girls were delighted to know that they would be fed well on this trip. Lidra said, "I am very impressed with this. The cooks must be busy all day to prepare food for so many."

"They work in their wagons all day to feed us. One of our slave girls who worked in the kitchen of a tavern is helping the cooks," said Melody. "She did such a good job for him and his wife that he thanked her and gave her some silver. I'm going to ask a friend of ours named Beldock if he would like to hire her to help his wife cook at the Laborer's Reward in Loadrel. Wherever I shop, I look for spices for them."

After dinner they sat sipping wine and watching the sky. Suddenly the wind started and the temperature dropped instantly. It was too cold to remain outside, so the girls took refuge in their wagons. Quickturn ran to Tall Sky and said, "This isn't normal. I sense something evil nearby."

Tall Sky replied, "So do I. This is demonic. Didn't you say that before Ahriman died, he called on the demon Melki-resha? You banished Melki-resha, but he has legions of demons at his command."

Quickturn looked up and saw a demon who said, "Karkotaka will destroy you!" His face turned into a funnel cloud racing toward the caravan causing the wagons to rock back and forth lifting wheels off the ground, tipping over some of them. The Bright Elves assembled and Tall Sky said, "We bind you in the name of Father God!" The Bright Elves held their hands up toward the funnel cloud sending forth beams of bright light forming one larger beam that circled around the funnel cloud. "We cast you out in the name of Father

God, and you may never return!" There was a scream as the funnel cloud dissipated and the demon sped away high into the sky.

The soldiers ran to the overturned wagons to get the girls out and then, with much effort, righted the wagons. The wheelright came out to check the wagons for damage. Some of the wheels needed repairs. Melody checked the girls for injuries and she and Tall Sky laid hands on their injuries and prayed for them to be healed. Then she gathered the girls together and Tall Sky explained what had happened. He told them about Ahriman and how he had tried to kill them in Orendia and how, when the dragon riders had torched him, he invoked the demon Melki-resha to avenge him. That demon was banned from Phayendar, but he had other demons stationed around Phayendar's moon. "One of those demons, Karkotaka, attacked us just now in the form of a funnel cloud and we bound him and cast him out in the name of Father God. I suspect that we may yet have trouble from the other three demons there," said Tall Sky.

Quickturn gathered his Bright Elves and said, "We must keep vigilance from now on. If I'm right, we will face three more attacks disguised as natural occurrences. I think they waited this long to get as many kills as possible. Some of our girls were hurt, but we are all still alive. Let's take care of the horses while the soldiers are putting things back in order and checking the roofs." When everything was repaired, they went to sleep with extra guards posted in rotating shifts throughout the night. The horses were tied to the wagons for safety.

In the morning, the cooks made porridge, ham and tea with pastries from the bakery. It was a welcomed treat. The girls talked about the funnel cloud and how the Bright Elves had tied it up with God's power and had cast it out. After breakfast, the soldiers hitched up the horses and Tall Sky drove back onto the road heading west toward the river.

When they reached the Sakina Rantu River, the earth began to shake and the ground rolled. The river ran backwards and fissures opened up spewing geysers high up into the air. The Bright Elves again went into action putting their hands on the ground and commanding it to be still in the name of Father God. The ground stopped shaking and the demon Paravataksha appeared to them as the figure of a man to the waist. From the waist down he appeared to be a large snake. He was shrieking with anger. The Bright Elves bound him and cast him out in the name of Father God. After checking the wagons, they turned north following the river.

After driving for a while, they didn't notice any more land damage, so the stopped for bathing and lunch. The girls had been through a lot and needed a refreshing distraction from the dangers they had endured. The girls bathed first, while the soldiers ate lunch on the other side of the wagons facing away from the river. The water was cold and clear and it was enjoyable to splash and immerse themselves in it. After bathing, they ate lunch while the soldiers bathed. Melody warmed some water and bathed and oiled Daisy. Then she put on daisy's harness and leash and walked her around for exercise. This made Daisy feel so good that she climbed into her velvet pouch for a nap. The girls felt the same way, so they climbed into their wagons for a nap.

Halden called, "Forward!" and Tall Sky pulled back onto the road going north. Melody, Andra, Faervel and Shanteel documented the last two demonic attacks. Some of the Bright Elves who had guard duty the night before took naps in the empty wagons. So far everything was going well. Tall Sky, Trinian and Gantio rode together on the wagon seat leading the caravan. Gantio asked, "When do you think the next attack will be?"

Tall Sky replied, "I think we will be alright for a while. The soldiers going through the hills might have some problems, though. I'm still leary of the hill people. Hopefully, when we get to Metos, we will gather some information about them and what to expect going through the hills. I think that Halden and Quickturn should remain here with us. I wish that you and Trinian could stay with us, but we need you to interpret. Make sure that you are surrounded by soldiers and Bright Elves at all times. They will all fight to keep you safe."

"What of dragons?" asked Gantio.

"Dragons are why I'm not going," said Tall Sky. "I've seen what dragons can do, and I promised to keep Melody safe. God told me that we will have a child, and she may be pregnant now, but don't tell anyone. She doesn't know yet. I'll wait for her to tell me."

"That's great! I'm happy for you. You will make a good father," said Gantio.

"It will be my first child, and I am very excited," said Tall Sky.

Gantio said, "Trinian wants to know if you have ever fought dragons."

"Yes, during my first hundred years, I fought with soldiers and other Bright Elves in the Aikasse Mountains. There were many dragons then, and they hated men, so they killed reindeer and their riders in Gullandia. They also attacked farms south of the mountains killing goats and sheep. Some farm houses were torched and they ate the humans as they ran from their flaming homes. I saw this gruesome scene as I stood in a field shielding myself. I killed a dragon with a well aimed arrow to its heart as it flew over me. We will know more about the possible dangers when we reach Metos.

There were no more attacks that afternoon, so they reached the outskirts of Metos safely and Tall Sky parked his wagon on the edge of town near the Sakina Rantu River. Trinian, Gantio, Halden, and two soldiers with extra horses rode into Metos and stopped at a tavern. They ordered ale and talked with the owner. Trinian asked the owner about the area and what types of business they conduct. The owner said that there were farms in the area that produce flax and that the seeds were good to put into breads and other foods. They use the stems of the flax to make fabric and this takes a long time and much work. The flax can also be used to make paper for scrolls. He said that he likes to wear flaxen clothing because it is comfortable. The farmers were good, hardworking people. Trinian asked about the people living in the hills and about any dangers in traveling to Galo. He said that the hills people didn't like outsiders, but that they have been known to let some outsiders travel through. He said that there was a guide who could get them through. Trinian asked if there were any slave girls in Metos. He said that there were a few. There were two at the brothel and two working at making paper out of flax. He said that the slavers went to Galo, but they did not return. He supposed that they had been killed in the hills. Trinian asked, "Would it be better to travel by sea to reach Pervati?"

The owner said, "I have never traveled by sea, but it is dangerous to travel near the Avika Plateau because of the wild dragons living there. The dragons hate people and kill them when they can. They fly over the plateau regularly to keep it free of humans."

"Do the hill people ever trade with others?" asked Trinian.

"Sometimes they trade for horses, but not for silver," said the owner.

"Is there a way to approach them for trading?" asked Trinian.

"There is a man in Metos who could arrange a meeting," said the owner. "He lives two houses down from here and trading is what he does. His name is Ramply."

Trinian showed him the king's edict banning slavery and told him about the sale of goods at their caravan. The owner said that the townspeople would love a sale like that, since they lived in an area that was so remote. Trinian, Gantio, Halden and the soldiers left the tavern and rode to the papermill to buy the slave girl working there. Trinian reached an agreement of price for her and they rode to the brothel to buy two more girls. The owner argued with Trinian, but they did arrive at a price, and the owner brought out two girls who were very surprised to be led out to horses by an Aksandan. They rode back to the caravan and left them with Melody, who explained their mission to return girls to their homes and showed them their wagon and men's clothing. The girls cried and thanked Melody.

Meanwhile, Trinian spread word of the sale and the soldiers set up tables spread with an array of merchandise. Soon, people arrived to shop. They were very excited and purchased amost everything. Afterwards, Halden said, "What a sale! I can hardly believe it! We have very little left. It's going to be so much better traveling without all of this stuff." The soldiers put away the tables and the caravan moved away fom the town to set up camp. Gantio and Trinian spoke with Halden.

Trinian said, "I met the trader Ramply. He agreed to set up a meeting with the hill people in exchange for some jewelry. He said that they might trade the girls for a wagon and a team of horses."

"That sounds good," said Halden.

"He said that we should meet him at the tavern tomorrow for lunch," said Trinian

The cooks brought out large pots full of meat and vegetables to cook at the fires. The girls took their caps off and wandered about the wagons talking. They were pleased that they would be on their way home. Melody gave the new girls some fabric and told them that she would place an experienced seamstress in their wagon to help them make clothes. Soon they filled their bowls with stew and flatbread. It had been a long day and everyone was very hungry. Tomorrow the soldiers would buy more supplies in town. After dinner they sat on some logs sipping wine and watching the sunset. Melody took Daisy for a walk.

The new girls could hardly believe their good fortune. It was like a dream come true and the answer to their prayers. They had good food and Aksandan people to talk with. When the sun went down, everyone went to bed. Tomorrow was another day without slavery. The new girls went to bed smiling and happily snuggled into their beds knowing that they were safe and cared for.

The next day Trinian, Gantio and Halden drove a wagon into town to meet Ramply. He was there and said that they could leave now and meet the hill people to make the exchange of girls for the wagon and team of horses. They just had to drive out of town a short way. They drove the wagon to the meeting place and met with the hill people. There were several very rough looking men with beards, long hair and dirty clothes. They agreed to the trade, but insisted that they took the girls' two babies with them. Trinian agreed and thanked them. He asked them if there were any slave girls north of the hills. They said that they killed the only slavers who had come this way. The girls mounted the two extra horses and they rode off toward the caravan.

Melody helped the girls clean up and bathe the babies. Then she looked for diaper material. Melody was going to get some first hand experience with infants. The other girls were delighted with the babies and took turns holding them. Melody said that the two girls should have a wagon together to have space to take care of the babies. The other girls wanted to make baby clothes. One girl decided to make cute little baby toys for them. This had energized the girls in ways that only babies can do.

Halden said that they should head south toward Dhuma and camp about halfway there, so they followed the river road until late afternoon. Then they stopped and set up camp. The soldiers took care of the horses and set up the cooks' fires. The cooks brought out the pots of food and set them on the fire. The girls removed their caps and walked around the caravan. The girls wanted to bathe in the river again, so they did while Tall Sky watched Daisy, and Trinian and Gantio held the babies. After the girls bathed, the soldiers bathed. Then the dinner bell rang. They had stew again, but Trinian had purchased all the sweets they had in Metos, so they had choice of an assortment of desserts and candy. It was his way of making the girls feel cared for and special. After dinner, they relaxed, sitting on their blankets and watching the sunset.

Melody and Tall Sky took Daisy for a walk and then sat on the wagon seat. "We only have one more town before visiting Queen Darshana," said Melody. "Trinian said that he saved the best necklace to give to her. I wonder how King Narendra liked his journey up the King's River."

Tall Sky said, "It's an enjoyable trip. I'm sure he was just fine with it. I would like to have heard the conversation between the two kings. That would have been interesting."

"It sure would have been, and I'll bet he heard some interesting stories from those girls. That would have been an eye opener for him," said Melody.

Tall Sky laughed and said, "It sure would have been. Trinian has been a surprise to me. It's great the way that he cares for the girls as if they were his own children."

"Yes it is. He is a really good man. Did you see how he played with the baby and talked to it?" asked Melody. "He will make a good husband and father. You know, the baby's mother learned to speak Fantolese. Maybe he could marry her. She's a very pretty girl and he likes her."

"It's possible," said Tall Sky. I've seen stranger things than that on this trip."

"Speaking of strange things, I wonder if we'll have any more trouble from demons," said Melody.

"I'm tired of that sort of thing, but it is possible. Demons are dangerous, but they are also stupid.

They should know by now that we will just banish them, but then they have to obey their master," said Tall Sky. "Don't worry. We have set extra guards for the night. We should go to bed now. Morning comes early and we have to travel tomorrow."

Overnight some clouds rolled in. They awakened to a loud crack of lightning that started a grass fire heading toward the caravan. The Bright Elves gathered in front of the caravan and commanded rain to fall in the name of Father God. In just minutes heavy rain fell stopping the grass fire. An angry demon appeared in the sky having the shape of a thin man with horns on his head and holding a bellows. He said, I am Zaphan and I will destroy you with fire. The Bright Elves went bright, holding their hands toward Zaphan and sent beams of light to bind Zaphan. Then they said, "In the name of Father God, we bind you and cast you out of Phayendar forever!" Zaphan screamed, flew into the sky and disappeared.

The rain had put out the breakfast fires, but the cooks had already made enough flatbread for ham sandwiches and they had fruit, so that's what everyone had for breakfast. After breakfast the caravan headed south to Dhurma.

They arrived at Dhurma before lunch and stopped at the edge of town. Trinian, Gantio, Halden and two soldiers with extra horses rode into town stopping at the tavern. The tavern owner said that he had a slave and that there were slaves at a brothel and at a bakery. Trinian showed him the king's decree and he sold his slave girl to

Trinian. Then they did the same at the bakery and at the brothel. They took four slave girls back to the caravan and brought them to Melody. Since there would be no sale today, the cooks handed out sandwiches for lunch. After lunch the caravan turned west onto a road heading southwest toward Kunola to visit Queen Darshana.

Melody, Shanteel and Andra stayed inside the wagon to document the latest events of their journey. The girls occupied themselves with sewing. The new girls learned sewing from a girl who was placed there by Melody. They also learned more about the caravan and about Father God. The soldiers rode on either side of the caravan for protection. Tall Sky, Gantio and Trinian rode up front in the first wagon as usual. It was a beautiful, sunny day with just a few travelers headed away from Kunola. It was good to be so close to the end of their journey through Fantolo. They reached Kunola around dinner time, but waited for dinner until they saw Queen Darshana. Trinian, Gantio, and Tall Sky changed into dress clothes and rode into town to the castle.

Queen Darshana had them taken to the study where they could talk. She said that she had not heard from her husband, but that she had collected a dozen more slave girls for them. Trinian presented her with a necklace of multi-colored gemstones and thanked her for the slave girls. She invited them to stay for dinner, but they declined saying that they should be on their way, as it was a long way home. She presented them with the girls, who all looked like princesses wearing long gowns. Trinian thanked her and they left the castle heading back to the caravan escorted by Darshana's soldiers who would bring back the horses. "It's a good thing that we emptied those wagons at the last sale. We're going to need them," said Tall Sky.

When they arrived at the caravan, Tall Sky spoke to them about their mission and the rules of the caravan. The girls looked relieved and happy. Melody showed them to their wagons and instructed them to change clothes. She said it was for their protection on the way through Orendia. Melody asked if they could put another empty wagon behind the cooks' wagon and have two girls experienced in baking to help the cooks. Halden said it was a good idea, so they talked to the cooks, who put the baking ingredients and pans into the empty wagon. Lindi and Lidra would be responsible for the making of flatbread. The young bakers were glad to have something to do besides sewing. Halden and some soldiers had gone shopping for supplies in Kunola and had purchased bakery and baking ingredients which they took to the bakers' wagon.

When all the supplies were put away, Halden called out, "Forward!" and the wagons pulled out onto King's Road heading west toward the Frothy Sea. About half way to Nola, Tall Sky pulled over to make camp. The cook's fires were made and while dinner was cooking, the soldiers took care of the horses and pitched tents. The sun was low in the sky when the dinner bell rang and a bunch of hungry girls descended on the cooks' fires. There was plenty of food for all. The girls were happy to be out walking around free. The new girls said that it was nice to live in the castle for a while, but it was much better to be on their way home and to be with Aksandan people.

After dinner, Tall Sky and Melody took Daisy for a walk. She padded about happily, fluttering her wings. Then they bathed and oiled her and she took a nap in her velvet pouch. They sat on the wagon seat watching the sunset and sipping wine. "We are more than half of the way out of Fantolo," said Tall Sky. "That's good. I hope we can see the dragon riders again," said Melody.

"I think we will. They keep a pretty close eye on the area, and they will undoubtedly want to see our girls," said Tall Sky. "Should we bathe again at the seashore?"

"Yes" replied Melody. "Many of the girls have never done that. I think they will want to. I know I do."

"We will camp at the seashore tonight before heading across the land bridge," said Tall Sky. Halden stopped by and told them that everyone was going to bed now. He wanted to get an early start in the morning. "Well, let's get some sleep. The sooner we sleep, the sooner we travel," said Tall Sky.

The next morning after breakfast, the caravan continued west stopping at Nola to buy more eggs and to eat a sandwich. Then they continued traveling until reaching the land bridge at the Frothy Sea. They pulled off the road and set up camp. Eighty-four girls immediately ran to the seashore, rolled up their pantlegs and waded in the frothy water. The soldiers took care of the horses and made cooking fires. It had been a long day of travel and everyone wanted to eat and rest. Melody let Daisy splash around at the water's edge. Dinner would take a while, so Halden instructed the girls to get their towels and soap and bathe in the sea. They frolicked and laughed and enjoyed the cool water. When they were done, they dried themselves and were dressing when a large octopus tentacle grabbed one of them and pulled her back into the water. It was a very large octopus with a bulbous head that surfaced holding the girl in the air and making a loud growling noise. The rest of the girls ran screaming back to the wagons. Quickturn commanded, "Release her in the name of Father God!" The octopus released her and she fell into deep water. Quickturn shielded himself, dove into the water and rescued the girl. Then the Bright Elves went bright and bound the octopus with beams of light encircling it. The octopus turned into a large face with menacing teeth. The Bright Elves said, "We command you in the name of Father God to leave Phayendar and never return!" The demon growled and snarled. Then it left quickly, flying up through the sky.

Tall Sky said, "At least that's the last of the demons. I think there were only four hovering about our moon." Then the dinner bell rang and two long lines formed for dinner. They ate sitting on blankets, watching the sea change colors as the sun set. The water reflected a pretty, rose color. Then the sun set and moonlight reflected a glint of silver on the waves. Everyone went to bed feeling tired and happy.

The next morning, breakfast consisted of ham and eggs and sweet rolls purchased at local bakeries. Everyone enjoyed this. After breakfast they packed up and headed east across the land bridge. It was a beautiful day with clear, blue skies and a cool sea breeze across the land. By lunch time they were in Orendia. They took a break for lunch and then continued along Seaside Road going south toward

King's Port. When they reached King's Port, they turned onto King's Road going toward Fallonia.

"When we get to Fallonia, I'm going to visit King Jahiz," said Tall Sky. "I need to find out how he's doing and ask if he has had any more slaves turned in to him. We were pretty thorough when we searched Orendia, but he could have a few more slaves. We should be there before dinner time."

"Do you think that I could meet the king and queen this time?" asked Melody.

"I will ask Gantio. It's possible," replied Tall Sky. "He and Trinian are busy translating scrolls right now."

"I remember the dinner and the ball that he gave the girls last time. If he offers that this time, I would prefer to just move on toward Aksanda. I miss my friends and it has been a long time," said Melody.

"I miss our friends, too," said Tall Sky. "I'm so glad you're with me. This trip would have been unbearable without you. I love you so much." He hugged her, pulling her close, and kissed her. "How are you? Have you been feeling well?"

"I feel great. Why do you ask?" said Melody.

"Just wondering," said Tall Sky.

"You think I might be pregnant," said Melody.

"It is possible," said Tall Sky.

"Well, I don't feel sick or anything," said Melody.

"Women don't always feel sick when they conceive," said Tall Sky.

"I hope we get home first," said Melody.

"It would be funny for you and Daisy to be pregnant at the same time," said Tall Sky.

# KING JAHIZ

The caravan reached Fallonia at dinner time and Halden, Gantio, Tall Sky and Melody went to see King Jahiz. He graciously received them in his study. "Who is this young lady with you?" asked King Jahiz.

"This is my wife Melody," said Tall Sky.

"I'm so glad to meet you," said Melody.

"I present Queen Dara," said King Jahiz.

Melody smiled and said, "I am honored."

"I have five slave girls for you. They were turned in to me last week," said King Jahiz. "How many girls did you find in Fantolo?"

"We have eighty-one girls and two infants. They are happy to be going home. My wife has a gift for you. It is a puzzle that we made of Phayendar," said Tall Sky.

"It is beautiful. Thank you," said King Jahiz.

"We are writing a book about Phayendar and I wish I had a painting or a drawing of you and Queen Dara to put in the book. We are making copies of the book and they will be in all the schools throughout Aksanda. Of course we will have a translation of this book sent to you," said Melody.

"I do have a small painting of us. I will get it for you," said King Jahiz.

Melody smiled and thanked him.

When he returned, he brought five girls dressed in long gowns. "I thank you, King Jahiz," said Tall Sky. "King Narendra is visiting King Aryante. He brought sixty girls from Fallonia on his ship. If you would like to meet with King Narendra and King Aryante, you could travel with us. The meeting you proposed before at Lake Inari is not far from Vivallen and you could discuss plans for introducing your people to Father God."

"It is a good plan. My son Prince Ravi can rule in my absence. I will pack and be ready to leave by tomorrow morning. I have my own travel wagon and I will have some soldiers with me for an escort home," said King Jahiz.

"We will be camped just outside of town waiting for you," said Gantio.

"I will see you then," said King Jahiz.

In the meantime, soldiers bought groceries in town. When everyone was back at the caravan, they drove out of town and made camp. The soldiers took care of the horses and made two cooking fires, and the cooks put out pots of food. The girls walked around the caravan. The plateau was to their left with its high, sheer rock face and there were rolling hills to their right.

Looking up they saw dragons circling far above them. The dragons circled lower and lower until they landed a short distance from them. Four women dismounted and walked toward the caravan. Gantio, Tall Sky, Melody and Halden walked out to greet them. Gantio greeted them and Melody hugged them.

Rana said, "It looks like you were successful in Fantolo. How many girls did you get?"

"Eighty-one girls and two babies," said Gantio. "Tomorrow King Jahiz will join us. He met Father God through us and wants to meet with the kings of Fantalo and Aksanda in Vivallen. King Narendra is already, there. "The dragon riders were visibly amazed by this. The kings will be devising a plan to introduce Father God to their people."

"That's great!" exclaimed Rana.

"Let's walk over to the girls. They would love to meet you," said Gantio. They walked over to the girls, waved and said hello to them. Gantio told them that Fantolo is better than Orendia in their treatment of women, but that there were still brothels and business men who use slaves for free labor.

"It would be wonderful for the two countries' people to follow Father God," said Rana.

"I would love to say hello to your dragon Kerberos again," said Melody.

"Alright, just follow me," said Rana.

She led her over to Kerberos and the dragon said, "Melody." Then the dragon touched his nose to Melody's tummy and said, "Baby."

"You're pregnant?!" said a surprised Rana. She motioned Gantio to come over to translate. "Kerberos says that Melody is pregnant."

Melody smiled and said, "I don't know."

Rana said, "Kerberos would know if you were."

Melody kissed Kerberos on his nose and stroked his neck and hugged him around the neck. "I love you, Kerberos," said Melody.

The dragon said, "Love you Melody."

Melody said to Rana, "I want a dragon so much. Maybe someday I can impress a dragonette and raise it and fly it to Home fire."

Tall Sky was standing there listening and said, "Maybe so, but not now. We have a mission to complete and schools to start."

"We have to go now, but we will see you again I hope. There will be eggs to impress someday and I would love for you two to learn dragon riding," said Rana. "And your child, too."

Melody laughed and waved goodbye as the dragons took to the air.

The dinner bell rang and everybody gathered for food. This time there were hunks of lamb in a stew, flatbread, and fresh fruit. They sat on boulders to eat. After dinner they sipped wine and talked among themselves. The girls who had stayed in the castle for a while told about being pampered. They said that there were women who helped them dress, do their hair and give them massages. There were always fresh fruit and sweets to eat, but there was no work to do and they couldn't communicate well with others because of the language differences.

Trinian sat with the young mothers and played with the babies. Gantio, Halden and Quickturn discussed the addition of King Jahis to the caravan. Halden wanted the king's wagon behind Tall Sky's wagon, because Tall Sky was leading the way to Vivallen and could sense dangers other than common ones. Gantio could relay any messages to the king and serve him if need be. They would take as good care of the king as possible. His own soldiers may also do that.

It was getting dark and Halden told the girls that they needed to go to bed. Melody left the girls she was talking with and she and Tall Sky took Daisy for one last walk before retiring to the wagon.

The next morning King Jahiz arrived in his wagon, which was very ornate looking with carved scenes on the wood and some colorful paintings on either side. There were silken curtains at the windows. Gantio and Halden greeted King Jahiz and told him to pull in behind Tall Sky's wagon. He said that this placement was for his protection. King Jahiz ordered his driver to do so. Then he asked for Gantio to ride with him for communication purposes. Halden agreed. With Gantio sitting in the king's wagons, Halden called out, "Forward!" and the caravan drove forward down King's Road.

King Jahiz said to Gantio, "This is quite an adventure. I've been wondering what caravan life was like. It's been a long time since I took a trip."

Gantio replied, "It's well organized. The soldiers take care of the horses and stand guard in shifts all night. They sleep in tents or in hammocks under the wagons."

"Soldiers?" said King Jahiz. "I thought they were merchants."

"They are soldiers trained as merchants. They trained in the Orendian language also. It took all winter to accomplish this and have all the wagons ready for the spring mission. The wagons had to be made. Tall Sky worked with the Loadrel blacksmith and the carpenter to make his," said Gantio. "They had to be soldiers to defend the caravan against bandits and Bitter Elves, not to mention giant mantises and wolves."

"That must have been horrible," said King Jahiz. "How did they get away from them?"

"They killed the mantises with well aimed arrows to their heads." said Gantio.

The caravan passed by Amby and kept on driving toward Tabira. Halfway to Tabira, they stopped for lunch, pulling the caravan off the road. Everyone climbed out of their wagons and walked around the caravan. King Jahiz and Gantio also walked. Then Halden called the girls together and introduced King Jahiz. He said, "Girls, I would like you to meet King Jahiz. He and his soldiers will be our honored guests for the remainder of our journey. He is going to meet with King Aryante and King Narendra to discuss plans to introduce Father God to their citizens. Treat them with the utmost respect and speak to him only with permission from Gantio and Gantio will translate."

King Jahiz said, "I know much about the suffering you have endured. I am glad for you to be getting safely back home. Now let's have lunch." King Jahiz ate his sandwich sitting on his wagon seat with Gantio. Everyone else sat on the boulders.

A large goup of bandits and Bitter Elves had been hiding in the rocks, and, seeing that many of the passengers were women, decided to attack. King Jahiz and the girls hid in their wagons and watched the attack in safety. The soldiers fought with swords in hand to hand combat, while the Bright Elves used arrows. There were so many bandits that the battle continued for some time. Then four dragon riders flew over torching some of them causing them to run for their lives. The dragons chased them a good distance and then flew back to the caravan and landed. The dragon riders walked up to the caravan, gifts in hand. They gave Halden bags of fresh meat and gave each of the girls a gemstone.

The dragon riders wanted to meet King Jahiz. When they saw him, they bowed and presented him with a pouch of gems. Rana said, "Blessings to you, our king. We wish you great success on your mission. This gift is to help you on your way."

King Jahiz said, "I am delighted to meet you. Thank you for your gift and for your protection. Could I touch one of your dragons?"

"Of course," said Rana. "They are your subjects too." Melody was already petting Kerberos, so they walked over to him. Rana said, "Kerberos, this is King Jahiz who is in charge over all our land."

Kerberos said, "King Jahiz," and he sniffed the king much the same as a horse would do. "Smells good."

The king stroked Kerberos' neck and Kerberos said," I like you too."

"It was nice meeting you," said King Jahiz. They all walked back to the wagons and finished lunch while the dragons departed, cirlcling into the sky where they could watch the bandits. "Now I see why they needed to be soldiers," said King Jahiz. "Those dragon riders were spectacular! They are courageous women. I'm glad they're on our side. I didn't know that dragons could talk."

"Only to a select few" said Gantio. "They have to be taught words. The dragon rider and the dragon have a very strong bond."

"I'm already glad that I came on this journey," said King Jahiz.

The soldiers were digging a pit to throw the bodies in. When it was finished, they gathered the bodies, taking from them anything of value and threw them into the pit and buried them. King Jahiz was impressed with this also. They washed up and remounted their horses. Halden called out, "Forward!" and Tall Sky drove back onto the road again heading toward Tabira.

Melody was sitting with Tall Sky and said, "When will thieves ever realize that it's better to work for a living? They sure would live longer."

"I know. It's ridiculous," said Tall Sky. "We lost some time back there, so I think we will be camping on the other side of Tabira. I was hoping we could get closer to Lake Inari."

"Does Daisy like the dragon?" asked Tall Sky.

"Yes, she does. She wasn't afraid at all. She rubbed cheeks with him. He knows her name, you know," Melody said with pride. "He thinks I'm pregnant. Do you think he's right?"

"Yes, I do," said Tall Sky. "You won't deliver until the spring."

"Gosh, that's a long time to wait," said Melody.

"I know," said Tall Sky. "You will have plenty of time to work on our school project so that our little one will be able to go to school and learn about his mother's exploits." He laughed. "You might even take up knitting and making baby clothes."

"Maybe I should. I could learn something about that by helping the girls who are making clothes for our two baby passengers," said Melody. "I'm going into the wagon to see how Andra and Shanteel are doing."

Melody climbed into the wagon. Andra was copying, Faervel was drawing, and Shanteel was drawing a picture of the battle. "You three are doing a great job," said Melody. "I guess I will write up the last battle. Where is Trinian?"

Andra said, "He is in the cabin with the two girls and babies. I think he is growing fond of one of them and they know Fantolese, so they can talk with him."

As they traveled down the road, everyone was busy with their projects and Tall Sky relaxed, enjoying the ride. It was a beautiful day, they had accomplished their mission of buying back the slaves, and they had plenty of food and silver left over to return to King Aryante. It was all good. He basked in this for a while and then turned his thoughts to the schools they were going to start. He was very pleased with the progress that they had already made with the gathering of school supplies and creating a history book. They also had documentation of their journey, and script and picutures of animals and plants. The scrolls were yielding medical information. When it was put together, three subjects of the curriculum would be completed. He would ask King Aryante for time with the other two kings to get historical information from them. This was an unprecedented opportunity to document the history of the three major countries of Phayendar, and it could be added to year by year.

Melody thought that she should ride with King Jahiz for a while and write as much history as he could remember. It would give him a productive way to spend his time as they traveled. He could tell her about the Orendian customs, and the previous kings and wars. She would have the Orendian history documented by the time they reached Vivallen. Then in Vivallen she could document the Fantolese history working with Trinian, Gantio and King Narendra. "What an opportunity!" she thought. She shared this with Tall Sky who applauded her idea. That night after dinner, Tall Sky presented this idea to King Jahiz who thought it was wonderful and thanked Melody for it.

The next morning brought a new feeling of excitement to Melody. She would be riding with King Jahiz and would be writing the history of his country. She was in awe of the king. Tall Sky fed and watered the horses, while Melody fed Daisy and took her for a short walk. After breakfast Melody took some paper and boarded the king's wagon. Gantio was there to translate. She began the history of Orendia with the list of the kings' names. He said that, when he was a boy, he had to memorize the king's names, what they had accomplished, and any wars that happened during their reigns. Melody was fascinated by all of this and enjoyed writing it. They were half of the way through the kings' list by the time that Tall Sky pulled over for lunch at the southern tip of Lake Inari.

King Jahiz thanked Melody and they climbed out of the wagon to stretch their legs. The girls walked around the caravan for exercise. "Tall Sky, this is very interesting," said Melody. "Give me Daisy now. Has she been a good girl?"

"She kept looking around for you, but she was good," said Tall Sky. Daisy chirred and rubbed cheeks with Melody.

"Melody, how are you getting along with King Jahiz?" asked Tall sky.

"He's wonderful," said Melody. "He is full of information and I think he enjoys talking about the history of his country. It's so exciting to be talking with a king."

"I'm glad you're enjoying it," said Tall Sky.

The cooks handed out the sandwiches and gave Melody a Daisy Plate. Tall Sky and Melody ate, sitting on the wagon seat. "You know, Vivallen is our next town," said Tall Sky. "Do you think that you and King Jahiz will be finished by then?"

"I think so," said Melody.

"How is our baby doing?" asked Tall Sky.

"How should I know?" replied Melody. Tall Sky Laughed.

Soon Halden told everyone to get back into their wagons and called "Forward!" They drove around the southern tip of Inari to the road leading toward Vivallen and drove until evening when they stopped for camp. The soldiers fed and watered the horses while the cooks put out large pots of meat and vegetables on the fires to cook. The bakers had flat bread ready to cook on pans to go on some hot coals. There were so many to feed that dinner was taking longer than usual, so baskets of fresh fruit were set out on a table for snacking.

Daisy was doing her hungry dance, so Melody got a dish of food for her. The cooks had saved her a pastry, so she was one happy dragon. Then the dinner bell rang, and there were two long lines of people waiting for food. King Jahiz was served first by one of his men. This was a time that girls from different wagons could get to know each other, so the sound of talking was fairly loud. After they ate, Halden called them together and said, "Tomorrow is the last day of our journey. When we reach Vivallen, we will spend one more night in the caravan. The next day we will go shopping for clothes and we will meet King Aryante. You will all be bathed and dressed properly as young ladies. Taking you to your homes will start shortly after that. I recommend that you tell your parents that you were forced to work and skip all the sexual abuse parts. Now let's all go to bed so we can have an early start in the morning."

Before any of the girls awakened, the cooks made breakfast of porridge and ham with fruit. After they had eaten and washed their dishes, they entered their wagons for the last part of their journey. The girls worked on their sewing, and Melody and Gantio worked with King Jahiz on the history of Orendia.

# VIVALLEN

After three hours of traveling, they pulled up in back of the castle. The girls were so excited that they climbed out of their wagons cheering and jumping up and down. Some of them kissed the ground. They were home!

Tall Sky, Melody, Quickturn, Halden, and Gantio escorted King Jahiz to the castle and announced their homecoming to King Aryante who, when he heard about King Jahiz being with them, came out of his study to warmly greet him. King Aryante invited them to his study and ordered wine to be poured. He sent for King Narendra who was in the garden with Trinian. When they walked in, King Aryante introduced King Narendra to King Jahiz. It was the first summit meeting in Phayendar history and Melody was there to record it. She sat at the end of the table taking notes. She had never felt so humble and honored as to be in the presence of three great kings at one time.

When King Narendra heard about the history of Phayendar being written, he said that he wanted Melody to write the history of Fantalo, too. She said that she would be honored to do so and that the book would be translated into Fantolese by Trinian and would be sent to him. Lunch was served in the study and the kings spent the rest of the afternoon visiting with each other. Then King Aryante took King Jahiz on a tour of the castle and showed him his rooms which were elegant with a large canopy bed with curtains, arched doorway, an overstuffed couch with velvet upholstery and paintings. King Jahiz was very pleased.

Meanwhile, the girls bathed, had their hair done and were dressed in gowns for dinner. King Aryante had ordered a feast and ball in their honor. Aleph and Faerverin were happy to be together again and Quickturn visited with Dawn Lace. Everyone got dressed up for an evening of festivities. Melody and Tall Sky went shopping for new clothes. Melody bought a lovely green satin gown with a V neckline and tall Sky bought new pants and shirt with a vest. Then they had a glass of wine at the Golden Chalice. "I'm tired, but I'm happy," said Melody.

"I am too," said Tall Sky. "We have much to do, but we are going to take it easy and get others to help us with the schools. We don't have to do it alone, so I want you to relax and enjoy being an expectant mother."

"That still seems weird to me. I haven't told Faervein yet," said Melody. "I'll bet she will be surprised. I wonder why she came back early."

"She must have heard from Father God about the return of Aleph," said Tall Sky. "They are both Bright Elves."

"That's right. It's like you knew I was pregnant before I did," said Melody.

Faerverin and Aleph walked in and sat at their table. Faerverin said, "I'm so glad that you're back. Aleph told me that you two will have a baby. It's wonderful. Maybe you can finally stay home for a while."

"I suppose we will. How is my kitten doing?" asked Melody.

"She is a happy little cat. She has grown some, you know. She knows more words and she can fly a bit," said Faerverin. "I think she will be delighted to see you and Daisy. Sometimes she says Daisy's name and looks around for her."

"I'm so glad. I thought she mght forget us," said Melody. "How are Princess Anya and Aranel?"

"They are fine and Anya is getting really good at painting," said Faerverin.

"We will be going to Loadrel tomorrow," said Tall Sky. "I've been gone so long and have been through so much, that Loadrel seems like a dream."

"What about the history of Fantolo?" asked Melody.

"Trinian and Gantio and Andra can write the rest of it," said Tall Sky. "I can't stand one more minute of this. Gantio can bring it to us and we can have someone make copies for the schools. Now let's go back to the castle and go to the celebrations."

By the time they walked into the castle, the girls were ready and seated at tables in the dining room. Soldiers in dress uniform were seated in between the girls. Tall Sky, Melody, Aleph and Faerverin went upstairs to put on their new clothes and went to the dining hall. They sat at the front table with Quickturn, Dawn Lace, Gantio, Shasta, Halden, Tilly and Grendamore. King Aryante's family sat at another front table with King Jahiz, Trinian and King Narendra with their partners for the evening.

King Aryante stood up and said, "I welcome all of you to this celebration of the return of our citizens to our country. Aksandans have long been concerned with this and will all rejoice with you. I hope that you will have wonderful lives from here on. My thanks go to the valiant men who traveled far and braved dangers to bring you home. Would you stand up Tall Sky, Aleph, Quickturn, and Halden. Also thank you to King Narendra and King Jahiz. Everyone applauded. Of course I thank my soldiers and Bright Elves for their bravery and dedication and our interpreters Gantio and Trinian. The girls applauded. Father God, I want to thank You above all for bringing our caravan safely home. Please bless this food we are about to eat. Amen. Now let's have dinner." They all sat down and waiters brought food in for everyone.

"That was a nice speech," said Melody. "I think we all owe a big thanks to our cooks. They did a marvelous job."

"We will thank them and give each of them a gift," said Tall Sky.

"Good idea," said Melody. "Will we really go home tomorrow? I don't want to insult the kings."

"I will tell them that you are pregnant and need to go home. They will understand. They all have children," said Tall Sky. "Gantio, would you finish up the history writing? I need to get Melody home. I want to leave for Loadrel tomorrow."

"I could do that easily enough," said Gantio. "You go ahead and go home. A pregnant woman needs her own home. I understand."

Dawn Lace said, "A baby. How exciting. Is it a boy or a girl?"

Tall Sky said, "It's a boy. I saw him in a vision. He has red, curly hair and green eyes. We have much to do before he gets here. We have schools to start in Loadrel and in Home Fire and I have to make a nursery out of one of our rooms. I want to have things ready for him."

The room was alive with conversation. Dawn Lace and Quickturn were talking about palace activities and some of what had happened on the caravan. The girls were talking about their homes and about the happier things like swimming in the sea. Gantio and Shasta were flirting with each other. They hadn't had much time together after being married at the last dinner with a caravan of girls from Orendia. Halden was telling his wife Tilly about the caravan journey. Aleph and Faerverin talked about her experiences with Princess Anya and Aranel. After dinner, King Aryante announced the dance in the ballroom. He and his family walked out of the dining hall and guests followed him to the ballroom.

The ballroom had tables on the edge of the room with a band already playing in the front right corner. King Aryante and Queen Svetlana began dancing, and King Narendra and King Jahiz joined in dancing with their partners. Then everyone else joined in. There were many colors of gowns whirling around the dance floor. The girls danced with the soldiers and were feeling like they were in a wonderful dream. Tall Sky and Melody were tired, but they danced the slow dances, holding each other close, feeling like they were a world unto themselves surrounded by a soft pink cloud that kept everyone else away. They said farewell to their friends and to the kings and walked to the Golden Chalice to order a room for the night. They fell asleep in each other's arms and dreamed of home.

# LOADREL AND EXPECTING A BABY

They awoke the next morning feeling better, and after having breakfast, Melody picked up her kitten, walked to their wagon and drove out of town. Melody took with her one copy of the writings and pictures that they had done so far and left one copy with Andra who would continue working with Gantio and Trinian. She had with her school supplies that she had gathered on the way through Fantolo and was looking forward to helping to set up the Loadrel School. They drove straight through to Loadrel without stopping to camp at the ruins, so Melody took a nap in the back of the wagon with Daisy curled up on her pillow. It was dark when they pulled up beside the Laborer's Reward. They walked in and hugged Beldock, who brought them some ale. "Mina!" Beldock called. "Tall Sky is home!" Mina rushed out and hugged them both.

"I'm so glad you're home. I've been worrying and praying for you. How's my little dragon? I've been missing all of you. I'll bet you're hungry. I'll go get your food and first the Daisy plate," said Mina.

"Tall Sky, did everything go as planned? Did you rescue many girls?" asked Beldock.

"Yes," said Tall Sky. "We rescued about one hundred and forty girls and two babies. I got so tired that I couldn't stand another minute of it, so I just drove home. There are more pregnant girls coming our way and there are girls going to Home Fire. I think Rando will be surprised. Talla will probably have to add on to the house."

Mina came out with the Daisy plate and Daisy hopped down on the table to eat. Then she went to the kitchen and brought out bowls of stew and freshly baked bread with jam. Melody sat there with tears streaming down her face. She was so relieved and grateful to be home. Mina saw this and said, "Come here child," and she held Melody in a motherly embrace for a while.

Melody said, "I'm pregnant."

Mina said, "Oh, I love you child. You are going to have a baby and you're home." Then tears came to Mina's eyes. She wiped them and they both laughed.

"I rode a dragon," said Melody. "I got to meet another king and we rescued lots of girls, but I got so homesick that I could barely stand it."

"Well, you sit down and eat your food while it's still hot, and we'll talk more in a while," said Mina.

Beldock went next door to get Laskron, Liadra and Elise. They came right over and sat down with Melody and Tall Sky. "It is so good to see you," said Laskron. "We have missed you."

"We missed our friends so much that we left without bringing any girls with us. The soldiers will bring them though," said Tall Sky. "Melody, Shanteel, and a slave girl named Andra documented the trip in words and pictures. Then Melody worked with Trinian and King Narendra to make a history of Fantolo. Andra and Gantio are working with King Jahiz on the history of Orendia. It's kind of complicated because of the language differences. I think we should offer Orendian as a second language for the older children. Did the school supplies get sent to Home Fire?"

"Yes, they did," said Trag. "I helped to load them."

"How are Rando and Alqua?" asked Tall Sky.

"They're fine," said Trag. "I haven't been out there, but they have been getting supplies from Loadrel and work crews report that they have been very busy out there. He has built a Vision Hall and they're making progress on the water system."

"That's good. I can hardly wait to see it, but Melody and I want to get more settled in at our house first. I want to order a rocking chair and a baby bed. Hopefully Ulrick isn't too busy to make them. I want to see your nursery, Arinya. I suppose we will have to order a baby bathtub and a changing table to dress him on. There is a lot to think about with a baby. I just want to be ready for him," said Tall Sky.

"Slow down there. You have plenty of time," said Trag.

"I can make you a baby bottle for water and juice," said Laskron.

"I can help you make clothes and small towels and other things," said Liadra. "We have a nursery, too, and I have made a lot of baby clothes. It's a good idea to have sizes going up to a whole year. Babies grow fast. You should get a chest of drawers for him."

"After breakfast we will visit Ulrick and the blacksmith shop and place our orders. Then we can choose some paint and go home," said Tall Sky.

"I thought to name him Eryn Alda which is elven for forest tree. What do you think, Melody?" asked Tall Sky.

"I like that name," replied Melody. "It's not too long and it sounds masculine."

"It's settled then. His name is Eryn," said Tall Sky. "It is also the name of a man who died saving me in battle long ago. Let's go buy that paint."

"When will we hear about the caravan?" asked Trag.

"After we get settled in," said Tall Sky as he was walking out the door.

Tall Sky and Melody walked to the store and chose some light blue paint for the nursery and walked home to begin their baby adventure. "I want to talk to Ulrick and the blacksmith," said Melody. They dropped off the paint at home and walked to Ulrick's shop to order the bed and the chest of drawers. Then they stopped by the blacksmith shop to order a baby tub. Satisfied with that, they went home to paint.

While they were painting, Twilric, Laskron's apprentice, walked in. "Hi, Tall Sky, Laskron sent me over to help. He said that he could spare me for a while because he is working on something complicated."

"Great! Grab a paintbrush, and you can work on that wall," said Tall Sky. Then Trag walked in, paintbrush in hand.

"I heard somebody could use some help painting. You two helped us so much, I thought I would return the favor. Liadra said that when you have time, she would get you started on baby clothes," said Trag.

"How do you have the energy to do this after being on caravans all summer?"

"We're just really excited about the baby," said Tall Sky.

"You have a long time to wait, you know," said Trag. "You will relax when everything is ready, and then you can start working on Eryn's school. Just think, all of our babies will go to school together and be friends just like we are."

"Sounds good," said Tall Sky. I'm going to ask Faerverin to paint a mural on the wall, and if she is too busy, I can have Shanteel paint one."

"I want one with trees and bunnies and butterflies, a flying cat and maybe a dragon," said Melody.

"There could also be a lake with mountains in the distance," said Tall Sky.

"Where is Daisy?" asked Trag.

"She doesn't like the smell of paint, so she's in her nesting box," said Melody. "She probably thinks that we have all gone crazy."

When they had finished painting the room, they walked to the Laborer's Reward for lunch, bringing Arinya and Liadra, Laskron and Elise on the way. After satisfying their hunger, they sipped some wine and talked. Tall Sky said, "I'm sorry about not telling you about our journey, but I couldn't get my mind back into it until I made some progress on the baby's room. It is all I've thought about since I knew for sure that Melody was pregnant. It's just so important, and I saw our boy in a vision riding on a dragon with his mommy. He looked to be about five years old and was really cute with red, curly hair and green eyes."

"Anyway, the journey was long and fairly uncomfortable, especially in the south of Fantolo. We saw plenty of wild animals like alligators, large water snakes, wolves, and a cougar that jumped on a wagon. Melody attracted a parrot that rode with us for a while. We killed some wolves that were chasing us. The people were nicer than the Orendians, but the brothel owners were pretty rough."

"In the north, we encountered four demons. One set off an earthquake that turned over some wagons and made the river run backwards. Some fishers opened up with geysers that went up pretty high. Another demon caused a grass fire. A third demon became a whirlwind bearing down on us. Of course, we bound them and cast them out in the name of Father God. "

"King Narendra signed the treaty and trade agreement making it fairly easy to buy slaves. The townspeople were anxious to buy our goods, so that freed up space for the girls. King Narendra accepted Father God into his heart and took many slave girls to Free Port on his own ship. He is in Vivallen now. When we were on our way back, we stopped at the land bridge to bathe in the sea and a fourth demon attacked us in the form of a large octopus and it grabbed one of our girls. Quickturn commanded it to release her in the name of Father God. Then he dove in and rescued her while the rest of the Bright Elves bound it and cast it out in the name of Father God."

"We stopped at the castle in Orendia to pick up some girls that King Jahiz had collected. He decided to come with us to Vivallen and on our way past the plateau, we were attacked by a large group of bandits. The soldiers were fighting them when four dragon riders flew down and torched them and chased them away. Then they landed and gave us bags of fresh meat and a gem to each of the girls. They gave a pouch of gems to King Jahiz and he asked if he could pet a dragon. Melody was already playing kissy face with the dragon Kerberos when it touched its nose to Melody's tummy and said, 'baby'. That's when I knew for sure that she was pregnant."

"By the time we reached Vivallen, I couldn't stand another day. I needed normalcy in my life, so after the dinner and some dancing, we spent the night at the Golden Chalace and drove straight for home in the morning. I'm still not over it, and I just want some peace and quiet," said Tall Sky.

"That was amazing," said Beldock. "No wonder you're tired. You need time to readjust to being home and you need to think about yourselves for a change. That much trauma for that long would take its toll on anybody."

"Guess what. Daisy mated while we were near the woods. She's pregnant too," said Melody.

"I'm pretty sure that you conceived in that forest," said Tall Sky. "It wouldn't be the first time that a dragon and its owner conceived at about the same time."

"Tomorrow we want to see your nurseries," said Melody.

"We have to see Talla and her girls tomorrow. I wonder if any of them delivered yet," said Tall Sky.

"She has several babies over there and several girls went to Home Fire," said Beldock. "When will the new girls be arriving?"

"I'm not sure, but I would think tomorrow or the day after," said Tall Sky. "Last time they started moving girls out right away. We should be getting home now. Do you want to walk with us, Trag?"

"Yes, we should be getting back home, too," said Trag. "It was a good dinner. Thank Mina for us."

"We'll see you tomorrow. Goodnight," said Tall Sky.

They walked out and down the street toward home, pleasantly tired and relaxed. When they reached home they went to bed holding each other in a loving embrace.

They awoke the next morning feeling rested and hopeful. "Let's go to the Laborer's Reward and stop at Jelsareeb's for a pastry," said Melody.

"Alright, but then I want to shop for baby room things," said Tall Sky.

They stopped at the bakery and walked to the Laborer's Reward. "Tall Sky and Melody, good morning! Do you feel better today?" asked Beldock.

"We do," said Tall Sky. He sat at a table and Beldock brought them some tea and went to get a Daisy plate for the agitated little dragon.

"Mina brought out the daisy plate. "There you are my little darling," said Mina in soothing tones. "It's hard to think of Daisy being out there in all that danger. She's so small."

"Yes, but as long as she's with me and I'm not chasing a grustabist, she's fine," said Melody. Mina laughed.

"I'll be right out with your breakfast," said Mina. She brought out plates of sausage, eggs and fried potatoes.

"We should see Liadra's baby room and Arinya's baby room first," said Melody.

"Alright, but keep in mind, their rooms are for girls. You might not get any ideas there," said Tall Sky.

After breakfast they stopped by Liadra's to see her nursery. As one would expect, it was full of pink things with fluffy curtains and white furniture. "I see what you mean," said Melody. "It's beautiful. Perfect for a little girl. We're going shopping for things for our baby's room."

"That's really fun. Have a nice time," said Liadra. They left and stopped by Trag's store first, because Trag usually has some interesting items.

"Hi, Trag. Do you have anything for a boy's room?" asked Tall Sky.

"Actually, I do," He went to the back of the store and brought out a small rocking horse suitable for a toddler. A lady brought this in last week and I put it aside for you," said Trag.

"It's wonderful!" said Melody. "Thank you."

"That's not all. She brought in some baby clothes and some of them are really cute for a little boy," said Trag. "Look at these."

Melody looked at the clothes and giggled. "They are so small. How fun!" she said.

"Here is a wall hanging that might do," said Trag. "It's a picture of the sea with a clipper ship and sea gulls. It's very well made."

"I like that. Where could I get a good rug?" asked Tall Sky.

"I know a lady who makes beautiful rugs with pictures on them. At the end of the road next to Ulrick's shop is a small house. You will find her there," said Trag.

"Thanks, Trag. We will take all of these and we will see the lady you mentioned." Tall Sky paid Trag and they left to drop off their things at home. Then they walked to the end of the road and bought a rug with a picture of a horse on a green background. They stopped at Ulrick's and he showed them the progress that he had made on the baby bed. He already had a chest of drawers, so Tall Sky purchased it and Ulrick drove it to their house in his cart.

"Thank you, Ulrick. You will be having more orders for baby beds soon. There are more girls being brought here from Vivallen and two of them already have babies," said Tall Sky. "Congratulations on your engagement to Jelsareeb. She's a good woman and will make you a wonderful wife."

"Thank you. I expect we will have a wedding soon," said Ulrick. "It is good that you are back home. Everybody missed you. I'm glad that you are safe."

"Ulrick, I can't tell you what a relief it is to be home again," said Tall Sky.

They placed the chest of drawers in the nursery and showed Ulrick their other items. They put the rocking horse in one corner and the rug on the floor. They fixed the picture of the ship above the dresser and put the clothes in the dresser. The room was starting to take on some character. "This is looking good," said Ulrick. "I will make you a changing table. You will need one of these and a baby bathtub, too," said Ulrick.

"I have one ordered. We can stop by the blacksmith shop and pick it up today," said Tall Sky. "How soon will you have the bed ready?"

"It will be ready in a few more days," said Ulrick. "I have to get back to the shop now."

"Thank you very much," said Tall Sky. "We will see you then."

"Melody, let's go choose some fabric for curtains," said Tall Sky.

They walked back to Beldock's inn and looked through the storage room. They chose a white fabric and some blue for ruffles around the edges. "This will look very nice," said Melody. "Can we get a baby doll to put in the bed until our baby comes?"

"Sure we can. We will look for one today," said Tall Sky, feeling just a bit heroic. "Let's take the fabric home and try to find a baby doll."

They bought a life sized baby doll in a store on the way home and set it on the little rocking horse. Then Melody went to work on making the curtains. By mid afternoon, she had finished the curtains and Tall Sky put a rod through them and put them on the windows. The room looked beautiful and both parents-to-be were very pleased. "Now I believe that we will have a baby," said Melody. Tall Sky laughed.

He said, "I knew that we had to get this done before we became caught up in other projects. More girls will be here soon, and I want to be with them when they go to Home Fire. I know you want to see Home Fire again and introduce the girls to Rando. I can hardly wait to see his face when we show up with more girls to settle there."

"Thank you for making this room. I love it and I can hardly wait to see Alqua," said Melody. "Now let's get that bathtub and some fabrics for a baby blanket and towels and clothes."

When they walked into the inn, Tall Sky talked with Beldock while Melody asked Liadra to help her. Liadra and Elise helped her to choose fabrics for the clothes and bedding, but the towels and washrags would have to be purchased along with some fatty soap and lotion. "There are many details to having a baby, but you will learn as you go along. I have had experience with helping to raise my brothers, so I will be here for you whenever you have questions," said Liadra.

"Well, right now I just have to feel secure knowing that we have things ready for him. Making the nursery was fun and now I have some real work to do making baby clothes," said Melody. "Tall Sky has done a really good job with it. The room is looking great."

Liadra said, "Soon you will have other things to do and you will relax. Keep in mind, that you should enjoy this freedom you have right now, because when the baby comes, you will be tired from taking care of the baby and having a lack of sleep for a while. Babies need to be fed sometimes in the middle of the night and they need to be held and rocked a lot. You will have to rinse out diapers as soon as they are dirty, but there is a woman in town who will launder them for you for a small price."

"Babies sure are complicated," said Melody.

"Yes, they are. They cry often, because that is the only way that they have of communicating with us. You will learn to recognize a cry as meaning that he needs changing or food or that he is just lonesome and wants to be held," said Liadra. "Now, let's go over to my home and look at some baby clothes that I have made." They walked next door to Liadra's house. Melody got some good ideas and asked if she could take home a few pieces to copy. "Here is a baby bottle that Laskron made for you."

"Thank you. Now I will get Tall Sky to help me take all of this home," said Melody. "I'll bring back the clothes when I am done."

She went next door and Tall Sky was drinking a glass of ale with Beldock. He said, "Melody, let's have dinner before going home. Where is all your fabric?"

"It's next door. Would you get it for me?" asked Melody who was quite tired from the day's activities.

"I'll get them now and you can start by feeding Daisy," said Tall Sky.

"I'll get the Daisy plate for you," said Beldock.

Mina came out with the Daisy plate and said, "I hear that you have made a cute nursery for Eryn, and that you are going to make baby clothes. That's good, but don't forget to get your rest."

"I won't forget. I do get tired more easily now," said Melody.

"Yes, and you have to get over all the traveling that you have been doing," said Mina. "That takes rest. Don't overdo it. You must think of the baby growing inside of you and take it easy."

"I will," said Melody, wondering if that would be possible.

"Here is your stuff," said Tall Sky. "It looks like you will be busy for a while."

Mina said, "Tall Sky, you must make her rest. I know that you have plans to make baby clothes, go to Home Fire, and make schools, but a pregnant woman needs rest, so you have to make that your number one priority. I mean it."

Tall Sky looked worried and said, "I will. I will make her lie down and take naps regularly."

"She must also limit her eating of anything sweet. It's bad for the baby and it will produce a larger baby to deliver," said Mina.

"She will. Won't you my darling," said Tall Sky. Melody looked unhappy about that, but said that she would.

"I'll bring you some dinner," said Mina feeling that she had done her duty. She brought dinner and Tall Sky and Melody ate some good stew and freshly baked rolls. Melody almost fell asleep sitting up and Daisy chirred in her ear and rubbed cheeks with her.

"That's it," said Tall Sky. "I'm taking you home." He picked up Melody's things and they headed for home where she took a nap. Tall Sky went to the blacksmith shop and bought the baby bathtub and brought it home. When Melody awoke, he showed her the tub and she was delighted. She spent the evening making a baby blanket, hemming all four sides.

# HOME FIRE

The next day at breakfast they were joined by a number of the girls from the caravan and some soldiers who were escorting them. There were ten girls staying in Loadrel and nine girls were going to Home Fire. They had arrived the night before after Tall Sky and Melody had gone home. The soldiers told Tall Sky that they would be heading for Home fire right after breakfast, so Tall Sky hitched up his wagon to go with them. When he arrived at the inn, they were ready to go. Tall Sky got a sandwich to eat on the way and they were off again on another adventure. He promised Mina that he would insist on Melody resting in the wagon on the way.

About four hours later they drove into Home Fire. Rando met them sayng, "What's all this?"

"We promised you some girls and here they are," said Tall Sky. "Do you have rooms for them?"

"I'll put a few of the workers in tents," said Rando. "I know some men who will be happy to meet them, but for now take them over to the circle and have them sit there. I will make sure that there are rooms for them. Could they stay two to a room?"

"I don't see why not. They did in Loadrel" said Tall Sky. The girls sat on the logs around the campfire and waited. Meanwhile, Melody went to Alqua's house to talk with her. "Hi, Alqua. How have you been?" asked Melody.

"Big and getting bigger," she said. "How did you fare on the caravan?"

"In the first place, I got pregnant and so did Daisy," said Melody. "I rode with a dragon rider on a dragon high up in the sky. I met another king and watched the soldiers fight off pirates and bandits and demons. It was quite an adventure."

"I'll bet you're glad to be home," said Alqua.

"I am, but now Mina and Tall Sky say that I have to rest. Do you rest more?" asked Melody.

"Yes, I do, but I think your body will let you know when you should rest. You can do any normal activities, but you do them more carefully and rest afterwards," said Alqua. "You will let me know when I should get one of Daisy's eggs, won't you?"

"Of course I will. They will need good homes. I think Faerverin wants one," said Melody.

"How is Faerverin doing?" asked Alqua.

"She is well and with Aleph in Loadrel. They are taking time to rest up from his journey. I'm going to ask her to paint a mural in my baby's room. We made one as soon as we got home. We are having Ulrick to make a bed and a changing table and I am making baby clothes," said Melody.

"How many girls did you bring us?" asked Alqua.

"Nine girls. They are sitting out by the fire waiting for Rando to make sure that their rooms are ready," said Melody. "You can meet them after they get settled in. How is Jalia doing? Does she like working with the children?"

"Yes, she does and she and Thogul are in love. She is teaching him Aksandan so they can communicate better and he is learning very quickly. Indra says that she has been a big help with the children," said Alqua.

"I'm glad to hear that. I like Thogul. He is a kind man and Tall Sky says that he will probably teach about God in the Vision Hall," said Melody.

"I know. Rando made building the Vision Hall a priority and we got that built while you were gone," said Alqua. "Would you like to see it?"

"I sure would," replied Melody. They left the house and walked over to the Vision Hall. It was about the same size as the one in Loadrel and already had thirty chairs in it. "Where did you get all these chairs?" "We had Steben's father make them. We have Emmy staying here for school, but she will be going home in another month.

271

She is smart and a fast learner. She is learning reading, writing and doctoring," said Alqua.

Melody said, "Shanteel, Andra and I have been writing a history book about the three main countries of Phayendar. We got most of the information from the kings. Also, we have written an account of our journey with pictures drawn by Shanteel. I hope to get them involved with the school at Loadrel. We are making copies of it, so you will have one for your school. Our idea is to have one town make copies of their materials and start a school in a neighboring town. Then that town will help the next town to start a school. That way schools will spring up all over the country. Hopefully, we can get Trinian and Gantio to write the materials in their languages too. There are very old writings about healing with recipes for herbal remedies that are translated and can be added to your medical information taught in your school. We brought some of this to you today. Thogul will be able to add the history of the dwarves. He might like that."

"This is amazing! What a wonderful idea!" said Alqua. "No wonder you need to rest. This was a working caravan."

"It was, and all my girls learned how to make clothes on the way so they can tell their parents that they learned how to sew in captivity. They have decided to not talk to people about their abuse. They are just going to say that they were made to work hard. That way people won't think about it every time they look at them," said Melody. "I'm getting hungry. Do you think the cooks have something made yet?"

"I'm sure they do. Let's go see," said Alqua.

They walked over to the fire and got a sandwich and a mug of milk. Then they sat down with the girls to listen. The girls were happy to be there and wondering what the inn was like. They also wondered what the men were like. Rando walked over to them and said, "Are you ready to put your things in your rooms?"

"Yes," they all said. They picked up their things from their wagons and followed Rando to the inn where he showed them to their rooms. They told Rando that they liked the rooms and left their things there to follow Rando on a tour of Home Fire. He showed them the houses, Vision Hall, and the animal enclosures. Then he showed them the cooks' building and they watched some food preparation going on there. He explained how everyone did their share of the work and that this arrangement made everything function smoothly. He told them that tomorrow they would begin working with a person who did the type of work that they would like to do. He had them write down their names and skills.

Tall Sky walked up to the waterfall to see how the work was progressing. They had made good headway on the canal and were still digging it. Thogul was supervising and Hafka was translating. Tall Sky said, "This looks good. You've come a long way. Thogul, you look great. Who cut your hair and beard?"

"Brilley did. She cuts hair when she isn't doctoring and helping at the school. We should be at the town in a few days," said Thogul. "Then we have to dig past the town a ways and also make some irrigation ditches. It's a big job. How did the caravan go?"

"The caravan was very successful, but we did have a few attacks from bandits, pirates and demons," said Tall Sky.

"It sounds exciting, but that would be too much excitement for me," said Thogul.

"How do you like the Vision Hall?" asked Tall Sky.

"I like it very much. I am going to speak there when I am better at the Aksandan language. I have a wonderful girl helping me to learn it. Her name is Jalia. We are very good friends," said Thogul. "Rando is going to build me a house next to the Vision Hall. I would like to stay here and get married."

"I thought you would," said Tall Sky. "You could speak at the Vision Hall and supervise the maintenance of the water system. It is a good paying job that would give you enough income to live on."

"That sounds good," said Thogul. "I want to ask Jalia to marry me, but I really need a home to take her to. I will ask Rando to have some workers build one."

Tall Sky said, "Rando has already lined up a work crew for it." Thogul smiled broadly and laughed.

"This makes me very happy," said Thogul.

Tall Sky said, "I will see you later at dinner. I want to get back to Melody. She is pregnant now."

"Congratulations," said Thogul. "Have a nice afternoon."

Tall Sky walked back to town to find Melody. She was sitting at the fire visiting with Alqua and sipping some tea. Tall Sky said, "Let's go see Indra and Jalia. I want to talk to them about the school and see what teaching materials thay have."

"The school building is not finished yet, so you will find them at the inn. I'll show you," said Alqua.

She showed them the classroom at the inn located in the back room of the first floor. There were pictures made by the children hanging on the walls, a long table with chairs, and a separate table for the teachers. They had supplies sitting on shelves. They were looking through papers that the children had written. Tall Sky said, "Hi Indra, hi Jalia. How did you like the supplies we sent?"

Indra answered, "They were very helpful. We have been using them."

Tall Sky sat down and explained the history project and his idea of having one school help the next town to build a school until all major towns in Aksanda have schools. "Of course, I would help with it, but I think it's extremely needed," said Tall Sky.

"I would do that," said Indra. "We will make copies of our materials for Yardrel and they will have something to work with. Also, I will write up some plans for daily lessons."

"I would really appreciate it. I will go to Yardrel and talk to the town chief about it beforehand and make sure that he has teachers lined up and a place for the school. That will make your visit fruitful," said Tall Sky.

"That would be good," said Indra. "Thank you. We use local people to teach things like sewing, art, and doctoring. They can do the same thing. Brilley has already taught them how to milk cows and how to churn butter. She has also taught them how to care for a wound. Cassie is teaching them how to clean game and smoke meat. Hilda will teach them how to sew and make decorations. All productive things that people do should be taught to the children."

"I agree," said Tall Sky. "I think that they should know everything to do to live well. If they really like one occupation or another, they will be able to choose."

"It makes sense to me," said Indra.

"Jalia, how do you like teaching?" asked Tall Sky.

"I love working with the children. It's fun to see them learn. We have some talented children here," said Jalia. "Thogul is doing very well, too. He enjoys learning the language, and the children like him, so they want to help. One of them drew a horse and wrote the name under it. Others do this and they quiz him on them every day. They are very excited about this."

"Did you know that Rando is having a house built for Thogul next to the Vision Hall?" asked Tall Sky.

"How wonderful," Jalia said with a big smile. "I was worried that he might leave after the water project."

"No, he is very happy here," said Tall Sky. "The house will only take a few weeks to build and maybe you could remind him to order furniture from Steben's Papa. That way he can bring it when he comes to get Emmy."

"I will do that," said Jalia.

"And I will teach him how to say 'I love you and 'Will you marry me' in Aksandan," said Tall Sky. Jalia blushed. "Now let's make a list of things that you need."

While they were working on the list, Melody and Alqua went back to Alqua's house and Alqua showed her the nursery. She had decorated it in greens and golds with a baby bed and a rocking chair. It was very pleasant. She opened the dresser and showed Melody some baby clothes that she had made.

"This is really pretty. You should order a baby bathtub and a changing table. Would you like me to do that for you when we get back to Loadrel?" asked Melody.

"I would appreciate that. I don't go on trips any more," said Alqua.

"I'm just starting to make baby clothes, but we have his room just about done. I want Faerverin to paint a mural on a wall," said Melody. "Are you scared to give birth?"

"A little. I know that it will hurt a lot, but Brilley assures me that most births are natural and without problems. She was working with a midwife before," said Alqua.

"I'll ask Tall Sky to be there. He might be able to help with the pain, and he can pray for you to healed. That really works well," said Melody.

"I would feel a lot better if he would be there," said Alqua.

Tall Sky walked in and Melody said, "Would you be here when Alqua gives birth?"

"Sure I will," said Tall Sky. "I want to be here to see Rando's face when he sees his first child."

"I feel much better about it," said Alqua.

"You will do just fine and I will pray for you to be healed afterwards," said Tall Sky. "Whatever the cooks are making smells really good. Is it too soon to go to the cooks for some food?"

"Let's go. I'm getting hungry and Daisy is doing her little dance on Melody's shoulder," said Alqua. They all went over to the cooks and got a bowl of stew and some freshly baked bread. Melody fixed a Daisy plate and set it on the ground beside her. Daisy happily gulped down her food and crawled into her pouch for a nap. Melody said, "Daisy sleeps more now that she is pregnant."

After dinner, Rando stood up and said, "We have nine girls who will be living here. Girls, would you stand up and introduce yourselves?"

"I am Shirl."

"I am Hanna."

"I am Adalia."

"I am Fauna."

"I am Chilia."

"I am Arda."

"I am Shantrel."

"I am Ashra."

"I am Larissa."

"They heard that this was a growing new town and chose to settle here. Give them a warm welcome," said Rando. Everybody applauded. "Now let's have some music and dancing." The musicians played and people started to dance. Some young, single men asked the girls to dance. They were very happy to finally meet some single girls. All of them were working on building houses. It was a great day for Home Fire.

Rando said to Tall Sky, "I wonder how many of the couples will choose to marry together? I like group weddings."

"So do I," said Tall Sky. "As you remember, Melody and I were married with three other couples."

"I remember," said Rando. "When these marry, it will make twenty-four homes here."

"Your water canal will reach town soon. I talked with Thogul. He wants to stay here and get married. When will his house be built?" asked Tall Sky.

"The work crew will be here tomorrow to build it. A house usually takes several weeks to build," said Rando. "I had to hire a crew fom Yardrel. I'll send word to have Papa make the furniture for him. You should perform their wedding. Then I can sit back and enjoy it."

"I would love to perform their wedding. He has been a friend for a long time," said Tall Sky. "Wouldn't it be fun to have King Farin and Heiki to attend?"

"That would be astounding," said Rando. "Thogul is a close friend of his. It won't hurt to ask."

"I think He will come," said Rando. "The new girls are having a good time," said Rando.

"I'm going to dance with Melody and then I'm going to bed. We'll sleep in our wagon. It's home away from home for us. We like it. Melody, let's dance," said Tall Sky. Melody and Tall Sky danced, holding each other closely. "I love you and I will always take care of you. Is it alright if we sleep in our wagon tonight?"

"It will be perfect," said Melody. "I love you too, and I will show you just how much." She kissed him passionately and cuddled close to him.

"Let's go to bed," he said. They climbed into the wagon, shed their clothes, and made passionate love. Afterwards, they fell asleep in each others' arms. In the morning, she felt better than ever. She was in love with her husband and she was carrying his baby. She had never felt happier in her life.

Aromas of bacon, eggs, fried potatoes and hotcakes wafted through the air. There was also porridge with apple pieces and cinnamon. "I am so hungry that I could eat all of this," said Melody.

Well, let's get some," said Tall Sky. Daisy was almost frantic with hunger, so Melody quickly put together a Daisy plate for her. After Daisy had eaten, Melody put her back in her velvet pouch for a nap. Tall Sky and Melody served their breakfasts and sat down outside to eat them. The Home Fire residents did the same. Emmy came over and sat down next to Melody. She said, "Mama and Papa are coming to get me soon. They have made me a desk for my room so I can continue studying at home. I miss them, but I have had a wonderful time here. We write and draw and teach a dwarf named Thogul how to speak our language. I can read a lot of words now. Indra is making a long list of words with pictures next to them so that I can continue learning them."

Tall Sky said, "Maybe you could make a list like that for the school in Yardrel. You could also include all of the words that you already know."

"Alright. That way kids who don't know any can learn them all," said Emmy.

"We are going to start a school there next and then help other towns to start schools," said Tall Sky.

Melody said, "Since we're already half way there, why don't we go to Yardrel and you can talk to the chief while I visit with Amidra. Then we could order Thogul's furniture from Papa while we're there. We could even take Emmy with us if she's ready to go."

"That's actually a great idea," said Tall Sky. "Indra, we're going to Yardrel to visit Steben and the town chief about starting a school there. If Emmy is ready, we could take her along and we could also order Thogul some furniture for the house that will be done in a few weeks. Would that be alright?"

"I think it would. Emmy has progressed well and I have some study materials for her to take home," said Indra.

"Emmy, get your things together and Indra will help you to the wagon with them," said Tall Sky.

He told Rando what he was doing and said goodbye. Then they climbed into the wagon and drove out onto the road leading to Yardrel. Emmy was excited to be going home and sat up front with Melody and Tall Sky. It was a beautiful day, but cooler than usual. Some of the leaves were turning red already. "We had better put on sweaters. They climbed into the wagon and put on sweaters. Melody even put one on Daisy who loved the sweater. She chirred and rubbed cheeks with Melody. Then they brought one to Tall Sky. It promised to be a pleasant trip to Yardrel. Daisy sat on Melody's shoulder looking for any little animals or birds. After a while, Melody and Emmy decided to take a nap.

After four hours of traveling, they pulled up in front of Steben's home. Emmy got down and ran into the house. "Emmy," said Amidra. "How did you get here?"

"Tall Sky and Melody brought me in the wagon," said Emmy. Amidra walked out to greet them.

"Hi, you two," said Amidra. "It's good to see you. Are you well?"

"Better than well," said Melody. "I'm pregnant. We are going to have a baby boy."

"I'm so happy for you. Steben is in the barn," said Amidra. "Come on in, Melody. Tall Sky can get Steben." Amidra and Melody walked into the kitchen and sat at the table.

"How is your pregnancy coming along?" asked Melody.

"I think that Arinya and I will give birth in a month or so. I feel uncomfortable, especially at night. It is difficult to sleep through the night. Other than that, I'm alright," said Amidra.

"Will you be able to travel to Home Fire in a few weeks? I think that King Farin will be visiting Home Fire for the wedding of his friend Thogul, who is there helping to develop the water system," said Melody. "He met a slave girl there who is very small and they fell in love. She had been the companion to a princess. She has been at Home Fire working with the children in the school and has been teaching our language to Thogul."

"I would love to, but I think it is wiser for me to stay at home until after the baby is born," said Amidra.

"We made a baby room that is so cute. It has furniture and a little rocking horse, and a tapestry of a ship on the sea, and a rug with a horse on it. Ulrick is making us a changing table and a rocking chair. Do you have a baby bathtub yet?" asked Melody.

"No, I don't," said Amidra.

"I will order one for you. You can set it on the changing table, bathe the baby and then dry him, oil and dress him on the changing table. It's very convenient," said Melody. "I plan to use mine for Daisy when we get back home. Daisy will be laying eggs soon and she is not as active as before," said Melody. "Faerverin will be in Loadrel for a while, so I plan to have her paint a mural on Eryn's wall and she will adopt one of the eggs."

"You named the baby Eryn?" asked Amidra.

"Yes, Eryn Alda means forest tree. We named him that for two reasons. He was conceived in the forest and it was the name of a man who died saving Tall Sky in battle," replied Melody.

"I don't know what to name my baby. It would help if I knew if it would be a boy or a girl," said Amidra.

"We can ask Tall Sky. He might know or he might ask Father God to tell him," said Melody. Tall Sky and Steben walked in and Melody asked him. He said that he would ask Father God. Amidra said that she would put out some food for sandwiches.

After lunch, Tall Sky, Steben and Emmy went to town to visit the chief. They presented the idea of starting a school in Yardrel. Emmy showed him how she was learning to read and write. She told him about the other things she was learning and said that it was really fun to do. Tall Sky explained the benefits of having an educated populace and how one town would show another how to set up a school. The chief was very impressed with this idea and knew where he could put the school. He even knew some women who could teach in it. Tall Sky said that Indra would come to help them get started and would bring some supplies with her, but that the chief should buy some paper, pens, and some art supplies also.

After the meeting, Tall Sky drove back to Steben's to drop off Emmy and Steben. They said goodby to Amidra and wished her well with having the baby. He told her that she would have a boy. "Then I want to name him Cliff to honor the man who was killed at Home Fire by Avidora's bushy bears," said Amidra.

"That is a good idea," said Tall Sky. "What do you think, Steben?"

"I like it," said Steben.

"We should be heading back. Don't forget to order furniture for Thogul's house," said Tall Sky. "You could also have Papa make a changing table for Alqua."

Melody hugged Amidra, and Tall Sky and Melody walked out to the wagon. "That was a good visit," said Melody. "While we were talking, I realized that I could use the baby tub and the changing table for Daisy. That would be alright, wouldn't it?"

"Anything you want, precious," said Tall Sky. They drove onto the road and headed south toward Home Fire.

"You had better go to the back and lie down, or I will get told off by Mina at dinner," said Tall Sky.

"I will, but only because you want me to. I feel fine," said Melody. She went to the back and lay down with Daisy on her pillow. They both fell asleep.

It was already dark when they pulled into Home Fire. People were still eating dinner around the fire. Rando said, "Get some dinner and then we'll talk. Alqua is eating indoors," said Rando. "Did you order the furniture?"

"Yes, we did and we met with the chief about starting a school. He knows where to put one and some women to teach in it. He's going to buy some supplies and I told him that Indra would help them with some lessons," said Tall Sky. "I told Jalia that I would teach Thogul how to say I love you and will you marry me in Aksandan." Rando laughed.

"He is right over there. Ask to speak with him. Hafka will interpret," said Rando.

"I'll just tell Hafka to teach it to him," said Tall Sky.

"That will work," said Rando.

"Have the boys been talking with the girls?" asked Tall Sky.

"They had lunch together today and they're sitting together across the fire from us. I guess they wanted some privacy," said Rando.

"That makes sense to me," said Tall Sky. "I think you should play some music," said Tall Sky.

"Good idea," said Rando. "He asked the musicians to play and soon couples were dancing."

Tall Sky said, "Would my lady like to dance?" Melody got up and slow danced with Tall Sky. The moon and stars were out lending a romantic atmosphere to the night. Thogul and Jalia danced and so did the men with the new girls. Rando went in to be with Alqua and gave her a back rub. Melody said that she was tired and wanted to go to bed, so they climbed into the wagon and snuggled under the covers with Daisy on the pillow purring them to sleep.

In the morning after breakfast, they headed back to Loadrel. They had completed their tasks and felt very good about it. "I am confident that our trip was a success. Now I think we can pursue our own interests of getting our school operational and finishing our home preparations," said Tall Sky.

"Yes, and we mustn't forget to order a baby bathtub for Alqua. We can send it to her with the next work crew," said Melody.

"You are so thoughtful," said Tall Sky. "I really like that."

"Thank you. You are thoughtful, too," said Melody. "I wonder how long it will be before Faerverin, Shanteel and Andra will be here."

"It should be soon. They didn't have that much to do. You know, you will have to go over the history and the pictures and organize them. Then we are going to need three copies made of them. We can have Shanteel and Andra help with it," said Tall Sky. "While you girls are working on that, I will get the physical school ready."

"Don't forget our house," said Melody. "I want all the rooms painted and new curtains at the windows and paintings on the walls. I want our home to look new and fresh, and I want a loom to make tapestries on. It will give me something to do while my body is busy growing a baby. I also need to learn how to cook and make jelly preserves and all that stuff. I expect that I can learn some of it from Mina."

"So you plan to turn yourself into a homemaker," said Tall Sky.

"Well, I will have to if I want our child to have a proper home," said Melody.

"Don't worry, we will still eat out a lot and take trips to help start schools," said Tall Sky. "There will always be things for us to do."

"You aren't ready to settle down yet, are you?" asked Melody.

"Yes, no, maybe," said Tall Sky. "It's just that it's all so new. I have been a wanderer all of my life. It takes some getting used to. Don't worry. I'll be alright. Besides, we can still take trips like going to see the dragon riders. We can still sail to Grace Island and learn about that culture."

"Then there is always teaching a little boy how to live, how to fish and hunt, and helping him to learn. He is your own little boy and you will love him. You will teach him about Father God and how to contact Him at all times. This boy will be an adventure in himself," said Melody.

"So young and yet so wise," said Tall Sky. "You're right, of course. You should lie down in the back and let me think about all of this. I'll talk to God and get my head back on straight."

Melody crawled into the back to lie down with Daisy. Soon she was fast asleep.

They arrived in Loadrel around lunch time and stopped at the Laborer's reward for lunch. Mina saw them and immediately brought out the Daisy plate and some sandwiches. "How is my favorite couple?" asked Mina.

"We're fine," said Melody. "Tall Sky makes me take naps in the wagon when we travel. Home fire is progressing quickly. It looks great. The nine girls have been dancing with some young men out there. They have an inn and a Vision Hall and more houses."

Tall Sky said, "The water system will be done in a few weeks. They have done very well out there."

"How is Alqua doing?" asked Mina.

"Alqua is doing very well, but she says that she is uncomfortable," said Melody.

"That's to be expected," said Mina. "She will be alright as soon as her baby gets here."

"Mina, would you let me watch you cook so that I can learn to make good food?" asked Melody.

"Of course you can, but you should wait until you have your house the way you want it," said Mina. "I'll go get your sandwiches. We have ham and cheese today and it's really good."

Mina brought the sandwiches and a mug of tea for Melody. They ate their sandwiches and went shopping for more paint. They bought the paint and a loom. Then they drove home and brought in their purchases.

The next morning Tall Sky hired some men to paint the inside of the house and bought some fall flowers to plant in front of the house. He was trying. Then he picked up the rest of the baby room furniture. Melody was at Liadra's visiting while he did all of this. At lunchtime he took Melody to the Laborer's Reward. She wanted to go home, but he insisted on taking a walk along the shore and then to Trag's Store to visit with Arinya. Then they went shopping for baby things like a pillow, some sheets, a few baby toys and some clothes for older babies. Then he took her to Talla's house to see the pregnant girls. Several of them had given birth and Melody played with the babies and talked with the women about childbirth. It was late afternoon and close to dinner time, so they walked home with their purchases. Melody said, "Look at all the flowers! Who did this?" asked Melody.

"I did. I hope you like them. There are more surprises inside," said Tall Sky.

Melody ran into the house to find that the inside had been painted and looked fresh and clean. They walked into the baby room and found the dressing table with a baby tub on it, a bed and a rocking chair. Melody was so happy that she cried and hugged Tall Sky. "Thank you. It's wonderful," said Melody. "You are wonderful."

"It's almost dinner time. Let's go get some," said Tall Sky. They walked hand in hand to the Laborer's Reward. Melody felt happy and loved, thinking of her new little boy with red, curly hair and green eyes running through the woods.

Printed in the United States
By Bookmasters